P9-DNP-467

A Gathering of Saints

A Gathering

of Saints

Christopher Hyde

All the characters and events portrayed in this work are fictitious.

A GATHERING OF SAINTS

A Felony & Mayhem mystery

PRINTING HISTORY
First U.S. edition: 1996
First U.S. paperback: 1997
Felony & Mayhem edition: 2007

Copyright © 1996 by Christopher Hyde
All rights reserved

ISBN 10: 1-933397-62-4
ISBN 13: 978-1-1933397-62-7

Manufactured in the United States of America

To Mariea,
with all my love,

To my mother,
Bettye Marguerite Hyde,
who told me tales of that
last summer before the end of the world,

And most of all,

To the memory of my father,
Laurence Evelyn Hyde,
the lonely little boy from Tooting Bec
who gave me *Sandpiper*
and so many other things.

Author's Note

Although *A Gathering of Saints* is a work of fiction, it is based entirely on historical fact. With almost no exceptions, the characters in the book are real people, and virtually all of the events took place as they have been described. Particular bombing raids during the Blitz, and their effects, have been re-created as accurately as possible, including information relating to times, damage, fatalities, and weather conditions.

More than three hundred historical books were consulted during the writing of *A Gathering of Saints*, as were a large number of military, intelligence, and political experts. Of the books consulted, a number were especially useful. These include *Secret Service* by Christopher Andrew; *A History of British Secret Service* by Richard Deacon; *The Double Cross System in World War II* by James Masterman; *A Letter From Grosvenor Square* by John G. Winant; *The Enigma War* by Jozef Garlinski; *Firewatch Diary* by John Betjeman; *St. Paul's Cathedral in Wartime* by Dean W. R. Matthews; and Browne and Tullet's biography of Sir Bernard Spilsbury, *Scalpel of Scotland Yard*.

Of the many people who helped me with the research directly, I would particularly like to thank Mrs. Betty Heller, who was kind enough to record her vivid memories of the Blitz for me. I would also like to express my deep appreciation for the help of a retired member of both the United States Office of Strategic Services, and later the Central Intelligence Agency, who provided me with invaluable information and corroborating evidence regarding the attempted "separate peace" of 1940 and the existence of the man who really was "The Doctor" during World War II. For obvious reasons, of course, she must remain anonymous.

Christopher Hyde
Point Roberts, Washington
1995

The icon above says you're holding a copy of a book in the Felony & Mayhem "Espionage" category, which features spies and conspiracies from World War I to the present. If you enjoy this book, you may well like other "Espionage" titles from Felony & Mayhem Press, including:

Who Guards a Prince, by Reginald Hill
The Cambridge Theorem, by Tony Cape
The Labyrinth Makers, by Anthony Price
The Romeo Flag, by Carolyn Hougan
Soviet Sources, by Robert Cullen

For more about these books, and other Felony & Mayhem titles, or to place an order, please visit our website at:

www.FelonyAndMayhem.com

or contact us at:

Felony and Mayhem Press
156 Waverly Place
New York, NY 10014

A Gathering of Saints

CHAPTER ONE

Saturday, September 7, 1940
4:30 A.M., British Summer Time

DETECTIVE INSPECTOR MORRIS BLACK awakened with a
start in the study of his flat in Shepherd's Market. He glanced
at his watch and saw that he'd been asleep for less than an
hour. Blinking himself back to full consciousness, he yawned,
frowning at the foul taste in his mouth. Two large tots of
brandy for his insomnia, or at least that's what he'd told himself. How long would it take for two tots to become three,
then four? How long until he lost count and any interest in
counting?

The book he'd been leafing through now lay on the floor
beside his favorite reading chair. Sighing, he bent down and
picked it up. It was one of his favorites: *The Life of the Hon.
William F. Cody, known as Buffalo Bill*, Cody's autobiography, a
rare Frank E. Bliss American first edition, with the frontispiece
engraving lavishly signed by Buffalo Bill himself.

Black closed the volume carefully. The book's falling off
his lap had probably woken him up. He checked his watch
again. An hour and a half before daybreak; barely worth going
to bed, but the swimming baths at the YMCA would still be

1

closed at this hour, so there was really no point in beginning his day. He stood up, stretching, yawning a second time. Bad habits. Too many and too often these days. He crossed to the window and stared out into the gloomy square. Ye Grapes and the other shops were dark and shuttered, shades drawn across the windows in the flats above. Cold night air leaked draftily around the window frame and he shivered, cinching the belt of his old silk dressing gown more tightly around his waist. He sighed, remembering. The dressing gown Fay had given him on their first anniversary. He closed his eyes, feeling the familiar tightening of loss in his chest, willing it to fade, not surprised when it did not do so. Outside he could hear the faint, rattling bell of a police car racing down Piccadilly, heading west toward Knightsbridge. At this hour it was more than likely a false alarm called in by some frightened South Kensington matron, or a burglary on the Cromwell Road. Not his patch, nor his concern, worse luck.

Black took a deep breath, then slowly let it out. The thought of a weekend away from the distractions of work at the Yard was hard enough to deal with; the concept of living out an entire lifetime without Fay was almost incomprehensible. After a long, silent moment, Morris Black turned away from the window. Another dash of brandy, just to rinse out his mouth, and then perhaps an hour or two of dreamless sleep. The best he could hope for.

The Number sat crouched at the end of the bed, arms wrapped around his naked knees, staring at the boy and silently counting in the darkness. In the last hour before the coming light he could hear everything. The distant rattling of the vans as they lumbered through the cavernous Great Eastern depot a mile away on Hare Street, the subterranean rumbling of the first tube trains of the day coming into Whitechapel-

Mile End Station only a few blocks away. Closing his eyes, he could even hear what he knew would come: soft moanings and louder shrieks from the patients in the asylum at the foot of the London Hospital grounds no more than a hundred yards from where he sat; the first summoning changes ringing on the bells of St. Philip's Chapel on New Street; the thundering hell that would rain down on this very spot exactly twelve hours from now; all of it joined by the perfect ticking of the clock, bound together by the immutable force of the numbers that stitched the universe together.

He leaned forward and began to chant the Nine Tailors softly, giving them to the sleeping boy as a parting gift, even though he knew they would not be understood. Tentatively he reached out one hand, brushing the tips of his fingers across the boy's foot. Cold now. The Number hesitated, almost losing the drifting count in his head, knowing in his heart that the boy wasn't sleeping at all, would never sleep again.

That part of the ritual was complete. The anticipation of pleasure, quick and hot, the dry mouth, the trembling wait for the perfect moment when the boy's handsome face was turned away against the pillow, neck bent to show the faint sunburned line not protected by the collar of his flight jacket, ringing his throat like a prophecy. Bristling black hair at the base of his skull, the first three vertebrae of his spine jutting up, bone sheathed in velvet skin.

Shivering with the joy of it, The Number slid forward, gliding over the boy's body, covering it, shrouding it, stealing it into the memory forever, the feel of his skin, hard flesh and muscle, the bloody palm, cool lips, eyes drying now, but still soft against his lapping tongue. Eyes as blue as the frightening skies of the coming day. Eyes he'd first seen a thousand years ago. X marks the spot.

Reaching the last Tailor, he rolled gently off the boy and smiled. X marks the spot. Z tells the tale.

❀ ❀ ❀

More than a year and a day had passed with the country poised at the brink. France had fallen, but who knew France? The Battle of Britain was cinema verité unreeling above the city's head in distant vapor trails with no more meaning than a game of cricket: *Biggest Raid Ever, Score 78 to 26, England Still Batting.*

The game was played in different ways. For the rich it meant shutting down the London house and moving to the country, missing the theater season and doing without the annual trip to the Continent. In the War Office there were opportunities to be had and uniforms to be fitted on Savile Row. For the poor, scratching out a living among the East End gasworks and warehouses, the game was cause for the older men to tell stories of Ypres and the Somme, and mothers to weep in the night for terrible fates yet to befall their sons.

On the afternoon of that first Saturday in September most people in London were sitting down to tea or lifting their first pint in the public house to celebrate the beginning of the weekend when the air raid sirens began to wail, but for the vast majority of Londoners anxiety about raids that were always false alarms had long ago turned to boredom, and boredom had finally become indifference. Wars were fought on battlefields, not in cities. The sirens were ignored, tea poured, bread buttered.

At 4:32 P.M. the first bombs began to fall, pale blue five-hundred pounders and incendiaries, invisible against the dusky sky.

In the city's East End, standing at the bar of the Seven Stars Pub nursing his second pint of Bass ale, Jack Champion, an aging villain retired to the secondhand clothing trade, heard the sound of the falling bombs less than a minute after their release. Three of the five-hundred-pound high-explosive bombs impacted within a hundred yards of the public house. When Champion realized how close the explosions were coming, he dropped his pint glass and ran outside, heading for his shop on the opposite side of the street. Like his mates in the low-ceilinged, dingy bar, he was astounded that the bombs were falling at all, let alone in a neighborhood best known for the size of its rat population. Hardly a target Uncle Adolf would be interested in.

The first of the three bombs struck the narrow, cobbled roadway less than thirty feet from the front door of the Seven Stars, vaporizing Jack Champion and any last thoughts he might have had in a twelve-thousand-degree inferno that briefly created an eight-hundred-mile-an-hour pressure wave. The whirlwind crushed the life out of the two men standing in front of the pub, exploded the street-facing windows, and turned the interior of the Seven Stars into a whirling horror of glass splinters, obliterating the eight occupants of the saloon bar.

Following the blast wave there was a secondary implosion as the vacuum created by the blast was filled by an inrushing fury of air. The front of the Seven Stars and the squalid houses on either side, already weakened by the blast, toppled into the street.

Eliza Champion, Jack Champion's wife, had died a split second earlier. Standing at the front window of the flat above the shop, she saw her Jack begin to move across the street, but was then blinded by the detonation of the bomb fifteen feet to his right. Her brain had only just given the order to raise her arm across her eyes when the window disintegrated three inches from her face and her chest wall collapsed under the force of the blast, crushing her heart and rupturing every major organ in her body.

At the same instant, a second bomb reached the ground midway between the high brick wall of the old Board School and the back of the Champion shop. The force of the explosion, trapped between the two walls, took the path of least resistance, blowing in the rear of the shop and the flat above it, burying what remained of Eliza Champion in a welter of tinder-dry debris, which then began to burn furiously, ignited by a clutch of incendiaries that had followed the larger bomb on its path down to Brick Lane.

The third bomb descended within fifty yards of the first two and entered the flat roof of the house two doors down from the Champion residence. It managed to carve its way down two floors and into the sodden, clay-floored basement before it exploded, completely demolishing that house and the ones on either side as well as shattering a ninety-two-year-old gas main. The entire area, little changed since the time of Charles Dickens, was turned into a nightmare landscape within the first few minutes of the raid, severed limbs and charred pieces of flesh littering the rubble like refuse from a slaughterhouse.

Within half an hour of the first explosions, huge sections of London's East End had been destroyed or were on fire, sending a dark pall of smoke more than a mile into the air, the thickness of it grounding fighter planes at Hornchurch, nearly ten miles away. With the exception of the lower dock area, almost no other areas were touched by the bombing. It was almost as though Hitler had conspired with the London County Council in a bit of expeditious slum clearance.

The bombing continued through the night as wave after wave of Heinkels, Dorniers, and Junkers descended on the city, guided now by the fires created by those who had gone before. Warehouses crammed with rum, molasses, rubber, and ammunition exploded, spreading the smoking horror even farther along the Thames, while thousands of firemen, 80 percent of them unskilled members of the Auxiliary, struggled to control the gigantic blazes. Hundreds died that afternoon and night, and hundreds more were wounded. Thousands, all from the East End, were left homeless. Within hours, these instant refugees were trudging west, desperate to escape the growing inferno and filtering into The City proper, many of them camping out in the underground stations at Charing Cross and Leicester Square, much to the horror of the local population, who had been watching the spectacle of the East End on fire from the rooftops of their Covent Garden flats.

The hellish night seemed to go on forever. As the fires raged, a million rats poured into the streets, fleeing the scorching heat, pouring over the firemen's boots in a black, chattering stream, vanishing into a thousand sewers, only to reappear again somewhere else as the fires spread. Bales of tea, tinder dry, began to smolder without flame, brought to the point of ignition by the incredible heat. Water doused on the bales turned them into a horrible sticky mass that began to ooze from the warehouses like molasses, making movement impossible.

The superheated air began to feed on the oxygen at ground level, scorching lungs and creating insane, swirling updrafts, melting the lead in the stained-glass windows of a hundred churches, turning their spires into furious, torchlike beacons as wave after wave of bombers droned over the city.

By 3 A.M. the last flight of bombers turned back toward France, but still the fires roared, and soon it was all the men could do to keep open a few escape routes for those still trapped by circling rings of flame. Water mains dried up, the thick tires of the hose and ladder trucks began to melt into the pavement, and finally, the hoses themselves began to burn.

Eventually though, the worst of it was contained, and dawn broke over the smoking ruins of a thousand buildings. Whole streets had vanished, and entire blocks of houses had been turned to rubble. In the first light of day a bird pecked at the upraised hand of a body crushed under a ton of broken brick. A woman, torn apart by the concussion of a high-explosive bomb, lay in a gutter thick with some glutinous horror spreading out of a warehouse loading dock. An old man in slippers sat with his back against a shattered wall, the hubcap from an automobile over his neck doing little to disguise the fact that he had no head.

Police spent the early-morning hours before the first trains began to arrive herding the homeless out of the underground stations, hosing down the platforms in an attempt to remove the foul odors left behind, but nothing they could do erased the deep, pervasive stink of fear that had been aroused by the previous night's attack. The impossible had occurred. England had been invaded for the first time in almost a thousand years. The aerial game played high overhead for the better part of a year was over. The rules, it seemed, had changed.

Later that morning a Civil Defense Heavy Rescue crew discovered a body while clearing a site just off Mount Street in Whitechapel on the eastern edge of the area hit hardest by the attack, not far from London Hospital. It soon became obvious that the young man had not died as a result of the bombings, and proper authorities were informed. The body was taken to the mortuary at University College Hospital where a post-mortem was arranged for the following day. The autopsy would be performed by Sir Bernard Spilsbury, the Home Office chief pathologist.

Also scheduled to be in attendance was Detective Inspector Morris Black of the London Metropolitan Police, Criminal Investigation Division, Scotland Yard.

CHAPTER TWO

Monday, September 9, 1940
8:15 A.M., British Summer Time

DETECTIVE INSPECTOR MORRIS BLACK made his way slowly down the green-walled, echoing stairwell that led to the basement of University College Hospital and tried to ignore the faint, cloying smell of formaldehyde drifting up from below. Instead he concentrated on his itching scalp and the sting in his eyes. Both were a result of his regular morning swim at the new YMCA swimming bath. His hair was already thinning and he was positive the chemicals in the water were hastening the process. Almost as bad was the requirement that those using the pool should do so naked. Black loathed swimming and always had.

On the other hand, it gave him the sort of energetic exercise deemed necessary for an otherwise sedentary police detective plodding wearily through his forty-first year. Even more importantly, it took his mind off Fay. His wife had been dead for more than a year, but the pain of her absence was as fresh now as the day she had been buried.

So he went swimming each morning before going to the Yard. Fifty lengths in the humid, green-tiled aquarium, surrounded by ghostly, naked strangers, all men much older than him. He never spoke to his companions beyond the exchange of politely murmured greetings. Sometimes he thought about the tragedies and loneliness that could bring old men to a place like that each day so early in the morning—presumably sad memories like his own, perhaps fainter and less painful—but mostly he just swam and tried not to think at all. It was easier that way.

Black reached the bottom of the stairs, turned left along a narrow corridor, and went through an open doorway halfway down its length. Spilsbury was already hard at work. He looked up as the detective stepped into the dank, chilly room.

"Ah, Black. Just in time."

"Yes, sir," Black agreed. Spilsbury was famous for his punctuality, which Black found somewhat ironic considering the man's profession.

"Interesting." The tall, slightly stooped man in the long white lab coat stared down at the body on the enameled autopsy table. Sir Bernard Spilsbury, chief pathologist for the Home Office, walked slowly around the table, hands jammed into the pockets of his trousers.

Spilsbury was in his mid-sixties, gray-haired, but still very handsome. He wore a pair of wire-rimmed bifocal spectacles perched on his forehead and bore a faint resemblance to a clean-shaven John Barrymore. The dark suit he wore under the lab coat was custom-made, expensive, and at least twenty years out of style, even though it was quite obviously new.

Morris Black smiled faintly as he watched Spilsbury pace around the table. Not only was the pathologist's suit decidedly out of fashion, Spilsbury was also sporting a tall celluloid collar like the one Black's father had worn in the early twenties. Black had attended a number of postmortem examinations with Spilsbury over the years, and the man always dressed the same way.

"Yes, sir. Interesting," said Black, unable to think of anything else to say that seemed appropriate. He shivered. The layout of the autopsy chamber was cold and austere: four dish-edged rectangular tables on wheels and fitted with blood gutters and drainage holes, green metal cabinets along the walls, steel counters laid with an assortment of tools ranging from scalpels and electrical saws to brutal-looking hammers and steel wedges, and more drains in the worn, stained floor.

Blowers in the low ceiling brought in gusts of freezing air, but even that wasn't enough to remove the dark, sour odor the room had been steeped in for the last eighty or ninety years. Spilsbury, whose poor sense of smell was legendary, didn't appear to notice, and the corpse on the table was long past caring. Black had witnessed dozens of autopsies in his time, but he could never get used to the stench of death. An image of Fay drifted into his mind, and he blinked it away quickly. Sometimes he found himself wishing he'd never met her at all; any sort of loneliness was better than the burden of love and loss he'd carried for the past year. The thought of her laid out on a table like this was unbearable.

"He was found this way?" Spilsbury asked.

"Yes, sir, according to the report."

The body, that of a naked man in his late teens or early twenties, was nestled within a dark blue rubberized bag fitted with a row of metal snaps. The letters *W.O./D.S.S.* and a serial number had been stenciled in white onto the upper-left quadrant. The bag, Black knew, was a standard-issue War Office Department of Supply and Services waterproof shroud manufactured by the government for use by the Ministry of Home Security (Air Raid Precautions Department). Black also knew that several hundred thousand bags just like it were stored in strategically located warehouses all over London. Although the bag had a serial number, he realized that it would be virtually impossible to trace.

"Found in a bombed-out building?" Spilsbury continued to move around the body. Black noted that the pathologist was on his third circuit. He began the fourth, then paused long enough to peel back one of the man's eyelids with a thumb and forefinger. He nodded to himself and moved on.

"Yes, sir. A block of cheap flats. Bed-sitting-rooms."

"Couldn't have been left there by a forgetful air-raid warden I suppose?"

"No, sir." Black shook his head. "The shroud, with the body inside it, was discovered *under* the debris from the house."

"So, we presume that the body was placed there prior to the bombing?"

"Yes, sir. There was no evidence that it was placed there after the fact. No burrowing or tunneling."

"Interesting," repeated the elderly pathologist. He glanced up at Black and smiled, the gray, intelligent eyes twinkling. "Do you know how much I get paid for doing this sort of thing, Inspector?"

"No, sir."

"Five guineas for each postmortem as a rule, with a pound to the mortuary keeper for his services. Each one takes the better part of half a day, not to mention writing it up and giving evidence at Coroner's Court if need be."

"Yes, sir." Black had no idea what the old man was getting at.

"What I'm saying, Inspector, is that I don't do this for the enormous financial benefit I derive from poking about in people's internal organs or mucking about in their brain pans with a scoop and trowel."

"No, sir."

"And after some twenty-five thousand postmortems, Inspector, I can assure you that I have seen virtually everything there is to see as regards the practice of homicide. I continue to do them, however, in the faint hope that there is still something which I have not seen. Something to pique an old gentleman's curiosity." Spilsbury beamed. "This," he said, nodding his chin toward the body in the blue bag, "is one of those rare occasions." He shook his head absently. "I must admit, Inspector Black, that I am confounded...quite happily so."

"I'm pleased the Yard could be of service, Sir Bernard." Black smiled. Despite Spilsbury's conservative style of dress, out of court and off the lectern he was remarkably informal and often showed signs of having a rather schoolboyish sense of humor. Once, it was said, when asked to carve the Christmas bird at a friend's house, he opened his famous "murder bag" and laid out a set of gleaming dissecting instruments. There was also an unsubstantiated story making the rounds that he'd recently given someone's dog a human thighbone done up with ribbon as a birthday present.

Black also knew that Splisbury had suffered a mild stroke the past summer, but it didn't seem to have dampened his wit or his enthusiasm. With the exception of the stoop, which Black had already noticed, and a certain weariness around the eyes, the chief pathologist seemed quite himself.

"Let's get on with it, shall we?" he said, finishing his final circuit of the table. "I have a lecture I really should be getting to at Guys."

"Of course."

The body, Spilsbury noted aloud, was that of a male in his late teens or early twenties, dark-haired, light-skinned, nude, and presently residing in a rubberized shroud. Notes made by the investigating officer, Detective Sergeant Windridge, regarding postmortem lividity, and corroborating photographs taken in situ, led Spilsbury to believe that the body had been dead for some eighteen to twenty-four hours. There was no visible cause of death. The only wound was the letter Z incised into the palm of the left hand with a sharp instrument. According to Spilsbury, the lack of bleeding suggested that the wound had been inflicted after death.

"Cause of death?" asked Black.

"Poison," Spilsbury answered, standing back from the body. "Nothing violent like strychnine or cyanide—there's no sign of vomitus in the mouth, and no bluish tint to the lips. I'd say a narcotic of some kind. Morphine in a large dose. I'll need to gut him to be sure."

Black nodded, already taking the diagnosis as given. Spilsbury's nickname at the Yard was The Pope; if Sir Bernard said it was morphine, then it probably was. Infallible.

"And the *Z*?"

"Yes, that really is very different," Spilsbury murmured. He dropped his glasses down onto his nose and peered at the dead man's hand. He used his scalpel to delicately peel back the pale, curling, labial edges of the wound. "No telling how a madman thinks."

"You think the murderer was insane?"

"Or wished us to think he was." Spilsbury shrugged. "This is ritual, premeditated. The man who did this was either mad or very shrewd, or both."

"A pervert of some sort?"

"Are you asking if there was some sexual element to all of this?"

"It occurred to me."

"I see no immediate evidence to suggest such a thing." The pathologist seemed to be a little uncomfortable with the subject. "Making that sort of assumption at this stage is premature I think."

Spilsbury picked up a pair of tongs from the counter behind him, carefully peeled back the front of the shroud, and bent slightly to take a closer look at the man's genitalia. The testes were small, nested like pale eggs in the dark brown pubic hair. The man's sex organ was engorged and much darker than the surrounding flesh. Using the tongs, Spilsbury lifted it by the foreskin.

"Blood tends to settle in the penis after death, makes it

swarthy like that." He glanced at Black, smiling pleasantly. "The only thing it really tells us is that he wasn't one of your tribe. As you see, he was uncircumcised."

"Yes, sir." Black nodded, trying to ignore the comment. During his twenty years on the Metropolitan Force, from his earliest days as a probationary constable at Peel House to his present position with CD, Morris Black had never thought much about being a Jew, at least as far as being a policeman was concerned. The last few months had changed all that.

Since early May and the enacting of the new Home Office regulations regarding refugees and so-called "enemy aliens," the latent anti-Semitism of his white Anglo-Saxon brethren had been given a hearty stamp of approval. People were seeing so-called "fifth columnist" saboteurs, most of them Jews, under every bed.

In a nervous response to the nation's sudden distemper, Scotland Yard's Special Branch had been given a mandate to investigate every individual of German or Austrian birth resident in England, and thousands—some of whom had been living here for decades—had been summarily arrested and interned under the all-encompassing Regulation 18B.

It was ludicrous, of course, especially since more than half of the fifty thousand already arrested were Jews fleeing Nazi persecution after Kristallnacht, and two-thirds of those were children under eighteen—hardly fertile ground for the nurturing of Gestapo thugs or agents of the Abwehr, the Nazi secret service. Black's intuitions told him that Special Branch interests had more to do with Communists than it did with Hitler's bully boys.

Whatever the case, it seemed as though he'd been hearing an increasing number of comments like Spilsbury's recently, or perhaps he had simply become more sensitive to them. He knew the elderly pathologist meant no real harm or slight by it, but not so long ago an aside like the one he'd just been offered would never have been made to his face.

"No obvious means of identification I suppose?" Spilsbury murmured, leaning over the dead man.

"No, sir," said Black, shaking his head. "His fingerprints were given to Central Records, but I don't hold out much hope."

"Quite right." Using a hooked dental pick, Spilsbury pulled back the corpse's lower lip to reveal a set of large, even teeth. He took another pick, poked the tongue back down into the throat and peered into the mouth. After a few moments he removed the picks and straightened. "I think you'll find that he's not on your files at all, Inspector."

"Oh?" Black waited patiently for the explanation. Spilsbury was like an overwound watch; you simply had to wait for it to run down.

"The dental work is definitely European. They use a much greater volume of silver in their amalgam. British dental work tends to tarnish rather more than this fellow is showing." Spilsbury plucked a cotton swab on an orange stick from the breast pocket of his lab coat and thrust it deeply into the dead man's left nostril. Black winced; it looked incredibly painful, even though he knew the man couldn't feel anything. The pathologist withdrew the swab and looked at it closely.

"Smoked." He nodded to himself. "And not Virginia tobacco, the staining is much too dark. Yes. European. At a guess, Polish."

"Interesting."

Spilsbury gave Black a brief, penetrating glance. "Do I detect a hint of doubt?"

"I just wondered how you came to that particular conclusion."

"It is not a conclusion, Inspector Black. As I said, it is a guess, and a speculative one at that."

"Sorry, sir."

"On the other hand, I didn't simply pull a nationality from thin air."

"No, Sir Bernard." Black waited, realizing that any further comment would simply delay Spilsbury's assessment. After a long moment the pathologist spoke again, firmly and without the slightest hesitation.

"A man who, by all appearances, was in good health until the time of his death, who shows no signs of having worked at hard labor, and whose teeth show care and attention given from an early age. His complexion is somewhat pale, and his features are Middle European rather than Gallic. We therefore rule out the French. He is far too tall to be Belgian, yet he is not robust enough to be of Scandinavian descent. We may also presume that he is not a German who fell out of the sky, already bagged for disposal. That leaves us with the Balkan countries, the Soviet Union or Poland. Given the present political climate, I would suggest the latter."

Black tried to suppress a smile. Spilsbury really was very good.

The pathologist poked one of the dental picks across the table in Black's direction. "Interesting indeed. And probably quite accurate." Spilsbury paused for effect. "If I were you, Inspector, I'd have a chat with the RAF about our friend here."

"Yes, sir? Why is that?" Black had had the same thought, but almost certainly for very different reasons.

"Stand over here," the pathologist instructed, motioning Black to come to the head of the table. He adjusted the large dish of the overhead light so that it shone directly down into the dead man's pale, waxy face. He used a pair of tweezers to gently fold back the left eyelid, tucking it under itself so that the entire eye was revealed. It was a cloudy blue, the pupil dull and dry. The white of the eye appeared bloodshot.

"Yes, sir."

"What do you see?"

"His eye. Blue. A little bloodshot."

"No. Not bloodshot. A bloodshot eye shows an irritation

of the surface veins. What you see are a number of ruptured blood vessels."

"What's the difference?"

"He was breathing pure oxygen on a regular basis. Too much blood being brought to the ocular area. And he was doing so at high altitudes. That's what caused the hemorrhaging."

"A pilot."

"Quite so," Spilsbury answered. "A Polish pilot."

CHAPTER THREE

Monday, September 9, 1940
11:30 A.M., British Summer Time

MORRIS BLACK MADE HIS APOLOGIES to Spilsbury and left the mortuary before the pathologist began "gutting" the rubber-shrouded, unidentified corpse. Even though the atmosphere was sour from the smoky pall still standing like a fog over Docklands and the East End, the open air was a welcome relief after the mortuary's dankness.

The bombers had come again last evening, but not in anything like the numbers that had appeared on Saturday. The raiders concentrated on the East End and the Docks again, and rail travel to the south was completely blocked, at least for now.

On the other hand, the *Evening Standard* was still advertising Lixen laxative and Wolsey socks across its front-page banner, and the wireless, commenting on Churchill's tour of the East End yesterday afternoon, said the prime minister had found the people to be "in good spirits, and defiant." Black wondered what sort of spirits and defiance the PM might have seen if he'd chosen to make his tour through the lower levels of the underground station at Leicester square. Thousands of

East Enders had forced their way into the subterranean tunnels and crammed the platforms, refusing to leave. The terrified refugees from the bombing raids had been on the verge of wholesale panic and had come close to rioting.

Black went on to the Yard and after making a few telephone calls discovered that the Free Polish Squadron of the RAF was based at Northolt, a few miles west of London. After filling out the necessary travel documents, Black then took the tube to Paddington, where he caught the one o'clock train to Northolt Junction. It was a half-hour journey, and sitting in his compartment, Black realized that filling out the forms for the trip had taken almost twice that long.

Arriving at the small, unattended station, the detective was met by a pretty, dark-haired Women's Auxiliary Air Force driver wearing goggles and piloting an RAF Norton motorcycle with a sidecar. The WAAF took him on a short, bumpy ride to the airdrome, dropping him off in front of a long, single-story brick building protected by an earth embankment on all sides and completely surrounded by trees.

"Ops Centre, sir," said the WAAF briskly as Black clambered out of the sidecar. "Flight Lieutenant Kent is waiting for you inside." Without waiting for a reply the woman put the Norton in gear and thundered off in a cloud of dust.

Black watched her go, squinting in the bright sunlight. He was amazed at the size of the place. Established in 1915, it was the oldest operational airdrome in the Royal Air Force and looked like a small town, complete with roads and streetlamps. From where he stood he could make out at least a dozen H-shaped, two-level barracks buildings, dozens of workshops, and in the distance, seen over the screening trees, he could see the jagged rooflines of the two giant hangars.

He was surprised at how neat and tidy things were. The newspapers had been reporting savage attacks on fighter stations by German dive bombers for weeks now, but there was no evidence of it here. He shrugged, then turned back to the

Operations Building and followed the short gravel path to the main door.

Opening it, he found himself on a small wooden platform with half a dozen steps leading down to a large open room, the floor covered in exactly the same shade of gray linoleum in his office. The single-storied appearance of the building from outside was a ruse—the center was actually built entirely below ground level.

A dozen large wooden tables on trestles were arranged on the floor, and a long low stage was against the far wall. The center of the wall was covered by a black felt curtain, probably covering a map board. In one corner a uniformed clerk sat at a radio table, headphones over his ears. He was reading a magazine and drinking tea from a thick pottery mug. To his left a doorway led to an inner office.

The only other person in the open area was a thin officer, the twin bars of a flight lieutenant on his jacket cuff and cap under his arm. He was reading notices pinned to a cork-board on the wall beside the clerk. The man looked up as Black came through the door. He smiled, his expression breaking into several sets of conflicting laugh, worry, and tension lines. He looked to be in his late twenties or early thirties, but the detective knew the man was probably much younger than that. They introduced themselves and Black had to make a conscious effort not to show his amusement at the man's flat, nasal accent. Even without the Canada flashes on his shoulders his nationality would have been obvious.

"Come on into the staff office, that's where we keep the files." The officer led the way into the office beside the radio operator. It was tiny, ancient filing cabinets against three walls, the remaining space barely large enough to accommodate a small desk and two chairs. There was no window and the cubicle stank of cigarettes. "Have a seat," Kent offered, waving a hand. Black sat down and watched as the Canadian flier began rummaging through the file drawers, talking while he looked.

"We've had at least nine different squadrons based here in the past year, so things get pretty mixed up, paperwise." He turned and flashed Black a quick grin. "It's a mess."

"Why do they have a Canadian in charge of a Polish squadron?"

"Dunno." Kent shrugged. "Just worked out that way. They only just got operational status for one thing, and also because they're all crazy. Urbanowicz is the worst. Like a mad dog, really. Sees a German and that's it, he's off, guns blazing, no matter what anyone else is up to. He says he doesn't speak English so he can't follow orders, but you should see him going after the girls. His English is pretty good then, let me tell you...Here we go."

Kent pulled a thick folder out of a file drawer and brought it to the desk. He sat down and lit a cigarette, staring curiously at Black over the bulky file. The policeman lit a cigarette of his own in self-defense as the little chamber filled with smoke.

"I've never met a real live Scotland Yard inspector," said the Canadian. "Kind of like meeting a descendant of Sherlock Holmes."

"Holmes was a private detective. He worked with a Yard man named Lestrade."

"Right, right." Kent puffed on his cigarette. To Black he seemed nervous, almost defensive. Finally he spoke again. "Look, I don't want to seem rude, but just why is it you want to know about Kosciuszko?"

"I beg your pardon?"

"Sorry. That's the squadron name. To us it's 303 Northolt, to the Poles it's Kosciuszko. He was a hero of theirs, in the States as a matter of fact, something to do with their Revolution."

"I didn't know."

"Me neither." Kent laughed. "For a long time I thought he was a flier who hadn't reported for duty. That language of theirs is a bit of a trick—like talking with your mouth full of marbles."

"Interesting," said Black, who wasn't interested at all. The flight lieutenant seemed intent on avoiding the reason for their meeting. "You asked me why I was interested. Group Captain Vincent didn't tell you?"

"Nope. Group doesn't talk with lowly flight lieutenants, not much anyway. I was given a note from Station Ops to meet with you here. That's all I know."

"There was a man murdered in London on the weekend. We have reason to believe he was a Polish airman."

Kent frowned. "What reason? And why 303? We've got Poles in half a dozen RAF squadrons." There was a defensive note in the man's voice.

"There was evidence of Polish ancestry at the postmortem. This is also the only squadron that's entirely Polish, and it's close to London." Black paused. "Have you got anyone from your squadron who's gone missing?"

"Yes, as a matter of fact." Kent flipped open the folder and thumbed through it. He removed a single sheet, glanced at it, then handed it across to Black. It was a Photostat copy of a man's service record. A small, square photograph was in the upper left-hand corner. Even blurred and badly reproduced, there was no doubt.

"Stanislav Rudelski," said Black, reading the spidery writing under the photo. "Born March 22, 1921, Warsaw, Poland. Not even twenty years old when he died."

"Your murdered man?"

"I'm afraid so, yes."

"Shit." Kent flushed. "Sorry."

"Quite all right."

"He was a good kid." Kent sighed. "Flew like he'd been born with a stick in his hand."

"He was very young."

"Old enough," Kent answered, frowning. "Fought in Poland, flying one of those idiot P-11s. Got out with a few others just in the nick, managed to get into France and flew for the Armée de l'Air. Six kills in a Bloch 152, which is saying something in itself. Flew one of them into Biggin Hill a few days before the Panzers rolled into Paris." The Canadian nodded firmly. "Oh, he was old enough all right, Inspector."

"Rudelski had a weekend leave?"

"Open leave. If the squadron stood down for weather or if we didn't have a kite for him. All any of us has to do is sign out with Ops."

"And he did?"

"Friday evening."

"Due to return when?"

"Sunday night."

"Any idea where he might have gone?"

"No." Kent looked embarrassed for a moment. "I...we don't socialize much with the men. Language."

"Did Rudelski speak English at all?"

"Only the orientation course they gave him at HQ. Enough to get by. 'Please' and 'thank you,' that sort of thing."

"Did he have any interests?"

"Not that I know of."

"A girlfriend in London perhaps?"

"I wouldn't know." Kent flushed again.

"A man friend?" Black asked gently.

"I really have no idea what sort of friendships he had." The flight lieutenant's voice was clipped and formal. Morris Black didn't pursue the point. Although he was curious by nature as well as vocation, it had taken him half a lifetime to learn a basic fact about his fellow man: people generally wanted to know less, not more.

Even Spilsbury, privy to the most unpleasant secrets the world had to offer, seemed to have been put off by Black's suggestion about Rudelski's sexual proclivities, and now Kent was clearly feeling uncomfortable about it as well. After more than two decades as a policeman, Black himself was completely inured to such things. In his book consensual sodomy rated as no more than a mild eccentricity. His own sexuality had been buried along with his wife at the Jewish Cemetery in Golden Green.

"Would it be possible for me to see Rudelski's billet?" Black asked. "His personal effects?"

"I suppose so. Snookie's around somewhere, I'll get him to show you."

"Snookie?"

"Captain Sznuk. He's on loan from Sikorski's bunch for a while. Speaks about a dozen languages from what I can gather."

Capt. Stefan Bronislaw Sznuk turned out to be a diminutive red-haired man in his mid-forties with an enormous nose and a cracked, high-pitched voice. He spoke in rapid-fire, heavily accented English augmented by an exhausting array of sweeping gestures to demonstrate his points. On the short walk from the Operations Centre to the main barracks building, the little man gave Black his entire military history.

"So Sikorski says to me, Snookie, how do you like this war? And I say to Sikorski, General, for me this is the fourth war I have been in, and I am always on the wrong side, yes? Russians, Prussian, Germans, French. Always the same. Poland is the foot-wiper of Europe."

"Doormat?" offered Black. Sznuk beamed, nodding and throwing his arms about.

"Quite, quite."

"You flew in the Great War?"

"Oh, yes! Sopwith Camel, Pup, Bristol." His left hand swooped in mock combat with his right. "Of course the Spitfire is far superior." He lifted his hands, thumbs upward, and made a rat-a-tat-tat sound. "Much better for killing Germans. Even better than ack-ack, you know, the anti-aircraft guns." He let out an unpleasant, cackling laugh. The look in his eyes wasn't quite normal, an impassioned fury and sadness for the homeland he'd been forced to flee. Kent had mentioned it—they were all crazy and fought like mad dogs. Not surprising under the circumstances.

They reached the nearer of the two large barracks buildings and went up to the second floor. Captain Sznuk led Black to a small cubicle at the far end of the dormitory, screened off from the other bunks by a makeshift partition built up with a large metal wardrobe and several steamer trunks. Other cubicles like it were scattered around the room. Except for Sznuk and Black the barracks was empty.

"Where are the men?"

"There is an alert. They are waiting at the dispersal huts on the field for the signal to scramble." The little man ran in place and buckled on an imaginary helmet to demonstrate. He pulled back a row of towels hanging on a sagging length of rope and ushered Black into Rudelski's tiny home.

A high window was at the end of the ersatz room, carefully covered with sheets of paper cellotaped in place over the glass in case of blast. Directly beneath the window was a narrow, metal-framed bed with a neatly rolled mattress at the end.

Several uniforms and shirts were in the wardrobe, but no civilian clothes. A steamer trunk had been converted into a bedside table complete with gooseneck lamp, a row of well-worn books, and a heavy glass ashtray. Beside the ashtray there was a packet of *tabac noir* French cigarettes; Spilsbury had been right about that too. A photograph was tacked to the door of the wardrobe. Rudelski at age twelve or thirteen, standing with an older man wearing a dark suit. Behind them Black could make out the corner of a large, stone house.

"His father was with the Warsaw engineering department. An important person I think," Sznuk commented.

"Did you know Rudelski well?"

"No. He was very...quiet, yes?" Sznuk made a slightly effeminate gesture, one palm against his cheek, head slightly tilted. The effect was so absurd Black almost burst out laughing.

"He was a homosexual?"

"Poof, pish, yes, almost certainly."

"He had a...friend, here?"

"No!" Sznuk shook his head violently. "The others in Squadron Kosciuszko are very..." He lifted one arm and squeezed the biceps with his other hand, frowning angrily. "Masculine. Very much for the ladies." Sznuk then made an astoundingly obscene gesture Black had never seen before and leered, lifting one eyebrow suggestively. Sznuk shrugged. "No one cared though. Rudelski made no great thing of it. He could fly. That is all that mattered."

Bending down, Black saw a footlocker under the bed and pulled it out. The simple hasp had no lock. He lifted the footlocker onto the springs of the bed and opened it. On the left there was a carefully folded, dark blue uniform with an officer's peaked cap resting on it. On the right there was a checkerboard, a small wooden box, a deck of playing cards, and a bundle of letters done up with a piece of twine. The lettering on the outside of the top letter was in Polish. There was no shaving kit.

Black handed the letters to Sznuk. "Who are these from?" The Pole pulled one out, removed the letter from its envelope, and read briefly. He took out a second letter, then a third. "They are from his mother. From when he was at flying school." The red-haired man smiled sadly. "He tells her that the food is very poor and that his stomach is missing her *barscht* and *kluski*." He paused. "You wish to know more?"

"Not at the moment. But perhaps you could have all his personal things removed from here and taken somewhere for safekeeping."

"Of course."

"I don't think there's anything else here."

"No." Sznuk shook his head sadly. "I think there is very little of Rudelski in this place."

Sznuk returned with Black to the Operations Centre. Kent had vanished, but the Pole arranged for another WAAF driver to run him across to the train station. He was back in London in time for a late tea. An hour later the Luftwaffe returned and the bombs began to fall again.

Dr. Charles Tennant, wearing the uniform of a captain in the Royal Army Medical Corps, sat in the small, darkened room staring intently through the small square of one-way glass. Beside him was Col. John Cecil Masterman, onetime prisoner of war, later censor of Christ Church Oxford, and presently head of B1(a), an obscure, utterly secret division of MI5, British counterintelligence, charged with the debriefing of downed airmen and the eventual "turning" of captured German spies.

Masterman was not in uniform. Instead the small, beak-nosed man wore a poorly fitted dark blue suit over a white shirt with frayed collar and cuffs and a Christ Church tie sporting two decades' worth of cigarette burns and jam stains—the prototypical dress of an Oxford don. Tennant's uniform on the other hand was exquisitely tailored, perfectly cut to the man's slight athletic figure. At forty-nine Masterman was only five years older than Tennant, but the psychiatrist looked considerably younger. What little hair Masterman still had was yellow-gray, his lean face seamed, lined, and stubbled. In contrast, Tennant's hair was thick and very dark, his handsome face perfectly shaven, nails neatly manicured.

The room the two men sat in was located in what had once been the administration wing of Wormwood Scrubs Prison in Hammersmith on the western edge of the city, taken over early in the war by MI5.

The Scrubs was a bleak Edwardian horror in brick and stone, surrounded by crouching gray cottage suburbs, freight yards, windswept cemeteries, and the rusting hulks of abandoned gasworks. For Tennant it represented the worst of Empire and British hypocrisy—the blight of hardship and mindless, grueling labor within a stone's throw of the lush Royal Gardens at Kew.

On the other side of the mirror a nervous-looking man in his late twenties and dressed in pajama-like gray coveralls was being interviewed by an interrogator wearing an RAF uniform completely devoid of any rank or insignia. The voices, both speaking in rapid-fire German, were being transmitted by a hidden microphone to Tennant and Masterman.

"His name is Zeidler," Masterman said quietly. "We've given him the code name Summer."

"Recent?" asked Tennant.

Masterman nodded. "Fresh as a daisy. Dropped out of the sky just before dawn on Friday not far from Oxford. We managed to get him within a few hours. Claimed he was Polish, but he couldn't find Warsaw on a map. Silly, really. I'm beginning to wonder where Canaris finds these people."

"He's very nervous. More than you'd expect."

"Really? You'd think nerves would be the order of the day under the circumstances."

"At this stage it's more likely that he'd still be in shock," the psychiatrist answered. "Numb rather than nervous."

"Well, you are the expert." Masterman shrugged. Like Masterman, Tennant spoke fluent German, held a commission in the Royal Army, and was the perfect choice to evaluate the psychological state of the poor unfortunates who had been caught in Masterman's web since the first days of the Double Cross counterintelligence group. The fact that he was a member of the same social set as Masterman and tended to the psychiatric needs of half the political and military wives in Mayfair and Belgravia made his appointment as psychiatric consultant to MI5 a fait accompli. The fact that he was handsome, enjoyed the company of women, and was an extremely eligible bachelor was also in his favor.

As well as monitoring the mental condition of captured spies and the odd downed Heinkel pilot, Tennant was also charged with interviewing prospective applicants to MI5 itself. In doing so he quickly came to realize that being brought into what Masterman referred to jovially as "the Land of Smoke and Mirrors" had far more to do with one's social acceptability than one's qualifications. Of the applicants he'd spoken to over the past year or so, almost two-thirds had attended Oxford or Cambridge, and an even higher percentage had gone to Eton before that.

"I wouldn't invest too much time and effort in this one," Tennant murmured, watching the man on the other side of the glass. "He might turn just to avoid the threat of execution, but he'll turn again."

"Interesting," said Masterman. "You're sure?"

"Positive." Tennant nodded.

The interrogation of the man Masterman had code-named Summer took several hours, and by the time Tennant passed through the main gate of the Scrubs, it was early evening. Far off to the east the Luftwaffe bombers were pounding Docklands again, the light from the East End fires pulsing on the horizon, explosions lighting up the underside of the low clouds overhead like gigantic flashbulbs.

The relentless sound of the bombs rolled across the sky in a stuttering funereal thunder, and Tennant smiled. Much more of this and the lags and lads of Spitalfields would win the war for Germany before the Germans had a chance to invade; there were already rumors of quickly stifled riots and talk that, just as it had been in the last war, it was the poor who were being used as cannon fodder, this time in their own homes rather than the trenches.

Chauffeured in the staff car provided by Masterman,

Tennant went to the station at St. Quintin Park, boarded an almost empty, blacked-out train, and began the slow journey through the darkened, waiting outskirts of the city. He spent the time contemplating the absurd construction of Masterman's organization. It was definitely an "old boys" network, and one that appeared to be populated by more than its fair share of homosexuals and self-confessed Communists. Not surprising really, when you considered the educational environment.

To Tennant it seemed an extraordinary way to run an intelligence service. If the Abwehr, the Reich Security Administration, was run that way, the European blitzkrieg would have ground to a halt before it began. This was no mere hypothesis, since, among other things, Dr. Charles Tennant had been in the employ of the German Secret Service for the past five years, working directly under the authority of the Nazi spymaster Reinhard Heydrich.

Born in Sheffield, England, in 1896, Charles Reid Tennant was the only child of Sir William Morpeth Tennant, an industrialist who'd made his fortune in steel and munitions, and Julia Steinmaur, the aristocratic sister of one of his Austrian partners. Shortly after Charles Tennant's fourth birthday his father died, and because of his mother's "nervous condition," the task of raising him fell to his widowed aunt from Vienna, Elizabeth Von Letz, followed by a succession of boarding schools.

Leaving Eton on the eve of World War I, Charles Tennant was accepted into University College, Sheffield, where he studied medicine for the next five years, specializing in mental diseases. He then interned as a resident in psychiatry at the Sheffield Lunatic Asylum for a sixth year and obtained his specialist's certificate.

In 1921 his aunt, Elizabeth Letts (the "Von" discreetly erased and the spelling of the name subtly altered in 1914), arranged an appointment for him at the newly created Vienna

Institute of Psychiatry, where he spent the next three years as a resident and, out of desire as well as necessity, regained his boyhood fluency in German.

In 1924 his mother, institutionalized for several years previously, committed suicide, and Charles Tennant came into his inheritance. After establishing a trust for his elderly aunt he used part of his newly acquired wealth to travel, spending the next four years in Canada and the United States, studying first at McGill University in Montreal, and then at Princeton in New Jersey.

Returning to England in 1928 following the death of his aunt, Tennant purchased a house in Cheyne Mews, Chelsea, a discreet, luxurious residence not far from the Royal Hospital and directly across the Thames from Battersea Park. Caught in the great Crash the following year, Tennant lost virtually everything except for the mews house and, for the first time in his life, found himself in the odd position of actually having to earn a living. Using his old contacts, he found a position at the Vienna Institute and returned to Austria in the spring of 1930.

During that year he met an old friend, Horst Kapkow. He and Horst had played together during Tennant's Austrian vacations before the war, forging a childhood friendship based largely on the availability of Horst's cousin Ingrid, her large breasts in particular. Horst was now a doctor himself, and more importantly, he was also a member of the fledgling National Socialist Party.

Tennant was converted to the Nazi philosophy almost immediately. Although he'd never practiced psychiatry on a clinical level, he had long been interested in the concept of shamanism among uncivilized races, and in Nazism he saw the perfect evocation of his own theories on the principle of sacrifice and its use on a practical level.

An African witch doctor, seeing that his patient was "possessed," would simply speak the necessary incantations to exorcise the demon, often using some sort of sacrificial object or totem to convince the possessed individual. Just as often, the symptoms of illness could be transferred to an object or another individual, thus solving the patient's problem with a brief and effective ceremony. Here too were the roots of Celtic ritual and the Wagnerian ring.

If Nazism was the sacrificial ritual, Adolf Hitler was the modern sorcerer utilizing it, taking the various ills of his troubled nation, distilling them into ritual, and then transferring them away.

Personally Tennant felt that the führer's attitude toward the Jews was overstated, but by the same token he saw the practical advantage of making a small and relatively benign segment of the population the sacrificial lamb for millions of others.

It wasn't a matter of right or wrong but of practical logic. The world was sick and that sickness had to have a cause. The Jew was the obvious tumor to be excised and Hitler the surgeon demigod wielding the knife. Not pleasant, but Tennant knew instinctively that it would work.

Over the next three years Tennant saw Nazism take hold in Germany and in Austria. These were exciting times, and through Horst Kapkow he began meeting the men who were the architects of this new world order. One of these was a young ex-naval officer named Reinhard Heydrich, who, by the spring of 1934, had become head of the Sicherheitsdienst or SD, the Nazi Intelligence and Security Service.

Tennant immediately recognized that Heydrich was a textbook paranoiac and sadist, but that took nothing away from the man's immense personal power. If Tennant was going to ally himself with anyone within the hierarchy of the Third Reich, he could think of no one better than Reinhard Heydrich.

Six months later, after a secret meeting in Paris, Charles Tennant went to work for the SD Ausland, or foreign department, acting, as Heydrich put it, to counterpoint the efforts of his chief rival, Wilhelm Canaris, head of the Abwehr, the Intelligence Department of the German Armed Forces High Command.

According to Heydrich, the white-haired admiral was not to be trusted, and his agents were both inept and amateur. When war came, as both men knew it would, the Reich—and Heydrich in particular—would need at least one competent and intelligent operative in England, even though Hitler, up to that point, had expressly forbidden any such activity. Tennant was to be that secret operative, Heydrich's personal cat among the pigeons.

In September of 1934, partially subsidized by Heydrich's steadily growing treasury, Charles Tennant returned to London and established himself as a practicing psychiatrist with offices at 6 Cheyne Walk Mews. Over the next five years he attracted a variety of patients, mainly women, many of them wives, daughters, and lovers of the British military, government, and industrial elite.

Following Heydrich's example, and using an extremely sophisticated wire recorder provided to him by the Telefunken Corporation, he began to amass extensive dossiers on all his patients, spending long hours cross-indexing hundreds of small morsels of intelligence to create a larger picture.

As well as assembling a monumental confessional of sexual peccadilloes, personal quirks, and professional secrets, he also managed to collect a great deal of hard information regarding the United Kingdom's general war preparedness, which he regularly transmitted to Heydrich's private listening post in Hamburg. Through his work with Masterman and MI5 he had discovered that the Abwehr spies run by Canaris had been prejudiced almost from the start, and just as importantly that the Abwehr itself had been penetrated by more than one of Masterman's people, including a supposed Welsh nationalist, code-named G.W., who was actually a retired police inspector. Just as important was the knowledge that

Masterman, through G.W., had co-opted the long-used method of transmitting important information using the Spanish embassy's diplomatic bag.

In keeping with his straightforward, well-ordered nature he had chosen the simple code name The Doctor for his transmissions. Only Heydrich knew Tennant's real identity. After learning about G.W. he had stopped using his Spanish contact, a buffoon named Del Pozo, who passed himself off as a journalist and who had access to the regular pouch to Lisbon. Over time Tennant developed his own system of getting information directly to Heydrich, and as far as he could tell, it had yet to be compromised.

The train from the Scrubs finally reached Victoria Station, and from there he hailed a taxi, settling back in his seat as the cabbie picked his way through the deserted streets heading for Whites, the ancient and relentlessly Conservative—with a capital C—gentlemen's club on St. James's Street just off Pall Mall, which Jonathan Swift had once called "the common rendezvous of infamous sharpers and noble cullies."

As well as being a discreet home away from home for half of Churchill's cabinet and most of the War Office, the bar at Whites was also a favorite watering hole for many of the euphemistically titled "junior Foreign Service officers" who worked for MI5. One, a handsome, cleft-chinned young man named Donald Maclean, was particularly interesting, but tonight it was dinner with a junior minister who worked with Beaverbrook and whose wife was completely indifferent to sex and just what the bloody hell was he supposed to do about it? Tennant smiled to himself in the dark interior of the taxicab. A spy's work, it seemed, was never done.

CHAPTER FOUR

Tuesday, September 10, 1940
10:00 A.M., British Summer Time

THERE WAS AN ORDINARY NAME on his National Registration Card, but he had more than one of those, and in his heart he called himself only The Number. He sat alone at a small table in the tea shop on the corner of Carter Lane and Burgon Street, polishing his eyeglasses with one corner of his dark blue tie. This was the heart of The City, scores of small, cramped buildings leaning over a thousand lanes and alleys and unnamed byways, all of them huddled around the glories of Wren's churches, most in the overwhelming shadow of the great dome of St. Paul's.

The Book was on the table in front of him, carefully kept to one side, out of the way of any possible spill. He'd ordered tea and scones but had tasted neither. From experience he knew that the tea would be thin and the scones stale, but it didn't matter; they were only an excuse to occupy the table.

Standing at the counter on the far side of the narrow room, the hugely fat woman who ran the shop was preparing sandwiches for the elevenses crowd who would soon be coming down from the Criminal Courts, Fleet Street, and the

Government Post Office. She snarled as she chopped and spread, browbeating the Italian cook, invisible in the kitchen, and ignoring her only customer.

"I told you, I don't give a flaming shit if the bloody milk's gone off! Use the powdered like I told you!" The woman glared into the aluminum bowl in front of her and dug into its contents, bringing up several large sections of pale, boiled chicken. She threw the pieces down onto the counter and began to chop them into salad, gripping the broad-handled carving knife with small, wet fingers, muttering under her breath as she worked.

The Number put his glasses on again, blinked, and looked out across the narrow street. Directly across from the Jo Lyons and occupying the other corner was the side entrance to a small public house, the Rising Sun. A tall, red metal sign had been wrapped around the corner bricks above the door, emblazoned with the name and advertising Trumans ale in even larger letters.

The pub, he knew, was owned by one Doris Luffington, a widow in her sixties who had inherited the business from her late husband. Sgt. Maj. Charles Luffington had died a slow, miserable death in Chelsea Hospital from the aftereffects of mustard-gas poisoning, leaving his wife to raise their only daughter, Jane, by herself, as well as operate the Rising Sun. Jane Luffington, twenty-two, was a member of the Women's Royal Navy Service, a "Wren," presently attached to a Motor Transport unit of lorry drivers and dispatch riders based in London.

It was all in The Book. Her unit number, commanding officer, even the license plate and Royal Navy serial codes of the side-valve Triumph 350 she rode and maintained with such loving care. All recorded in the small, precise hand he'd developed years ago at City and Guilds College.

Without taking his eyes off the entrance to the Rising Sun, he reached out with his left hand and put his palm down on the worn buckram cover of The Book. In the daylight his power was greatly diminished, but The Book and its contents was a constant source of strength.

It told him, for instance, that Jane Luffington had a some-time lover, a handsome lieutenant commander (Royal Navy Volunteer Reserve) who worked for Admiral Godfrey in Naval Intelligence. Her numbers also told him that her menstrual period was almost exactly aligned with the lunar cycle, and that without the clandestine visits she made to the Rising Sun, she would not be able to afford the flat in Bayswater she shared with three other Wrens.

Without thinking, he removed his eyeglasses and began to polish them again, smiling vaguely to himself. Sometimes he wondered if The Names really mattered at all, since they were nothing more than false constructs without any true value in a world where numbers meant so much. Numbers had no emotion and told no lies. A Number was, or it was not, without equivocation.

He heard the motorcycle well before he saw it, the power-ful engine echoing off the brickwork as she thundered onto Burgon Street from Ireland Yard. Without undue haste, know-ing he had time, The Number replaced the glasses on his nose and took his watch from his waistcoat pocket. One-handed, he flipped open the engraved silver case and checked the time. A little early, but well within the limits he'd established. The extra minutes meant she'd almost certainly spend more time with her mother, which would make it all the easier. He closed the watch and slipped it back into his pocket, then turned toward the window once again.

The motorcycle appeared, a dark blue, heavy-chassied beast, brightwork painted flat gray, the bulbous eye of the headlamp shielded by a blackout cover. Below the pillion seat, steel-framed pannier baskets contained large canvas dispatch bags, strapped tightly shut.

Leading Wren Jane Luffington braked in front of the entrance, switched off the engine, and climbed down from the Triumph. She was dressed as usual in her full dispatch-rider uniform of dark blue jodhpurs, high, tightly fitted boots, short serge riding jacket, and long, flared gauntlets. She stood by the motorcycle for a moment, lifted up her goggles, and snapped them down over the brim of her old-fashioned tricorn hat. Stripping off the gauntlets, she tucked them under the strap of her gas-mask bag. She was pretty in a boyish way, oval faced, dark eyed, with short, dark hair.

Jane leaned over the motorcycle, grasping the handgrips, and wheeled the machine into the narrow passage between the Burgon Street side of the Rising Sun and the neighboring building, a small office block. She reappeared a few seconds later and vanished into the pub.

The Number watched her go from his vantage point across the Street. He'd witnessed her routine seven times in the past three weeks. She never spent more than eleven minutes with her mother, or fewer than seven. Calmly he tucked The Book into the side pocket of his jacket, picked up his large, civil-service-issue briefcase from the floor beside the table, and left the tea shop.

Four and a half minutes later, his task successfully accomplished, The Number reached the Blackfriars underground station and began his long journey back to Dollis Hill. Three minutes after that, as he began to choose new numbers for the night ahead, Jane Luffington climbed back onto the Triumph, tramped down hard on the kick starter, and prepared to complete her own journey, turning the motorcycle down the hill to New Bridge Street, then wheeling it north toward New Fetter Lane and the Public Record Office.

"I don't think we're going to get through." Dick Capstick slowed as they drove down Middlesex Street and eased the ten-year-old Fordson van to a stop in front of a makeshift timber barrier. A warehouse on the left of the wooden barricade was a charred ruin, while a smaller shed on the right appeared to have weathered the previous night's bombing unscathed. The barrier blocked the entrance to Strype Street, a narrow lane of row houses running a single despairing block between Middlesex Street and Bell Lane on the border between Spitalfields and Aldgate. Another slum slowly easing west into The City, a cancer unnoticed for the moment, but growing with time.

"A little walk won't hurt you." Morris Black smiled at his companion. Capstick was thirty-seven, three years younger than Black, and at least two stone heavier. He looked more like a circus strongman than a detective, and the effect of his broad shoulders and heavy, square-jawed face was intensified by his dapper Savile Row suits and the trademark white rose he wore in his lapel. Black had known the burly, expansive man since joining the Metropolitan Police. Capstick was one of the very few people at the Yard whom Black considered to be a friend. Even at that the relationship was a distant one, almost exclusively confined to work. Fay had been both best friend and lover, and Black had long ago come to the conclusion that he would never have either again.

Capstick set the handbrake on the Flying Squad vehicle, and both men climbed out into the smoky, late-morning sunlight. Black's nostrils were instantly assailed by the heavy stench of wet ash and sodden, charred wood. Much more of this, thought Black, and the entire city would stink like a crematorium. The drifting shroud of smoke hanging over London was becoming a permanent part of the landscape.

"Hold tight, Morris, we've got a little Hitler to contend with this morning." Capstick poked his broad chin in the direction of the barrier. A slight, round-faced man in his early forties was parading back and forth in front of the obstruction dressed in a long greatcoat and a tin helmet with the letters

W.R.P. stenciled in white on the front. A War Reserve Police constable.

He was carrying a long truncheon in one hand, smacking it lightly against one leg as he walked. Capstick and Black moved toward the barrier and the constable stepped forward. He was wearing lightly tinted eyeglasses, and Black noticed that his complexion was flushed; a drinker, or someone with very high blood pressure.

"You can't stop there. Police business." His voice barely rose above a whispered squeak. He gestured with the truncheon, almost threateningly.

"Oh, bugger off," Capstick growled. The red-faced constable stepped in front of the much larger detective and held up one imperious hand. His color heightened even more; Black thought he was going to have a stroke.

"That's enough of that. You'll have to move along."

Capstick dug into the inside pocket of his jacket and pulled out his warrant card. He thrust it under the man's nose.

"Detective Inspector Capstick, CID." He gestured toward Black. "This is Detective Inspector Black." Capstick scowled. "Who the hell are you?"

"Special Constable Christie." Seeing the warrant card, the man had come rigidly to attention. "I'm terribly sorry, Inspector, I..." The squeaky voice faded into silence.

"Bloody right you're sorry," snarled Capstick. "Now step aside." Special Constable Christie did as he was told, and the two men went by, stepping over the low barrier.

"A bit hard on him, weren't you?" said Black as they headed down the street.

"Drives me right round the twist," Capstick answered, sidestepping a pile of rubble. "We're fighting a bloody war, with bloody bombs raining down out of the bloody sky, and they go out and hire a thousand silly buggers like that one. Officious little shits. All they do is get in the way."

Black said nothing. Capstick was perfectly right. The worst

of it was that almost no care was taken in vetting the hordes of new recruits, so God only knew whom they were actually hiring on. One man, using his newly acquired authority, had taken to testing tap beer in public houses to see if it had been tampered with by fifth columnists. He'd managed to get away with it for the better part of a week before someone saw fit to check up on him.

Only the first few houses in the block had actually been hit by high explosives, but evidence of incendiary activity was all the way along: puddles of fused pavement tar where incendiaries had fallen into the road and burned unchecked, sooty streaks above shattered, burnt-out window frames, scatterings of charred bedding and furniture lying in the street. No children anywhere, that was the most disconcerting thing.

The address they'd been called to by Central Dispatch was the last house in the row, with nothing beyond but a high wrought-iron fence that separated the house from a small piece of waste ground opening onto Bell Lane. The foundations of what had once been a school stood at one edge of the waste, weeds growing up around the tumbled stones. Black paused for a moment and gazed around; this place had been a ruin long before the bombings began.

Several uniformed coppers were standing around the entrance to the house, as well as a pair of plainclothes types from Records, their cumbersome Speed Graphic cameras in hand. Black caught a quick, flicking motion and a tiny arc of sparks as one of the constables surreptitiously tossed away a cigarette, seeing them approach.

The house itself was two storied and narrow, the doorway flush against the crumbling, yellow bricks, Three cement steps, edges rotted and flanked by thick patches of weed, led up to the dark green door. The color of the door matched the window frames and was exactly the shade of the filing cabinets at the Yard and every other government office in Whitehall and Westminster.

A quart or two pinched from stores and brought home hidden at the bottom of a briefcase. All of Bermondsey and most of Tooting had the same petty-theft decor. Paint was hard to come by these days; lead was being used for more important things like bombs and bullets.

"This it?" asked Capstick unnecessarily. One of the photographers nodded. Capstick and Black climbed up the steps and went into the house.

Reg Perrin, the detective sergeant from Bishopsgate who'd caught the Strype Street call, was on his hands and knees in the dark, narrow passage just inside the door. A single, low-watt bulb hung from the ceiling, operated by a length of string knotted to a short pull chain. The walls were green over rough plaster. The floor was covered with thin brown carpet, worn through in places to show the darkly varnished boards beneath.

"Find anything?" Capstick asked. Perrin grunted and climbed to his feet, brushing grime from his trouser knees.

"Nothing but rising damp." Perrin was in his mid-thirties, a wiry, hatchet-faced Welshman, his thinning hair inevitably hidden under an ancient bowler. "Christ, I don't know why we bother with places like this. Bloody Hitler's doing us all a favor if you ask me."

"No one's asking you anything," said Capstick, his voice flat. Perrin ran Bishopsgate like a feudal lord, collecting tithes from every pub and rooming-house brothel in the district. Capstick thoroughly disliked the weasely little man.

"Cats," said Black, sniffing the air. The atmosphere in the dank little passage reeked of ammonia.

"Takes a man from CID to figure that out." Perrin grinned. "Cats belong to Wardle, the old gent who lives in the flat above." He nodded back toward the stairway behind him. "Brakeman. Retired."

"Let's have a look inside," Black suggested.

Perrin lifted an eyebrow. "You'll have company, best manners, mind."

"Who?"

"The Pope and the Archbishop." Black nodded. Spilsbury and his longtime friend Bentley Purchase, the East London coroner.

"They're very quick," said Capstick, suddenly alert. "Who brought them along?"

"Your lot."

The two Scotland Yard detectives went into the ground-floor flat. The door off the passage led directly into a small sitting room that looked out onto the street. An oval, braided rag rug was on the floor, with a sagging chesterfield along the far wall and an armchair at an angle to the small gas fire. There were no decorations on the walls except a Lloyds Bank calendar. The front window was cracked from side to side and filthy. The wallpaper had a floral motif that might once have been light blue. Now it was the color of nicotine.

A doorway led down a short passage to a three-step landing. An open door was on the right. A tiny bedroom. The mattress had been stripped of its linen. A small window set high on the wall looked out onto a bare patch of dull sky. Once again the glass was filthy.

The steps took them down into a kitchen area. Spilsbury, hands stuffed into the pockets of his overcoat, was standing with the coroner beside a white enameled stove. There was a refrigerator beside the stove, and just past it, a door, probably leading out into the back garden.

On top of the refrigerator there was an alarm clock in a bright yellow Bakelite case. The only other furniture in the room was a pair of wooden, straight-backed chairs and a square table covered with a drooping sheet of dark blue oilcloth. On the oilcloth there was the naked body of a young man in his mid-twenties.

In life he had been taller than the table was long. His head hung down over the near edge of the table while his legs hung over the far side. His mouth and eyes were open. Blood had settled into the face, turning it a mottled blue and bulging the eyes. The tongue, fallen back against the man's hard palate, was almost black. The bulging eyes were brown. He was fair-skinned and had light, corn-silk blond hair, cut long.

"Interesting, don't you think?" said Spilsbury, speaking to Black. There was no greeting or introduction. Morris Black felt a twinge of claustrophobia. The four live men stood in a room twelve feet wide and fourteen long. Between them and the body on the table there was barely room to move.

"No visible cause of death," said Purchase. Black had met the coroner on one or two occasions, but knew him mostly by reputation. From what he understood, the pinched man with the small eyes and heavy glasses had trained for medicine at Cambridge, then switched to law. A good combination for a coroner, a quick mind and a fair hand, but what were he and Spilsbury doing here so quickly, and for that matter, what were they doing here at all? Definitely odd, as out of place as the corpse they were examining.

"Rather like our Polish friend," said Spilsbury. Black edged around Capstick and took a closer look at the body on the table. Naked, like Rudelski, and without any sign of what might have killed him. There was no shroud, but the sense of the body's having been prepared for its discovery was the same, the altarlike display on the table replacing the theatrics of the Polish flier's rubber bag.

Black leaned down. The positioning of the limbs was strange. The left arm lay splayed out at a forty-five-degree angle relative to the torso while the right arm had been brought over the hairless chest to lie parallel to the shoulders. He felt something niggling at his memory, but he couldn't quite grasp it. Ignoring the feeling for the moment, he took his fountain pen out of his jacket pocket and gently lifted the hands, checking the palms.

"Nothing," said Spilsbury. "Mr. Purchase and I have already made a preliminary examination. I'm afraid there is no *Z* this time. Too much to hope for, I suppose."

Black stood away from the body. It was almost there. He let his eyes drift over the room again and finally settled on the little clock perched on the refrigerator. The hands hadn't moved since he'd come into the room. He had an alarm clock much like it beside his bed; they ticked loudly when they were wound up. He couldn't hear anything in the kitchen. The clock on the refrigerator was stopped at 3:25. He looked down at the body again and imagined the arms as the hands of the clock. The positioning was the same. Twenty-five past three.

He felt a sick, hollow twinge in the pit of his stomach and simultaneously a quickening excitement. He had it now and knew what it meant, at least on one level. Time and circumstance might eventually have explained Rudelski's murder— the rubber bag, the narcotic poisoning, even the letter carved into his hand, but not this. He felt himself flushing, embarrassed by the animal depth of his feeling. A tracking hound with a fresh scent in his nostrils. The passion that could make him forget his pain.

Black nodded to himself. Unsolved, the death of the Polish airman would have been charged off as an aberration, a case file left irritatingly open for a time, eventually to be forgotten, buried under a dozen, then a hundred, then a thousand more pressing matters. The stopped clock and the position of the dead man's arms changed that irrevocably.

Frowning, Black stared down at the body, wondering if either victim or killer had once been a Boy Scout. That or a Sea Cadet. Both the clock and the body had been positioned to mimic the semaphore signal for the last letter in the alphabet.

"No, Sir Bernard," Black said finally, sure of himself now. "Not one *Z*. Two."

CHAPTER FIVE

Tuesday, September 10, 1940
7:30 P.M., British Summer Time

"**B**Y GOD, MORRIS, I THOUGHT the old man's eyes were going to pop out of his head! Semaphore, imagine that!" Dick Capstick sprinkled more cheese onto his pasta, wound up an enormous forkful, and popped it gleefully into his mouth.

The two men were dining together at Gennaro's on Dean Street in the center of Soho. The popular Italian restaurant was almost empty. The bombings were forcing a new schedule on London; movie theaters closed at seven, and even the most popular restaurants and clubs shut down by eight. Soho, that bastion of the avant-garde squeezed in between the Bloomsbury literati and Mayfair high society, was no exception. Only in hotels with basement shelters were the old hours maintained.

Morris Black smiled and sipped his glass of wine. His own meal, a thin veal Parmesan, had turned into a glutinous, untouched mass on his plate. To Black, who'd been a Boy Scout for several years, the semaphore secret had quickly become obvious—the position of the clock hands and the dead man's arms were identical: semaphore for the letter Z. Both Spilsbury and Purchase the coroner had missed it altogether. Sir Bernard congratulated Black on his observation; Purchase only scowled.

"It doesn't bring me any closer to finding out who did the deed."

"Still..." Capstick washed down the spaghetti with a swallow from his glass. "Put him in his place a bit." Black smiled again. Capstick was Labour Party born and bred, and putting his superiors "in their place" was an ongoing crusade.

"I'm just wondering what's going to happen when the newspapers find out about this." Black toyed with the stem of his glass. At the rear of the dim-lit room someone put on a phonograph record of moody violin music. "It's the kind of thing that could start a panic. A madman going about killing people during the raids."

"I shouldn't worry about it." Capstick shook his head as he scraped up the last of the spaghetti. "Mark my words, that's why Sir Bernard and Purchase were there so quickly. Word's come down from the top; this is to be kept hush-hush. Bad for morale and all that. Not a word gets out or heads will roll. The canteen was one great whisper about it today at tea." The large man wiped his plate with the last bit of bread from the basket between them, ate it, then leaned back in his chair and lit a cigarette. "It'll be D-noticed already unless I'm very much mistaken."

"Something always gets out." Morris Black shrugged. "D notice or not, you know that." The ubiquitous D notice was an across-the-board censorship blanket used by the War Office. Black wondered what the Nazis called their version of the news blackout. A *Goebbelsröte*?

Capstick shrugged. "I think they're making too much of it. The fiend in question is only killing queers, after all."

"We don't know that for certain."

"Safe enough to assume. Pretty young lads left dead with their peters lolling about in the breeze. Not going to worry the vast majority of the great unwashed, Morris."

"No, but maybe it's going to worry a few well-placed MPs and the odd first secretary."

Capstick grinned. "Not to mention half the old Etonians in the Home Office. That is, if you believe Nosey Smith and the lads in Special Branch. Smile at one of them standing at the pissoir and he'll have you up on charges for gross indecency." One of the Gennaro's waiters was singing along with the violin music now as he swept crumbs up off the tables.

Capstick shook his head again and spewed out a long plume of smoke. "I'm glad it's your patch and not mine, Morris. They'll want you to clear this one off with all due speed." The detective made a face. "Meaningful looks from the chief superintendent. Concerned memoranda from the Office of the Commissioner. Deathly stuff."

"I didn't notice you staying on to lend a hand."

"I've got my own villains to pursue...thank God." He smiled across the table at his friend. "No joy from the upstairs lodger?"

"Wardle? He's half-blind and almost deaf. The flat was let through an agency, two months' rent, cash in advance, paid through the post and arranged over the telephone. Wardle only spoke once to the man who took the rooms."

"Doesn't remember anything?"

"*Nowt a bleeding fing,*" said Black, imitating the old man.

"Nothing to go on then?"

"No."

"Which means you'll have to wait for him to do it again, I suppose."

"I'm afraid so." Black nodded.

Capstick consulted his watch. "Well, that shouldn't be long. The Nazi hordes will be along any minute now. Maybe Queer Jack will strike again tonight."

"Oh, God!" moaned Black. "Now you've gone and given him a name!"

"And if you see the name tomorrow in the *Standard*, you'll know where it came from, D notice or not."

"In which case I'd hand you over to Special Branch as a fifth columnist."

"Come along, Morris." Capstick laughed, pushing back his chair and climbing to his feet. "I'll drive you home before the bombs begin to fall."

They drove through the dark, empty streets, heading west toward Shepherd's Market. Black stared moodily out through the windshield, lost in thought. Finally he spoke.

"Another thing's been bothering me," he said quietly.

"What's that?"

"How did he know?"

"Who?"

"Queer Jack. How did he know that part of the city would be bombed? First Rudelski and now this one."

"The whole bloody city is being bombed, Morris. It's just coincidence."

"I don't think so." Black shook his head. "Rudelski was murdered before the first big raid on the seventh." He glanced out the side window at the darkened streets. "Before all this started. The same with the second one. He knew in advance."

"What are you on about? You're making this lad out to be some sort of magician. Next thing, you'll be telling me he flies about on bat's wings and sleeps in a bloody coffin at night." The heavyset detective snorted loudly. "Either that or he's one of Special Branch's Nazi spies and knows when the raids are going to come." Capstick let out a barking laugh. "Christ! That's all we need, Morris! Imagine what would happen if the newspapers got hold of that idea—a bloody homicidal Nazi gone round the bend." He shook his head. "Trust me, old fellow, it's just coincidence."

Black shrugged. "Perhaps. I suppose we'll just have to wait and see."

He had Capstick drop him off on Curzon Street, then went through the carriageway beside the Ye Grapes and onto Market Street.

Black paused for a moment at the corner, listening to the muted laughter from the pub as it leaked out around the blackout curtains into the cooling night air. He thought about having a quick nightcap, then decided against it. He'd begun drinking shortly after Fay's death, mostly as a sure way of dulling his feelings and bringing on sleep. Since then it had become an easy habit, and soon, he knew, it would become a necessity.

He'd seen it happen to others often enough; colleagues at the Yard bringing their fat briefcases to and fro, bottles within tinkling as they stepped onto the lift or climbed the stairs, raspberry filigrees of broken veins growing on their cheeks and noses like rosy patches of lichen spreading on a stone.

In the far distance he heard the sirens begin, but there was no sound of approaching aircraft. Since mid-afternoon the sky had patched over with gray clouds, and the Met. Report from Greenwich had mentioned overcast across most of France and Central Europe. There would be no big raid tonight. He thought about Queer Jack again, nagged by the murderer's apparent ability to predict the future. He tried to shrug it off. Capstick was probably right, it was nothing more than coincidence.

Black stepped off the pavement and crossed to the three-story building on the corner of Market Street and White Horse Street. A bakery and a greengrocer were on the ground floor, with two flats on the first floor and a third, larger one above.

His father had purchased the building and half a dozen others like it during the Depression, then deeded it to his son as a wedding present. Morris Black had lived in the uppermost flat for the entire duration of his marriage, the rents from the two other flats and the shops on the ground floor adding up to more than twice his annual salary at the Yard.

The income had always made him slightly uncomfortable, and from the beginning he'd had an arrangement with his bank to collect the rents and put them into an interest-bearing trust account for his children. The children had never materialized, but he continued with the arrangement after Fay's death. He had no idea how much money was now in the account, nor did he care; without a rent or mortgage of his own to pay, his salary was more than sufficient.

Unlocking the plain wooden door between the two shops, he went up the two steep flights of stairs and let himself into his flat. Since he often returned home well after dark, he'd taken to drawing the blackout curtains before leaving each morning, so the short hallway was utterly dark.

He closed the door behind him and threw the bolt. Still working blindly, he bent down, gathered up the day's post from the floor, then walked into the living room. Only then did he turn on a light, choosing a lamp on the small table close to the gas fire rather than the switch for the much brighter wall sconces and the overhead.

The flat was reasonably large, but without too many rooms. A kitchen stood to one side of the hall and adjoined the living room. A second hallway led to a good-sized master bedroom and a smaller room he now used as a study, but which at one time had been intended as a nursery. In addition to the main rooms there was a WC, a bath, and a cupboard-sized box room.

One way or the other, every square foot of the flat, box room included, bore Fay's indelible stamp. To Black it had never been anything more than a place to live and a mild embarrassment of riches; to Fay it had been an ongoing work of art, a work in progress.

The large rug on the living room floor was a Marian Pepler geometrical in soft shades of blue and gray, the lacquered, streamlined bar on the opposite side of the room was a British version of Bauhaus, and the rosewood and moiré silk armchairs on either side of the gas fire were done in the style of Paul Follot, the Parisian art deco designer. In the far corner, partially hidden behind a Japanese folding screen, was Fay's small easel and paint table, set up close to one of the tall windows that looked out onto Shepherd Street.

Before she died, the walls had been covered by small paintings and working drawings done by the artists she'd met in her job as assistant to the director of the gallery in the basement of Sunderland House, only a few blocks away on Curzon Street. People like Victor Passmore, John Piper, Roy de Maistre, and his "friend," Francis Bacon, whom Black had never seen sober during the entire time Fay had worked at the gallery. Some, like Bacon, had achieved recent fame, while others had drifted into alcoholic obscurity, but neither their fortunes nor their varying talents made any difference to Black.

A week after burying Fay within the peaceful confines of the Jewish Cemetery on Hoop Lane in Golden Green, all the paintings had come off the walls, replaced by the small, delicate watercolors Fay had painted of daily life in Shepherd's Market, seen from the easel by the window. Paintings she'd always been too shy to show to anyone, himself included. Paintings he had grown to love, not for what they depicted, but as small jewels of frozen time, each stroke and wash of color bringing the brush and the hand that had held it briefly back to life. The last of her. Christ! Letting her go was so bloody hard!

Going to the bar, Black made himself a small Scotch and soda, then took it back to one of the chairs beside the cold iron hearth of the fire. He lit a cigarette, sipped his drink, and went through the post.

There was little of interest: a statement from his bank, which he didn't even bother to open, an invitation to the bar mitzvah of a boy he'd never heard of—undoubtedly the grandson of one of his mother's unbearable friends—and a discreet announcement of an upcoming auction of rare stamps at Gibbons. Leaving the bank statement and the invitation on the table beside his chair, he slipped the Gibbons notice into his jacket pocket, then took his drink and cigarette down the hall to his study.

It was very much a man's room. Fay's only contribution to it had been the elegant ebony desk he used for sorting through new acquisitions. The chair was a monstrosity of scarred wood and cracked green leather upholstered with brass tacks, the carpet was a buffalo skin complete with head and horns, and the nap on the hideous blue velvet club chair was so worn that Fay had insisted on shrouding the entire object with a throw of gray-and-black-striped mattress ticking.

The oddments of furniture had been in the flat when he took it over, and wisely Fay had never even suggested that he get rid of them. The desk took up one wall, floor-to-ceiling bookcases took up two more, and the fourth wall, bracketing the door, was occupied by several tall wooden storage cabinets for his stamps.

He sank wearily down in the club chair, balancing his drink on the broad arm, and glanced at the ranks of neatly ordered books on his shelves. Two of Stevenson, including a uniform edition of his complete works in sixteen volumes. A shelf of Dickens, another of Mark Twain, one shelf shared by Dumas and Defoe, one more for Conan Doyle.

James Fenimore Cooper, Melville, a dozen or so volumes on Drake, more on James Cook, Bligh's diaries, Darwin's voyages and recent studies of Scott's expedition, the strangely vanished flight of the *Eagle* from Spitsbergen and the equally ill-fated Nobile expedition in the Italian dirigible *Italia* only a few years ago.

Fawcett's disappearance on the Amazon. The search for the Nile source. A thousand adventures, from Lindbergh's transatlantic flight to the discovery of the Indies by Christopher Columbus.

All the places he'd never go, the people he'd never meet, the things he'd never do. A secret cosmology all his own, its beginnings rooted back in his childhood and represented by the first book he could remember buying with his own money—a well-worn copy of Verne's *Journey to the Centre of the Earth*, purchased with his father at a bookstall in Farringdon Road, Clerkenwell. Fay had teased him about his adventure stories, but she'd never made an issue of it. Now it seemed almost foolish. Perhaps it was time to grow up and put away childish things.

The first bombs began to fall, the sound reaching into the windowless study like the urgent muted rumblings of an approaching storm. The East End again tonight; if they were lucky, the clouds would make the raid a short one.

Black drained the last of his drink and stubbed his cigarette out in the pedestal ashtray beside the chair. No gliding up rivers in a canoe with Radisson or *The Last of the Mohicans* tonight; the Luftwaffe was knocking at London's door and there was Queer Jack to think about.

He cursed Capstick silently; the name was firmly in his head now, and Black knew that it had almost certainly taken up permanent residence. The detective lit another cigarette and sat back in the chair, staring at the ceiling. His quarry had been named; how long would it be before he had a face as well?

Black peeled off his eyeglasses and squeezed the bridge of his nose with a thumb and forefinger. One thing was certain: the face, when it was finally revealed, would be grotesque, only in its ordinariness, as mild and unassuming as the bland features of a salesclerk at Harrods.

Stevenson's Hyde had been a bull-necked, thick-jawed monster in evening clothes, but the reality of murder was usually dressed in the camouflage of normalcy—Crippen's neatly trimmed mustache, Seddon's starched collars, and the so-called Tiger Woman, Winnie Judd, the trunk murderer with apple cheeks and a permanent wave. In the end, of course, what the murderer looked like didn't really matter a damn, but Black found that being able to visualize his quarry seemed to help. It was part of the Sight.

Over the ninety-eight years of its existence the Criminal Investigation Division of the Metropolitan Police had employed hundreds of detectives. Most of them had been at least competent, some had been very good, and a very few qualified as great. Richard Capstick, for instance, was the epitome of the "good" detective. He wasn't "bent" like Perrin, for one thing—and avoiding corruption was no small feat for a man who worked within an organization rife with bribery and whose members had been faced with three separate salary cuts in the past ten years.

He was hardworking, methodical, accurate, and intelligent, and, equally important, he was the soul of patience, willing to spend weeks and months pursuing the shreds of evidence and testimony necessary to build a strong case. He had a good eye, a flair for detail, and he got along well with colleagues and villains alike.

But Capstick lacked the one thing that made the difference between a "good" detective and a "great" one. He lacked what was generally referred to at the Yard as the Sight.

The Sight wasn't something ever found mentioned in the popular press, and if asked, few if any detectives employed by Scotland Yard would ever admit to its existence. But everyone knew it was real, and anyone who'd ever worked with Morris Black knew that he had it in abundance. Some of his coworkers thought of the Sight in almost metaphysical terms—an extra sense that some were given and others denied—but

Black himself viewed it as the subtle difference between craft and art.

The majority of his colleagues saw their work as nothing more than a job, a multilayered process of time and labor during which the much larger bureaucracy of authority pitted itself against the smaller forces of larceny and defeat. The villains had the mobility of lawlessness, but the Yard had a world of time and endless patience.

Black saw his work as something else. He knew and fully appreciated the skills of a man like Dick Capstick, and he also knew the value of hard-slogging work; but for Morris Black there was always a point within an investigation where a sudden theoretical leap beyond the evidence could succeed where a hundred interviews had failed. It was imagination and intuition combined. It was the Sight.

But it wasn't working now. He had no sense of Queer Jack, no tickling itch about the murder victims. Jack was a faceless phantom without character and motive, who left nothing behind pointing to his personality except the enigmatic Z.

Typically the investigation of a murder centered on elements of fact both prior and after the act. How had the murderer and his victim come to the place of execution and who had seen them? What was done to the victim, and what evidence of those actions might have been overlooked by the murderer trying to cover his tracks? Who was the victim and how did he relate to his killer? On leaving, who had seen the murderer depart?

Eventually one of those questions would be answered, and the answer to one would almost inevitably lead to the resolution of the others. With enough effort put into the investigation a pattern would appear, shimmering up out of nothing like a line of ghostly footprints leading inexorably to the murderer.

It seemed, however, that Queer Jack wasn't playing by the rules. Capstick had concluded that both victims had been homosexuals, but nothing really proved that. In Rudelski's case there was at least the same presumption by the people who'd known him, but for the young man this afternoon there was nothing except his fey good looks and his nakedness. While both men had been unclothed, there was no obvious indication that their nudity had any direct sexual implication.

Jack the Ripper at least had the common decency to disembowel his victims, paying particular attention to their genitals; his latter-day namesake wasn't being so clear as to the motive fueling his madness. It was as though Queer Jack didn't really exist at all. Two young men had simply taken off their clothes in the midst of a raid, gone to sleep, and died.

Black frowned, listening to the crumpled roar of the exploding bombs in the distance. Follow that way of thinking and he'd be attending séances before he knew it. He shook his head. There was no magic here. Any unsolved murders, those two included, were nothing more than music hall illusions. It was only necessary to discover how the trick was played.

He sighed, stood up, and went to the toilet. Returning to the living room after relieving himself, he switched off the lamp, then crossed to Fay's easel. Drawing back the blackout curtain, he opened the window and looked out. On the far side of Market Street he could still hear laughter drifting up from Ye Grapes. He leaned out a little and took a deep breath. It was probably only his imagination, but it seemed as though the very smell of London had changed these past few days. The drab odors of the city had been added to. Something primitive was in the air as well as petrol fumes. Old tangs of ancient clay, brought to light after ten thousand years by order of the German Air Force. The smell of burnt wood and roasted flesh. Must and mold and coffin planking.

He looked up over the rooflines of the buildings at the end of the street. Every few seconds there was a brilliant flash, followed by a jarring clap of thunder. He wondered if Queer Jack was watching as well, seeing the same sheets of brilliance burning across the sky, hearing the same furious roaring of the bombs.

Black shivered as a faint gust of autumn air blew up the street. Maybe Dick Capstick was right; his frustrations about the case made it easy enough to let his imagination run loose. Lighting another cigarette, he continued to stare out at the flashing sky. Maybe it was time for him to get out of the game altogether. Fay had been dead for more than a year, but he still couldn't shake the deeply rooted malaise of his grief. Perhaps with her death some part of him had died as well. Could he have been robbed of the Sight by the anguish of his broken heart? Or was it something else? Was the Sight showing him something he didn't want to see? Despite what Capstick had said, Black was sure that Queer Jack knew when the bombing raids would come. And that seemed impossible. Madness.

The Number frowned with concentration as he worked in the semidarkness. The grinding wheel gave off no feathery gush of sparks as he pushed the tip of his instrument against it. The machine had originally been designed for jewelry fabrication, and the dull black Carborundum wheel had been coated with a thick layer of dark green rouge. Number 6, about midway in terms of its abrasiveness. Each time he brought the gleaming edge of the tungsten steel against the wheel, it created a tiny wisp of smoke, filling his sensitive nostrils with the scent of burning oil. The smell made him think of his mother's bright kitchen, and he frowned, pushing the razor-sharp vanes harder into the rouge.

His mother's bright kitchen, flies swarming, gathering delicately above the skins, blackening in the terrible heat. Dust motes hung in the still air, gold flecks in the brighter sun. Motar, seated at the door, brown legs curled up under him like twisted pieces of old dark wood, the pocks on the skin of his narrow face like deep craters, his gnarled hands steadily puffing on the handle that moved the fan in the kitchen ceiling round and round, while the desperate child watched the slowly spinning blades, too terrified to let his eyes touch Motar's eyes, but hypnotized by the fan blades, which were in turn connected to the sawing motion of the rope as it traveled through the pulleys, down to Motar's shriveled arms and brown root fingers; and then one hand would slip like a dry brown spider, scuttling under the stained cloth bound about his hips and under it to stroke and squeeze and stroke and pull, and the unoiled mechanism of the fan and that awful rhythmic squeak and the crackling of blistering oil as Ata the old cook dropped in the pieces of speckled plantain to sputter and hiss and fill the air with that wonderful sick smell, and faintly, faintly, somewhere in the golden light outside the groan of the pipes and the thrill of the drum, the bark of the Sarmajor's voice and the stamp of the Sarmajor's booted feet in the dark, hard-packed earth of the parade ground. And nobody knew. Nobody ever knew.

The Number blinked, staring into space, then turned back to the grinder. He switched it on again and studied the wheel turning to a blur as it came up to speed. He went back to his work, watching the razor edge magically becoming mirror bright between his fingers, seeing the frayed rope pass between the pulleys, smelling the hot oil in his nostrils again, and the hotter fear.

The words from the fairy tale his mother used to speak when they walked through the narrow streets and watched the bent widows in their dark saris squatting in the dust, spindles twirling between dark fingers aged to the color of blackened bone.

"Toil and spin, toil and spin, my name is Rumplestiltskin. Toil and spin, toil and spin."

The frayed rope between the pulley wheels. The smell of hot oil. Motar's hands and the dusty slap and thunder of the

Sarmajor's boots, too far away on the parade ground to help. The spinning wheels, counting each traverse, counting each movement, counting each dust mote in the air. Toil and spin, like a prayer never answered. Until now.

Straw into gold, toil and spin.

Steel into death.

CHAPTER SIX

Wednesday, September 11, 1940
9:30 A.M., British Summer Time

BLACK FOUND AN URGENT MESSAGE from Spilsbury waiting for him when he arrived at the Yard the following morning. Slipping a copy of Rudelski's RAF photograph into his pocket, as well as a mortuary photograph of the second victim, the detective left the building on the Thames Embankment and took a taxi to the main building of University College on Gower Street.

The laboratory occupied by Sir Bernard Spilsbury was surprisingly small considering the pathologist's status and reputation. It consisted of a single, narrow little room with a window overlooking the courtyard in the north wing. His microscope was on a wooden bench under the window, with a sink and glass-doored cabinets along the left wall and another bench for Bunsen burners to the right. There was also a long table close to the door, stacked with boxes containing Spilsbury's case cards—a meticulous record of sudden death spinning back for more than thirty years.

Dressed in his usual white lab coat, Sir Bernard was hunched over his microscope when Morris Black stepped into the room. The blackout shutters were still up over the window, blotting out the sun. The only light came from a green-hooded gooseneck lamp on the bench beside him and the steady blue flames of the Bunsen burners to his right.

"Sir Bernard?"

Spilsbury lifted a hand and waved, his eye still pressed to the microscope. He adjusted a knob, then reached out blindly, picking up a small tool. He used it to poke at something on the specimen platform.

"Take a look at this." The pathologist straightened, then shifted slightly on his stool, leaning to one side. Black approached, then leaned over, squinting through the eyepiece of the microscope.

He found himself staring at what appeared to be an Indian arrowhead made out of a dark, highly polished metal. Instead of two, or perhaps three, cutting edges, there were six, each one slightly flared, thicker at the base and narrowing to a perfect point. At that magnification he would have expected to see nicks or flaws on the cutting edges, but there were none.

The base of the arrowhead was circular and tapped for a screw. A few flecks of something were caught within the minuscule threads. Black blinked as Spilsbury plucked the miniature weapon off the platform with a pair of surgical tweezers. Black stood up. The pathologist was holding the tweezers under the bright light of the gooseneck lamp. The arrowhead was barely visible between the pincers. Base included, it was no more than a centimeter long.

"Astounding," said Spilsbury. "The craftsmanship is quite extraordinary."

"What exactly is it?"

"A murder weapon."

"Rudelski?"

"Yes. I expect to find the same thing with the newer victim."

"I thought you said he'd been drugged."

"That was my original hypothesis. Tests proved otherwise. All I could find was a mildly elevated alcohol level. I went back and checked again." He held up the deadly little projectile. "And found this."

"It hardly looks as though it could cause a fatal wound."

"The puncture was almost invisible. Hidden by the hair on the nape of the neck. Sliced through the upper quadrant of the trapezius, entering between the third and fourth cervical vertebrae, severing the spinal cord and the autonomous ganglia. Death was paralytic and virtually instantaneous. No time to react at all."

"Powerful."

"Extremely. There was no sign of powder burns. I suspect the projectile was delivered mechanically. Compressed air, or a very strong spring. The point itself is made from tungsten steel. Difficult to acquire these days, I'd think."

"That should narrow things down a bit."

"The weapon was hand-tooled and machined. Whoever created it has a near-genius mechanical aptitude and ability. Machinist, technician, engineer. Highly skilled at any rate."

"I didn't see any nicks or scratches. I would have thought there'd be some evidence of it striking bone."

"It didn't," said Spilsbury, sitting back on his stool. He dropped the miniature arrowhead into a petri dish beside the microscope. "Your man is either very shrewd or very lucky. The neck was bent when the weapon was used, opening a space between the vertebrae. When he was laid out in the shroud, his neck straightened, closing the space and hiding the weapon within the gray matter."

"The same for the second victim."

"Quite so." Spilsbury nodded. "Without an obvious wound, there would be no reason to look for a severing of the cord, and neither victim showed any evidence of spinal trauma. Even a gross dissection of the spine wouldn't have revealed it."

Black nodded. Spilsbury wasn't making excuses for himself, he was simply stating a fact.

"Would the killer need some special medical knowledge?" Black refused to use Capstick's nickname. The associations with Jack the Ripper were too obvious. He winced inwardly, thinking again about what would happen if news of this leaked to the press.

"Not necessarily. Some basic anatomy perhaps. Nothing you couldn't get out of a copy of *Gray's*. It's the mechanical knowledge that sets him apart."

Black thought about that for a moment, wondering how many members of the Royal Society of Engineers were presently in England, and how many of them had access to an ounce or two of tungsten steel. Thousands. And that wasn't counting thousands more technicians and machinists in scores of laboratories and factories around the country.

"Anything else you can tell me about the man?"

"Yes." Spilsbury's voice was emphatic, almost respectful. "He's a perfectionist. The edges on that device are sharp as razors. You could drive it through your palm and never even notice." The pathologist frowned. "And from the workmanship I'd wager that he has small hands. Long fingered and very strong, like a pianist, or like a surgeon." He held up his own hand, pale in the light from the lamp. "Like mine."

Leaving Spilsbury's laboratory, Black spent the rest of the morning canvassing likely haunts where Rudelski and the unidentified second victim might have come into contact with the killer. Third on his list was the Mandrake, an afternoon drinking club on Meard Street, just around the corner from Gennaro's, the restaurant where he'd eaten with Capstick the night before.

Soho before noon displayed none of the slightly sinister romance offered up to its patrons during the evening. In daylight, Meard Street was a flyblown narrow byway connecting Dean Street to Wardour Street, dustbins overflowing, shops shuttered, pavement cracked, the street itself deserted.

Black knew the Mandrake by reputation. It was owned by "Overcoat" Charlie Waters, a notorious trafficker in stolen goods, and managed by a Russian émigré named Boris, who'd previously operated a sordid little café in St. Giles High Street called the Coffee An'.

As a private drinking club, the Mandrake was able to bend its way around the regular licensing hours and also provide a convenient rallying point for the prostitutes, impoverished sailors, and Guardsmen seeking likely prospects of an evening. The Mandrake, like most of its brethren, was located in a basement. Black took a deep breath before going down the steps, closing his eyes briefly. Half the art of interrogation was acting a part, assuming a role depending on whom you were interrogating. Boris Watson and the Mandrake would need a little of the street copper combined with a darker dose of Reggie Perrin. Unlike Capstick, Morris Black took no particular pleasure from the play-acting, but long experience had made him very good at it.

Skirting a pile of refuse, Black went down the rickety staircase and pushed open the low, heavy door at the foot of the steps. The inside of the club was dark. Black had only barely managed to pass the Metropolitan Police height requirements, but even so he found he had to duck his head to avoid smacking into the wooden ceiling rafters.

The main room was small, no more than twenty feet on a side. Half a dozen round tables were pushed tightly together, a roughly made bar along the right-hand wall and a doorway at the end of the room. Behind the bar, bottles were stacked three deep on several shelves. A dart board hung on the near wall, and the table beside it was inlaid with a checkerboard pattern; so much for "club" amenities.

A tall man in shirtsleeves was reading a newspaper spread out on the bar near the rear door, lit from above by a single dangling bulb. The man was thin to the point of emaciation with narrow shoulders and thick, snow white hair. He looked up as Black stepped into the room.

"Closed," he said, then went back to his paper. Black walked to the end of the bar.

"Boris Watson?"

"Closed."

"I don't want a drink."

"I wasn't offering you one." He looked up again, scowling.

Black took out his warrant card and placed it on the scarred surface of the bar. "CID."

"So?"

"I'd like you to answer a few questions."

"Why should I?"

"You're Boris Watson?"

"Yes. Not that it is any of your business." The Russian's English was good, but there was a slight stiffness to it. "I pay my drink to Stillman, it should be enough." That was interesting. Ronald Stillman was a detective sergeant with the Vice Crimes division. Bent. A useful bit of information under the proper circumstances.

"I hear you've been poncing." A fair assumption if he was bribing Stillman on a regular basis, not to mention the fact that Boris *looked* like a procurer.

"You hear wrong. I don't let prossies in here." That was a lie. Even under the best of circumstances it would have been impossible to keep them out. Black ignored the comment. People like Boris Watson lied on principle.

"I also hear you've been purchasing illicit supplies of liquor." Black glanced at the shelves behind Boris. Another good guess. Scotch was almost unavailable these days, but the Mandrake appeared to be knee-deep in Dewar's and Pinch Bottle.

"Why don't you just ask your questions?" Boris sighed and closed his newspaper, giving in to the inevitable. Black took out his photographs and laid them on the bar.

"Know them?"

"No."

"Do us a favor, Boris. You haven't even looked."

"Don't need to. I don't know anybody. I see a hundred, two hundred people every day. All kinds. Young, old, rich, poor. I sell them drinks, Inspector, I do not ask them for references."

"Look anyway."

The Russian spread his fingers over the photographs and spun them around. He bent down, examining them carefully.

"This one," he said, tapping the photograph of the second victim.

"You know him?"

"He looks dead."

"He is."

"Accident?" The Russian smirked.

"Murder."

"I do not know him."

"But you've seen him?"

"Perhaps. I think..." Boris was weighing the benefit of truth against another lie.

"What?" Black pressed.

"Upton."

"His name is Upton?"

"No. No." Boris Watson shook his head firmly. "Upton helps here sometimes. In the evenings."

"What about him?"

"I think I have seen them talking, Upton and this dead man of yours."

"Talking?"

Boris lifted an arm and let his wrist droop. "Upton is..." Boris raised an eyebrow.

"A flit?"

"I do not know the word."

"Queer. Limp wrist. Nellie."

"Maybe, I have not asked him. But I think so, yes."

"And...?" Black let it hang.

The Russian shrugged. "They talked."

"No more?"

"Not that I saw."

"When was this?"

"A few nights ago. After the big raid. We were not so busy."

"Sunday?"

"Perhaps."

"What time?"

"Late. One, maybe two o'clock in the morning."

"They left together?"

"I did not see."

"Can you remember anything about him?"

"He was pretty. Too pretty for Upton." His lip curled. "Upton is a pig."

"Anything else?"

"He was in uniform."

Black felt his pulse quicken. Rudelski was a flier, and now a second uniform.

"What branch of the service?"

"How should I know?" Boris lifted a hand. "It is dark in here."

"RAF?"

"Perhaps. It is possible. All I know is that he was in a uniform."

"Color?"

"Gray, blue, stripes?" Boris made a snorting sound. "I told you. I did not notice."

"All right. Tell me about Upton then."

"He works here sometimes. Helps with the tables."

"Do you know his first name?"

"Henry."

"Where does he live?"

"I have no idea."

"Will he be coming in here today?"

"Perhaps. Late in the afternoon. After his work."

"He has another job?"

"Yes. In a bookstore on Charing Cross Road."

"Do you know the name of the store?" There were scores of secondhand bookstores on Charing Cross Road, from Tottenham Court Road down to Foyles at Leicester Square.

"No. Only that it begins with *Q.*" Boris made a face. "I hire him to wash dishes and clean tables. I do not socialize with him, Detective."

"Quaritch's?" Black pressed. Quaritch's was probably the oldest and most revered antiquarian book dealer in London.

"No." The Russian shook his head again. "Odd like that, but no." He frowned, his mouth drawing down. "I can't remember. Sorry."

"What about Quilleran's?" There weren't that many antiquarian shops beginning with the letter *Q.* Boris nodded eagerly, relieved.

"Yes. That's it. The place is called Quilleran's."

Black took a taxi to the Vine Street Police Station on the far side of Regent Street. He placed a call to the Yard and waited while a clerk in Criminal Records checked through the index for any information on Henry Upton. A few minutes later he had what he needed.

According to his card, Henry Upton was twenty-three years old, lived in rooms on Little Earl Street in Seven Dials, and was exempt from National Service due to extremely poor eyesight and a serious asthmatic condition. He also had two convictions with fines for indecent behavior in the public toilets at Kew Gardens. A third conviction and he'd go down.

Black made a few notes in his logbook, checked the address for Quilleran's in the directory, then begged a ride across to Charing Cross Road with the Vine Street traffic sergeant.

By then it was noon. The streets were clogged with vehicles of every description, and the pavement was equally thick with pedestrians. Except for the whitewashed strips along the curbs and the rings around the lampposts for the blackout, there was no sign that the city was effectively under siege. It was an illusion of course; darkness and the bombers would bring reality home with a vengeance. The streets would be empty except for the racing fire engines, and the only people on foot would be roving ARP wardens and tin-hatted policemen.

The bookstore was located just off the Charing Cross Road on Denmark Street. Most of the other shops appeared to be dealing in musical instruments of one kind or another, and the offices above were all music publishers.

Like every other secondhand bookseller in the district, Quilleran's had several narrow tables laden with books outside its door, and more books stacked in the dusty windows. It was narrow-fronted and dimly lit with stoutly built, dark-varnished bookcases set up in rows of aisles running the length of the shop.

Just inside the door to the left there was a long, glass-fronted bookcase that also served as a sales counter. Behind it, seated on a low stool, was a small, round-faced man with thinning brown hair and thick, tortoiseshell-rimmed spectacles. He was wearing a baggy tweed suit that looked badly in need of cleaning and sat with his back against shelves loaded down with parcels wrapped in butcher's paper and tied up with string.

He was reading a book, held close to his face. Black read the title off the spine: *Guilty Men*, a simpering, pompous bit of twaddle published by the Gollancz Left Book Club just after Dunkirk, blaming every British ill on Chamberlain and his cabinet.

The distinctly stated message in the book was "Never again," but after browsing through it himself a month or so ago, Black had found himself wondering just how the authors of the book would have stopped Herr Hitler in his tracks. Not by producing slim little tracts like *Guilty Men*, that was certain.

"Henry Upton?"

The man lowered his book and stared owlishly up at Black. He blinked, then smiled, showing two rows of small gray teeth. A careful look, wary, like a rabbit. Upton was a man who lived in moral twilight, ready to bolt at any moment. Familiar turf to Morris Black.

"Yes?"

Black showed his warrant card and watched the blood flush into Upton's cheeks. Guilty men indeed; more than one MP had been arrested in a public toilet.

He reached into his pocket, took out the pair of photographs, and placed them on the counter in front of Upton, watching carefully for a reaction. Huge behind the thick lenses, Upton's eyes flicked over Rudelski's photograph, then touched on the other, widening for an instant, then fluttering away, trying to settle anywhere else, finding only Black's face.

"You knew him." A fact.

"I..."

"You met him at the Mandrake club. You work there. For Boris Watson. He saw you talking."

"I don't..."

"He's dead. Murdered."

"Oh, God." A whisper. Black put his forefinger on the photograph and pushed it closer to Upton. The frightened man stood up, the stool scraping on the wood floor. There was nowhere to go. From rabbit look to cornered rat.

"Tell me." Black said it softly, praying that no customer came into the shop to break the fragile moment. The confessional instant between a sinner and his priest. Upton sat down again. He swallowed—sharp, stubbed Adam's apple bobbing—then plucked off the glasses. He pulled up his tie and wiped the lenses furiously. Black knew the habit. Remove your spectacles and the world recedes. The universe blurs.

Upton was escaping the only way he knew how, the only way left to him.

"I don't know what you're talking about." The relief of confession hadn't been enough; fear of the penance he'd receive still outweighed it. Only threats remained. Black assumed the Reggie Perrin mantle once again, this time mixed with some of Dick Capstick's blunt edge.

"Two convictions for indecency." Black smiled as wickedly as he was able. "I can cobble up another, you know that, Henry. You're a wretched little curb crawler, and I'll have you unless you give it up. That's a promise. I'll see you in Dartmoor with all those old lags on you, slobbering in the dark. Five years? You won't last five days, Henry. You'll have a bung hole you could drive a lorry through. They'll put springs in your jawbones and felt pads on your knees. No chatting up the lads in the local, no bill and coo between silk sheets for you, Henry my boy. Rough and tumble, that's where you're headed."

It was enough. Upton looked as though he was going to be sick. When he spoke, his voice was weak and hoarse. "What do you want to know?"

"The truth."

"I only met him once."

"When?"

"That night."

"Sunday?"

"Yes. He'd just come down for the day. He had to get back."

"Come down from where?"

"Cambridge."

"He was a student?"

"Yes."

"What was his name?"

"David."

"David what?"

"He never said." A pause. "They never do."

"You went home with him?"

"No."

"Don't lie to me, Henry."

"I'm not. I wanted to, but he said he had a previous engagement. A match."

"What sort of match?"

"I don't know."

"You're lying."

"I'm not!"

"Boris said he was in uniform."

"Yes."

"What uniform?"

"I didn't notice…I was looking at his eyes." Upton looked down at the photograph and then away.

"Spare me."

"It's true. I didn't notice."

"Close your eyes. Think. Think about the uniform."

Upton did as he was told. Black could see sweat forming up in tiny beads in the hairs of his short sideburns. A slick of it was on his upper lip. The flush in his cheeks had vanished, the blood drained away. His face looked like damp chalk.

Henry Upton was no killer, or at least not the kind of killer he was looking for, Black was sure of that. If Upton ever committed murder, it would be in the lukewarm heat of some small passion, a killing of the moment, meaningless and without thought. Queer, but not Queer Jack.

Henry Upton would snivel on the dock and cry when the executioner slipped the bag over his head. Catch Queer Jack and he'd laugh out loud when the trap was sprung, all the way down to the hard last snap of the rope as it cracked his neck and sent him dancing and twitching off to hell. Upton opened his eyes wide, tears pooling on the rims of the lower lids.

"I remember something."

"What?" Softly now.

"The uniform was tailored, expensive."

"You can do better than that, Henry."

"Yes. Something else."

"Yes?"

"A patch. On his shoulder."

"Describe it."

"It was dark."

"The patch?"

"No. The room. The Mandrake. I can't..."

"Yes, you can, Harry. His Majesty's prison awaits."

"There were four letters in the middle, intertwined. RAAF."

"Anything else?"

"Below the letters, in a scroll. Cambridge University Squadron. Some numbers, I can't remember..." Upton slumped down on the stool, narrow shoulders rising in defeat, head telescoping down like a turtle. He slipped the spectacles back onto the bridge of his nose, hooking them over his ears, fingers trembling, waiting for the ax to fall.

"You still keep rooms in Seven Dials?"

"Yes."

"Stay in them. Try to slip away and I'll find you no matter what."

"Yes."

"You did well, Henry."

"I'm sorry." He looked down at the photograph, then reached out and tentatively touched the dead mouth with a bony finger.

"Sorry that he's dead?"

"Yes. He was..." Henry Upton swallowed again. The tears had overflowed, tracking down the cheeks. "He was very beautiful."

Black slid the picture gently out from beneath Upton's hand.

"Yes, he was."

CHAPTER SEVEN

Thursday, September 12, 1940
11:30 A.M., British Summer Time

THIS, MORRIS BLACK KNEW, was the definition of a nightmare: a dream in which he cannot awaken when the Furies finally come. Now England slept, and those terrors were fast approaching.

His train had been steaming through the fens and valleys of the countryside north of London for the better part of an hour, and from his window Black could see the passing landscape, delicately molded, rich in pastures and corn-bearing fields, hills dark with trees, small ponds and streams gathering into gentle, willow-fringed rivers winding slowly on their way to the distant sea. It was the most English of scenes, pastoral, softly colored with quiet beauty, utterly at peace.

Cambridge lay a few miles ahead, and beyond it, Ely and the Wash. Behind him was London, poised on the brink of war, the quick, harsh whispers at the Yard tense with rumors of invasion. They even had a name for it: Sea Lion. The secret memoranda circulated to senior staff referred to invasion preparations from Rotterdam to Boulogne; barges, artillery, munitions, fuel, and men were being assembled at twenty Channel ports.

The presumption was that when it came, the invasion would center off the eastern coast. To defend against it, barbed wire had been strung for miles along the beaches, mines had been buried in the sand, and every road sign and railway halt placard removed or painted over.

Poles had been planted in farmers' fields to prevent gliders from landing, and plans had been made to put obstructions along every roadway that might be used as an airstrip by the enemy.

A top-secret resistance battalion had been formed, complete with weapons caches, hidden burrows, and radio transmitters buried under rural chicken coops. Ten million pamphlets had been distributed to the general population, giving instructions on what to do when the first paratroops were sighted.

Even the church bells had been stilled—when they sounded again, it would be to announce the coming of the Nazi invader. Fear crouched like an invisible wraith on the shoulders of each and every man and woman he saw, yet here, in the bright, late-morning sun, there was no sign that these same fields and pastures, hills and valleys, would soon become a bloody killing ground.

Black wasn't entirely sure why the various military leaders in Whitehall assumed that the invasion would come via the eastern approaches. To his mind he saw no reason why Hitler wouldn't follow the examples of Julius Caesar or William the Conqueror, the only warriors to have successfully invaded England in the past. Dover and Hastings were closest to the coast of France, and from there the way was clear to the obvious main objective—London. If the city fell, the rest of the nation would follow. It seemed an obvious choice, especially in light of the Luftwaffe's continuing bombardment along the same path.

Sitting in his compartment, alone except for the young woman dozing opposite him, Morris Black sighed. Who was he to offer an opinion about an invasion? He was a policeman, not even a soldier, much less a general. His mandate was Queer Jack, not Adolf Hitler and his black minions.

The bombers, regular as clockwork, had returned the night before, scattering their destructive seed across the city somewhat more democratically than on previous raids. The East End and Docklands had still taken the brunt of it, but this time bombs had also exploded in Greenwich, Deptford, Lewisham, and Woolwich Arsenal.

Some damage had been done to St. Thomas's Hospital, but overall there was less destruction and fewer casualties than on the nights before. Up until the time he'd left for Cambridge, there were no reports of anything leading him to believe Queer Jack had been at work again. Perhaps, thought Black, he's disappeared down some black rabbit hole, never to be seen again. He sighed. Not bloody likely.

The train lurched slightly as they went over a crossing, and the bag in his fellow passenger's lap slid onto the floor, bursting open. The woman awoke with a start. Black knelt down and helped her retrieve the contents of her handbag.

"Sorry about that," she said. The accent was flat, the voice pleasant. Black noticed that among the things spilled out was a recent Field's Postage Stamp Catalogue from their shop on Dover Street.

"You're a collector?" he asked, handing over the small, dark green brochure.

"Stamps?" She smiled. "No. My uncle asked me to bring it up to him."

"You're American." The woman nodded. For the first time Black noticed that she was extremely attractive. Late twenties or early thirties, her hair cut unfashionably long, dark blond with lighter streaks as though she'd spent some time in the sun. She was wearing a man's belted trench coat over a simple dark blue skirt and matching sweater. He felt something close to panic clutching at the base of his throat. He was sitting with an attractive woman and he felt like a stumbling schoolboy. Worse, he felt guilty that he was enjoying the sensation.

"You're a stamp collector?" she asked as she filled her purse again.

"Yes."

"But that's not what you do."

"Do?" He smiled. "No. I'm a policeman actually."

"I'm a warco." She smiled back. "Katherine Copeland." She held out a hand and Black shook it. Her skin was smooth and the grip surprisingly strong. The panic surged again at the touch of her hand. This was how it had been with Fay so long ago, and it was something he thought he'd never feel again. Didn't want to feel again.

"Morris Black," he said, clearing his throat nervously. "I'm afraid I don't know what a warco is."

"War correspondent." She flushed lightly. "I tell a lie. Actually I spend most of my time writing about the 'woman's angle.' Twenty exciting ways to cook potatoes, that kind of thing. *Washington Times Herald.*"

"It sounds very interesting," Black answered politely. It never ceased to amaze him how Americans could give you their entire life story within two minutes of first meeting.

"Not half as interesting as being a bobby."

Black shrugged. He didn't bother telling her that policemen in London hadn't been called bobbies for the better part of a hundred years.

"Your uncle lives in Cambridge?"

"For the last year. He's a visiting lecturer. American history. Caius College."

"I believe it's pronounced 'Keys,'" Black said, correcting her gently. She'd be a marked woman if she went around Cambridge saying "Ky-us."

"Is that right?" she said brightly. "Well, I guess you learn something new every day." She dug into her bag and pulled out a dark blue box of DuMauriers. "You mind?"

"No, of course not." Black reached into the pocket of his jacket for his lighter, but she'd already used her own by the time he got his out. He lit a cigarette for himself and glanced out the window.

"You think the Germans are going to invade?" said the young woman.

Black turned to look at her again, surprised. Had she been reading his mind? "I don't know. I hope not." As though his hopes meant anything, or his fears.

"Me too," she said, and smiled.

Black arrived in Cambridge a quarter of an hour later, said good-bye to the woman he'd shared his compartment with, and took a cab to the Blue Boar Hotel. In the interests of discretion he'd agreed to meet Hawkins there rather than at the college itself. Rupert Hawkins was a Trinity don, but he was also the acting head of the University Squadron and in charge of its flight training program.

The drive from the station was brief. There was almost no traffic, and the streets were empty; Michaelmas term wouldn't begin for another two weeks, and the war had provided its own form of summer holiday. The nightmare and the dream of peace persisted here; reading medieval history or studying ancient languages, even contemplating the scholar's life, seemed utter madness in the face of what lay so near at hand.

The Blue Boar was a small, very old hotel almost directly across the cobbled street from the Kings Gate of Trinity College. Hawkins was waiting for him in the dark, oak-paneled bar, a small sherry on the table in front of him.

The Cambridge don was in his mid-thirties, slightly thick

around the middle, sandy hair thinning at the temples. He had the berry cheeks of a drinker, and a pipe was clamped between his teeth under the canopy of a bushy, RAF-style mustache, tips curled and heavily waxed.

Underneath his dark gown he wore the light-colored blazer that marked him as a onetime Cambridge Blue. Cricket from the looks of him, Black thought, or maybe rowing. Black often silently chided himself for jumping to conclusions about people based on first impressions, but half a lifetime spent as a policeman had taken its toll. Rupert Hawkins was every inch a pompous ass, and probably worse.

Black handed his warrant card to the man and sat down across from him without waiting for an invitation. A waiter appeared and Black ordered coffee. Hawkins handed back the warrant, then took a minimal sip of his sherry. The cheeks told a different story; without an audience the drink would have vanished in a single swallow followed by a two-fingered wave to the barman for another. Black's coffee appeared. He ignored it for the moment.

"Detective Inspector Morris Black." Hawkins made the name sound like a carpet stain.

"That's right."

"When you telephoned me yesterday, you intimated that you were seeking identification of someone in relation to a...case?"

"Correct, Mr. Hawkins."

"*Doctor.*"

"I beg your pardon. *Doctor* Hawkins."

"You have reason to believe it might have been one of my boys?"

"There is evidence to suggest that the person in question was a member of the Cambridge University Flying Squadron. Yes."

"What sort of evidence?" Black saw a momentary flash of apprehension cross Hawkins's face. Perhaps it wasn't the first time one of "his boys" had jumped the rails.

"The person in question was wearing a Cambridge University Flying Squadron uniform."

"Ah." Another sip of sherry. A bigger one this time. Black took the mortuary photograph from his pocket and placed it beside Hawkins's sherry glass. He picked it up and glanced at it without curiosity for a moment, then frowned.

"Good Lord, young Talbot."

"You know him then?"

"Certainly. David Talbot. Among other things I'm one of his tutors." The frown deepened. "Perhaps you'd better explain what this is all about, Inspector."

"He's been murdered."

Hawkins blanched. He kept his eyes on the photograph, picked up his sherry, and drained it away. "I thought perhaps..."

"What did you think?"

"Well, boys will be boys after all. Pranks are played. I thought perhaps a member of the squadron might have been involved in some...escapade."

"No escapade, Dr. Hawkins." Black saw no reason to be genteel. "He was found naked with his spinal cord severed in the kitchen of a cheap flat in Spitalfields."

Hawkins's eyes widened. "I don't understand."

"Nor do I," Black answered dryly. "Which is why I'm here. I'd like to know anything you can tell me about David Talbot."

"He was such a quiet boy," Hawkins mumbled, still looking at the photograph. "I can't believe this."

"It's true." Black paused. "He was a flier?"

"Yes. A damned good one."

"What about his age, background, interests, that sort of thing? Who were his friends?"

"He was nineteen. Canadian. His family has something to do with the railroads I think."

"A good student?"

"Exceptional, especially considering the deficiencies of his previous education. Early days of course, but he seemed intent on working in the aeronautical engineering field after the war."

"Farsighted of him, since the war hasn't really begun, at least not for people like him."

"Wars end, Inspector. Life goes on, you know."

"Not for him." Black paused again, taking a moment to light a cigarette. "Hobbies?"

"Flying of course. Reading, games, that sort of thing. Nothing in particular."

"Friends?"

"None that stands out."

"No one close? A girl perhaps?" Black cast that line into the stream, wondering what it would reel in.

Hawkins shrugged. "Between his studies and the squadron he didn't have much time for a social life." The answer was cool and formal. The bait hadn't been taken; if there had been anything untoward in Hawkins's relationship with Talbot, the tutor wasn't about to reveal it openly.

"Time enough to go down to London."

"Term hasn't begun yet...or perhaps you're not aware of the university calendar." Another condescending note; after all, an uneducated policeman couldn't be expected to know the vagaries of a scholar's schedule.

"Where did he live? Rooms at the college, or lodgings?"

"He has a set at the college."

"I'd like to see it if that's convenient."

"It's convenient enough. But I'm not sure that it's wise."

"Why is that?"

"Cambridge is a small town, Inspector. Very much a closed shop as the saying goes. There's already a great deal of concern about the progress of the war; a policeman treading about is hardly the thing to lift morale. Not to mention the squadron." Hawkins gave Black a small, condescending smile. "I'm sure you understand."

"I know that a young man has been murdered, Dr.

Hawkins. An examination of his rooms is in order, questions of morale and your squadron's honor aside. And I can assure you that I won't be 'treading about.'"

Lighting his pipe, Hawkins sat back in his chair and stared coolly at Black for a moment, squinting at him through a thickening haze of smoke.

"You're a Jew, aren't you?"

Black stared at the man seated across from him. "I beg your pardon?"

"I said, you're a Jew, aren't you?"

"I don't see how my religion has any relevance to this discussion."

"Oh, but it does." Hawkins waved a hand through the cloud of smoke drifting between them. "Don't misunderstand me, Inspector; I have a great deal of respect for your people—Disraeli, for instance, was a Jew—but historically you are a race without roots. Cambridge is a university of tradition and continuity, something I suppose you can't really be expected to understand. You find it a simple thing to put morale and honor aside; I'm afraid I cannot do the same."

It was one of the most absurd speeches Black had ever heard, and for a moment he was struck dumb by the placid assurance of Hawkins's offensive attitudes. He was the worst sort of bigot—the kind who cloaked his hatred in false logic and pat generalities. For Hawkins, Judaism was akin to being born with a withered leg or a port-wine birthmark—it was a handicap to be overcome, or at the very least, accepted philosophically. He wondered how the arrogant little shit would react if he knew about the Gestapo list intercepted by Special Branch a few months ago. The 350-page document contained the names and addresses of those who were to be arrested, interrogated, and interned following the invasion—all Cambridge and Oxford faculty were included. Swallowing his anger, Black reached out, took the photograph away from Hawkins, and stood. He'd have the officious little bugger served up on toast.

"Presumably the head porter will be able to direct me to Talbot's rooms?"

Hawkins stared up at him, color rising to his already pink cheeks. If Trinity College was anything like the Yard, the porter would also be the surest way to spread tales about the investigation from one end of Cambridge to the other. Hawkins looked away from Black. He knew his arrogant little bluff had been called.

"There's no need to bring Maskell into this," he muttered. "I'll take you." They left the hotel and stepped out into the warmth of the early-afternoon sun.

While the invasion barges assembled in Calais, the late-blooming cherry trees were blossoming on Trinity Street, showers of pale pink petals cascading down onto the cobbles in the face of each trembling gust of wind, filling the air with their gentle scent. Black felt a brief tug of sadness, as though he were witness to the exact moment of summer's passing. Everything now would be autumn, cool and dying, and nothing lay ahead but bitter winter.

Talbot's rooms were on the second floor of the college's south wing, overlooking narrow Trinity Lane and the stone walls and angled chimney pots of Gonville and Caius College a few yards away. At the foot of the stairs leading up to Talbot's lodgings, they met Mercy Reynolds, the thin-faced "bedder" in charge of housekeeping for the second floor. She was wearing a long apron, stockings rolled down over thick-heeled shoes, and a shapeless, dark green Tyrolean hat pinned to a tightly curled cap of iron gray hair. She had a coal scuttle in one hand and a dustpan in the other.

"We'd like to see David Talbot's rooms," said Hawkins stiffly. "Are they locked?"

"Course they are." She gave Black a long inquiring look. "Clean as well. Bed made, basin filled."

"Do you have the key?" asked Black.

"Yerss."

"Then perhaps you could open the rooms," Hawkins suggested.

"Don't like to do it without the young master's permission."

"It's quite important, Mrs. Reynolds, please..."

"I'm sure David wouldn't mind," Black said quietly. "And it is quite important, just as Dr. Hawkins says."

The old woman gave Black another long look, then shrugged her narrow shoulders. "Just as you say then." She sighed, turned, and headed back up the narrow stone steps.

Reaching a darkly varnished door just past the head of the stairs, she put down the scuttle, fished deeply into the pocket of her apron, and brought out a ring of heavy iron keys. She unlocked the door, then stood aside, waiting.

"I don't think we'll be needing you any longer," said Black.

"I'll let you know when we're done," Hawkins added. "Then you can lock up."

"Yerss." She frowned, picked up her scuttle, and shuffled off toward the stairs. Hawkins pushed open the door and Black followed. Talbot's "set" was made up of two rooms and a small, oak-paneled vestibule with a narrow shelf for shoes and an elephant's-foot umbrella stand. Beyond it was a larger, white-walled sitting room, the pale wood floor strewn with half a dozen thin rugs, two sagging armchairs set in front of a cast-iron, coal-burning fireplace.

On either side of the hearth there were tall bookshelves, roughly made from bricks and boards. A long table stood under the window, its surface piled with books and papers. More books were stacked around it on the floor. The window, high and narrow, looked down into Trinity Lane. A doorway on the right led to a small bedroom, sparsely furnished with a wardrobe against one wall, a plain wooden washstand with a white enameled basin, and an iron bedstead. The window here also looked down onto the lane.

Opening the wardrobe, Black briefly inspected the contents: half a dozen white shirts, a spare gown, a blazer with the

Trinity crest, and a silk-lined leather flying jacket with the Cambridge University Flying Squadron emblem stitched onto the left breast. There were also two suits, one gray, one chalk stripe, and a set of evening clothes. The suits were from a company in San Francisco, and the shirts came from H. J. Nicholls on Regent Street. The late David Talbot had expensive tastes.

Black went back into the sitting room and scanned the bookshelves. Engineering texts, the *R.A.F. Handbook*, a manual for the Harvard training aircraft flown by the Cambridge Squadron. A dozen or so modern novels in paperback, some history, and a great deal of poetry. There was also a Muirhead's *London* and last year's Royal Automobile Club guide. Tacked to one of the shelves was a snapshot of a graceful cantilevered bridge spanning a wide, placid river.

Black pulled out the drawing pin and examined the back of the photograph. *Levis, Quebec, 1937*. He replaced the picture and crossed the room to the table beneath the window. Hawkins stood by the door, pipe jutting out between his lips.

Black sifted slowly through the papers, looking for some artifact that would tell him about David Talbot. Most of what he saw related to his studies—notes taken during lectures, portions of essays, both typed and handwritten, thumbnail sketches of architectural and engineering detail, and a cleverly designed proposal for a punt operated by foot pedals rather than a sculling oar or pole.

A small box on the right-hand side of the table was used for writing equipment: erasers; four Eagle pencils of varying hardness, two unsharpened; a mechanical pencil; and a tortoiseshell Swan fountain pen. Beside the box a German-made set of drafting instruments nestled in a blue-velvet-lined wooden case. On the inside of the lid a small brass plaque was engraved with an inscription: *To David Struan Talbot from his Father, Christmas, 1938.*

The detective smiled, remembering the gift his father had given him on his acceptance into the Police Training College:

a butter-soft, blue Morocco dispatch case, his initials embossed in gold beneath the handles. He still had the case, but the lettering had worn away years ago. Black carefully closed the lid, wondering if fathers really knew how important those gestures were and how long they lasted in their children's hearts.

On the right-hand side of the table a silver-plated toast rack had been converted into a letter stand. There were several envelopes from an Angus Talbot, 1333 Haro Street in Vancouver, British Columbia, presumably David's father, several more from Mrs. A. Talbot at the same address, a statement from the local branch of the Westminster Bank, a membership renewal notice from the RAC, and a sheaf of postcards held together with a metal spring clip. Ignoring the letters, Black picked up the postcards.

There were seven in all, each depicting a different English cathedral in garishly colored rotogravure—Gloucester, Carlisle, Coventry, Liverpool, Durham, Ely, and Hereford. Black had seen them before, sold in packets at places like the W. H. Smith bookstall in Victoria Station and his newsagent's shop in Shepherd's Market.

He shuffled through them slowly. Each one had been mailed from the Government Post Office in King Edward Street, London, addressed to David S. Talbot, Trinity College, Cambridge, in a perfectly formed, meticulous hand. There was no return address. The messages on the seven cards were brief and cryptic: *3-17, 12-28, 14-30, 5x30, 1-17, 1x22, 16-32.* Black jotted down the number messages in his log, then turned to Hawkins, who was still standing by the door.

"Are you quite finished?"

"Almost." Black nodded. "Did Talbot own an automobile?"

"Not that I'm aware of. Undergraduates under the age of twenty-two are forbidden to keep a motor vehicle within twenty-five miles of the center of town."

"He has a membership in the RAC."

"How interesting."

"Do these mean anything to you?" Black held up the postcards. Grudgingly, Hawkins crossed the room and took them from the detective's hand. He glanced at them quickly, then shook his head.

"No."

"Did Talbot have some particular interest in cathedrals? Was he religious at all?"

"No. He was interested in bridges as I recall. And flying."

"The messages mean nothing?"

"Not to me." Hawkins shrugged. "A code of some sort? Dimensions for a building? They could mean anything, Black. Or nothing." He handed back the postcards. Black slipped them into the pocket of his jacket, then took the rest of the correspondence out of the silver rack.

"I'm going to bring these along. I'll give you a receipt for them."

"All right." The two men left the set of rooms. Hawkins said good-bye at the foot of the stairs without shaking hands and went off in search of Mrs. Reynolds, leaving Black to make his own way out of the college. Half an hour later the Scotland Yard detective was on his way back to London.

This time his compartment was empty, and for most of the journey into the city he found himself thinking about Katherine Copeland. It was ridiculous of course; why waste time thinking about a chance encounter on a train when nothing could possibly come of it? Beyond that, he had far more important things to occupy his mind. He was almost relieved when the train reached the sooty outskirts of the city. The late-afternoon sky was overcast, but it wouldn't be enough to stop the Luftwaffe. In another hour or so the raids would begin once more. The train lumbered onward, squeaking and rattling over the switch points as it headed slowly through the suburbs toward Paddington.

Out of the dream and into the nightmare once again.

CHAPTER EIGHT

Thursday, September 12, 1940
9:30 P.M., British Summer Time

Less than an hour after Black's return from Cambridge late that afternoon, the duty sergeant at the Yard informed him that his immediate presence was required by Chief Superintendent Cornish. The meeting with his direct superior was short. He was to gather up all his notes and files on Rudelski and the newly identified Talbot, then present himself at the underground motor pool of 55 Broadway Buildings. Cornish had no idea what any of it was about beyond the fact that he'd been sent a rocket from the commissioner, who, it appeared, was having his strings pulled from even higher up. The only thing Black knew for certain was that 55 Broadway was the barely disguised headquarters of the Secret Intelligence Service. Arriving there, he was vetted by an assortment of anonymous, serious-faced young men, then escorted to an equally anonymous Wolesley sedan driven by a dark-haired Wren. As dusk began to settle and the sirens began to wail, they left the city and headed west.

Morris Black sat in the back of the unmarked Wolesley staring out at the silver thread of the Thames on his right hand, narrow and placid here, only a few miles from the city, like something out of a fairy tale in the last light of evening. Robert Louis Stevenson had called it the children's hour, a moment of growing shadows creeping toward nightfall, time suspended, a promise or a warning, a final blessing from the setting sun. But there were no fairy tales, not anymore. It was dusk, a cloudless sky, and soon to rise, a bomber's moon.

They had passed through the outskirts of Richmond a moment before. The suburban village was shuttered against the bombers, empty except for a phantom ARP warden on his bicycle searching for illicit chinks of light, silent except for the steady droning wail of the sirens. Far behind, muted by distance, Black could hear the faint sound of giants' footsteps as the first of the bombs began to explode.

Black looked out into the darkness as they drove through the sleeping village of Petersham, moving away from the river and following the dark, wooded length of the Upper Ham Road down to Ham Common. The Wren piloting the Wolesley hadn't said a word since leaving the city, and Black didn't have the slightest idea where he was being taken, or why. Presumably it had something to do with Rudelski and Talbot, but he still hadn't been able to make the connection.

The Wren turned onto Church Road, then turned again at Latchmere Lane, a secluded byway enclosed by trees on both sides that led down to a large estate screened by hedges, the old, stone-pillared entrance gate further secured with a newly built guard post and a pair of uniformed sentries, both armed with machine guns. Black noted that the high walls on either side of the pillars were strung with concertina wire. The Wren offered a pass to one of the guards, and they were waved through.

"I don't suppose you can tell me where we are?" Black

asked as they went through the gate. It was the first time he'd spoken since leaving the motor pool.

"Latchmere House," the Wren answered, and said nothing more.

Past the hedges and the barbed wire a narrow graveled road led for a quarter mile through a scattering of trees. Beyond them Black could see a large, brooding mass of stone hunched on the brow of a low hill, almost invisible in the growing darkness—an English country house as one of the Brontës would have imagined it, stained and worn with half a dozen generations of ill will, bad blood, and whispered scandal. A rough concrete citadel, three stories high and windowless, had been added to the west wing of the house, ringed by its own crude barbed-wire fence.

As they approached, Black could see that the large main building was surrounded by two barriers. The first was a head-high palisade of unpainted planking topped once again with barbed wire and set out with guard posts at each corner. Within that wall was a second perimeter made up of two lines of concertina wire with a no-man's-land between. Here there were guard posts every thirty feet—wooden huts at the corners and raised platforms between. A prison.

They paused at another checkpoint and the Wren showed her pass again while a second guard swung the shaded beam of a torch into the rear of the Wolesley. The car was waved on and the Wren pulled up at a side entrance to the main building. A man in Signal Corps uniform with corporal's stripes on his sleeve opened the door for Black, then took him through the doorway. Except for the rank insignia there were no badges on the uniform.

The corporal silently led Black down a narrow flight of stone steps into the basement. At the bottom of the stairwell a chain-link enclosure had been erected complete with a locked and bolted swing-gate. Another soldier, this one wearing sergeant's stripes, was seated at a scarred wooden desk.

The corporal handed Black off and the sergeant opened the swing-gate, ushering Black through. He closed and locked the gate behind him, then led Black down a long, dimly lit corridor. The walls on either side were newly built of raw concrete blocks. Every ten feet there was a heavily constructed metal door, painted pale green, each one secured with an enormous padlock and a wrought-iron drop bar. The doors were fitted with covered peepholes.

The lights overhead were nothing more than bare bulbs hanging from dangling lengths of twisted flex and shielded by sheet-metal pans painted the same color as the doors. Except for the echo of the sergeant's booted feet on the stone floor, the passage was deathly quiet. The stale, uncirculated air smelled faintly of mold and urine.

A high metal door barred the far end of the corridor. The sergeant unlocked it, pulled it open, then stood aside. Black went through the doorway and found himself standing in a small office, the cream-colored walls lined with rows of filing cabinets. A young man, once again wearing an unadorned Signal Corps uniform, was seated behind a desk, pecking at a typewriter. He looked up as Black entered, smiled, and stood up.

"Inspector Black?"

"That's right."

"Your people are waiting inside." The young man gestured to a door on his right.

"My people?"

The uniformed man ignored the question. "You're to go right in."

"Thank you."

The clerk sat down and began typing again. Black crossed the office and opened the door.

The room beyond was a dispensary. The walls were white and hung with supply cabinets. Counters below the cabinets were outfitted with sinks, a shining autoclave for sterilizing instruments, and a small X-ray viewing screen. Tonight the large room was doing double duty as a morgue. In the center of the gray-tiled floor there was an examination table, and on it there was a body, its obvious shape covered by a dark green surgical sheet. The sharp, antiseptic tang of rubbing alcohol filled the air, and cutting through it there was the rich, sick odor of overcooked pork.

Three other people were in the room with the anonymous corpse, only one of whom, Sir Bernard Spilsbury, was familiar to Black. The pathologist, his back to the body on the table, was examining an X-ray film of a human skull and upper spine.

To his left, keeping one wary, monocled eye on the shrouded body, was a bull-necked, gray-haired man in his middle fifties wearing colonel's crowns on the shoulder boards of his uniform, powerful arms crossed over his chest. His pale face was cut deep with lines, and his downturned scowl appeared to be a permanent expression.

Leaning on the counter opposite the uniformed man was a thickset figure in a tweed suit about Black's age with thinning, light brown hair and a neatly trimmed mustache. He smiled as Black entered the room, but the heavy-lidded, almost sleepy eyes were distant and reserved.

Spilsbury turned, spotted Black, and waved at him with the X-ray film. "Ah, Black, you've arrived finally."

"Yes."

"I gather you've put a name to the young fellow from Spitalfields."

"Yes, sir. A Cambridge student named Talbot."

"No connection to our Polish pilot?"

"None that I can find, Sir Bernard. Yet. Talbot flew with the Cambridge Squadron, but I don't think it means very much." Black glanced casually at the two other men in the dispensary. Spilsbury noticed the look and made the introductions.

"Colonel Stephens, commandant of Latchmere House, and Captain Guy Liddell." Liddell extended a hand to Black, but Stephens stood his ground, arms still resolutely crossed, steel-framed monocle tightly screwed into the socket of his right eye. "Colonel Stephens has offered us his hospitality and his discretion," Spilsbury continued. "Captain Liddell is here to…observe." No attempt was made to explain Liddell's function, but considering the origin of his transportation to Latchmere House, Black assumed that the pudgy man worked for one of the civilian intelligence organizations, the Secret Intelligence Service (MI6) or MI5. He was far too well dressed to be a Special Branch "watcher."

"I see," Black said finally, not seeing at all. What could his investigation of Queer Jack possibly have to do with either organization?

"Let's get on with it," said Stephens harshly. "I've got better bloody things to do than to play at being nursemaid to a corpse."

"Quite so," said Spilsbury. He dropped the X ray on the counter behind him, then pulled away the sheet covering the body on the table. Black stared, then swallowed the sudden rush of bile that had risen instantly to the back of his throat.

"Sweet fucking Christ!" Stephens groaned. He pulled the monocle away from his eye, paling visibly. The face of the thing on the table was barely human. The hair was almost completely burned away, the flesh on the right side of the skull turned to lumps and ridges of carbonized gristle revealing the yellow bone beneath.

The ear was gone and the skin and fat of the right cheek had split like roasted meat, opening up the mouth, palate, and teeth. The tongue, blackened and charred, hung back limply down into the throat. The right eye had liquefied, leaving a dark, empty socket, pink-edged and swollen like an angry, open sore.

Spilsbury smiled pleasantly. "As you say, Colonel, if you have better things to do…"

"I'll be in my office if you need me." Stephens jammed the monocle into place, nodded once in Black's direction, and rushed out of the room.

"Sauce for the goose and all that," Liddell said quietly. "Tin Eye doesn't like to see this kind of damage unless he's inflicted it himself."

Black swallowed again and cleared his throat. "Presumably this has something to do with my investigation."

"Yes." Spilsbury nodded. "We believe it does."

"His name is Eddings," said Liddell, taking out a well-used pipe and a box of matches. He lit the pipe and puffed, staring down at the body on the table. "Merchant seaman, twenty-three years old. His papers, National Registration Card, and passport were on his person when he was discovered."

"Discovered where?" asked Black, trying to keep the irritation out of his voice. If the body in front of him really did connect with his investigation, then that investigation was being interfered with by Liddell, and obviously with Spilsbury's blessing.

"Portsmouth. Stonehouse Backs to be precise. In what the local constabulary politely referred to as a 'lodging house.' Place called the Ant and Bee. Well-known, apparently."

"When?"

"This morning. There was a raid in Portsmouth last night. A lot of incendiaries. A fire at the Ant and Bee. At first they thought it was from the bombings—"

Spilsbury was bent over Eddings's body, poking away at the cooked flesh around the nostrils with a long metal tool. "An incendiary would have caused more generalized burning," he said. "From the preliminary report it would also seem that the fire was localized in the room occupied by Eddings." Black looked away quickly as part of Eddings's face crumbled under pressure from the pathologist's hand. Spilsbury continued, unperturbed, bending low and delicately blowing away the ash obscuring his field of view. He sniffed, his wide nostrils flaring. "Phosphorus, that's clear enough," he muttered. "Something else as well. Thermite." He stood, wincing slightly and putting one splayed hand over the small of his back.

"So it was an incendiary," said Liddell.

Spilsbury nodded painfully. "Yes. A homemade device." He grunted.

"But it wasn't the cause of death," said Black.

"No." Spilsbury shook his head. "The X rays I had taken show a projectile lodged between the second and third cervical vertebrae, just as before."

"Queer Jack," said Black.

"Who?" asked Liddell.

"A name he's been given," said Black, embarrassed by the slip.

"Good enough for the time being." Liddell smiled, his face wreathed in smoke from his pipe. Black was thankful for the masking smell of the tobacco.

"I would have liked to have seen the body in situ," said Black, frowning. More interference from above; first Spilsbury and Purchase at the Talbot scene, now Spilsbury again and Liddell. It was more than simply irritating; it was suspicious. Trying to ignore his rising annoyance, Black tried to concentrate on the job at hand. He glanced at the cadaver, then looked back up at Spilsbury. "He was naked, like the other two?"

"Yes. Sitting in a chair close to a window. If you look, you can detect ligature marks on the wrists and ankles."

"He was bound?" That was something new.

"Postmortem," said Spilsbury. "Just enough to keep him upright in the chair."

"Like a display at Madame Tussaud's," put in Liddell. Black turned and looked at the tweed-suited man. The anonymous intelligence officer had the air of a mildly condescending schoolmaster.

Black held himself in check again; Cornish been nothing more than an errand boy, relaying the order for him to come here. Liddell, whoever he was, and whomever he represented, clearly had powerful connections, and this was neither the time nor the place for Black to make a stand; better to find out what he was up against before stepping out of bounds.

Black turned back to the pathologist. "Is there anything else to connect him with Rudelski and Talbot?"

Spilsbury nodded and crooked a finger in Black's direction, motioning him toward the examination table and its horrid cargo. Gathering himself together, the detective stepped forward. Spilsbury lifted up Eddings's right wrist. A narrow blackened area zigzagged around the otherwise unblemished skin, banding the wrist like a tattooed bracelet.

"Quite ingenious," said Spilsbury. "It was done using electrical current. Postmortem again, like the other wounds."

"This was found in the room at the Ant and Bee," said Liddell. He moved aside and picked up a large manila envelope from the counter behind him. He tipped it up and a length of electrical cord spilled out. One end of the flex had been stripped of its insulation and connected to a length of heavy wire, bent in the shape of the burn on Eddings's wrist. The plug end was intact. Liddell held up the bent-wire end. "You see it?"

Black looked, then nodded. "Yes, I see it." It was easier to spot than it had been on the dead man's wrist—the wire, bent back and forth, formed a jagged row of Z's, three of them. "He's adding one for each victim."

"He'll add one more," said Liddell. "*ZZZZ*. We're almost certain of that."

"Really," Black answered flatly. "Perhaps you should tell me just who 'we' is, Captain Liddell, and why you're so sure of what this man is going to do."

"Yes," Liddell said pleasantly. "I suppose I should at that. In due time." He turned to Spilsbury. "You're all right here, Sir Bernard?"

"Yes, yes, quite all right. Plenty yet to do. I'll send you up my report tomorrow." The pathologist was now deeply engrossed in measuring the burn on Eddings's wrist, using a pair of scaling calipers.

"Good," Liddell said briskly. "We'll be getting on then. If Tin Eye asks for more information about this, you can refer him to me." Spilsbury nodded absently without looking up from his measurements. "Come along, Inspector Black, I'll run you back to the city."

Liddell drove Morris Black back into London, taking the eastern route through Brentwood and Hammersmith to avoid the inevitable traffic problems caused by the nightly bombings. Black waited for his companion to make his explanations, but none were forthcoming, and he wasn't about to beg for information. They drove most of the way in silence.

As they neared Shepherd's Market, Black finally spoke. "Odd way to wage a war."

"Pardon me?"

"Without knowing who your enemies are, or your allies for that matter."

Liddell smiled blandly. "You sound a little put out."

"You might say that. Moonlight rides into the countryside. Anonymous assignations with members of nameless organizations. I cobble villains for a living, Captain Liddell, if that really is your name and rank. I'm not much for cloak-and-dagger games."

"It's not a game, Inspector Black, I can assure you of that."

"Why is Secret Intelligence interested in my investigation?"

"What makes you think I work for SIS?"

"I don't really care whom you work for, one way or the other. I do want to know why you're putting your oar into Scotland Yard business." Black paused. "My business."

"I told you, Black, all in due time." Liddell pulled to the

curb and threw the gearshift into neutral. The quiet burble of the idling engine was barely audible over the thump and thunder of the bombs exploding in the eastern end of the city. The sky was alive with the flaring light from bursting detonations and the rising fires. They were a block away from Black's flat. "Close enough?"

The detective nodded. "Yes. Thank you."

"We should continue our little conversation under less fortunate circumstances. Luncheon perhaps?" Liddell paused. "Tomorrow. Grill Room at the Royal Palace." He smiled. "My treat of course."

Black nodded again. "All right." He pulled down on the door handle, then turned back to Liddell. A shot in the dark, just to see how the tweedy little bastard reacted. "It's because he knows, isn't it?"

"I beg your pardon?"

"It's because he knows about the bombings."

"Who?"

"Queer Jack. That's why you're interested, isn't it? Because he knows when the raids are going to come. You want to know how he manages it."

Liddell's bland expression was a frozen mask. "What makes you think that?" he asked quietly.

Black smiled pleasantly. "The look on your face." He pushed open the door. "Good night, Captain."

"The Grill Room. Tomorrow."

The detective slammed the door and then stood on the pavement, watching as Liddell drove off. He'd touched a nerve and had at least one question answered. Good enough, at least for the moment. He turned and made his way cautiously through the carriageway leading to Market Street, then stumbled through the darkness toward home, using the intermittent bomb flashes to guide him on his way. Except for the crumpled sound of the explosions and the moaning rise and fall of the sirens, the city was silent. Pausing in front of his building, Black brought the glowing dial of his wristwatch up to his eyes. Just past midnight—it had been a long day.

He opened the door to his building, then turned, startled as a bomb exploded only a few blocks away, close enough for him to feel the shock wave pressing at his eardrums. The pavement shivered beneath his feet and windows rattled overhead.

A single anomalous bomb or was the Luftwaffe shifting its sights away from the East End? He stood for a moment, heart beating hard in his chest, listening tensely. All around him the sirens wailed in terrible broken harmony, the sky lighting up beyond the chimney pots, clouds slashed in a blinding symphony of lurid pink and green.

To reach the nearest refuge he'd have to make his way along White Horse Street and Shepherd Street to the large block of flats with the designated shelter for the area in its basement. A night awake surrounded by nervous, chattering strangers or a few hours' rest in his own bed? He went up the stairs. He'd had enough of the world's savagery; all he wanted now was the short-lived oblivion of sleep.

That night he dreamed of Fay again, sitting by the window this time, painting quietly, her face lit up in brief flashes as the bombs fell and the city burned around her. In his dream Black prayed for the bombs to keep falling, keeping her face so brightly alive. Somewhere in the dream the face of his wife became the face of the woman he'd met on the train, and then, horribly, transformed itself into the charred, ruined corpse of Eddings, Queer Jack's third victim, seated in Fay's place, bound to her chair with wire, the ghastly, empty eye sockets draining down over the split and oozing jaws.

Black awoke to utter silence just before the gray breaking of the dawn and wondered for a moment if the world had somehow ended while he slept, or if he had gone mad. Outside, rain spattered against the bedroom window, and on his cheeks he could feel the drying traces of his tears.

CHAPTER NINE

Friday, September 13, 1940
10:30 A.M., British Summer Time

JOAN MILLER HAD THE TAXICAB drop her at the main entrance to the Botanical Gardens on Royal Hospital Road, then traveled on foot the short distance back along the Chelsea Embankment to the rows of aristocratic town houses on Cheyne Walk and the narrow entrance to Cheyne Mews. There were two reasons for her discretion: Potts, the ex-Guardsman Max had taken on as a driver, was as much a watchdog as he was a chauffeur; and even now, after the better part of half a century's acceptance, visiting a psychiatrist was still cause for embarrassment and even shame.

The strikingly attractive brunette gripped the lapels of her long lamb's-wool coat tightly as she made her way quickly along the pavement. There was no sun today; the sky was a dull shade of lead, and a stiff breeze was blowing, ruffling the surface of the river to her left.

The raid last night had been a bad one, and the breeze was carrying the wet-ash stink of the still smoldering East End fires. Another smell was in the air as well, a darker, richer scent. The smell of an open grave.

The young woman shivered and kept on. The Embankment was deserted, and traffic was eerily absent except for the occasional taxi hurrying along, usually headed away from the city center. Everything was silent except for the rustling of the trees above her and the faint, intermittent moaning of the sirens.

The warning had been sounding regularly from the moment Potts let her off at Waterloo Station on the Lambeth side of the river, but so far she'd heard no bombs. Perhaps the poor weather was keeping the Germans at bay for the moment. It wasn't something she really worried about; there was as much chance of being bombed in the little house in Camberley as there was of being blown to bits on the Chelsea Embankment.

So far the raids had scrupulously avoided any targets west of Charing Cross Road, still concentrating on the East End. Bombing by caste as Maxwell called it. Leveling the lower-class slums of Spitalfields and Shoreditch, but leaving the upper-class confines of Mayfair alone. Not that it would last. If it went on long enough, no one would be safe, at least that's what Max said, and if anyone should know, it was him.

She turned down the narrow passage leading into the Mews and came out into a small cobbled courtyard. Number 6 stood to her right, a tall Edwardian house in patterned brick and terra-cotta, much like the other homes in the prestigious riverside community. She felt herself relaxing for the first time since beginning the drive up through the Surrey countryside; she was alone.

According to Dr. Tennant, Numbers 1 through 5 were empty, abandoned by their wealthy owners for safer residences in the country, part of last year's great exodus out of the city by anyone who could afford to leave. She walked across the courtyard, pressed the brass button to the right of the tall black door as she always did, then let herself in.

She closed the door behind her, hung her coat on the

ornately carved stand, and went down the short hall to Dr. Tennant's office. The large, high-ceilinged room had a single, narrow window looking out onto the mews. As usual the heavy curtains were pulled across the glass, the room lit by several softly glowing lamps.

The exotic feel of the office always excited her. The thick, deep blue and gold Chinese carpet, the lacquered cabinets, and the perfectly arranged collection of small, pre-Raphaelite paintings on the moiré silk walls were a far cry from the heavy Victorian furniture she'd grown up with, and further still from Max's plain, rustic tastes.

At the far end of the room there was a large, black-lacquered table Dr. Tennant used as a desk, and a modest display of his diplomas and degrees was mounted on the wall behind his chair. Eton, Cambridge, the Vienna Institute of Psychiatry, McGill University in Montreal, Princeton, and his framed commission as a captain in the Royal Army Medical Corps. She sighed; Charles Tennant was barely ten years her senior, yet he'd already seen and done so much with his life. Still a man's world and likely to remain so.

To the left and right of the desk, on flanking walls, there were floor-to-ceiling bookcases filled with all the texts and tomes that were the totems of the psychiatrist's art. In the four months of her relationship with Tennant she'd leafed through most of them while she waited for the doctor to come down from his upstairs flat.

Freud, Jung and Adler, Otto Rank, Wilhelm Stekel and Sandor Ferenczi. Books by Franz Alexander of Berlin, Karl Abraham, Max Eitington, and Ernst Simmel. Wexberg's *Individual Psychology* nestled beside Nietzsche's *Also Sprach Zarathustra*. D. H. Lawrence cheek by jowl with Rob May and Father Wilcott's *Catholic Thought and Modern Psychology*. There was even a copy of the Van de Veldes's *Ideal Marriage*. Representative, according to Dr. Tennant, of his membership in what he called the "Eclectic" school of psychiatry.

"Hello, Joanna." She turned as Tennant came into the office. He was shorter than average, like Max, but dark, and darkly handsome, wearing a perfectly cut pinstripe suit and Eton tie with a cream-colored silk shirt. His thick black hair was cut just a little longer than was stylish, and his large, hazel eyes were ringed with a faint corona of gold that she found almost hypnotic. His voice had the same effect, a perfect baritone, accentless and almost ethereal.

She flushed at the name he'd called her. Max didn't have the slightest idea she was seeing a psychiatrist, but she knew that his obsession with security demanded the false identity.

So to Tennant she was Joanna Phipps, and she had the documents to prove it. She hated the subterfuge, but some things she couldn't divulge, even here.

"Hello, Doctor."

"Charles, please, I've told you that."

He smiled, gestured with a small, perfectly manicured hand toward the leather-covered chaise to the right of his desk, then seated himself. Joan lay down, letting her head drop gratefully against the back of the couch, arranging her long blue skirt around her ankles and placing her hands together on her lap. She closed her eyes, then opened them again, promising herself that she wouldn't cry this time, although, God only knew, she had enough to cry about.

"I heard the sirens," said Tennant, invisible behind her. "Raid still on then?"

"Umm. False alarm, I think. I didn't hear any bombs raining down."

"It was bad last night."

"So I understand."

"Do you feel safe out in the country?"

"I suppose I am. *Lonely* is a better word."

"Mr. X not spending very much time with you, then?"

"No."

"Nor his wife, I suspect."

"No. Neither one of us. He came down for an hour or so last night and then he was away again."

"Any progress?"

"With Mr. X?"

"Umm," Tennant murmured. Joan could feel him settling back into his chair, his eyes half-closing.

"I suppose you mean sexually."

"Anything you'd like."

"I bet you say that to all your patients."

"I'm saying it to you." His voice was firm. Fatherly? No. Deeper than that and not so obviously Freudian. Caring. Or was that just wishful thinking? She could feel the familiar heat spreading out across her chest. A tight, heavy knot began to form below her stomach. The feelings she had for Max. The feelings she couldn't express to him.

"No progress."

"Any attempts?"

"No. Not recently anyway. If it looks to be going that way, he has some excuse for hurrying off."

"Do you ever…initiate relations?"

"Once or twice. It never comes to much, and it makes me feel dirty. I know that's silly but…"

"It's not silly, Joanna. We all have needs."

"Not him. He pets his little furry friends more than he does me."

"His animals, you mean."

"Yes. Sometimes I think he cares more for them than me. Or any woman for that matter." She let out a long breath, squeezing her eyes closed, trying to keep back the tears.

"Perhaps it's because they make no demands on him."

"Then why did he want to live with me? Why did he make me move to that wretched little cottage where I never see him?"

"Why do you think?"

"Because he's bloody well ashamed of me!" she blurted. The tears came then, and there was no way to stop them.

"Or ashamed of himself," suggested Tennant. His chair scraped as he stood up. His hand came over the back of the couch, holding a linen handkerchief, touching her shoulder for an instant. She took the handkerchief, her fingers brushing his. She wiped her eyes.

"I feel so selfish," she whispered.

"Why?"

"His work. It's so important. I mean, my God, Charles, we're fighting a war, and he's fighting harder than anybody, and here I am worrying about…"

"The fact that your relationship remains unconsummated." The tone was matter-of-fact.

"Yes." She sniffed. "I must sound a fool."

"Not at all."

"I mean, really, he's under so much pressure. From all sides. And now…"

"Now?"

"There's something new. A problem. He's very distracted. More than usual."

"What sort of problem?"

"I really don't think I should talk about it, Charles. I mentioned—"

"Yes. I'm aware that his work is highly secret."

"I don't mean to be offensive." Her throat tightened. She didn't know what she'd do if she couldn't come to these sessions every week.

"I'm not offended, Joanna, I assure you. But you really do have to understand—I'm bound by my own vow of silence, not to mention the Official Secrets Act. I have my cloak-and-dagger side as well you know." Gently chiding.

"Still…"

"To solve your problem I have to know a certain amount about his." Tennant's voice was soft now, not demanding, but still forceful somehow. "You know that honesty between us is absolutely essential, Joanna, or we'll never get to the root of things."

"Yes, I know."

"You mentioned his new problem?"

"There have been several murders recently."

"Not his responsibility surely."

"No. Normally that would be true." She hesitated. Max hadn't been very clear himself.

"But now?"

"They're connected with his work."

"How?"

"I'm not sure. A security breach, I think. It must be important; they've roped in Spilsbury and a detective inspector from the Yard. All very hush-hush."

"And you feel this is causing him more anxiety than usual?"

"Yes. I'm sure of that. He said if it leaked to the press, it would make Dunkirk look like a garden party."

"I see." Not skeptical, but not excited either. Neutral. A good thing, too. She bit her lip and stared up at the intricate designs in the ceiling molding. She'd said too much already. A small sound rose in her throat. If Max knew...

"All right," Tennant said after a moment. "Enough of Mr. X for the moment, let's talk about you. I seem to remember that you had some concerns about your mother."

Seated behind his desk, Dr. Charles Tennant allowed Joanna Phipps's voice to recede from his conscious mind as she prattled on about some imagined episode from her childhood. Listening wasn't important; the microphone built into the small cabinet beside the couch would pick up every word and feed it to the wire recorder hidden in his bookcase.

He picked up a pencil from the table and tapped it gently against his teeth, leaning back in the chair and letting the few small morsels of information swim about in his brain.

Joanna Phipps, of course, was actually Joan Miller, and Mr. X was none other than Maxwell Knight, who, according to his entry in the most recent edition of *Who's Who*, was an ex-naval officer and author of several rather poorly received crime novels including an abomination called *Gunman's Holiday*.

In point of fact, the resolutely impotent Knight was director of MI5's Department B5(b), in charge of all counterintelligence operations in England, and Joan Miller was his virgin mistress as well as an employee of the same department. Through Knight she was also acquainted with Dennis Wheatley and his wife, who was Tennant's patient as well. It was all a very small circle.

From his casual investigations over the past three or four weeks, Tennant had come to the conclusion that Knight was suffering from a homosexual neurosis that had almost certainly led to the suicide of his first wife and his separation from the second, not to mention Joan Miller's unresolved frustrations. A hint from Joan the week before had led him to believe that Knight was carrying on an illicit, and illegal, sexual liaison with his driver, Potts.

The possibility of a senior intelligence officer being a homosexual was useful enough information, but this new "problem" was even more promising. Tennant smiled. His initial intuitions about the beautiful young woman lying a few feet away were being borne out; of the forty or so patients he saw on a regular basis, she showed every indication of becoming the most valuable.

Tennant blinked, held back a yawn between clenched teeth, and glanced at his watch. The timepiece was one of his few affectations, a Rolex Oyster Perpetual with a military-style wire-mesh cage over the crystal and a black, lizardskin strap.

Glancing over in the direction of the couch, he was suddenly aware that Joan Miller had stopped talking. He wondered briefly if she'd posed a question he was supposed to answer, but then he heard the measured rhythm of her breathing and realized that she'd fallen asleep. He smiled; it had happened several times before during their sessions, an indication both of the depth of her anxiety and her trust in him.

He stood, walked around the desk, and stood over her. She really was quite beautiful, and an utter waste. What did she see in a man like Knight? His weakness, disguised by the sensitivity he showed his animal friends? Or did she somehow sense his homosexuality and, like so many women before her, assume that she could "cure" him of it?

Then again it might be something more complex, a Christ scenario, for instance, with herself in the role of Mary Magdalene, ready to bathe her master's feet and give him aid and succor on the cross as he martyred himself for a great, just cause.

There was no doubt in his mind that he could have her himself. She was already well into the process of transferring her sexual feelings from Knight to him and had even begun to show some tentative signs of seductiveness. It was tempting of course—she was extremely attractive, and he had no difficulty in seeing it all in his mind's eye, but it was also out of the question.

To engage in any sort of sexual liaison at this point would destroy the magic bond between them, the fragile thread of fantasy that promised to reveal far more as the classic unrequited transference of a patient than by any writhing, passionate embrace. Perhaps he could indulge himself when he knew a little more about the murders that were causing her false lover so much anguish; but not yet. Extending a hand, he teased himself by letting it brush gently over her breast before he tapped her lightly on the shoulder. Her eyes flew open.

"Oh, dear. I've gone and done it again, haven't I?" She blushed fiercely, and from her reaction he could easily imagine what she'd been dreaming. "Fallen asleep, I mean."

"That's quite all right, Joanna. But I am afraid our time is up."

"I can come again on Tuesday?" Her eyes were pleading. An opium addict about to be denied her pipe.

"Come any time you like, Joanna," he said, smiling. "You know I'm always here if you need me."

Morris Black sat in the restaurant of the Royal Palace Hotel and gazed out at the bleak, windswept view of Kensington Gardens and Round Pond, waiting for Liddell to return. On the table in front of him was the remains of their luncheon, including a thick document that included the entire text of the Official Secrets Act, an empty bottle of wine, and an overflowing ashtray.

Before the war such poor service would never have been tolerated in a place like the Royal Palace Grill Room, but now it was the norm rather than the exception, like oleomargarine, meatless stew, and powdered milk. Waiters were either arthritic pensioners or pimply youths, and by the looks of things the cooking staff had been recruited from a Barnardo Home for homeless waifs.

He shook his head; war, it seemed, intruded well beyond the battlefield, reaching into every corner of life. Last night the war had brought him Guy Liddell; today it had given him the Official Secrets Act and a watery minestrone made from tinned vegetables and Oxo broth, three shillings and sixpence, less the wine. His dreams of the previous night had been touched with madness, and waking life was just as lunatic in its own bland way.

"Awful weather," said Liddell, returning to the table and following Black's gaze. "Can't come too soon as far as I'm concerned. Our best defense is going to be the weather I think. Keep the bombers at bay."

"The alert was on all morning." There was a long silence. The mediocre seduction by way of the minestrone was done with; Liddell was preparing to come in for the kill.

"You've spoken with your people at the Yard?" he said finally.

"Yes. They confirmed that I've been seconded to a Colonel John Masterman at something called B1(a)." Black paused. "I'm not entirely sure what's going on, Captain Liddell, and I'm not sure I like the idea of working for this mysterious colonel of yours."

"He's not a colonel. He's an Oxford don," Liddell answered, a slight note of bitterness in his voice. "And by the way, the secondment is just a bit of smoke and mirrors, old man. Masterman works for me, I don't work for him." Liddell paused. "He's another amateur. His only real qualification for the job is the fact that he was captured by the Germans twenty-five years ago and plays a better than average game of cricket. Stupid really."

"Masterman?"

"No. Far from it. It's the idea of people like that working in the intelligence game that's so idiotic."

"What does he do?"

"You've signed the dreaded document?" Liddell pointed at the sheaf of papers with the stem of his pipe.

"Yes."

"Well done, that's over with at least." Liddell paused and lit the pipe, tilting his head back and blowing a great billow toward the ceiling. "Colonel John Cecil bloody Masterman is director of B1(a) and chairman of the so-called Twenty Committee."

"Twenty?"

"As in the roman numerals double X, double cross. It's his job to take German spies dropped into our laps and 'double' them. Turn them about so they appear to be working for Uncle Adolf while they're actually working for us."

There'd been some vague rumors emanating from Special Branch about such a group, but this was Black's first confirmation of it. "How many has he 'doubled,' as you call it?"

"Thirty-odd so far. He has most of them in the Scrubs tapping away like mad at their Morse keys. What our Soviet friends refer to as *dizinformation*. He's given them all sorts of code names like Rainbow and Giraffe."

"They do this willingly?"

"They have a strong incentive," Liddell answered, grinning. "Remember Tin Eye from last night?"

"Vividly." A man better suited to one of those Gestapo leather greatcoats than His Majesty's uniform.

"After the agents are captured, they get sent to Latchmere for a few days. Bread and water, no heat, foul sanitation, sometimes a bit of rough treatment for good measure. Then Tin Eye screws in his monocle and gives them the gen. Work for Masterman or face a fixing squad at the Tower."

"Guarantees a high success rate, I should think."

"Umm." Liddell nodded. "Very impressive so far."

"Interesting, but I don't quite see where I fit in, or Queer Jack. I told you before, I'm a policeman, Captain, not a spy catcher. And I have no intention of becoming one." That was certainly true enough, not to mention that he'd seriously been considering leaving the police force as well. At forty he'd come to the conclusion that every human being has a finite capacity to accept tragedy, and he was reasonably sure he was close to the limit, professionally as well as personally. Time to grow roses in Dorset or something equally unassuming.

"I'm afraid the problem is Masterman's ego. He's absolutely convinced that B1(a) has managed to capture every single German agent in England. Without exception."

"Seems a bit much," said Black. Liddell was off on another of his roundabout explanations. The only thing to do, it seemed, was sit back and wait for him to get to the point—if there was one.

"Quite so." Liddell nodded. "But that's what he thinks—and will continue to think. He really thinks he's managed to nip each and every one of them in the bud."

"I gather you don't agree."

"No. In the first place it presumes that the German intelligence service is utterly incompetent and naive to the point of idiocy. It also presumes that Masterman and his troop of amateurs have been scrupulously efficient. I have firm evidence that neither statement is true."

"You think they've placed agents Colonel Masterman hasn't discovered?"

"Yes. At least one. A year or so ago we discovered some serious leakage of information that seemed to be coming from the United States embassy here in London. We had our own source in the German Foreign Office in Berlin, who said the material originated with a mysterious agent outside the regular Abwehr sphere known as The Doctor. At the time we had one of the embassy cipher clerks under surveillance, a fellow named Tyler Kent. We thought he might be our man, but it turned out that he wasn't."

"I remember the case." Black nodded. Kent was still being tried in camera. As he recalled, a Russian émigré woman had also been involved.

"There was even some thought that Ambassador Kennedy might have been The Doctor, but that didn't prove out either. The only thing we do know is that he continues to exist."

"What does Masterman say?"

"Masterman thinks The Doctor is a figment of my overfertile imagination." The portly man took the pipe out of his mouth and stared into the bowl for a moment. He frowned, then looked across the table at Black. "The state of my imagination aside, Inspector, I can assure you that The Doctor is an active German espionage agent, probably living in London." He used another match and relit his pipe, poking it back between his lips. "Masterman thinks looking for him is a waste of effort, but he continues to humor me, at least for the time being. I am his superior, at least on paper, although certainly not as much of a 'gentleman.'"

"That still doesn't answer the question of my involvement in all of this."

"You're part of the humoring process." Liddell smiled. "Something to keep me busy and out of Masterman's hair. Evidence points to the fact that your friend Queer Jack is in possession of extremely important information relating to the war effort. In your opinion the man is a homicidal maniac. That's quite a volatile combination, don't you think?"

"You're afraid The Doctor will find out about him and this 'evidence.'"

"Precisely. The Doctor managed to penetrate the hallowed halls of the United States embassy. Presumably Scotland Yard would be as easy as turning the key on a tin of sardines. If we assume that to be the case, it follows that the detective in charge of the investigation should be removed from a potentially vulnerable position. Hence your seconding to B1(a). Masterman thinks it's all a lot of jiggerypokery, but he's willing to go along with it for now." Liddell smiled again. "As I said, the man's not a complete fool. If I am right about The Doctor..."

"You could end up saving his bacon," Black said, finishing the thought. The whole sordid little picture was coming into focus now. This was the kind of thing he'd tried to avoid at the Yard—mixing police work with politics. He was a pawn being played by Liddell for his own ends, and Black was under no illusions about his expendability. Whether or not he managed to find Queer Jack and bring him to book was of no concern to Liddell or anyone else. He felt his temper rising, and for a brief moment he seriously contemplated getting up from the table and walking away.

"I rather think it's my own bacon that's at risk," Liddell said finally. "Masterman would like nothing better than to prove me wrong."

"I don't suppose I have much choice in all of this, do I?"

"Not really." Liddell shrugged. "But that's the way of things these days. We all have to do our bit."

"Ours not to reason why and all that?"

"Umm. I'm afraid Kipling still runs rampant at the War Office, Inspector."

The two men stared at each other silently, then Liddell looked away. He scanned the table in front of them. Black's soup bowl was still almost full. Three or four spoonfuls had been enough. "Bloody awful wasn't it?" said Liddell.

"Umm," said Black, and smiled.

Liddell laughed. "Come along," he said, pushing back his chair. "I'll show you your new digs."

Number 6-7 Kensington Park Gardens was a five-storied, broad-hipped mansion across from the shadowed wing of the Royal Palace Hotel on the west side of the private road that ran from Kensington High Street north to Notting Hill Gate. The house was surrounded by a rudely constructed plank fence at least fifteen feet high, topped with a scrolling, twisted roll of barbed wire. The gateway was open and Black could see a collection of vehicles parked along the curving driveway leading to the front entrance. According to Liddell, most of the mansions on either side of 6-7 were embassies and legations. A pair of uniformed policemen patrolled the south end of the street, and Black spotted the familiar shape of an unmarked, gray Fordson van parked by the curb. It was the only vehicle on the street.

"Special Branch?" he asked as they turned in toward the mansion.

"The Lithuanian consul thinks it's for his benefit. Good luck to him!"

Liddell pressed the buzzer by the front door of the large house and let himself in. A heavyset man in a dark, ill-fitting suit sat close to the entrance, leafing through a copy of *Picture Post*. He glanced up at Liddell and Black as they entered, nodded briefly, then went back to his reading.

Black followed his companion along a wide, carpeted corridor to the rear of the house. Closed doors stood to the left, and a broad staircase ran up the right-hand wall. Between the stairs and what might once have been the solarium of the house, a private lift had been installed. They entered the small cage and Liddell swung the handle to the fourth-floor notch. The lift began to climb slowly upward.

"What goes on here?" Black asked.

"Very little at the moment," Liddell murmured. "It's destined to be an interrogation center for captured airmen."

The lift slid to a stop at the fourth floor, and the two men climbed out. More closed doors and a narrow, plain staircase leading upward. Liddell led the way to the fifth, and top, floor of the mansion.

It was little more than a garret and had obviously performed the function of rubbish heap for the rest of the house. Stacks of boxes were scattered over the plain wood floors, and the three small rooms facing the skylit landing were choked with rolls of carpet, tangled chairs, trunks, and other detritus from the previous owner. Liddell took Black into the largest of the three rooms. The wallpaper motif was a repeating pastoral scene done in various shades of pale blue and paler green. The small, soot-spattered window faced a blank-walled central airshaft.

"I'm to conduct my investigation from here?" Black asked, appalled. He'd do better working out of the coal bin at Central. Being a pawn was one thing, being glued to one's spot on the board was another. He felt his temper rising again.

"We'll have it cleaned up in a day or so. Telephones installed, desks, chairs, that sort of thing. There's even a FANY type named Bronwyn who brings around tea and biscuits from time to time. Marvelous girl."

"Marvelous," Black repeated dully. It was going from bad to worse. He suddenly found himself thinking about the pretty young American woman he'd met on the train to Cambridge, envying her the freedom she was enjoying. He forced himself back to the job at hand.

"You'll need an assistant," Liddell said. Oh, God, thought Black. Not Bronwyn the First Aid Nursing Yeoman, spare me that.

"You had someone in mind, I presume." Someone to watch the watcher? A spy among spies? He saw his investigation of Queer Jack spinning off into a bleak, impenetrable blackness of bureaucratic ink.

"Not really." Liddell shrugged. Black sneezed. There was an inch of dust on everything. "I thought perhaps you might like to have someone of your own about. A familiar face."

Black thought about it for a moment, his spirits lifting slightly at the thought of employing an ally. Dick Capstick was the obvious choice, but the bearlike man would go mad in a place like this. He was also wrong for the job when you got right down to it, and he'd have a hard time keeping his mouth shut. No. Black needed someone without a lot of baggage. A plodder, but one with an imagination, and one who'd follow orders.

"I think I'd like to bring in a recruit from Hendon, a clean slate," he said after a moment. "Any restrictions?"

"None whatsoever," Liddell said expansively. "Just so long as he signs the Act." He smiled. "The world, for what's it's worth, Inspector Black, is your oyster."

"Thanks." There was a long pause. Looking out through the grimy window, Black watched as a fragment of newspaper soared up the airshaft, whirling around like the pale, bodiless wing of a bird.

"Do you think you can really do it?" Liddell said quietly. He looked at the detective strangely, like a butcher bird choosing which thorn to impale its victim upon.

"Run down Queer Jack?"

"Umm."

"Is that a serious question?" asked Morris Black, unable to stop himself from risking the question. "Or are you just following the form for this sort of thing?"

"What sort of thing?"

"I may be new to this, Liddell, but I'm not a complete fool. You and your people aren't the slightest bit interested in bringing a murderer to book, you're all too bloody interested in each other's job."

"Good Lord." Liddell smiled. "Still waters run deep, it appears."

"I just want to get on with my job," Black answered coldly. "And frankly, I don't see how I'm to go about it closeted in a place like this, presumably because I won't be treading my great bloody copper's boots across the wrong toes in Whitehall."

"Believe me, Inspector, Whitehall can find you at Scotland Yard just as easily as here. Whether you believe it or not, what I said before is true. The chances of you bringing your investigation to a successful conclusion, successful by your terms as well as mine, would be hampered and perhaps prejudiced if that investigation was carried on at the Yard." Liddell looked at Black seriously. "I can assure you, Inspector Black, that all of this is for your benefit as much as ours." The policeman said nothing. The speech sounded like a set piece, as though Liddell had been prepared for Black's outburst.

"Your assurances are no guarantee I'll be given a free hand."

"None of us has a free hand in anything these days, Inspector, you know that as well as I do." Liddell paused. "And you still haven't answered my question."

"About the chances of finding Queer Jack?"

"Yes. Can it be done?"

Black thought for a moment, then nodded. "Yes, I think so." It surprised him that he'd never really considered any other possibility. He stared at Liddell. "I still have some questions of my own I'd like answered."

"All in good time."

"Bloody rot."

Liddell patted Black lightly on the shoulder. "Welcome to the world of spies and stratagems, Inspector."

At seven-thirty that evening, Katherine Louise Copeland left the offices of the *Washington Times Herald* on Northumberland Avenue and climbed into the dark blue, chauffeur-driven Lincoln Zephyr waiting for her at the curb. With its headlights hooded, the enormous American sedan was virtually invisible as it slid quietly up to the roundabout at Trafalgar Square, and the driver piloted the vehicle cautiously, peering anxiously through the windshield as the wipers thumped back and forth with monotonous regularity.

There weren't many people about on a night like this, but since the blackout restrictions had gone into effect a little more than a year ago, they had caused more fatalities in London than the Luftwaffe. It would be extremely bad publicity if the latest traffic accident was caused by a United States embassy car.

The driver wheeled the Lincoln around Trafalgar Square, then headed west between the palatial clubs that lined Pall Mall, heading for Green Park, Park Lane, and finally, Upper Grosvenor Street on the western edge of Mayfair. Ten minutes after picking her up, the driver deposited his passenger in front of number 47, a plain-faced 1800s brick mansion, its two lower stories refaced with stone at the turn of the century. Like several other houses scattered throughout the resolutely upper-class district, it was owned by the United States government, although not part of the embassy proper.

Katherine Copeland was ushered into the house by a stiff-postured young man wearing plainclothes but sporting a very military haircut. After giving the man her raincoat, she followed him along a wide, richly carpeted hallway to the main drawing room. The large salon, blackout curtains in place over the front windows, was lit with pools of light cast by half a dozen table lamps standing on small tables scattered here and there, the lamps and tables placed as eccentrically as the upholstered chairs, sofas, and ottomans.

The walls were covered with ornately framed paintings, large and small, arranged with even less sense than the furniture. Altogether it was an oddly skewed and poorly decorated facsimile of an English drawing room taken from the pages of a glossy magazine.

An electric fire, its open coil burning a furious cherry red, was hissing angrily in the hearth of a huge, marble-faced fireplace at the far end of the room. Standing in front of it was a tall, hawk-faced man dressed in evening clothes, named Lawrence Bingham. Ostensibly he was the new first secretary at the embassy around the corner on Grosvenor Square. In fact he was London operations chief for the embryonic intelligence service that later became the Office of Strategic Services under the overall direction of Gen. William J. "Wild Bill" Donovan. Bingham turned as Katherine Copeland walked into the room.

"Kat." His voice was dry as old leaves, sandpaper rough from too many cigarettes.

"Larry." He hated being called that, which was precisely why she did it.

"Did you make the contact?"

"Yes."

"Where? When?"

"Yesterday. On the train to Cambridge."

"How did it go?"

Katherine shrugged. "Well enough. I kept it pretty soft. He's not a fool."

"We don't have a lot of time."

"I know that. But I repeat, Larry, your Detective Inspector Black is not a fool. Come on too strong and he's going to smell something rotten in the state of Denmark. He's a cop after all."

"Can you arrange another meeting?"

"It shouldn't be too hard. I moved into a flat on Shepherd Street just around the corner from him. Lots of newspaper types in the building. Never fear, Larry, I've set the stage. We're bound to run into each other sooner or later."

"Make it sooner. This could be important." Bingham turned toward the electric fire once more, spreading his hands out over the coil.

"I'm aware of that," she answered, speaking to his back.

"Christ!" Bingham muttered, rubbing his hands together, ignoring her comment. "Why do they have to make this country so goddamn cold?"

The Number stood with one hand gripping a leather strap in the middle carriage of the Bakerloo tube as it clattered southward toward Piccadilly. His other hand was pushed deep into the pocket of his long waterproof, wrapped around the cold, reassuring cylinder of the Wand.

He stood, even though the carriage was virtually empty at this time of night, and stared blankly at an advertisement for Barclay's London lager, his tongue, a secret abacus behind his lips, tapping out the fluttering numbers of the safety lights strung along the tunnel wall as they whisked past the glass panel in the door beside him.

Out of the corner of his steadily blinking eye he could see the pulse beating in the anterior ulnar artery at his wrist; all part of the Count, telling him that they were within a few seconds of arriving at Piccadilly, despite the slowdowns and stoppages all the way down from Dollis Hill and Hampstead.

The Number smiled; no matter how deviously the distractions were presented to him, the Count remained. His magic cloak and singing sword against the black, swirling forces bent on his destruction. Tonight he was Prometheus, envoy of fire, and he would let nothing stand in his way.

The train slowed and jerked, then rumbled into Piccadilly Station. It pulled noisily to a stop and he stepped out onto the platform. It was becoming an eerie, familiar scene, the dim lights revealing a living set piece of despair, the result of some terrible catastrophe or plague.

The platform was a whispering mass of human bodies, people of both sexes and all ages sprawled on coverlets and rugs, most of them awake, some talking quietly, while others stared mutely at the curved ceiling overhead. The men were in shirtsleeves, their jackets folded for pillows, while the women were fully dressed, the poor quality of their clothing identifying them as East Enders.

On his left, a young boy was pouring tea from a thermos for his mother, while beside them a man in a bloodstained butcher's apron was trying to read his newspaper with the aid of an electric torch. Younger children were asleep, clutching favorite toys, their faces hollow and gray in the dismal light.

The heat was almost overwhelming, and the foul stench of human waste filled the torpid air, fusing with the reek of too many bodies pressed too closely together in too small a space. At either end of the platform, high, Hessian screens had been erected around lavatory buckets that had begun to overflow hours before, when the hordes had begun to gather, disappearing into the underground like frightened rats going down a hole. Thick sludge was spreading out now from under the screens, stanched by cofferdams of sodden newspaper.

A girl, no more than ten or eleven, faced by the horrors of the makeshift lavatories, was squatting by the stairs leading back into the tunnel, defecating in the darkness, her eyes clenched tightly shut with embarrassment. There were a dozen coughs and a score of moans. Sneezing, the mutterings of shallow sleep, and children's whimpering cries. It was a sewer.

Pleased by what he saw, The Number made his way carefully down the yard-wide path between the crush of shelterers to the escalators. Here too there were hunched figures sleeping, the electrically operated stairs switched off for the night.

He began to climb, counting the steps and the advertisements mounted on the walls, eventually reaching the large, circular expanse of the upper station. Hundreds more had gathered here, too late for the relative safety of the lower platform, tucking themselves around the row of automatic ticket machines and under the empty showcases. A single bomb, a fire, even ordinary panic, and a thousand souls would be gathered up like scythed stalks of winter wheat.

Counting each lift and fall of his feet, he went around the circle and through the exit, finally climbing the stairs leading to the street. He paused at the top of the steps and pulled up the collar of his thin raincoat against the faint breeze and spattering shower, breathing deeply to rid his nostrils of the ghastly odors drifting up from below.

Piccadilly Circus had become its own ghost. In the deepening twilight of the huge Wrigley's, Guinness, Bovril, and Schweppes signs were dark exoskeletons bolted to the walls of the London Pavilion and the Criterion. A single omnibus shuddered flatulently around the Circus, windows dark, shuttered headlamps barely visible in the mistlike rain.

In the center of the darkened square stood the shrouded statue of Eros, his cast-aluminum bow aimed up Shaftesbury Avenue, the figure covered since last New Year's Eve by a gigantic canvas drop cloth. He smiled again; another of their lies. He knew that the canvas covered nothing but a rigid wire frame; the statue itself had been taken away for safekeeping months ago. All an illusion.

He looked upward into the iron sky, rain pebbling the lenses of his spectacles and wetting his smoothly shaven cheeks. His pulse and tongue, tapping fingers and beating heart, told him all that he needed to know of truth. It was almost time. He would spit in the jaws of death as the Twelfth Key was turned and come alive once more. He breathed deeply, feeling the memories swarm around him like gathering flies around a corpse. Such a bright day, so long ago.

Transported into the past, he knelt again in the dark copse that grew behind the chapel in Stanmer Woods, knelt over the still, small body of the little boy, one hand holding the slim, smooth neck, pressing nose and eyes and mouth down into the dying moss and the wet broken leaves of autumn, passing on the terror and the burning pain that had once been his alone.

They found the child eventually, after searching for days, using all the boys from school, and dogs.

CHAPTER TEN

Saturday, September 14, 1940
9:30 A.M., British Summer Time

TRUE TO HIS WORD, LIDDELL had seen to the cleaning of the fifth-floor offices at 6-7 Kensington Park Gardens almost immediately, and Morris Black spent most of his Saturday morning supervising the placement of a grisly assortment of Department of Works surplus furniture and sorting through the relevant files and dossiers on the Queer Jack killings. He found himself enjoying the various housecleaning chores; it was a refreshing change from his gloomy office at the Yard, and it kept him away from the flat with its constant reminders of the past.

After leaving Liddell the previous afternoon he'd gone to Central Records at the Yard and spent a frustrating hour sifting through possible recruits from the nearly defunct Police College at Hendon. There weren't many to choose from; the war had seen to that. In the end only one person on file seemed at all suitable—PC Swift, Simon George, twenty-three years of age and unmarried. Hoping for the best, Black placed a call to Hendon and asked that Police Constable Swift be sent down from the college the following day.

The recruit appeared shortly before noon, limping up the last flight of stairs, slightly out of breath. He was dressed in civilian clothing as Black had requested, looking like an owlish solicitor's clerk.

He was on the short side, probably a fraction of an inch taller than the five-feet-six-inch regulation minimum, prematurely bald with a fringe of light brown hair, a round face, and an oddly pointed chin. Large, pale blue eyes were made even larger by the steel-rimmed spectacles perched on his long, narrow nose, and he had the plump potbelly of a much older man. As he appeared in the doorway of the office, Black noticed that he walked with a strange jerking limp as though he were dragging the lower end of his right leg after the rest of his body.

"PC Swift?"

"Yes, sir."

"Take a seat."

"Yes, sir."

Black had placed his large, heavily varnished desk in the center of the room with the window at his back. Swift seated himself in the plain chair on the far side of the desk, using both hands to shift his right leg into a comfortable position. When the foot came down, it made a harsh thumping sound. Black glanced down at the open file on his desk.

"Dunkirk?"

"Yes, sir."

"What happened?"

"Little town called Arques, sir. We were caught napping, I'm afraid. Stayed back to help some civilians trying to reach the beaches. Ran into a German advance unit." Swift's tone was bland as tapioca; he might just as well have been giving the bus schedule for the Edgeware Road and Maida Vale.

"That's where you were injured?"

"Yes, sir. I was separated from my bunch. Walked right into one of them."

"A German."

"Yes, sir. Frightened him as much as me, I think. Couldn't have been more than nineteen or twenty. Didn't even have his weapon at the ready. I just came around the corner and there we were, a foot apart. I'm pretty sure he squeezed the trigger by accident."

"What happened then?"

"He shot my foot off. The right one. With a Schmeisser."

"What did you do?"

"I fell down, sir."

"What about the German?"

"I grabbed him."

"And?"

"I killed him, sir. It was him or me."

"How did you kill him?"

Swift shrugged calmly, his hands fluttering briefly in his lap. "I strangled him, sir. There wasn't time for anything else."

"And then you managed to rejoin your unit?"

"Yes, sir. That was June third. We were evacuated the next day. Spent a month or so in hospital and then they gave me my new foot."

"You went back to Hendon."

"It was either that or a disability pension, sir. I like to work."

"Your file says you're a qualified typist."

"Yes, sir." Swift smiled. "Before I joined the police I was a salesman for Imperial, sir. It was part of the job."

"Typewriter salesman, soldier, and now a detective?"

"It's the only section of Hendon still in operation. And you don't need to be a sprinter to track down villains, sir. It seemed like a good idea, all things considered. Bit of a future and all that, such as it is."

"Do you know what any of this is about?"

"I know what I've heard."

"And what's that?"

"You're looking for a murderer. Multiple. Something has the brass all a flutter, but no one's quite sure why. Most people are saying it's a spy or a friend of Winston's gone off his nut."

"Do you believe that?" The sort of person who believed rumors was the same sort who spread them.

"I haven't thought very much about it, sir. All I really know is that it's very hush-hush." Swift paused. "And important." The last was almost a question. The large eyes behind the spectacles blinked slowly.

"Yes, important. And I need an assistant." Black lit a cigarette, offering one to Swift, who refused politely. "Can you drive?" he asked finally.

Swift nodded. "Yes, sir. Bit of a lead foot these days, but I can manage well enough."

"All right." Black nodded. "The job is yours if you want it. Set yourself up in the room next door and find us a car, would you?"

The young man lifted himself out of the chair, a flash of pain appearing on his face for an instant. A pain he'd probably be feeling for the rest of his life, Black thought. The young man headed for the door.

Black stopped him. "You won't be able to tell anyone about what we're doing. Girlfriend, family, friends."

"I don't have a girlfriend at the moment. And my parents emigrated to Australia three years ago." Friends, it seemed, were not part of the equation at all.

"All right, Simon. After you've signed the Official Secrets Act I'll fill you in on the details. Then we can get down to it."

"I've already signed it, sir. They insisted downstairs. Inspector Black?"

"Yes."

"I'd prefer Swift, sir, if you don't mind. Simon is a name I never much cared for."

"Swift it is then."

"Thank you, sir." The young man smiled briefly. "I'm sure

that when I find out what it is I'll actually be doing, I'll find it most interesting." He nodded once, then left the room.

Black sat back in his chair and stared upward, thinking about his new assistant and watching the coils of smoke from his cigarette curl slowly up to the oppressively low ceiling. Swift was a man adrift on the sea of life without a tiller, without a focus, his world a dream ever since he'd killed that young German soldier with his bare hands. His life was never going to be the same and he knew it. Like Black himself ever since the death of his wife. Sad men in a sad world, with sadder times to come.

Black allowed himself the luxury of a single sigh, sat forward, and reached for the newly installed telephone on his desk. He'd been given virtual carte blanche in his investigation of Queer Jack; now it was time to put it to the test. The telephone rang loudly before he touched it and he jerked back, startled. It rang again and he picked it up.

"Yes?"

"Black?"

It was Liddell.

Dressed conspicuously in his Medical Corps captain's uniform and armed with the appropriate "essential services" petrol warrant sticker on his windshield, Dr. Charles Tennant drove his dark Bentley Speed Six out of London, heading west on the main road to Maidenhead. He left the highway at the newly built Colnbrook bypass and stopped for a short luncheon, then continued on, still moving westward until he reached Burnham Beeches Station.

Just beyond the tiny railway halt he turned south on the narrow secondary road leading down through woodlots and small farms to Burnham Abbey, Dorney Village, and the Thames at Queen's Eyot, his final destination.

He stopped again, opened the ancient gate, and drove the last few hundred yards along the rutted track that wound through the screening ash and beechwood to Rooksnest, the simple, plain brick farmhouse that served as his country home.

The house was neat and square, two and a half storied, slate roofed, the windows veiled by simple white shutters, the pale brick covered with a veinlike network of spreading ivy.

The spaces between the stone steps leading to the white, Georgian-styled door were sprouting with willow herb, and the narrow beds around the foundation were a tangle of meadow grass and briar rose.

To the left of the house were the overgrown, skeletal remains of an old apple orchard, and on both sides of the two-acre property, high, ancient hedgerows ran down to the water's edge, two hundred feet away at the end of a sloping meadow that had once been a croquet lawn and was now a patchwork breeding ground for scatterings of campion and convolvulus.

Overall, the property had a look of elegant neglect. Not quite abandoned, but not a proud man's castle either. Rooksnest had the air of an afterthought, which was precisely the impression Dr. Charles Tennant wanted to give his distant neighbors beyond the hedgerows and any curious passersby on the river.

Tennant took his overnight bag out of the Bentley and went to the front door, pausing for a moment to examine the small security devices he'd left at the end of his last visit to the property. Satisfied that they hadn't been disturbed, he unlocked the door and went inside.

Two rooms were off the main hall on the ground floor, a drawing room to the left and a dining room to the right, both low ceilinged, plaster walled, and plainly decorated. At the rear of the house, facing the water, there was a larder, kitchen, and scullery with a door leading outside.

Narrow stairs ran up from the hall to the first floor, which contained three small bedrooms, only one of which was furnished. On the upper landing a counterweighted ladder gave access to the half-storied attic above, empty except for a few trunks and bits of bric-a-brac left there by the previous owner.

Taking his bag up to the first-floor bedroom, Tennant changed out of his uniform and put on a pair of dark twill trousers, heavy wool socks, and a dark blue roll-neck sweater. Returning to the ground floor, he went to the kitchen, slipped into a well-worn pair of Wellingtons, and stepped out of the house through the back door, leaving it unlocked behind him. Humming quietly, he went down the long gravel path to the small dock at riverside and his boat, *Sandpiper.*

The twenty-foot Thornycroft motor sailer had been part of his purchase agreement for the house and was ideally suited for his purposes. *Sandpiper* was as old as she was long, planked with Oregon pine and decked in Burma teak. Her shallow keel was English elm, the tiller was oak, and the original solid-core single mast and boom had been made of straight-grained Norway spruce.

Altogether a very cosmopolitan little boat, which wasn't surprising since the original owner had been a lumber importer and had supplied the wood used in *Sandpiper's* construction to Thornycroft at a discount. The Bermuda-rigged vessel slept two on narrow bunks in the small forward cabin, was fitted out with a gas cooker and a small WC between the cabin and the bow, and was powered by an inboard three-horsepower Stuart-Turner petrol engine that was capable of pushing her along at a demure six knots without excessive noise or vibration and ten knots if really necessary.

The only major change Tennant had made in *Sandpiper* had been the replacement of the solid-spruce mast. The boat was now stepped with a hollow-core laminated mast of the same height with an aluminum spine running from top to bottom. The rigging, once hemp, was now plough-steel wire of a type normally used on much larger craft.

Even the most practiced eye would never have noticed the almost invisible wire leads connecting rigging to mast spine and mast spine to a cable under the cabin floorboards that led under the portside bunk. Nor would that eye have spotted the equally well-hidden power line stretching from the aft engine well and storage battery to the same location.

Since the first part of his journey was downstream with the current, Tennant only raised the foresail mizzen, leaving the mainsail furled for the moment. He cast off his lines fore and aft, stepped down into the boat, and pushed off, seating himself on the wooden jump seat beside the small wheel. He turned *Sandpiper* into the stream, watching as the slight breeze caught the triangular sail, then settled back against the small padded cushion on the gunwale. To all intents and purposes he was every inch the Saturday sailor, off for an afternoon cruise along the Thames.

Pushing back the sleeve of his sweater, he checked the time and smiled, then lit a cigarette. He was right on schedule. Tennant nudged the wheel slightly, putting himself into the deep-water channel, pointing *Sandpiper's* stubby little bow toward the playing fields of Eton and the looming fortress walls of Windsor Castle, slightly less than five miles downriver.

He'd learned a great deal since his appointment with Joan Miller the previous day. Immediately after she left his office the psychiatrist had called George Smith at Special Branch. That evening several large glasses of Scotch followed by an unrationed and hideously expensive meal of roast lamb at the Junior Carlton loosened the priggish little man's tongue, adding to the few intriguing morsels provided by his attractive patient.

According to "Nosey" Smith, there had been three murders so far, two in London and one in Portsmouth. He wasn't certain about the details, but he did know that it was being assumed that all three deaths were related and that somehow the killer knew the locations he chose for the murders were about to be air-raid targets.

The first two murders had been given to a detective inspector named Morris Black to investigate. Following the third death, Black had suddenly been given indefinite leave from his duties at the Yard, and all files relating to the murders had been quietly removed from Central Records and the Home Office Coroner's Index. Rumor had it that Black, or the "Jewboy" as Smith called him, had been seconded to MI5 and put under the wind of an ex-Special Branch man named Liddell.

Liddell of course was the connection to Maxwell Knight, but Tennant had heard the name before, and not from Joan Miller. Another of his patients, a friend to one of the younger Rothschilds, had spent an entire homophobic session with him discussing the grotesque antics of a group of young men and women who rented a maisonette on Bentinck Street just off Oxford Street in Bloomsbury.

The large three-storied flat, owned by the younger Rothschild, had been let to a Cambridge Apostle who was vaguely related to the King and was supposedly an art historian. The art historian in turn had opened the doors of number 5 Bentinck Street to a veritable who's who of revolutionaries, most of whom had indeterminate sexual habits and were what Tennant's patient sneeringly referred to as "cabinet ministers to be, honored gurus of the extreme left to be, connoisseurs extraordinary to be, Etonian mudlarks, and BBC God-knows-what-have-you."

Other visitors to the flat included several War Office "civil assistants," which, in the language of Whitehall meant MI5 (Counterintelligence) and MI6 (Secret Service) operatives. Liddell fell into this group. According to Tennant's source, Liddell's marriage to the well-known debutante Calypso

Baring had collapsed long before the war, and he sought regular solace at Bentinck Street, using it as a place to relax, discuss the progress of the war, and practice the cello.

That a man of Liddell's station spent a fair amount of his
free time at what Tennant's patient described as a cross
between a "Bolshie drinking club and a high-class male brothel" was valuable information and a potential source of lever-
age, but at this point Tennant wasn't quite sure what to do
with the knowledge. The fact that a detective inspector investigating a trio of murders had been transferred to Liddell's
care was even more interesting.

If Liddell had taken control of the "Jewboy" Morris Black,
presumably at the insistence of Maxwell Knight, it meant the
murders had to have a strong intelligence value of some sort.
At any rate, it was something Tennant intended to pursue, and
something his people in Hamburg needed to know about as
soon as possible.

After an uneventful hour's sailing Tennant reached Boveney Lock, paid his shilling to pass through, then went under
the railway bridge, joining the throng of punters and day-trip-
pers in their electric canoes, intent on enjoying a last taste of
cooling summer on the river as they darted about like frantic
water beetles in the midafternoon sun, all under the gloomy
watch of Windsor Castle on the southern heights.

Climbing onto the foredeck, Tennant dropped the mizzen,
then returned to the wheel and started up his engine. Tooting
Sandpiper's horn he turned across the main stream and came
up alongside the tea garden of the Thames Hotel, a large,
mock-Tudor building fronting on Barry Avenue at the foot of
River Street, almost directly under the castle walls.

The Thames was more a public house than a real hostel-
ry, specializing in luncheons for riverine Hornblowers like
Tennant, and passengers from the narrow, fringed-awning
steamers that carried holiday travelers up to Maidenhead and
beyond to Oxford. Two of the steamers were already tied up at

the hotel dock, and as Tennant sat down at the table he'd reserved before leaving London, he saw that a third steamer was sliding out from under the shadows of Windsor Bridge a few hundred feet away. He glanced at his watch. The military-style Rolex showed 4 P.M. Teatime.

He ordered a bottle of Courage and a steak and kidney pie, then inquired after a newspaper. The best the waiter could do was the most recent edition of the *Illustrated London News*. Sipping his ale and searching almost in vain for meat among the vegetables on his plate, Tennant spent the next three-quarters of an hour reading quietly and watching the river.

For a nation poised on the edge of invasion and with its greatest city having endured a full week of aerial evisceration by the Luftwaffe, the contents of the slim magazine were remarkably banal. A full-page illustration demonstrating how the ill-equipped Home Guard practiced shooting at model Stukas launched toward them on strings while Boy Scouts flung firecrackers about to provide authenticity; a review of a book entitled *Barbarians and Philistines, Democracy and the Public Schools*; a ludicrous article by Arthur Bryant in which he used a muddled metaphor about a chair factory to demonstrate the immorality of the Nazi regime; and to finish off, a peculiar treatise, more than sufficiently illustrated, concerning the "rasping tongues of fruit-eating moths." Scattered throughout the magazine in grotesque counterpoint were photographs of hardworking firemen, ruined buildings, and blown-up views of insects' digestive tracts and mouth parts. It was insane, like something out of Lewis Carroll seen through the eyes of Gustave Doré.

The psychiatrist smiled at that and dropped the magazine onto the table. He wondered if Guy Liddell, cello-playing intelligence officer with MI5 and friend to "Bolshie fairies," was any relation to Alice Liddell, the source of Carroll's inspiration for his looking-glass world. He glanced out at the placid, genteel scene before him. Wonderland, indeed, and naive enough to be the setting for any number of innocent children's tales. Or the work of a Reich Security Administration spy.

Tennant paid for his meal, then returned to *Sandpiper*. He cast off fore and aft, started the little engine, then turned the boat upstream and returned to Boveney Lock. During his meal, several more Thames steamers and three or four smaller vessels like his own had created a queue at the entrance gates, waiting for the lockmaster to finish his own tea. Maneuvering *Sandpiper* expertly, he throttled back the engine and took his place at the end of the line. By the looks of things it would take another twenty minutes or so before his turn through the locks came. More than enough time.

Tennant looped *Sandpiper*'s aft line over a bollard on the lock wall, then ducked down into the small cabin. Immediately through the hatchway there was a tiny galley, gas stove on the port side, sink to starboard. Beyond that, a pair of leather-covered banquettes doubled as bunks, a small fixed table between. Hidden behind the louvered doors of the cupboard forming the divider galley and saloon there was a built-in wireless, complete with a set of headphones, and below that a storage drawer.

Working quickly, the psychiatrist sat down on the port banquette, opened the louvered doors, and took down the headphones. He unscrewed both earpieces, exposing the small, heavily varnished speakers and the connecting screws fixing the wires. Twisting off the screws he pulled the wires free, then set the headphones aside.

The drawer beneath the wireless was crammed with an assortment of odds and ends that you might expect to find on a vessel like *Sandpiper*. An old knife switch, the tattered, salt-stained remains of the manual for the Marconi set, a pencil stub, a broken mousetrap, a few loose wires, a rusted butter knife minus its handle, a bit of coil spring and other parts from an ancient alarm clock...nothing to arouse suspicion during even the most meticulous of examinations. Not that Tennant was expecting *Sandpiper* to be searched, but it never hurt to be careful.

He removed the knife switch, the coil spring, and the butter knife from the drawer, laying them out in front of the wireless. He wrapped one of the wire ends around a contact nut on the knife switch, fit the butter knife and the bit of alarm-clock spring under the switch's metal flange, and joined the second wire from the headphones to the handle end of the butter knife; it looked a little bizarre, but he now had a perfectly workable telegraph key.

The jack end of the headphones appeared to be plugged into the faceplate of the wireless, but the connection actually ran down to the high-powered Telefunken transmitter hidden between the cabin sole and the keelson beneath his feet.

The transmitter was powered by the same storage batteries used by the inboard engine, and more hidden wires were connected to and within the new mast he'd stepped, transforming it into an extremely effective dipole antenna easily capable of reaching Heydrich's private listening post in Hamburg. Since Tennant always sent his transmissions from a different spot on the river, he was safe from even the most sophisticated radio-detection devices in use by RAF Air Intelligence, which, Tennant knew, was actually a ghostly division of MI6, headquartered at 55 Broadway Buildings in London and the huge Victorian pile at Bletchley Park.

Unstrapping his Rolex, he twisted the outer bezel to give himself an elapsed-time count, switched on the wireless, which in turn activated the hidden transmitter, then bent over his ersatz telegraph key. Tapping quickly, he sent out his brief identifying call sign, then began to transmit his message.

For the better part of half an hour Morris Black had been following Guy Liddell through a maze of subterranean pas-

sageways and corridors that ran under the streets and buildings of Westminster. Their bizarre, Alice-down-the-rabbit-
hole progression had started deep in the underground station
close to SIS headquarters at Broadway Buildings, and Black
had long ago given up on trying to figure out where they were
going. As usual, Liddell said nothing. From somewhere high
above them Black could faintly hear the sound of the sirens
announcing the evening's first raid.

Eventually they went through an unmarked blast door,
along a dingy, ill-lit concrete-block passage, then up a spiraling flight of metal stairs bolted to the walls of a circular shaft.
They finally reached another vestibule set with yet another
metal door and went through. Black found himself standing in
what seemed to be the corridor of someone's house. A thin,
Oriental-style carpet runner was on the floor, some ornately
framed prints of famous naval battles on the walls, and proper lights in the ceiling.

"Where exactly are we?" Black asked finally, tiring of the
anonymous trek.

"The basement of Number 10," Liddell answered blandly.
"Come along, Black, mustn't keep these fellows waiting." The
policeman blinked. Number 10 had to be Downing Street, the
prime minister's residence. My God, what had he let himself
in for?

Liddell paused in front of a varnished door, knocked once,
then pulled it open, standing aside and ushering Black forward. He stepped through the doorway and Liddell followed.
The room was large, low ceilinged, and dark, the only light
coming from a row of spotlights pointing at an enormous
mapboard filling one wall, and small desk lights ranged
around a massive, rectangular table. The mapboard was
screened by floor-length, black, felt curtains hooked to a ceiling track.

In the center of the table there was a raised bank of telephones in three colors, red, black, and white. Four men were seated at the table, three of them in uniform, and one in a dark blue, very conservative suit. One chair, the only one with arms and set in the center of the table with its back to the large, shrouded mapboard, was conspicuously empty.

Liddell took Black across the room and seated him at the empty end of the table, then settled into the chair on the detective's left. The sound of the sirens was now mixed with the steady crumping impact of the German bombs. No one else at the table appeared to take any notice. Liddell made the appropriate introductions.

At the far end of the table was Stewart Menzies, head of the Secret Intelligence Service (MI6), a craggy, dark-haired man of fifty or so with a downturned mouth and a Guards mustache looking totally suited to the uniform of an Army colonel. To his right, on the same side of the table as Liddell, was Squadron Leader Frederick Winterbotham, director of the SIS Scientific Division, and beside him was Comdr. Alastair Denniston, the handsome, slightly tubercular-looking head of something called the Government Code and Cipher School. The well-dressed, sandy-haired man with the mustache sitting between the table and the mapboard was Maj. Desmond Morton, introduced as the prime minister's personal assistant and lately the head of the Industrial Intelligence Center, which, like the GC&CS, Black had never heard of before.

Sitting there at the far end of the table, Morris Black realized just how appropriate it was that he had come here by such a convoluted, troglodyte path. These men were the knights of ghost and shadow, military demigods of an inverted Mount Olympus, their faces and names unknown to the general public aboveground. He also knew that any one of them could destroy his career, and perhaps even his life, with a simple nod or the single stroke of a pen.

"Inspector Black. Welcome." It was Menzies, his accent clearly Eton and Sandhurst. A member of the old guard before his time, as much politician as soldier.

"Sir."

"Did Captain Liddell give you any indication of why we wished to see you?"

"No, sir. None at all."

"You have no idea?"

"Presumably this has something to do with Queer Jack," Black answered. On his right Desmond Morton smiled. For the first time Black noticed that the prime minister's assistant had a rectangular wooden file box in front of him. It was yellow.

"Ah, yes, that's the name you've given this fellow," said Menzies, the basset mouth turning up briefly.

"Yes, sir. I'm afraid so."

"I rather think we should get down to cases," put in Winterbotham crisply. "I've quite a bit of work to do."

"As do we all, Squadron Leader," answered Menzies, glancing at the ferretlike little man to his right. "Still, there's no point in dragging this out. Since you seem so eager, perhaps you should begin, Winterbotham."

"As you like." The man in the RAF uniform looked down the table at Black. "From what Captain Liddell tells us, this Queer Jack of yours has now committed three murders."

"That we know of." No sense being too specific at this stage of the game.

"Indeed." Winterbotham nodded. "It would also appear that the murderer has prior knowledge regarding the location of Luftwaffe raids."

"It would seem that way, yes." Black fought to keep his expression blank. By God! His instincts had been right. Queer Jack's knowledge was the source of their interest.

"This is disturbing."

"Yes, sir." *Disturbing* was hardly the word; a madman on a murdering spree who also happened to have the ear of the Nazi High Command.

"Particularly to me and the other people at this table, not

to mention the prime minister." Winterbotham glanced at Desmond Morton on the other side of the table.

"Yes?" said Black, trying to sound noncommittal.

"Yes," snapped Winterbotham. "This Queer Jack is in possession of information he should not have. We would very much like to know how he gets it. At the very least it represents a very serious breach of security...security I am ultimately responsible for."

"Oh, for God sake, Fred, tell him!" said Denniston, laughing harshly, the sound like a bark.

"Allow me," said Desmond Morton, his voice calm and smooth. As he spoke, he reached out and touched the yellow box on the table in front of him. "What Squadron Leader Winterbotham alludes to is something which we presently refer to as Boniface, also known as Ultra."

"I'm afraid I don't understand," said Black.

"Nor should you," Morton continued. "Boniface, or Ultra, are the code names given to messages to and from the German General Staff and sent between German field officers utilizing something the Nazis call Enigma, a coding machine. Thanks to the best efforts of Commander Denniston's people at GC and CS, we have managed to break those codes. Virtually all of them—Kriegsmarine, Wehrmacht, and Luftwaffe."

Black couldn't help himself. His eyes widened as he sat back in his chair, stunned. "Good Lord." Beside Morton the empty armchair seemed to have a presence of its own. Black could almost see the portly figure of Churchill sitting there, cigar end drooping in the corner of his mouth, the huge map behind him stuck with the pins and flags that marked his secret knowledge of the war. In a single explicit sentence Black had been given what he knew must be the most important piece of intelligence information extant in England—some of Denniston's people had managed to break the Nazi staff codes and were privy to every move the Germans made—well before they made them, presumably. Incredibly, it seemed that Queer Jack was equally well-informed. It was a security breach of enormous proportions. No wonder these men were so worried.

"Good Lord, yes, quite so," murmured Morton, one hand still on the yellow box. He shifted his eyes toward Menzies for a slow moment, then turned his attention back toward Morris Black. "Captain Liddell is convinced that the so-called Double Cross system has not been entirely effective and that there is at least one German intelligence agent at work here in London. According to him, it also appears likely that this agent is not working for the Abwehr, which leaves the esteemed Herr Heydrich of the SD, the Reich Main Security Office, as the man's, or woman's, most likely superior." Morton paused for a moment, eyeing the box in front of him. He sighed. "The point of all this, Inspector Black, is that if there is such an agent, and if he learned about our knowledge of the Ultra codes—perhaps through the activities of this Queer Jack fellow as you call him—it might well lose the war for us. At the moment there isn't very much standing between us and a rout. If the Nazis took it into their heads to change their present system, we would have nothing at all." He looked carefully at Black. "There is no doubt about it, Inspector. If the Ultra secret is revealed, either by your Queer Jack or Liddell's 'Doctor,' we will lose the war."

Black felt a wave of nausea sweeping over him. This was no melodrama. He was being told in no uncertain terms that his investigation was the linchpin on which the war was hinged.

"Of course there is nothing to actually prove Captain Liddell's contention about this so-called agent," countered Menzies.

"Do you want to take that risk?" asked Morton dryly.

"We're taking an enormous security risk bringing a Scotland Yard inspector into this," Winterbotham muttered.

"Churchill's own private secretaries aren't privy to Ultra. Even the King doesn't know about it."

"Somebody does," Liddell said calmly, speaking for the first time. "Queer Jack is proof of that."

"Perhaps," said Menzies. "It could be a coincidence."

"I somehow doubt that." Morton opened the lid of the yellow file box and took out a single onionskin flimsy. He handed it down to Black. "What do you think of this, Inspector?"

The policeman read the slip of paper he'd been handed.

REF: CX/MSS/T266/67   XL 4708
ZZZZ
XL 4708 SH88 SHA34 TK22 YU26 YK ZF EF 32 32 16
FLIVO 21 EARLY FOURTEENTH HEIGHTS
THREE NOUGHT ONE, THREE TWO ONE AND
TWO NOUGHT FIVE. SEVEN YOUR SIX, YOUR
NINE NOUGHT SEVEN TWO ONE TWO FIVE
FOUR.
CONFIRM.

CAZ/RFB
EVB   14/1054/9/40

"What you have in your hands," said Morton, "is the original decrypt for the raid that's going on over our heads as we speak. It refers to an adjustment in heights for the bombers concerned. The first message, giving the actual number of aircraft and their specific targets, was received several hours earlier."

"The four Z's across the top of the message," asked Black. "What do they mean?"

"That's our own priority system for incoming messages," said Denniston. "One Z for the lowest-priority general information and so on."

"A signal ordering an invasion would have five," put in Morton. "Up until now we've only used four."

"Queer Jack's use of the letter Z was our first clue," said Liddell.

"The Germans don't use it?" asked Black.

"No," said Menzies.

The implication was clear. "Then Queer Jack is getting his information after it's been received here."

"That would seem to be the case."

There was a long pause. Black handed the flimsy back to Morton, who returned it to the yellow box. Everyone at the table was watching Black, looking for an answer, or perhaps an excuse. It was his moment and the choice was his—accept the challenge or back off. These were cold men, capable of anything. To them Black was nothing more than a pawn being moved across a chessboard, useful to attack but equally available for sacrifice if the game required it. They were asking him to risk everything. He took a deep breath and let it out slowly. If they were asking him to risk so much, then his own demands would have to be equally great. This was power, raw and unadorned.

"I'll need to know everything," said Black finally. "A list of everyone who is privy to this information to begin with, and a complete overview of how the material is transmitted to the people on that list after it is decoded. I'll also have to have authority to interview anyone on that list. Without exception." He sat back in his chair, waiting for the response he knew would come.

"That's absurd!" snorted Winterbotham "You'd be turning my entire security system on its ear."

"I'm afraid it's the only way," Black answered, trying to keep his voice even. He knew he was on shaky ground. "And there's one more thing. My assistant will have to know about this, at least in general terms."

There was another long pause. Desmond Morton eventually broke the cold silence. "He's right. Give him what he wants. Everything."

Morris Black felt a sudden, almost overwhelming surge of pleasure, replaced almost instantly by a cold and terrible fear. In that moment he knew that he had lost some part of himself that could never be regained and that he had seen something in himself he never knew existed. Power had been offered to him and he'd taken it gladly. The mark of this place would be on him forever.

He brushed the thought away as quickly as it had come, listening to the dull and impotent clamor above his head as the raid continued, then realized, to his horror, that he was smiling. He was still no more than a pawn in the game, but he knew that a single pawn in a chess match could mean the difference between winning and losing, success and failure. The men around the table stared at him and he stared back. The game was going to continue, and for the moment, the pawn was still in play.

CHAPTER ELEVEN

Monday, September 16, 1940
9:00 A.M., British Summer Time

WITHIN TWENTY-FOUR HOURS of being employed as Morris Black's assistant, Police Constable Swift had accomplished a great deal. Returning to the Kensington Park Gardens garret on Monday morning, Black found it transformed. Several large maps now covered the walls in the smaller office next to Black's—a gigantic Ordnance Survey chart of England, an equally large GPO map of London, and a third map showing central London and The City. The maps were dotted here and there with colored flag pins. In front of the maps a small metal secretary's desk had been set up, complete with a large and very old typewriter. In Black's own office he discovered a low pile of neatly typewritten sheets—his notes from the dockets on Rudelski, Talbot, and Eddings, neatly transcribed.

As well as putting the offices in order, Swift had managed to liberate a rather nice Alvis sedan from the stolen-car impound yard, and he'd also tracked down David Talbot's car, a 1936 double-entrance Ford Saloon. According to the secretary at the Royal Automobile Club, Mr. Talbot kept the vehicle at a place called the Stag Motor Garage in East Finchley. The proprietor was a man named Gurney.

The Stag Motor Garage was located just south of the intersection of the East Finchley Road and Fortis Green Road in north London. The place was completely anonymous, its yard hidden behind a high wooden fence. The sagging gate was hanging open, and Swift drove the Alvis directly through, pulling to a stop beside the twin green iron pillars of the garage's petrol pumps.

An assortment of vehicles was scattered around the rear section of the yard in various states of repair, the hard-packed ground around them black as pitch with a decade or more of oil stain. A large, windowless corrugated iron shed leaned against the south side of the fence with a row of smaller stalls and sheds facing it on the far side of the pumps.

Black climbed out of the car and glanced around. Anything made out of wood was in need of painting, and any metal he could see was patched and speckled with rust and grime. At least half of the vehicles at the rear of the yard had been relieved of their tires and sat on blocks of wood, and any free space between the sheds was piled with rusting wheel rims, bits and pieces of chassis, and other spare parts. An automotive graveyard.

Swift followed Black out of the Alvis and said, "I'll see if I can locate Mr. Talbot's vehicle." Black nodded absently and Swift went off across the yard toward the collection of motorcars.

A tall, blond-haired man in his early forties stepped out of the main shed, a wrench in one hand, a gray-faced, glowering dog at his feet that looked like a cross between a large wire-haired terrier and a bull mastiff. Its large paws were stained with oil, and the mustard-colored fur on its flanks and lower legs was matted with it. The dog began to growl, baring a set of long, mismatched yellowing fangs as Black stepped forward. The tall man moved his free hand slightly and the dog quieted.

"Good morning," he said, smiling pleasantly. "Something I can help you with?" The man was handsome in a gaunt way, a cross between Sir Walter Scott's Ivanhoe and a star from an American western film. The boilersuit he was wearing was filthy, but the signet ring on the hand holding the wrench was solid gold. His accent was definitely Oxford, plummy tones and all.

"You're Mr. Gurney?"

"And you'd be from the police," the man answered, glancing at Swift as he vanished into the ranks of cars at the other end of the yard. He turned back to Black, still smiling.

"Perceptive of you," said Black.

Gurney shrugged. "Not really. Someone from the Yard rang me earlier this morning, asking about a Ford being stored here." He paused, the smile turning into a broadening grin. "And you have the look." He extended a large, grimy hand. "George Le Fanu Gurney."

"Detective Inspector Morris Black." He took the proffered hand, ignoring the grime. The dog took one step forward and sniffed at Black's trouser cuff, then backed away.

"Don't mind Sam." Gurney laughed. "He's been waiting for a burglar for years. Yearns to sink his teeth into human flesh just once before he dies." He paused. "You wanted to know about David Talbot?"

"That's right."

Gurney nodded. "Come into the shop." He turned and went back into the large shed. Black followed.

The shop interior was the complete antithesis of the yard outside. Shelves to waist level filled the far wall, an enormous collection of tools neatly arranged along them. More shelves lined the walls on either side, stacked with engine parts and electrical components. A space had been made in one corner for a desk, two chairs, and several old-fashioned wooden filing cabinets.

Directly in front of Black in the center of the floor was a huge automobile raised five feet into the air on the fat, oil-slick tube of a pneumatic lift. The enormous vehicle was at least eighteen feet long, the majestic, curving body painted a gleaming dark blue with bloodred side panels to match the smooth leather interior. The side-opening bonnet was pulled up to reveal an enormous gray and chromium engine that would have looked at home in an airplane. The silver grille was topped by a sculpted crane in full, swept-wing flight with an enameled badge below.

"Nineteen thirty-five Hispano Suiza J12," commented Gurney, standing in front of the desk and noting Black's interest. "Picked it up from Whitney Straight, the race driver. Said he needed the money."

Black bit back the urge to ask how much. It had to be in the three- or four-thousand-pound range, if not more. And even he knew the name Whitney Straight, mostly from the pages of *The Sphere* and the *Illustrated London News*.

Straight was an upper-class society sportsman who appeared to spend as much time in Monte Carlo at the casinos and drinking champagne as he did racing cars. Not the sort of man you'd think would be found consorting with an East Finchley garage mechanic—even a mechanic with an Oxford accent who could afford a vehicle like the one in front of him. Gurney caught the expression on Black's face and read it perfectly.

"I do this sort of work because I enjoy it, Inspector Black," said Gurney, looking up from the open file drawer in front of him. "Not because I have to." The blond man glanced briefly at a framed photograph over the desk. "And because..." He bit off his sentence and went back to the files.

Black crossed the floor of the shop and joined him. He leaned forward and peered at the photograph over the desk. An extremely good-looking, dark-haired woman in her late thirties, wearing a tweed skirt and a sweater, seated on a picnic blanket. Behind her, barely in focus, were the ruins of an ancient castle. Beside her, one on either side, were two boys, one nine or ten, dark as his mother, the other a few years older and very blond. They were smiling, eyes crinkling as they stared into the camera and the sun.

"Your family?"

"Yes," Gurney answered stiffly. "Karen and the lads."

"Good-looking boys."

"Yes. They were." Gurney saw the expression on Black's face at his use of the past tense and smiled coldly. "Karen was an American, you see. I thought it would be a good idea if they spent the war there." He paused and looked at the photograph again, almost as though he expected the flat, black-and-white images of his wife and children to move within the frame. "I booked them passage on the *Arandora Star*. It was the only ship I could find. I thought they would be safe."

"I'm terribly sorry," Black said quietly, looking away from the man. The *Arandora Star* was an Italian passenger liner that had been confiscated when Mussolini joined the Axis. She'd been sunk less than two months before, loaded with more than fifteen hundred internees and others being evacuated to Halifax. Many of the passengers had been children. None had survived.

"Well, Inspector, you didn't come round to hear about my little tragedy." Gurney twitched a file out of the cabinet and opened it on the desk. Black looked over the man's slumped shoulders at the contents of the docket. Receipts, copies of work orders, a paper-clipped list of parts. "Not very much, as you can see." He looked up at the detective. "Is he in some kind of trouble?"

"You might say that. He's been murdered."

"Dear God." Gurney seemed genuinely shocked. "How did it happen?"

Black ignored the question. "How long did he have his car here?"

"Almost a year. They have a rule at Cambridge about keeping private motorcars within a certain radius."

"You knew about that?"

"Yes. Before he told me. They had the same sort of regulation at...at the college I attended." Black nodded. Gurney seemed embarrassed.

"Can you remember very much about him?"

"He was bright." Gurney thought for a moment, sweeping one hand through his longish hair. "He'd come down most weekends, chat for a bit, then take the car into town."

"Anything else?"

"He liked chess."

"How do you know that?"

"We used to play." Gurney reached down and pulled open one of the desk drawers. He took out a small hinged box and opened it on the desk. The box contained a miniature chess set, each square drilled with a small hole for pegs set into the base of each tiny piece.

"Was he any good?"

"Very. I think we had a dozen matches over the year. I might have won two or three."

"I see. Anything else, Mr. Gurney?"

"I can't remember very much. He was Canadian, we talked about that. He was from the western coast."

"Vancouver."

"Yes, that's right." Gurney nodded.

"You played chess, talked about Canada..." Black let it dangle.

Gurney shrugged. "He liked to work on his own car." Gurney smiled. "Said he couldn't afford my rates. I let him use one of the stalls on the other side of the yard."

"Did he ever talk about friends he might have had? Ones in London?"

"No, not that I can recall" Gurney frowned. "He did meet someone here once, though. I remember that."

"Yes?"

Gurney seemed to be struggling with some decision. He

hesitated for a moment, then spoke. "Um. Older fellow. He must have come by train because he went off with Talbot in the Ford."

"You say older fellow. How much older?"

"Thirty, thirty-five. It's hard to say. I wasn't paying a great deal of attention. The man did seem very interested in my workshop, though. Knew his way around tools."

"Talbot never called him by name?"

"Not that I can remember."

"How long ago was this?"

"A week or so ago. Just before the first big raids. That was the last time I saw him, actually." Gurney looked sharply at Black. "You think this man had something to do with the murder?"

"It's quite possible. Do you remember anything else about him. Anything else at all? A bit of a physical description perhaps?"

"Well dressed. A suit. Dark hair, thinning a bit on the sides. Average height and weight."

"Voice?"

"He didn't say much. Nothing out of the ordinary that I can recall."

"They went off together?"

"Yes."

"In the car?"

"Yes. I went out to my...to the country that weekend. When I returned, the Ford was back. I remember now, I gave him a key to the gate in case he returned the car before I came back to town." Black nodded. No key had been found on David Talbot's body. It seemed likely that the car had been returned by Queer Jack after the murder. Black heard a sound and turned. It was Swift.

"Did you find the car?"

"Yes."

"Was there anything in it?"

"Just this." Swift held up a luridly tinted postcard. The cathedral at Bath. Like the postcards in David Talbot's rooms at Cambridge.

Dr. Charles Tennant sat in a café almost directly across from the modern, white concrete mass of Broadcasting House, occasionally letting his glance drift slightly north to the gloomy mansion a few doors up from the BBC head-quarters. Like Broadcasting House, the main entrance of the building was fronted by head-high piles of sandbags. Over the double doors a large, limp Swedish flag hung motionless in the still, early-afternoon air.

It was the lunch hour and the café was crowded, mostly with BBC employees desperate for a change from the over-cooked, officially sanctioned diet offered up by the basement canteen. Several times in the past quarter hour Tennant had been given sharp looks by people wanting his table by the window, but he had studiously ignored them, sipping at the small, lukewarm glass of lemon squash in front of him and smoking, keeping watch on the Swedish embassy.

Tennant was nervous. Socially he knew quite a few people who worked for the BBC, and although he had a perfectly rea-sonable excuse for being in the area—a tea break after visiting one of his colleagues on Harley Street—the last thing he want-ed was to meet someone now.

There was another, much more serious reason for his growing anxiety. Ten minutes before, a green, unmarked Fordson van had pulled into a clearly marked fire zone a few yards up the broad thoroughfare and shut off its engine. Almost immediately the van had been approached by a uni-formed policeman, but the man seated on the van driver's left had showed the patrolman something, at which point he nod-ded and moved on. The van remained. The two men in the

Fordson were either Special Branch, plainclothes detectives from the Yard, or something even more dangerous.

Prudence suggested that Tennant leave the area at once. He was reasonably sure that the two men in the Fordson weren't on to him, but if, as he now suspected, they were "watchers" from MI5's B(6), it was almost certain they were keeping the Swedish embassy under surveillance, just as he was—which meant in turn that they knew about his contact.

The man, a flight engineer for Swedish Airlines, was also a diplomatic courier and supposedly had immunity, but these days both the police and organizations like MI5 had virtual carte blanche when it came to search and arrest procedure. Sweden was a neutral country, but it was also known to have strong pro-Nazi ties, if only because of that country's fear of imminent invasion.

If MI5 wanted to scoop up the man and take him to Latchmere or one of the other interrogation centers nearby, nothing would, or could, be done to stop them. The courier knew nothing of Tennant except his code name, but even the smallest shred of information in the wrong hands was dangerous. Tennant, so sure of his invisibility up to now, had suddenly become vulnerable. One way or the other the connection had to be severed before it was too late.

Looking out the window of the café, the psychiatrist froze in his seat as he saw his man step out through the main doors on the opposite side of the broad thoroughfare. He'd been through the same procedure several times before, and normally he would have waited for a moment, then trailed after the tall, blond man at a distance, just to make sure he wasn't being followed. This time he stayed where he was, his eyes now on the parked Fordson van.

Thirty seconds after the courier left the embassy, the passenger door of the van opened and a heavyset man in a tan overcoat stepped onto the pavement. He had an ill-fitting dark homburg pulled low over his eyebrows, and his hands were thrust deeply into his pockets. He headed north, walking parallel to the Swede and twenty or thirty yards behind. There was no doubt about it now; the courier had been blown.

Trying to stay calm, Tennant rose to his feet and made his way through the crowded café to the door. He stepped inside, pausing for a moment as though trying to decide which way to go. In fact, he knew exactly what his destination was going to be; at that moment it was his only advantage.

Taking two steps toward the curb, he raised his arm, preparing to hail a cab, then felt a large hand clap down onto his shoulder. His heart leapt into his throat and he turned, muscles in his shoulders and legs bunching, a thousand alternatives streaming through his brain in a mad, incoherent current. He could run, but how far, and how long?

"Tennant, old man!" His assailant's breath reeked of alcohol. The psychiatrist found himself staring into a florid, beaming face he couldn't quite put a name to. He frowned, trying to regain control of himself, the man's hand like a huge weight on his shoulder, pinning him down. Then he had it. He swallowed, tried to smile.

"Burgess."

"Quite right! Quite right!" The pale, ginger-haired man let his hand slide away from Tennant's shoulder. Guy Burgess was someone he'd met briefly at Emerald Cunard's country estate. Lady Cunard was known for the eclectic, eccentric assortment of people who traveled in her wake, but Guy Burgess was bizarre even by her standards. He dressed like a circus clown who slept in his clothes, drank huge quantities of liquor, and made no bones at all about his homosexuality; in fact he flaunted it.

Tennant vaguely recalled that the man had some sort of job in radio. He was also one of the regular group who spent time at the Rothschild flat at 5 Bentinck Street. Burgess was a BBC "God-knows-what-have-you" at the "Bolshie drinking club and high-class male brothel" Liddell favored. Even in the present situation Tennant could see the irony of it, and at any other time he would probably have taken advantage of the chance meeting, but at that particular moment the pasty-faced drunk was his worst nightmare come to life.

Burgess blinked, his thick, damp lips pursing. He gripped Tennant by the upper arm and turned up the wattage of his bleary smile as he began urging the psychiatrist down the street.

"Come along, Tennant. I'll buy you a large gin at the George. You can tell me all about your loonies and I'll entertain you with stories about all the fairies at the Bloody British Buggering Corporation." The smile had become a loose grin now. "My private name for the place," Burgess slurred. He blinked again and squinted as though he were standing in bright sunlight rather than a brooding gray overcast. It was barely noon and the man was already falling-down drunk. "Three-B C. The BBBC, don't you know? Maybe you can cure us all, what?"

Looking back over his shoulder, Tennant could see the Fordson begin to move off, keeping close to the curb. Tennant stopped in his tracks and firmly pulled Burgess's fingers off his arm.

"Some other time perhaps," Tennant said quickly. "I've got a bit of an emergency right at the moment." He smiled briefly and then turned away in the opposite direction.

"Charming," snorted Burgess. A few seconds later Tennant managed to flag down a cab. He climbed in and slammed the door, feeling the sweat begin to pool in his armpits. Another few minutes with the drunken homosexual and he might never have been able to get away.

"Where to?" asked the driver.

"The zoo," Tennant instructed, leaning back against the seat. He turned and looked out the rear window. Burgess was still standing there, weaving slightly at the curb. He made a rude gesture in Tennant's direction, then struck off through the heavy, midday traffic, holding up one imperious hand as he staggered back toward Broadcasting House.

"Fool," muttered Tennant.

"Beg pardon?" asked the driver.

"Nothing."

"Which entrance, Guv?"

"Main gate. And hurry."

They moved north up Portland Place, heading for the semicircle of elegant Regency mansions at Park Crescent. They passed the slow-moving Fordson, the MI5 watcher, and finally the tall, blond-haired courier, then bore to the right, following the wide avenue to the Outer Circle of Regent's Park, arcing up to the main entrance to the Zoological Gardens.

Tennant's cab dropped him in front of the main gate on the Outer Circle Road across from the crescent-shaped car park. He paid the driver, gave his shilling to the man at the ticket wicket, and went through the turnstile. The rear of the monkey house was directly in front of him, and his nostrils were instantly assaulted by the stench of several hundred of the creatures all assembled in one place.

To left and right were large aviary buildings, their occupants keeping up a steady, idiotic screeching. A light drizzle had begun to fall, and the graveled pathways meandering around the cages, pavilions, and small treed areas were almost empty.

Not that the zoo was doing any great business these days—since the evacuation of London's children, the Zoological Gardens had lost their most loyal customers. Over the last twelve months the daily admissions had dropped from eighteen thousand to less than a quarter of that number. On a rainy Monday afternoon there'd be even fewer people about.

Tennant pulled up the collar of his jacket and glanced over his shoulder. Still no sign of the Swede and the watchers following him. From past experience the psychiatrist knew that the courier always walked up to the Regent's Park tube station, then took a cab to the main entrance or more often a No. 74 omnibus to the north entrance on Albert Road. Either way, Tennant still had a few minutes to prepare.

Desperately trying to organize his thoughts, he turned left toward the east aviary and the clock tower. If the Swede and the men following him arrived at the main entrance he'd be ahead of them, and if they came via the north entrance and the connecting tunnel beside the teahouse, he'd be waiting.

The clock tower was a stunted Victorian structure located at a widening in the path between the east aviary and the camel house. It looked like an armless, clapboard windmill poking out of a gardener's potting shed, the shed in turn topped by a green-shingled minaret.

Across from it was a large, thickly treed circle of ornamental gardens split down the middle by the broad processional way of the elephant walk. At the edge of the circle there were a number of conveniently placed wood and wrought-iron park benches. Tennant chose a relatively dry one, protected by the spreading umbrella of a tall Dutch elm. He lit a cigarette, stared at the pale face of the tower clock, and tried to think.

The protocol for his communications with Heydrich's organization in Hamburg and Berlin was simple and supposedly safe. All radio transmissions were made by Tennant, using *Sandpiper*; there were no return messages. This ensured that Tennant would never find himself entrapped by the roving radio direction finders of the RAF Signals Intelligence Service.

Instead, any response from Germany would come through a small advertisement in the *Daily Sketch* on the third, fifth, and seventh days after his transmission. The advertisement, extolling the virtues of a Swedish herbal laxative, had a Stockholm mailing address and was presumably placed by Heydrich's contacts in Sweden.

On seeing the advertisement Tennant would then go to one of three locations depending on the day the advertisement appeared. The third appearance of the ad meant he should go to the Ring Refreshment House in Hyde Park, the second appearance meant the All Weather Golf Practice Course just off Holland Walk in Kensington, and the first appearance meant the zoo. By watching the paper on all three days, he always knew his spot.

The most basic rule was that there would be no direct contact. Depending on the circumstances, the courier would leave his message hidden in the toilet tank of a specific cubicle in either the WC discreetly hidden in the artificial hill between the fox and jackal pens or the larger facility at the entrance to the underground aquarium beneath the Mappin Terraces.

When Tennant was sure that the way was clear, he could retrieve the reply to his transmission at his leisure. The messages were coded using a mutually agreed upon key. The entire procedure was supposedly foolproof, with no possible risk to Tennant.

Supposedly. But now it was obvious that MI5 knew about the courier, and there was a good chance they also knew about the messages in the *Daily Sketch*. If that was the case, one of the two watchers would follow the Swede while the second would check any possible place a message might be dropped. There was also a reasonably good chance that the Swede would be picked up after the drop had taken place and then interrogated. At the very least such an interrogation would lead MI5 back to Stockholm and a connection with Heydrich, even if it didn't reveal his identity. His lifeline to Hamburg and Berlin would be severed.

Tennant dropped the butt of his cigarette onto the gravel path in front of him and ground it out with the toe of his shoe. He glanced at the clock tower. He'd been sitting there for almost five minutes. The Swede would be arriving at any moment. He had to make a decision. Standing up, he turned, then headed through the trees behind him.

Coming out from under the trees, he hunched his shoulders against the spattering rain and crossed the elephant walk, swinging south across the open lawn on the far side of the avenue, moving toward the lion house and the antelope paddock.

At the end of the lawn he followed a wide pathway to the left, walking in the direction of the south entrance leading out to Broad Walk. Before he reached the entrance gate he turned left again, taking the narrow walkway that led between a trio of small hilled pens used by the resident prairie dogs and the long narrow building that contained the birds-of-prey aviaries.

Continuing on for another fifty yards, he cut in behind the low, wood-sided refreshment concession and paused in front of the raccoons' cages. He lit another cigarette, watching as half a dozen of the masked, sharp-nosed creatures paced back and forth in their enclosures, fat bellies and high back legs giving them the look of shambling, ring-tailed sailors.

Behind him, less than ten feet away, were the cages containing the foxes and jackals. There was no sound except for the patter of the rain and the distant jungle hoot and caw of the monkey house and the main aviaries close to the entrance.

Fifty feet to his left, screened by the fox and jackal pens, was the sloping walk leading to the tunnel beneath the Outer Circle Road. If the Swede came through the north entrance, as he had on the last three occasions, he would leave his message in the WC here.

The psychiatrist looked cautiously to left and right; he was alone on the pathway. He glanced over his shoulder; a jackal, fur matted with the rain, ears pricked nervously, watched him from beneath a ledge of concrete built into the ten-foot-high hill. It lifted its narrow head, tasting the air. Tennant shuddered with a sudden chill and wondered if the creature could smell his fear.

He turned on his heel and walked quickly toward the hidden entrance to the men's lavatory. Ever since he'd come through the gate, he'd tried to identify his options; now he realized there were none. There was only one course of action he could take. Reaching the door of the lavatory, he took a last look around. To his right the bandstand in front of the large teahouse was empty, rain dripping from its gingerbread eaves. To his left an old man in a long black coat and worn galoshes stood in front of the small-cat house. Tennant pulled open the door and went inside.

The lavatory was a long, narrow bunker, its eastern wall forming the rear of the fox and jackal pens, its roof covered with soil and vented through two small metal chimneys. Three lights recessed into the ceiling, wire-mesh guarded, threw pools of sick yellow light around the white-tiled chamber.

There were three porcelain sinks and a long, polished metal mirror just inside the plain swinging door, a row of urinals on the left and five toilet stalls on the right. The Swede would leave the message in the tank of the farthest stall. The place stank of disinfectant and old urine.

Tennant turned on the taps of the nearest sink and stared at his dim, streaked reflection in the mirror. His suit jacket was damp with rain, his hair plastered down on his skull. A mess. He knew it was his imagination, but he could almost swear that dark rings had suddenly appeared beneath his eyes.

The fear he felt was as palpable as the aching throb of his heart pounding against his ribs, as terribly real as the hot rip and tear of the blood coursing through his veins. His mouth was thick as oiled cotton, and looking down, he saw that the dark hairs on the back of his hands were rising. Adrenaline, a heightened sensory awareness brought on by massive anxiety—there were a score of physical and psychological manifestations and precedents for what he saw and felt and heard. Madness. Control.

He reached into the inside pocket of his jacket and took

out the fountain pen he always carried, unscrewed the top, then placed it carefully on the edge of the sink close to his right hand. He bent his head low, splashed water on his face, then froze, hearing the yawning creak of the door as it swung open behind his back.

The Swede entered the lavatory and Tennant raised his head, looking into the mirror. The tall, blond man paused for a moment, then let the door swing shut behind him. He glanced at Tennant, and then, instead of moving to the stalls, he went to the row of urinals and began undoing his flies. Christ! What was he doing?

Tennant pushed up the lever to drain the sink, his face still dripping. The Swede finished, then came back toward the psychiatrist. He chose a sink to Tennant's left and began to wash his hands. The psychiatrist picked up the pen, gripping it in his clenched fist.

"Where is it?" Tennant asked, turning toward the Swede, keeping the hand holding the pen at his side. "You're being followed. Give it to me, quickly!"

The Swede frowned. *"Forlat? Vad sade ni."*

"The message, man!" Tennant hissed. "I'm the Doctor. Give it to me!"

"Doktor? Jag talar inte engelska."

Tennant groaned. The idiot didn't speak English. Sanity was deserting him, spinning away on a whirling flood of rising panic. *"Ich bin der Doktor,"* he said, switching to German. *"Du hast ein—"*

"Nej! Nej!" said the Swede, backing away from the sink, suddenly realizing whom he was speaking to, his hands coming up defensively as the implications of meeting Tennant face-to-face dawned on him. *"Jag gar—"*

There was no more time. The psychiatrist reached out, gripped the man's left wrist, and pulled it aside, simultaneously bringing the pen up in a sweeping arc, burying it deeply in the socket of the courier's eye.

The man screamed, struggling horribly, but Tennant held on, pushing the pen even deeper into the socket, the gold nib slicing the optic nerve and finally embedding itself in the soft tissue of the man's brain. There was a sudden terrible odor as the man's bowels voided, and then he died. The Swede slid away, dropping to the floor as Tennant withdrew the pen, stuffing the gory instrument into his jacket pocket.

He bent over the dead man and began going through his pockets, muttering half to himself and half in apology to the man he had just murdered.

"You saw my face. You knew who I was. They were following you. It was necessary. Necessary." His breath was coming in ragged, panting gasps, and he felt the sour taste of vomit rising in his throat.

Clear fluid was draining down from the man's eye, slowly turning crimson as it tracked down his cheek and dripped onto the floor. The smell filling the lavatory now was a hideous mixture of blood and excrement strong enough to blot out the scent of the chemical disinfectant.

Tennant felt as though he was going to be sick at any moment. He went through the last pocket. Nothing. The messages were invariably carried in a small Bakelite tube, sealed and coated with paraffin.

Tennant moaned. "Christ, man! What have you done?" And then he knew. Instead of coming in through the north entrance and using the tunnel under the Outer Circle Road, the courier had chosen instead to use the main entrance. He'd deposited the message in the lavatory beside the stairs leading down to the aquarium, then cut along here. He'd used the urinal in earnest.

"Oh, God," Tennant whispered, standing, staring down at the dead man. By now the watchers would have gone into the aquarium lavatory, and one or both of them would be close by, watching for the Swede to reappear. He was trapped in this evil-smelling hole. Doomed, a murderer, a spy, a traitor.

They'd post him against a wall within the Tower, pin a paper target over his heart, and then six stone-faced soldiers would blow him to hell and his life would be over. The last shred of reason fled. He had to get away. He turned and bolted, racing for the door.

It swung open before he reached it, and Tennant had the fleeting impression of a heavyset man wearing a hat pulled low over his brow. The passenger in the Fordson. The psychiatrist slammed into the man, who was already reaching under the long flap over his overcoat.

The two went down, sprawling on the floor beside the first of the toilet cubicles. The watcher was at least six inches taller and much heavier, but Tennant had the advantage of surprise and the panic-stricken strength of his overwhelming terror. He smashed at the man's face and pushed his free hand under the overcoat, feeling the hard metallic shape of a pistol in the man's hand.

They rolled sideways and the watcher's shoulder smashed against the supporting stanchion of the cubicle door. For a split second his grip on the pistol loosened. Tennant's fingers scrabbled madly for the trigger, and then the weapon fired, the sound muffled by the overcoat and the watcher's own bulk. The watcher let out a single, sharp exclamation and then sagged to one side. Less than a minute had passed.

Tennant crabbed madly away from the body on all fours, reached the row of sinks, then pulled himself upright, breathing hard, lungs fighting for air. He turned, leaning back on the edge of the sink, and looked back. The watcher lay like a bundle of rags next to the toilet cubicle. Dead. The psychiatrist felt the world spinning away under his feet, almost overcome by nausea, the meat of his tongue like a choking gag. In the space of five minutes he'd murdered twice. Two men were dead at his feet and it wasn't over yet.

He pushed away from the row of sinks, forcing himself to move through sheer power of will. Wooden legged, he reached the door, took one deep breath, and stepped out into the open air again. Letting the door swing shut behind him, Tennant paused and looked around, trying to look as casual as he could.

The old man in front of the small-cat house was gone. The path leading back past the raccoon cages and behind the refreshment concession was empty, as was the bandstand and the teahouse terrace. He was alone. Thank God for that; there was still a chance. Gritting his teeth, he walked away, his pace as calm and slow as his terrible fear would allow. He moved toward the dark mouth of the tunnel leading to the middle garden, trying not to think of what he was leaving behind.

At each step he expected to hear the crack of a bullet or the harsh screeching of a policeman's whistle, but nothing came. There was only the wet-bone crunch of gravel under his shoes and the small tapping whisper of rain in the trees. He reached the shadows of the tunnel entrance and disappeared. Safe.

But for how long?

He ran, his pelting footsteps echoing in the darkness, and then he was gone.

Katherine Copeland sat at the writing desk in the sitting room of her anonymously furnished flat on Shepard Street, smoking an endless series of DuMaurier cigarettes as she went over the dossier Bingham had given her on Detective Inspector Morris Black, occasionally making notes on a tablet of lined paper.

She took a long, deep pull on her cigarette. Donovan had once told her, and not too kindly, that she smoked like a man, holding the cigarette low between her fingers instead of high, and exhaling through her nostrils. Katherine made a snorting sound under her breath. It wasn't the only thing she did like a man if truth be told. She stared down at the open folder, frowning.

Black, at least on the surface, was every inch the plodding, ordinary policeman and very little more. She'd combed through the libraries of half a dozen London newspapers, eking out a bare-bones history of Black's career, and had come to the conclusion that he was very good at his job and shied away from any sort of publicity.

More detailed information picked up by Larry Bingham seemed to indicate that by dint of his methodical nature and an ability to glean useful knowledge out of seemingly irrelevant detail, Morris Black was often given the most difficult, if not the most exciting, cases.

Digging a little deeper, Katherine had also decided that Black's work was more a way of life than a way to make a living. According to Bingham's sources, Black came from quite a wealthy family, owned the building he lived in only a few blocks from her flat, and had a sizable income outside of his salary at the Yard. He didn't bother to collect the clothing allowance due to plainclothes detectives and rarely if ever put in vouchers for work-related food or travel.

Since the death of his wife the previous year, he'd also taken on an ever-increasing caseload, working almost twice as many open dockets as his friend Capstick. The lonely widower burying his sorrow in work? It was a possibility, and if Black's reaction to her on the train to Cambridge was any indication, it might also be a vulnerable soft spot in his character that she could use to her advantage.

Twisting out her cigarette in the already overflowing ashtray, Katherine glanced out through the gauzy curtains and shook her head. She was starting to think like Bingham and she didn't like that one little bit. Maybe Donovan was right; smoke like a man, think like a man, drink like one, next thing you know she'd be sprouting a mustache. What the hell had happened to Charlie Copeland's little girl, the senator's pride and joy in pigtails, riding around their West Virginia estate on her pony Cimarron and smiling at the photographers?

She'd grown up, that's what, cursed as her father once said with as much brains as beauty. Balking at a Southern belle's debutante future, she'd gone to Sarah Lawrence looking for an education, not a Harvard husband.

Six months after receiving her degree, Katherine Copeland ended an instructive and almost violently passionate affair she'd had with her European-history tutor, placed a telephone call to her father in Washington, and landed a job as a research assistant in the Georgetown branch of the law firm headed by William J. "Wild Bill" Donovan. The rest, she thought wryly, was history, and history had brought her to this, playing the role of a Yankee Mata Hari, mixing with gray-faced horrors like Lawrence Bingham and planning the seduction of a British bobby who was probably still in mourning for his wife. A long way from pigtails and pony rides.

And too far to go back.

Katherine took a deep breath and let it out slowly, watching the curtains moving slightly in the soft breeze. Maybe tonight those same curtains would be blasted to shreds by a whirling storm of flying glass as a German bomb exploded in the street. She'd always wanted to come to London, but not this way.

Somewhere along the line, her feelings, her hopes and dreams, had faded. She'd told herself often enough that she was the victim of events, and her personal life had to be put aside, at least for the moment. Which was all horseshit, of course. School had been a way to get away from home, and working for Donovan had been a way of getting away from school. It had been exciting at first, but after a while she saw that Washington society wasn't much different from Sarah Lawrence; given time she would have succumbed, letting herself be married off to a son of one of her father's well-connected friends. London was just another place to run to.

And now that she was here, Bill Donovan and Larry god-damn Bingham were doing their level best to turn her into a whore. Katherine looked down at the file on Black again. She and Black were a lot alike, flotsam and jetsam drifting on a sea of war, caught on a rising tide of other people's plots and plans. She'd met Black once and liked him almost immediately; now she was supposed to betray him. She lit another cigarette and stared at the photograph of Black clipped to the file.

"We really are a pair of sorry sons of bitches, aren't we, Morris?" she whispered.

Liddell was waiting in the Kensington Park Gardens office, smoking his pipe and staring at the large maps pinned to the wall. He turned as Morris Black and his assistant returned from the Stag Garage and entered the narrow room.

"There's been another one," he said quietly.

"Where?" Black asked.

"Southampton. Last night."

"You're sure?"

"Yes. There's no doubt, I'm afraid. I came round to collect you. There's an airplane waiting for us at Croydon."

"We're flying?" Black felt a flutter in the pit of his stomach; he'd never flown before.

"Yes. It's all laid on."

"Has Spilsbury been told?"

"No." Liddell looked down into the bowl of his pipe, frowning. "St. Thomas Hospital was hit during the raid last night. Two of the on-call physicians were killed. One of them was Peter Spilsbury, his son."

"My God."

"Umm," Liddell murmured. "Spilsbury had no idea. He was at an inquest this morning and someone delivered a note of condolence to him in court. It must have been a terrible shock." The intelligence officer cleared his throat noisily and tucked the pipe into the breast pocket of his jacket. "Fortunes of war I suppose," he said philosophically. "Strikes home from time to time." He paused. "The point is, I don't think we'll be able to count on his continuing assistance in this matter. Not for the time being at any rate."

"No," said Black. There was a long silence. Slipping silently past his superior, Police Constable Swift went to the ordnance map of England, chose a large drawing pin set with a red-enameled, tin-plate flag, and stuck it into the map over the large circle indicating the port city of Southampton on the Channel coast. He stood back and eyed his handiwork. Liddell looked sideways at the map, then turned back to Morris Black. Liddell's brief moment of sympathy for the pathologist's sudden grief had passed.

"Come along then," he said, smiling. "Mustn't keep the RAF waiting."

CHAPTER TWELVE

Monday, September 16, 1940
2:30 P.M., British Summer Time

MORRIS BLACK AND GUY LIDDELL flew out of Croydon in an RAF Walrus, an aging, scarred amphibian with retractable landing gear. The aircraft was usually ship-launched by catapult, and to Black it seemed as though the ungainly, incredibly noisy single-engine biplane would never leave the ground.

The Walrus hadn't been designed for comfort either, and the detective endured his first flight crammed into the tiny rear gunner's compartment, squeezing himself between the two main wing struts while Liddell occupied an equally uncomfortable position in the small navigator's compartment almost under the feet of the pilot.

The sound of the large, wing-mounted engine was so loud that conversation was impossible, and Black had to endure his maiden flight in silence, trying to ignore the stomach-churning smell of petrol and exhaust, staring out through the small porthole as the slow-moving machine lumbered over the North Downs, heading southwest toward the coast. Forty minutes after leaving Croydon, the Walrus reached Southampton Water, circled once, and dropped down onto the River Itchen, its boat-hulled fuselage sending up a huge rooster tail of spray as it slammed down onto the sluggish, oily surface of the river.

To port, behind them, were the piers, cranes, and loading sheds of Southampton's Empress Docks, while to starboard Black could see the soot and grime expanse of Woolston, the port city's southern industrial suburb. The pilot steered the aircraft up to the Vickers-Supermarine pier and finally cut the engine. They had arrived, and for Black it was none too soon. With Liddell in the lead, he crawled out of the Walrus and clambered up the narrow companionway to the head of the pier.

The smell of charred, wet wood was even more overpowering than the stench of the aircraft's fuel. To his right, looking south toward the floating bridge beyond the coal dock, there was nothing but rubble and debris. Twenty yards of the main pier had been blown to splinters, and the huge warehouse directly in front of them was a sagging ruin. A crisp breeze was blowing down the river, and the sky overhead was a cloudless blue, but all Black could see was the devastation of the dockside wasteland.

"I had no idea," he said, staring at the ruins of the Vickers warehouse. It stretched for blocks along the waterfront, its roof collapsed in a dozen different places, every window shattered.

"They've been getting it for the better part of six weeks now," said Liddell. "Every second or third day since the beginning of August." He shook his head wearily. "No bloody defenses at all. Six balloons and an ack-ack battery to defend the only Spitfire works in the country. Madness."

A battered, mud-stained gray sedan was creeping down the debris-strewn pier in their direction, picking its way carefully. It was carrying official license plates and flying a blue pennon from its left mudguard. The car stopped and a uni-

formed Southampton Police driver stepped out into the sunlight. The man saluted smartly as Liddell and Black walked
toward the vehicle. He opened the rear door of the sedan and
stood aside as the two men climbed in.

"Allen will meet us at the scene," said Liddell as they
turned down the pier and headed up a narrow alleyway
between the wreckage of two large buildings.

"Allen?" asked Black.

"The chief constable." Liddell leaned forward and tapped
the driver on the shoulder. The man behind the wheel turned
his head slightly.

"Sir?"

"How far?" asked Liddell.

"Just this side of the Bridge Road. Not far at all."

They drove on in silence.

It was far worse than anything Black had seen in London.
Whole blocks of industrial buildings had been destroyed.
Here and there steam rose as small groups of firefighters
doused still-fuming embers, and demolition workers were
using cranes and chains to bring down blackened sections of
unstable walls. Small streets lined with workmen's houses had
been utterly laid waste, the streets themselves invisible below
heaps of madly strewn rubble. They passed the burnt-out
skeleton of a lorry, its tires melted into the cobbles, and a little farther on, Black saw a telephone pole leaning drunkenly
across a doorway. It was being used as a message center, a
score of paper scraps tacked onto it; desperate queries and
faint hopes.

"Bad was it?" asked Liddell, leaning forward and speaking
to the driver once again.

"Bad enough." The man shrugged. "Bowling to an empty
wicket. Lots of them came in no more than a hundred feet off
the ground. Couldn't miss and no one to fight back." The
driver snorted. "Surprised the whole bloody city didn't burn to
the ground when it comes to that."

The driver stopped the car at the entrance to a narrow lane a few hundred feet from Bridge Street. Before the raid the street had been lined on both sides with small, four-room row houses built just after the First World War to house workers from Vickers-Supermarine and the Thorneycroft Boat Works along the river to the south of the bridge.

Of the dozen or so houses on the lane, only three were standing, and two of those were little more than gutted shells. The third house, protected by the high wall of a warehouse directly behind it, was still intact except for the roof, which seemed to be badly burned along the front, long licks of black soot rising up the yellow brick above the shattered windows facing the street. A black, windowless van was parked in front of the house, and a uniformed policeman stood at the front door, helmet pulled low over his eyes, hands clasped behind his back.

Liddell and Black left their car and walked up the short path through what had once been the front garden, now littered with scraps of wood, broken furniture, and a sea of broken glass, the splintered shards glittering like ice in the midafternoon sun. Liddell showed his warrant card to the policeman at the door, and they ducked into the gloomy interior of the house.

Two rooms were on the ground floor with a narrow hallway running past the stairs that stood against the wall adjoining the next house over, now nothing more than a heap of bricks and burnt timbers. Two plainclothes detectives were sorting through the front sitting room, turning over pieces of broken furniture, their feet crunching on still more broken glass.

"Chief Constable Allen?" asked Liddell.

"Upstairs," said one of the men.

They climbed to the upper floor. Black could feel the stair treads giving slightly under his feet, and from the way the plain wood banister moved under his hand, he could tell that the house was on the verge of collapsing. Like the house in London where they had discovered the body of David Talbot, the bombing had broken this place, forcing it to reveal its secrets. The sour smell of old wallpaper paste, the rot-musk of things stored too long in the cellar. Dry wood, dust, brief lives lived and not remembered.

Chief Constable H. C. Allen of the Southampton Police was waiting for them at the top of the stairs. He was a tall, broad-shouldered man, slab-faced and clean shaven, wearing a trench coat over civilian clothes. He introduced himself and then ushered Liddell and Black into the nearest of the two rooms on the upper floor.

It was a bedroom, little more than a large windowless closet with just enough room for a single iron bedstead, a freestanding wardrobe, and a washstand with a mirror on the wall above it. An oval rope rug was on the bare wood floor. The walls were papered in a pale blue stripe yellowed with nicotine.

A fully clothed man was on the bed, eyes carefully closed, hands clasped over his waist. He was small, no more than five foot three, white haired, and appeared to be in his late fifties or early sixties. He was dressed in trousers, a collarless white shirt, and a gray cardigan. He was shoeless, the dark green stocking on his right foot rudely darned by a man's hand. A pair of felt slippers had been neatly arranged on the floor beside the bed. At first glance he seemed to be sleeping, but his skin had the faint paraffin cast of the newly dead, and the pillow behind his head was soaked through with blood, dried to the color of old rust. There were no visible wounds.

On the wall above the bed, roughly drawn in the same color as the blood on the pillow, were four Z's arranged in a swastika-like pattern. Like every corpse Morris Black had ever seen, this one had a sad, tired air of abandonment about it, like an empty house closed for the winter, curtains drawn, dry leaves blowing through the eaves.

"We had your advisory from a few days ago," said the chief

constable, looking down at the body. "When this came in, I thought I should see to it. Fit the description of the sort of thing you were after."

"Yes." Liddell nodded. "It would seem so. You've kept this quiet?"

"Yes."

"Good."

"Do you have any idea who he was?" Black asked, frowning. Rudelski, Talbot, and Eddings—the sailor from Portsmouth—had all been young. This man didn't fit the pattern at all.

Chief Constable Allen tugged a small notebook out of his trench coat and flipped it open. "According to his National Registration Card, his name is Ivor John Dranie."

"Welsh?" asked Liddell, frowning. Black knew what he was thinking; there had been a fair bit of talk in the first days of the war about the possibility of a Welsh nationalists' fifth column. As far as Black knew, it had never materialized.

"Welsh, yes, if his name means anything," Allen answered. "Fifty-nine years old. Retired machinist at Vickers-Supermarine."

"Fifty-nine is a bit young for retirement, isn't it?" asked Black.

"I asked them about that at Vickers. He had some sort of liver disease. They pensioned him off, I gather."

"How long ago?" asked Black.

"A little more than a year ago."

"Was he married?"

"A widower. Two grown children. Boys. One dead at Dunkirk, the other with the Army in North Africa."

"What do his neighbors say about him?"

"Very little," the chief constable said dryly. "A good few died in the raid, and we haven't interviewed the others yet. They might think it a bit of an imposition under the circumstances."

"He lived alone?"

"From the looks of things."

"When was he discovered?"

"This morning. Dawn. One of the ARP wardens had a look round after they put out the fire." The tall man paused. "Odd that."

"The fire?" asked Liddell.

"Umm." Allen nodded. "Come along and I'll show you." He led the two men out of the room and across the small landing. The second room was even smaller than the first, one window looking out over the street. The front of the room had been partially consumed by fire so intense that it had burned down through the plaster walls to the lath. The ceiling overhead was open to the sky, the burnt ribs of the charred rafters clearly visible. A patch of wood flooring under the window had burnt through completely, leaving a gaping, black-edged hole.

"We thought it was an incendiary at first," Allen explained as they stepped into the room. "But we couldn't find the bomb container and then we saw that the fire had burned up, not down. It was set in this room." His eyebrows lifted. "Arson in the middle of a firestorm."

"The same as Eddings," Liddell murmured. Black looked around the room. Dranie had obviously used it as some sort of study. There were several bookshelves on the left, only partly burnt away, a wooden table, a pair of wooden straight chairs, and a large, comfortable-looking upholstered armchair with a matching ottoman. The walls were papered in the same blue stripe as the bedroom.

On the right there was a gas fire with a plain wooden mantel. A small framed photograph was over the fire. Black stepped across and examined it more closely. The photograph appeared to have been cut out of a magazine and showed a dozen oddly costumed figures crossing a cobbled square. The houses and buildings in the background looked vaguely

Germanic. Along the edge of the picture there was a small credit line: *Photo Union, Paul Lamm.*

Black turned and went to the bookcase. Nothing very interesting. A few popular novels, an eight-volume set of Audel's *Engineers and Mechanics Guide*, the softbound edition of the *Thomas National Road Atlas*. The detective picked up the map book and flipped through it. No penciled markings, no turned-down pages.

"Did Dranie have a car?" he asked.

"No," answered the chief constable. "Not that we know of. There was no driver's license or registration slip among his papers, at any rate."

Black went to the plain table in the center of the room and looked down at it thoughtfully. The surface of the table was bare. Both chairs were neatly pushed in. No cups or glasses, nothing to say who Ivor Dranie's last guest had been. Black glanced around the room. Dranie had used it for something, and not just reading. It had a purpose of some sort. But what?

Still thinking, Black wandered out of the room and went down the stairs to the ground floor. The two men in the front room had moved back into the kitchen. He was alone.

The sitting room looking out onto the street had been simply furnished with a dark Victorian settee, a small circular dining table with four matching chairs, and a desk under the window. The fire in the room above had come through the floor, and flaming debris had ignited the settee and the table, partially destroying them. The desk was covered in a layer of soot and fallen plaster. The two Southampton policemen had uncovered enough of the desktop to reveal an old Underwood typewriter. The desk drawers were all open and empty.

Black went into the small kitchen at the rear of the little house. The two men were searching through the cupboards. "The desk in the front room," said Black.

The taller of the two men looked up from his work. "What about it?"

"Was there anything in the drawers?"

"Nothing out of the ordinary. Paper, stamps, pencils, and pens. Letters, that sort of thing."

"Official papers?"

"Just what you'd expect. We've packed it all up."

"All right."

Liddell and Chief Constable Allen were waiting for him at the bottom of the stairs. Allen gripped the banister newel post and shook it firmly. The entire banister creaked and moved.

"It'll have to come down," he said.

"What about the body?" Liddell asked.

"That's up to you, Captain. We have our own coroner's courts of course, but if you'd like…" He let it dangle; from the expression on his face Black could see that the man would like nothing better than to turn the case over to MI5. Liddell turned to Black.

"Inspector?" The responsibility was being passed again.

"I think I'd like to have the body taken to London."

"That can be arranged," said Allen.

"St. Pancras Morgue," said Black. "And I'd like to have any of the material you've gathered up here as well, if that's all right."

"Certainly." Allen nodded. "No trouble at all."

"I'll give you the address," Liddell offered.

"Anything else?" Allen asked. "We can continue to investigate Dranie's background if you want."

Black thought for a moment, then shook his head slowly. The offer was sincere enough, but it was obvious that the chief constable had other, far more pressing matters on his mind. "No. I don't think that will be necessary," he answered finally.

"We'll let you know if there's anything more you can do for us," said Liddell. He handed Allen a small card with the Kensington Park Gardens address printed on it. "If you could see to the other?"

"We'll have it on the train this evening," Allen promised.

They shook hands. Allen joined his detectives in the kitchen. Liddell and Black went outside.

"Well?" asked Liddell as they stepped out into the sunlight. "What do you think?"

Morris Black frowned, looking down the blasted remains of the narrow street. He shook his head. "It doesn't fit," he said quietly. "None of it."

By the time Black returned to London it was already early evening, the weak, lowering sun turning the sprawling city into a hazy, pewter-shaded invention of itself, hollow and unreal in the silvery half-light, its population invisible behind closed doors and blackout-shuttered windows. Over it all a thousand barrage balloons drifted at the end of their taut cables, as though trying to lift the entire city up from the ground and out of danger, and once again the sirens had begun their nightly caterwauling, announcing the imminent arrival of the Luftwaffe's grumbling, dark-winged hordes.

Black paused briefly at his flat on Market Street, but after examining the meager contents of his refrigerator, he went out again. The market shops were long since closed for the night, and he had no appetite for the strained bonhomie and watery meat pies served at Ye Grapes across the way, so he walked up to Piccadilly and turned east, arriving a few minutes later at the below-street-level entrance to the White Horse Cellar between Dover Street and Albemarle Street, a few blocks short of the Circus.

Ignoring the temptations of the bar, he went directly into the dark, low-ceilinged restaurant and was taken to a small table at the rear of the almost empty room. He ordered, allowing himself the nerve-soothing balm of a pint of bitter, just as the first bombs began to fall in the distance.

The White Horse was located below the bulk of an office-converted mansion, so he felt reasonably safe, but even so he could feel a nagging tic begin to pull at the muscles of his cheek as the raid continued. He finished his beer before the food arrived and ordered a second with his meal. The restaurant was only a hundred yards or so away from Whites on St. James Street, and he consoled himself with the fact that if he was bombed in the midst of his cutlet, he'd be going in good company.

As he ate, he pondered the anomalous fate of Ivor John Dranie, the retired Vickers machinist from Southampton. There was no doubt that he'd died at the hands of Queer Jack, but with the exception of the telltale letters on the wall behind his head, there seemed to be no continuity between his death and the three previous murders. Rudelski, Talbot, and Eddings all appeared to have lived in the twilight world of underground homosexuality, while Dranie was a widower. The three others had all been young, less than twenty-five, while Dranie was twice their age. The three had been murdered in anonymous, rented rooms, but the older man had been slaughtered in his own house. Dranie had been laid out on his bed fully clothed; the others had been naked. It didn't add up.

It would, of course, in the end. Queer Jack wasn't the first multiple murderer, nor would he be the last, but no matter what form their madness took—the Borgias' poisons, the Ripper's evisceration of Whitechapel prostitutes, or George Smith's grisly use of the mundane bathtub—there was always a pattern, a link that bound the chain together. The pattern might be obscure, even invisible to the "normal" eye, but it would be there, of that Morris Black was absolutely sure. In the end it was simply a matter of perception: what Morris Black saw as an inconsequential detail might be glaringly obvious to Queer Jack.

"Hello." A woman's voice. Black looked up, startled. "It's

the policeman from the train, isn't it? The stamp collector? 'Keys' and 'Ky-us'?"

"That's right." Black was surprised at how well he remembered her, and how quickly. "You're the 'warco' who writes about potatoes and has an uncle in Cambridge."

"That's right." She smiled. "Katherine Copeland."

"Morris Black."

"I think we've gone through this before. Mind if I sit down?"

"No, please do." Black gestured toward the chair on the opposite side of the table. She slipped into it gracefully, one hand slipping automatically under her thighs to smooth her dark gray skirt. Black found the gesture startlingly intimate, and he cleared his throat to cover his embarrassment.

"I was in the bar. I took a peek in here and saw you."

"You're waiting for someone?"

"For almost half an hour. I think I've been stood up."

"I'm sorry."

"I'm not," she said frankly, smiling across the table at him. He picked up his napkin and brushed it across his shirt-front, desperately hoping he hadn't spilled gravy on his tie or dragged a shirt cuff through the soup. Idiotically, he felt guilty about the mess on the table, and then, magically, the Italian waiter reappeared and began to clear away the dishes. Relieved, Black sat back in his chair.

"Would you like some coffee?"

"That would be nice. Do you think they serve that frothy stuff here?"

Black turned to the waiter. "Two cappuccinos, please."

"Certainly." The waiter nodded and then shimmered away, his arms loaded down with dishes and cutlery.

"Is the food good?" Katherine asked as the man disappeared into the gloom.

"Quite good, considering the circumstances." Ironically, Black could feel the meal souring in his stomach as he spoke.

He couldn't think of a damn thing to say. Once again the stumbling schoolboy. He suddenly remembered that she'd smoked on the train, and he fumbled in his jacket pocket, finally producing his lighter and a partially crushed packet of Gems. He held the packet out to her. "Cigarette?"

"Sure." She took them, shook one out, and put it between her lips. He flicked his lighter on and she leaned forward, the dancing flame cutting deep shadows under her cheekbones. She really was beautiful. He lit a cigarette for himself and then the coffee arrived. The waiter withdrew and Black glanced around the room. They were the only people in the restaurant now.

With the cigarette still between her fingers, Katherine lifted the cup using both hands and sipped cautiously. A thin line of froth coated her upper lip. She smiled and licked it away slowly with the tip of her tongue. Black remembered Fay doing the same thing a few months before the sudden onset of her disease made going to places like the White Horse impossible, and suddenly there was a bitter edge to the pleasure he'd begun to feel.

"A penny for them."

"Pardon me?"

"Your thoughts." Katherine smiled. "A penny for them. You look...bemused."

"Old memories."

"Good or bad?"

"Neither, really. Sad, perhaps."

"Bit of a luxury these days, don't you think?" She glanced up. Outside, in the middle distance, the bombs continued their thundering symphony.

"Perhaps you're right." He managed a weak smile. "I had my first trip in an airplane today, maybe I'm still in shock from that."

"Where'd you go?"

"Southampton." There was no reason not to tell her that much.

"Something interesting?"

"Murder." Still safe enough, even though she did work for a newspaper.

"That's almost funny."

"Not to the dead man."

"I didn't mean funny like a joke. It just seems strange that policemen are investigating murders at a time like this. The war and everything."

"People still have lives. Wives murder husbands and vice versa, villains burgle houses, cars get pinched."

"I suppose so. My father fought in the last war. He said he used to sit in the trenches at dusk and watch the swallows and nighthawks flying above him. He said it seemed very strange that birds were going about their business while thousands of men were dying below them. I guess it's the same thing."

"I think the war makes it worse. We've all been thrown into a different world. Some people seem to think the old rules and laws no longer apply."

"I know a few like that." Katherine paused, drawing on her cigarette. "There was another murder today," she said after a moment. "Two, actually. At the zoo."

"Oh?" said Black, both interested and annoyed. Since his abrupt departure from the Yard, he'd been cut off from the day-to-day gossip, and her comment reminded him of how much he missed it. "I hadn't heard."

"One was an American, the other worked for Swedish Airlines." She frowned. "I'd have thought you would have known all about it."

"I'm involved with other things right now," Black answered vaguely. "Where exactly were they killed?"

"One of the toilets."

"Oh."

She caught his intonation and shook her head. "No. I don't think it was anything like that. They say the American was a cop of some kind."

"Really? And just who is 'they'?"

Katherine grinned and stubbed out her cigarette. "I work for a newspaper, remember? We've got all sorts of 'theys' lying around. First cousin to the well-known 'high-ranking official' and brother to the 'unimpeachable source.'"

"What sort of American policeman would be wandering around the London zoo?"

"Somebody from the State Department presumably. The FBI has a liaison office here as well. Who knows?"

"Interesting."

"I suppose," she sighed. "Not my beat though. I'm supposed to be doing something on Princess Elizabeth and her dollhouse or something." She sighed again. "Which reminds me. I should be getting home."

"Not much chance of finding a cab with the raid on."

"I'll walk." She shrugged. "It's not far, really."

"Where do you live?"

"Hertford Street."

Black smiled, pleased. "Shepherd's Market?"

"Yes."

"I've got a flat on Market Street, just around the corner from you."

"We're neighbors then." She smiled warmly.

"Why don't I escort you home?"

"All right."

Black gestured for the waiter. He gave the man a five-pound note and the Italian went off to make change.

"I've just had a thought," said Black. "Maybe you can help me out. One of those 'theys' you have lying about."

"Shoot."

Black took his notebook from the inside pocket of his jacket and flipped it open. "Have you ever heard of something called Photo Union?"

"Sure." She nodded. "It's a picture agency. One of the big ones."

"And the name Paul Lamm? A photographer?"

"Never heard of him." She smiled. "Which doesn't mean much."

"How could I find out about him? Does Photo Union have an office in London?"

"I don't know." Katherine shrugged. "Probably. I could ask around. What exactly do you want to know?"

"I saw a photograph credited to him today. It might have some significance to my investigation. I'd like to speak with Lamm, or at least find out more about the picture."

"I'll see what I can do. Can I see the photograph?"

"Certainly." Black nodded. "I'll have a copy made and send it around to your office."

"Great."

They went up the short flight of steps to street level and paused. Night had fallen and it was fully dark, but to the east the sky was bright as day. The East End and the docks were obviously taking the brunt of the attack, but Black could see thick clouds of roiling smoke and huge tongues of flame rising much closer at hand.

Two people appeared out of the gloom: a man in his twenties, one hand firmly gripping the elbow of a much older woman, hurrying her along. The woman's long gray hair had come undone and was flying in all directions. She was wearing a man's topcoat over her nightdress. Her eyes were wide and panic-stricken. Her mouth was a puckered, toothless O of fear. Black caught a fragment of their conversation as they passed.

"Hurry up, Mum, we've got to get to the shelter."

"My teef!" the old woman moaned, lisping. "We've got to go back and get my teef!"

"They're dropping bombs, Mum, not sandwiches." And then they were gone, swallowed by the darkness. Black and Katherine continued down the street.

It looked as though at least one bomb had fallen in the area around Piccadilly Circus. As the explosions continued there were enormous flashes of brilliant light, and they could see the plump shapes of the silvery barrage balloons strung up over Covent Garden and Leicester Square. The ack-ack batteries in St. James's Park added their own steady barking to the raging noise surrounding them, and Black could feel the muscles in his jaw tensing.

"Maybe we should find a shelter until this lets up a bit," he said. Insanity piled on insanity, he thought; he was making the raid sound like a summer shower.

"Not on your life!" said Katherine, raising her voice above the pounding din of the bombs and the antiaircraft guns. "This is incredible!"

"Hardly the time for sight-seeing."

"I want to get closer." She took Black's hand in her own and headed east, her eyes wide with excitement. Feeling like a fool, but bound by the soft warmth of her palm and fingers, he let himself be dragged along.

Keeping close to the questionable security offered by the buildings beside them, the couple walked quickly up Piccadilly, crossing Albemarle Street and then Old Bond Street.

Piccadilly was deserted, blind windows all around them reflecting the leaping light from the fires farther east, and Black knew that they were putting themselves in terrible jeopardy. He prayed for the sudden appearance of an ARP warden to force them into a shelter, more than willing to suffer the humiliation of an officious dressing down when it was discovered that he was a police inspector.

He gritted his teeth; another few steps and then he'd insist that they go to a shelter. There had to be one close by, and he looked around, searching for one of the ubiquitous signs posted on the side of a building.

Suddenly Katherine drew up short, staring. "What's this?" Black followed her glance. They were halfway down the block between Old Bond Street and the portico entrance to the Royal Academy of Arts. She was looking down a long, arch-roofed alley, two stories high and less than twenty feet from side to side, lined with bow-windowed shops. A series of darkened lamps hung between the glassed-in skylights, dangling on long chains.

"Burlington Arcade," said Black. "It runs down to Cork Street."

"It's wonderful!" Katherine released his hand and began walking down the covered mall. Black followed. "It's like a cathedral, or a shrine."

"I think that was the intention. A temple of excess."

Burlington Arcade was home to some of the most prestigious and expensive shops in the city, selling everything from hand-rolled cigars and cigarettes to fine jewelry and custom-made saddlery. He'd once bought Dick Capstick a dusty bottle of cask-aged port for his birthday in one of the vintage-wine shops here, knowing that his large friend would consume it like so much home-brewed beer, smacking his lips all the while. He bought it for him anyway. The gift had been Fay's idea; most of his best thoughts seemed to have come with her gentle prompting.

Watching this other, far more beautiful woman wandering bright-eyed along the arcade, Black felt a sudden, terrible longing wrenching at his heart, and he hated himself for the small pleasure he'd felt at the touch of Katherine Copeland's hand.

"We have to get back," he called out. "This is too dangerous."

She turned, facing him, smiling widely. Even from that distance Black could see the thrusting movement of her chest beneath the fabric of her jacket and blouse. She was excited, and God help him, so was he.

"Another minute, please."

"Now." Black held out his hand and she came forward, taking it. Beneath their feet the stone paving was shaking, and above them the glass in the skylights was rattling as the raid-

ing bombers droned across the night sky, their engines changing to a louder, ear-numbing scream as they turned abruptly
at the end of their run.

"You're no fun at all!" Katherine grinned as she joined
him, squeezing his hand hard. He ignored the comment, returning the grip and pulling her back toward Piccadilly.
Somewhere he could hear the sound of approaching sirens
and then a groaning, broken roar as a wall collapsed. He
pulled her close in under his arm as a fist-sized piece of white-
hot metal ricocheted off the wall of the building beside them
and skipped out into the street, cutting a scarring zigzag
trench into the asphalt. Pushing her forward, Black risked a
glance back over his shoulder and saw that the roadway
behind them was now littered with the blinding flares of at
least a dozen phosphorus incendiaries. Above the city the
clouds flashed and flared in pink and orange, fire raining from
the sky.

He felt the blast before he heard or saw anything and
reacted instinctively, pushing Katherine away from the yawning opening leading into the arcade. The bomb, a five-thou-
sand-kilogram high-explosive monster, had impacted at the
far end of the enclosed passage almost a block away, and the
searing, superheated pressure wave of air acted like a huge
invisible fist as it pistoned down the long, open-ended tunnel,
shattering the glass in a hundred windows and turning the
bow-fronts of a score of shops into a hail of lethal slivers.

Every one of the wire-reinforced skylights in the roof was
torn from its wooden frame, and the hanging lamps and
chains were ripped from their fixtures and sent whirling into
the deadly maelstrom.

Dragging Katherine to the ground, Black threw himself on
top of her as the fuming, flaming tumble of flying debris vomited out of the Piccadilly end of the Arcade, blowing a hundred-
foot-long blast-furnace tongue of fire to lick against the sculpted front of the Egyptian House on the far side of the avenue.

Black felt a stunning weight fall on his back, and beneath him Katherine screamed. He had the sudden, brief sensation of soft flesh pressed against his hand and then his nostrils were filled with the lavender scent of soap as his face was buried in her hair.

Ignoring the pain in his back, he pushed hard, lifting his shoulder and freeing one hand. He clawed madly, thrusting aside the litter of plaster, brick, and mortar that covered them, finally managing to free them from the choking mass. He lurched to his feet, pulling Katherine up, and they stood there for a moment, clinging to each other desperately.

The world around them had gone mad, lit by a thousand fires, and everywhere there was the sound of roaring flame and snapping timber. Out of the corner of his eye Black saw a fire engine come to a screeching stop, and half a dozen helmeted men ran toward them, dragging unraveling lines of canvas hose. A second truck appeared, then a third.

"Oh, Christ!" Katherine moaned. She pressed her cheek into Black's chest, then lifted her face and kissed him hard, pressing her mouth onto his, her breasts crushed against him. For an instant he could taste the cool sweetness of her tongue, and then he felt a wrenching hand on his upper arm, whirling him around.

"What the bloody hell do you think you're up to then!" Black found himself staring into the face of a helmeted ARP warden, the man's features twisted into a furious scowl. There was a hiss and roar behind him as the first of the hoses went into operation and a long arc of spray began to play against the burning entrance to the arcade. The warden pushed Black hard.

"Fuck off out of here, mate! I've got no time for the likes of you!"

Still holding on to Katherine, Black staggered away. He took a few steps and then Katherine stumbled, tripping over the twisted remains of one of the arcade skylights.

"Are you all right?"

She nodded. "Yes. Fine." She shuddered and gripped his arm. "Another few seconds—Jesus!" She stared up at him, her eyes wide, the excitement gone, replaced by shock and fear. "You saved my life."

"I'll take you home."

Twenty silent minutes later they reached the dark entrance to her building in Hertford Street. Behind them, hidden now in the distance, the raid continued. Standing in the doorway, Katherine was nothing but a darker shadow.

"You're sure you're all right?" he asked.

"Yes." He could hear her take in a long shuddering breath and then she sighed. "Would you like to come in for a drink? I could do with something to calm my nerves."

Morris Black remembered the smell of her hair and the quick cool taste of her mouth. For no good reason that he could think of, he felt ashamed.

"All right," he said. Which didn't make much sense, either. Katherine turned her key in the lock, and Black followed her up the dark stairway to her flat. She ushered Black into the front sitting room, pulled the blackout curtains across the windows and switched on the lights. The room had been furnished with flea-market economy and lacked any kind of real personality. A desk was in front of the windows, piled high with news clippings and neatly stacked file folders. Katherine showed Black to a large, overstuffed chair on the far side of the room, then went to a small, cream-colored cabinet that stood close to the kitchen door. She opened the cabinet and took out two bottles.

"I can give you Scotch, or Scotch," she said, turning to face him, smiling, a bottle in each hand.

"I think I'll have the Scotch."

"Ice?"

Black smiled. "No thank you." Cold beer, and ice in their spirits. Americans did strange things to their drink.

"Good, because I don't have any." She poured two glasses of neat liquor, gave one to Black, then settled down in another upholstered chair across from him, tucking her legs up underneath her and pulling down her skirt. Black sipped at his drink, then put it down on a small table beside him.

"Rather a coincidence, don't you think?" he said after a moment.

"What?"

"Meeting up like that in the White Horse."

Katherine shrugged. "Not really. I go there quite a lot. It's close."

"But you asked me about the food. You didn't sound very familiar with the menu."

"I meet people in the bar. I don't eat there." The woman frowned. "Why do I have the feeling I'm being interrogated?"

Black smiled. "Professional habit. Sorry." And he was sorry, which was the extraordinary thing. Here he was, sitting with a woman he found extremely attractive, and he was doing his best to ruin the encounter.

"I suppose you think I lay in wait and followed you to the restaurant."

"It crossed my mind."

Katherine shook her head. "Are you always that suspicious of people you meet?"

"Usually." Black shrugged. "I generally meet people who are involved in criminal activities of one kind or another. That sort tends to lie a great deal, even when there's no need to."

"You think I'm 'that sort'?"

He smiled. "You're a journalist."

"And therefore not one to be trusted?"

Black shrugged. "A basic tenet of the policeman's creed."

"You must spend a lot of time being depressed."

"I'm a Jew, Miss Copeland. Jews are supposed to be depressed. People expect it."

"And I suppose that's meant to be funny?"

Black shrugged again. "Jews are supposed to be funny as well. People expect that too." My God, he thought, where did *that* come from? He almost never made reference to his religion, and certainly not twice in thirty seconds. Was he really that nervous being alone with an attractive woman?

Katherine swallowed the remainder of her drink. She stood up, went back to the liquor cabinet, and poured herself another. She sat down again and looked at Black.

"I think you're full of it, Mr. Policeman. I think you enjoy being depressed. You wear it like a uniform."

Black burst out laughing, surprised at how much he was enjoying their verbal fencing. "You sound more like an alienist than a newspaperwoman."

"Alienist?"

"Psychiatrist."

"You sound as though you need one, Inspector." She took a long swallow of her drink. "All angst and anguish, worrying about being pursued by devious American reporters hell-bent on seducing you." Katherine laughed. "You probably think I arranged for that bomb to go off in the arcade, or whatever you called it."

"Are you really hell-bent on seducing me?"

The young woman shook her head. "Not at the moment, but I do like you." She smiled. "Or is that grounds for suspicion?"

"No." Silence stood impatiently between them. In the distance he could hear the muffled explosions as the raid continued. "I should be getting on," he said finally. "It's late." He stood up and Katherine walked him to the door of the flat. He was about to step out into the hallway when she put a hand on his arm. He turned and suddenly she leaned forward, tilted her head to one side, and kissed him softly on the cheek.

"I really do like you," she said quietly, and then she closed the door. Katherine stood there for a moment, then turned and walked back into the sitting room. She switched off the lights and went to the window, pulling the blackout curtain back a few inches. A moment later she saw Black's shadowy figure as he stepped out of the front entrance of her building and turned down the street, heading for his own flat.

"God damn you, Larry Bingham!" she whispered. "And you too, Morris Black!" She let the curtain fall back into place and turned away.

Below her, on the pavement, Black walked slowly toward Market Street. He was halfway home before something Katherine Copeland had said made him stop and look back the way he'd come. They'd met twice, once on the train to Cambridge and then again a few hours ago at the White Horse. On both occasions he'd introduced himself simply as Morris Black, identifying himself as a policeman and nothing more.

But a few moments ago, upstairs in her flat, Katherine Copeland had called him "inspector." He stood there for a long moment, tracing his memory back along their conversations, almost positive that he'd never mentioned his rank at Scotland Yard. But she'd known. How? And even more importantly, why had she been interested enough to find out?

CHAPTER THIRTEEN

Friday, September 20, 1940
9:00 A.M., British Summer Time
10:00 A.M., Central European Summer Time

LIDDELL PICKED UP MORRIS BLACK at the offices on Kensington Park Gardens just after nine and headed south toward the Thames Embankment. As they moved down Gloucester Road, Liddell reached into the pocket of his tweed jacket and pulled out a folded sheet of Photostat paper. He handed it to Black.

"Malmstrom, the Swede, hid this in one of the other WCs at the zoo."

"The Americans picked it up?" Black glanced at the copy; it was a solid block of numbers.

"The second watcher found it."

"The Americans just handed it over to you?"

"It wasn't quite that simple." Liddell smiled. "Bit of a farce, really. We were watching Malmstrom ourselves—another matter entirely—and stumbled on the Americans. In return for us covering up the matter of their agent having the bad taste to get himself killed in the loo, they agreed to 'share' information with us."

Black looked up from his examination of the sheet of paper. "You think this might have some connection to Queer Jack?"

"I think it might have some connection to The Doctor, which is almost as good. I've sent another copy of the message to the people at Bletchley, but so far they haven't managed anything. We need the key to break the code. It's early days yet, but I thought we should inform Knight anyway."

"Maxwell Knight?"

Liddell nodded. "Yes. That's who we're going to see now."

"I saw his name on your Magic Circle list." True to his word, within hours of their meeting, Desmond Morton had provided them with a list of everyone who had officially been informed about Ultra.

"That's right," said the intelligence officer, nodding again. "Specializes in the Communist Party and fifth-column work. Odd fellow. Bit of a loner. Sometimes disappears for days on end and then pops up without a by-your-leave, but he might be able to throw some light on who Malmstrom was going to meet. As you said, he is on the list, so you'd have to talk to him eventually."

"All right."

Maxwell Knight kept his office on Dolphin Square, a massive block of more than a thousand flats in dull red brick spread across eight acres overlooking Grosvenor Road and the Thames. The complex, built only a few years before the war, was the largest of its kind in Europe and completely self-contained with a cavernous underground parking garage, a dozen shops, and several restaurants.

To Black, Dolphin Square, surrounded by Pimlico's time-weary terraces and rooming-house mansions, was like a dreary, monolithic evocation from H.G. Wells's *The Shape of Things to Come*. For Maxwell Knight, éminence grise of B5(b), it had the obvious advantage of total anonymity.

The flat, when they finally found it, had the name Coplestone below the bell push. "His wife, Lois," explained Liddell, poking the button. "Such as she is."

"Such as she is?"

"Separated. Never had much luck with women from what I hear. His first wife committed suicide."

The door opened, and Black found himself staring into the brutally burn-scarred face of a man wearing trousers with suspenders and a white shirt with the sleeves rolled up. A neat, bright red bow tie bound his collar. It looked as though someone had taken a blowtorch to his face. The eyebrows were gone, the nose was no more than a shiny stub, and the lips were nonexistent. The raw skin was tautly drawn over his jaw and cheeks like pink patchwork sheets of parchment.

"Captain Liddell," the man said, standing to one side.

"Hello, Baines. His lordship anywhere about?"

"In the back." From the gravel whisper of Baines's voice it was apparent that whatever flames had eaten away his face had also damaged his vocal cords.

"School chum of Knight's," Liddell said softly as they walked down a short hall to the flat's sitting room. "Got that lot flying Spits in France."

The curtains were drawn over the large front windows, and an attractive blond woman was busily typing at a desk in one corner, her work lit by a tall gooseneck lamp. There were several other desks in the gloomy room, a row of filing cabinets, and a large chalkboard on an easel.

A small, clean-shaven man with a large nose and a wide mouth appeared in a doorway leading off to one side. He was wearing an Army officer's uniform, complete with a row of service ribbons. He was also wearing leather bedroom slippers, expensive ones from what Black could tell. The man smiled thinly, seeing Liddell.

"Hello, Guy. Come to set the cat among the pigeons?" A pair of very pale blue eyes surveyed Black for a moment, then looked back at Liddell. The detective was surprised; he'd expected Knight to be cut from the same Eton-Cambridge cloth as Liddell, but his voice was flat and provincial with a crisp military overtone. An Army brat, raised on some desolate post in a godforsaken colony?

"No cats and no pigeons, Max, we're here about Malmstrom. This is Detective Inspector Morris Black. He's been seconded to us for the time being."

"Malmstrom." Knight nodded. "Our literary Swede." He flashed on his brief smile again. "Come into my office."

He ushered them into what had probably been intended as a bedroom but was now fitted out with desk, chairs, and more filing cabinets. Knight sat down behind the desk while Black and Liddell seated themselves opposite.

"Why literary?" asked Liddell. "Have you come up with something new?"

"We've just had the preliminary autopsy report from Purchase at the Coroner's Office. Malmstrom was killed with a fountain pen."

"Good Lord!" said Liddell, startled. He laughed. "I suppose this means the pen really is mightier than the sword." Knight frowned at the terrible joke.

"How did they find that out?" asked Black, ignoring Liddell's comment.

"It wasn't difficult," Knight responded dryly. "The nib snapped off in his brain. Might be useful."

"Why?" asked Liddell.

"The nib was Italian. Gold. Rover brand. Rover apparently stands for *Rodolpho Verlicchi*, a firm in Bologna. Not many pens here use the brand. We may be able to trace it."

"Not much to go on," said Black.

Knight lifted a bushy eyebrow. "There never is, Inspector."

For no real reason, Black found that he'd taken an instant dislike to the uniformed man. It was nothing specific, just a sense that Knight looked down on everyone around him. He couldn't imagine that the man had very many friends.

"Anything else?" Liddell asked hopefully.

Knight shrugged. "Nothing beyond the obvious. According to the Americans, they were following Malmstrom because he'd once worked as a pilot for Axel Wenner-Gren."

"Oh, dear," said Liddell. "Not him again."

"I'm afraid so."

"I don't recognize the name," said Black. Knight's supercilious eyebrow lifted again. "No reason why you should, Inspector. Not the sort of pond I'd expect to find someone like you swimming about in."

Black resisted the urge to ask the man what he meant by "someone like you" and lit a cigarette instead, perfectly aware that there wasn't any ashtray in sight.

"Wenner-Gren owns a huge company called Electrolux," Liddell explained. "Invented the vacuum cleaner or some such."

"He also owns a large interest in Bofors, the Swedish armament company," said Knight. "And he takes care of the Krupp interests in Sweden as well. Trades with both the Americans and the Germans." The short man frowned. "He's a Nazi." There was a small glass dish on the desk, filled with drawing pins. Knight emptied it into a desk drawer and slid the dish across to Black.

"Is that the extent of your interest in him?" asked Black, tipping his ash into the dish.

"Of course not."

"He's close friends with another man named Charles Bedeaux," put in Liddell. "A naturalized American. Bedeaux has interests in several banks including Banque Worm in Geneva; half of its board of directors are members of the Nazi Party."

"I still don't quite see..."

"Bedeaux is also a friend of His Royal Highness the Duke of Windsor," explained Knight. "He was partially responsible for arranging the Duke's visit to Germany in 1937. He and the Simpson woman were married at Bedeaux's château in France."

"We've had a watching brief on the Duke and his associates since well before the war," Liddell continued. "Bedeaux gives us Wenner-Gren, Wenner-Gren gives us Malmstrom. By all appearances it would seem that the Americans simply wound up in the net we'd cast."

"It doesn't explain the murders."

"Malmstrom didn't go to the zoo to see the animals," said Knight. "He was going to meet someone; the message is proof enough of that. Perhaps the person he was going to meet saw that Malmstrom was being watched and killed him."

"What about the American? Why was he killed?"

"Bad luck," Knight answered. "According to the remaining American, he went into the lavatory at the aquarium entrance to see if Malmstrom had left anything there, which he had—the message packet. Meanwhile the second man followed Malmstrom to the WC near the tunnel. Whoever the Swede was meeting was probably waiting for him there. When Malmstrom didn't come out, the American went in...and died."

"Why do you make the assumption that the man who killed Malmstrom was a Nazi agent?" asked Black.

"Because Malmstrom didn't just work for Wenner-Gren, or even Charles Bedeaux. He had another employer as well." Knight put on a pair of spectacles, opened a folder on his desk, and extracted a grainy photograph. In it, two men were seated at an outdoor café in bright sunlight. From the looks of it, the picture had been taken with a telephoto lens from a car parked on the far side of the street.

"The blond man seated on the left is Malmstrom," Knight continued. "The darker-haired fellow opposite is a man named Ernest Filbert."

"Like the nut," said Black innocently.

"Quite," said Knight coldly. "That photograph was taken in June of this year." He handed Black a second picture. This one was much clearer. It showed Filbert and a second, taller

companion exiting a car in front of an imposing stone build-
ing. A huge swastika flag hung over the entrance. Both men
were in black, SS uniform. "The man with Filbert is Walter
Schellenberg. Filbert is Schellenberg's assistant, and
Schellenberg is second-in-command to Gruppenführer
Reinhard Heydrich, chief of the SD, the Nazi Party
Intelligence Service. The photograph was taken in Lisbon, late
July."

"So you think Malmstrom was working for Schellenberg?" asked Black. He was swimming in a sea of names and
interconnections. Much more and he'd drown.

Knight nodded. "I think that's a reasonable conclusion."
Black handed him the photographs. "All right," he said slowly.
"Malmstrom is working for Schellenberg. What does that tell
us about the man he was going to meet—The Doctor?"

"Schellenberg is being groomed to take over the Foreign
Intelligence Division of the SS under Heydrich. If Heydrich is
running an agent here, Schellenberg would be the likely man
to be his control. For a man at Schellenberg's level to actively
take on that role, the agent in question would have to be of
enormous importance, and probably very highly placed."
Knight paused and glanced at Liddell. "Well beyond the sort
that Masterman and the Twenty Committee has been reeling
in."

"It still doesn't tell us anything about who the man might
be," Black insisted.

"Not yet perhaps." Knight shrugged. "Hopefully, the message left by Malmstrom will give us a direction to follow."

"We need more than a direction." Liddell's tone was dark.
"We need an answer."

Sitting at a window table in the café of Stockholm's Grand
Hotel, Charles Tennant smoked another cigarette and stared

out across the narrow inlet at the sunlit walls and towers of the Royal Palace. A few small sailboats coursed brightly back and forth through his line of sight, and a little sightseeing packet chugged steadily southward into the open water of the Saltsjon.

God only knew who would be sightseeing in these mad days, he thought. The packet probably carried more spies than innocent passengers. Germans asking questions about Russians, and Russian military officers chatting with British diplomats. Norwegian exiles negotiating with Swiss bankers, Swiss bankers having secret meetings with American business interests. Everyone watching everyone else.

With the exception of Switzerland, Sweden was the only neutral country in central Europe, and after the invasion of Poland a year ago it had quickly become a Scandinavian version of Lisbon, a northern hotbed of intrigue with safe, albeit irregular flights to and from London, Moscow, and Berlin. Tennant shook his head, then butted his cigarette into the already overflowing ashtray. He'd been a fool to come here, but he'd seen no other choice. If his cover in London had been jeopardized, he wanted to be taken out of England immediately.

A short journey on one of those flights to Berlin and he'd spend the rest of the war doing something obscure for Heydrich's office in that converted Jewish old-folks home on Berkaerstrasse they used as a headquarters. Perhaps he could spend his days reading the *Times* and the *Evening Standard*, analyzing their content for psychiatric clues about the state of England's morale.

He glanced at his watch. Almost time. He stood, tossed a five-krona coin onto the table, and left the café, making his way to the main lobby and then the street. A stiff breeze was blowing off the water and along the quay; he turned up the collar of his jacket against the chill.

Tennant found a taxi waiting at the stand on the corner

and told the driver to take him to Skansen, Stockholm's unique open-air museum on the Djurgarden peninsula a mile or so to the east. The taxi went through the complex, ultra-modern "three-leaf clover" at the Slussen, then followed the broad Strandvagen along the water to the Djurgarden Bridge. They crossed over to Djurgarden, swung around past the castlelike Nordic Museum, and finally stopped at the Skansen main entrance.

Tennant handed the driver a ten-krona note, waved away the change, and climbed out of the taxi. He joined the small line of people at the turnstile, paid for his ticket, and stepped into the seventy-acre park. Skansen was roughly circular, crammed with examples of an extraordinary number of native trees, plants, birds, and animals as well as examples of various types of Swedish architecture, including a typical dairy farm, ancient Lapp huts, craftsmen's workshops, a church, and a manor house.

An entire Swedish village had been reproduced, and visitors could watch appropriately costumed people making butter, cheese, and bread, weaving baskets, operating old-fashioned printing presses, wood-turning on foot-operated lathes, and blowing glass. More than a hundred buildings were within the hilly enclosure, almost ten times more than when the park first opened.

Tennant didn't have the slightest interest in any of it. Ignoring the sights around him, he trudged up the steep hill directly beyond the entrance, turned left and went past the Lapp camp, then followed a narrower path along to the Seal Basin.

He found a bench, sat down, and waited. From behind, screened by a wall of trees, he could smell the rich, heavy scent of the model tar works. In the bright, crisp sunlight with the breeze rustling through the trees around him, the scene was idyllic.

A platoon of children dressed in lederhosen and brightly

colored dresses swarmed over the fence surrounding the Seal Basin while a plump, large-busted matron in a nurse's cape and cowl brooded over them, making sure they didn't fall in among the small cavorting beasts. Couples meandered by, holding hands, arm in arm, smiling. A trio of white-bearded old men went by, their severe dark clothing and walking sticks from another time, talking loudly to each other in lilting, musical Swedish.

A quarter hour passed, and finally, looking up, he saw the man he was to meet walking slowly along the path, playing the idle tourist. Tennant almost laughed aloud when he saw who Heydrich had sent to meet with him. It was Schellenberg, Heydrich's young deputy, dressed in a dark blue suit and a ludicrous little trilby hat. Without the highly polished jack-boots and dead black SS uniform, he looked as unassuming as a junior stockbroker in The City or a solicitor's clerk. He was fit enough, reasonably tall and trim, but his boyish features were soft, almost effeminate, his skin too pale and smooth. The only hint of hidden strength was the broad dueling scar running from the left side of his chin to a point halfway up his jaw.

Tennant had no illusions about the man, however. At thir-ty, Walter Schellenberg had risen swiftly through the SS hierar-chy to his present position. He was intelligent, quick-witted, and had degrees in both medicine and law from the University at Bonn. He'd been a member of the Nazi Party since they came to power in 1933, and he was totally committed to German hegemony over Europe at any cost. Wisely, he'd never shown any obvious interest in usurping his master's position and seemed content to stay where he was, resting on his laurels won the previous year at Venlo in Holland, where he'd mastermind-ed the plan to kidnap two British agents, Payne Best and Richard Stevens. The interrogation of the captured men had brought on the collapse of the entire British espionage network in Europe, all accomplished in a single afternoon.

Schellenberg sat down on the bench beside Tennant and

watched the children hovering around the Seal Basin. The psychiatrist did the same, and they sat there for a long moment, silently. Out of the corner of his eye Tennant watched the Nazi smile, the upturned mouth deepening the dueling scar to a dark, shaded slash. When he spoke finally, it was in flawless, barely accented English.

"Well, Doctor, here I am, as you requested." Tennant assumed that Heydrich had kept his word and that Schellenberg was referring to him by his code name and not alluding to his actual identity. On the single occasion the two men had met before, his real name had not been used. For that matter, Schellenberg hadn't used his real name either.

"Hauptmann Schaemmel."

"You remembered." Schellenberg smiled broadly.

"I have a very good memory."

"I too." The young intelligence officer reached into his jacket pocket, took out a small, leather-covered case, and removed a cigarette. He lit it with an ordinary kitchen match, igniting it on the nail of his thumb, and leaned back against the bench.

"I have an urgent problem," said Tennant.

"Malmstrom? The Swedish courier?"

"I never knew his name."

"It doesn't matter." Schellenberg smiled again. "And neither does he."

"You know about his death?"

"Of course."

"I was the one who killed him."

Schellenberg looked shocked, then pleased. "Good Lord. It never occurred to us that you were the one responsible. Interesting."

"There was another man."

"You killed him as well?"

"Yes. An MI5 watcher. There were two of them. Malmstrom was being followed."

"MI5? What makes you think that?"

"Who else would it be?"

"As it turns out they were American." Schellenberg puffed on his cigarette and stared at the rowdy group of children on the opposite side of the gravel path. Their matron, exasperated, caught one by the ear and led him away. The others followed. For the moment Tennant and Schellenberg were alone.

"American?"

"They belonged to the new group being organized by William Donovan. 'Wild Bill' I believe they call him. Amateurs."

"Why would the Americans be following Malmstrom?"

"For the same reason MI5 might have had him under surveillance. Putting the staff at the Swedish embassy under surveillance is an obvious precaution. They do the same with the embassy of Portugal in Portman Square and the Swiss legation at Montagu Place. Standard operating procedure; it's the same in Berlin."

"That's all well and good. But I was compromised."

"Did anyone see you?"

"Not that I'm aware of."

The younger man shrugged elegantly. "Then how were you compromised?"

"Presumably Malmstrom was carrying a reply to my earlier transmission, is that correct?"

"Yes."

"He didn't have any message on him. Presumably he dropped it earlier."

"You didn't check the other mailbox?"

"No. And I can't go back there now. They'll be watching, surely, and so will MI5."

"I see." Schellenberg thought for a moment, then nodded. "You're right."

"So now the Americans have the message. The message intended for me."

"It was in code."

"Codes can be broken."

"It will take them weeks. The Americans' cryptanalysis capabilities aren't what they once were. Without the key text it will be very difficult."

"Difficult but not impossible."

"No. Not impossible," Schellenberg agreed.

"The message presumably includes my code name; it could be traced, given enough time."

"Perhaps." Schellenberg reached up and traced the line of his dueling scar thoughtfully. "That is the operative word of course—time." He turned and looked at Tennant directly. "I suppose it's up to you. Return to London or give up your position and come back to Berlin with me."

"I don't like giving up. But if there's to be a risk, I need to know the benefit."

"The transmission you sent was extremely interesting. Especially considering the people who seem to be involved. British intelligence wouldn't involve itself in an ordinary murder investigation under normal circumstances. There's something very strange going on. We'd very much like to know what it is. We have some other information that..." Schellenberg paused, censoring himself abruptly, his mouth hardening. "Ever since you told us about their system of turning agents, we've had to utterly discount any information coming from the Abwehr." Schellenberg laughed harshly. "Not that SS Gruppenführer Heydrich ever has believed a word from Canaris anyway." He paused. "Frankly, Doctor, you are our only real source. We're depending on you."

Tennant nodded, but he didn't take the blandishment seriously. For all he knew, Schellenberg and Heydrich had half a dozen other agents in London, all running independently. Whatever the case, his breaking of the conversation in mid-sentence was telling. Plots and counterplots, schemes within schemes. Something was going on, and suddenly the thought of retiring to Berlin seemed fraught with danger. What might happen to him there? He'd seen enough of men like Schellenberg and Heydrich to know that, win or lose, the life of a pawn caught within even the mildest Nazi internecine squabble could be very short. Freud might have his weaknesses and shortcomings, but Tennant was a firm believer in the power of the subconscious and the value of the blind, unsubstantiated hunch. He made his decision.

"If I'm to remain in London, I'll need a new system of communication."

"That can be arranged."

"The message Malmstrom was bringing to me. Is there any way you can find out what happened to it?"

"Of course. At this point we still have a source in the American embassy. Quite a good one, actually. We'll keep you advised."

"All right."

"You'll go back? Investigate this murderer MI5 is so interested in?"

"Yes." Tennant nodded, letting out a long breath. "I'll go back."

Returning to his desk in the garret of the Kensington Park Gardens mansion, Morris Black went over Liddell's Magic Circle list again, groaning inwardly. Next door, in what they were all now calling the Map Room, Police Constable Swift was studiously cataloging each and every piece of evidence gathered from the four murder scenes, filing it all neatly in the growing collection of metal cabinets that now spilled out into the landing at the head of the stairs.

Black had been staring at the row of names on the page in front of him for several hours, smoking cigarettes and listening to the intermittent clatter of Swift, hard at work on his battered Royal. The sound was gratingly accompanied by the limping policeman's relentless, off-key whistling and the staggered tap of his regulation boot clips on the creaking floorboards as he went from typewriter to file cabinet and back again. It was all slowly driving Black to distraction, mostly because it pointed up his own lack of concentration and inability to buckle down.

Ever since the night of the bombing at Burlington Arcade, it seemed as though almost every thought was intruded upon by flickering memories of those moments. Not the fear or the panic or the terrible exploding images, but the smell of Katherine Copeland's hair, soft flesh, cool mouth crushed on his.

Next door, Swift went from "The Lambeth Walk" to a mutilated *Peter and the Wolf.* "Bloody hell," Black grunted. His mouth tasted like the bottom of a canary cage. He took a bitter swallow of the cold, ungodly tea Swift had brewed an hour before, lit yet another cigarette, and looked at the list again. It had been waiting for him on his desk the morning after the raid.

According to Liddell, it was relatively complete, naming virtually everyone included in Churchill's so-called Magic Circle of those who knew about the Ultra secret. Somewhere down the row of names, Black knew, was the first turning of the key that would lead him to Queer Jack. All he had to do was go through them one by one, starting with the boffins and their minders at the Government Code and Cipher School headquarters at Bletchley Park, an estate fifty miles northwest of London:

Fred Winterbotham, director of SIS Scientific Division
Comdr. Alastair Denniston, director, GC&CS
Edward Travis, Denniston's second-in-command
Dillwyn Knox, senior assistant, GC&CS
Oliver Strachey, senior assistant, GC&CS
John Cairncross, senior assistant, GC&CS
Hugh Alexander, mathematician

Stuart Milner-Barry, mathematician
Gordon Welchman, mathematician
Alan Turing, mathematician

In addition, according to Liddell, a score or more of people were actively involved in the deciphering of messages at Bletchley, some being members of one of the three services, but mostly civilians of every imaginable stripe from lawyers to stockbrokers and archaeologists.

After the Bletchley group came the longer list of high-ranking military and intelligence personnel:

John Masterman, the donnish head of the XX Committee
Stewart Menzies, head of MI6
Miss Kathleen Pettigrew, his ironclad secretary
Col. Valentine Vivian, deputy chief, MI6
Lt. Col. Claude Dansey, assistant chief, MI6
Brig. "Jasper" Harker, acting head of MI5
Guy Liddell, director, B Division, MI5
Anthony Blunt, his senior assistant, an art historian
Maxwell Knight, head, B5(b) Department, MI5
Gen. George Davidson, director, Military Intelligence
Air Marshal "Stuffy" Dowding, Fighter Command
Air Vice-Marshal Keith Park
Charles Medhurst, director, Air Intelligence
Archibald Boyle, his deputy
Air Commo. Gerry Blackford, Air Ministry, Plans Division
Jack Slessor, Blackford's second-in-command
Adm. John H. Godfrey, director, Naval Intelligence
Comdr. Ian Fleming, his assistant
Winston Churchill, prime minister
Desmond Morton, Churchill's personal assistant

Thirty names in all, but as Liddell had bleakly pointed out in his covering memorandum, this didn't account for between eighty and a hundred other people who came into direct contact with the daily intercepts somewhere between Bletchley Park and Whitehall.

That list, when Liddell's people completed it, would include a score of Wrens at Bletchley, two dozen dispatch riders, and an assortment of teleprinter operators at the Air Ministry, Fighter Command HO at Stanmore, the War Department and the Admiralty, the Air Intelligence Office, the Department of Military Intelligence, and Admiral Godfrey's DNI.

As far as Morris Black was concerned, the Magic Circle was more like an endless series of concentric rings spreading out across an almost infinite pond. Regardless of what Denniston or anyone else said about the absolute security around Ultra, Black knew that, with so many people involved, someone, somewhere, would talk. Everyone on Liddell's list had friends, family, lovers, or confidants. Absolute security in such an environment was as unlikely as Masterman's contention that a clean sweep had been made of every Nazi agent in England.

A happy conclusion, devoutly desired, but so far unachieved. Even with the help of the Government Code and Cipher School experts at Bletchley, the answer would take time, if it came at all. Maxwell Knight, who, the detective now concluded, was an arrogant, condescending little prig of the worst sort, seemed content to wait for a miracle. Black knew it wasn't going to be that easy and was even beginning to consider the possibility that tracking down Queer Jack and finding Liddell's mysterious Doctor weren't going to happen at all.

Blinking and fighting off a yawn, Morris Black realized that he'd been woolgathering yet again. He also realized that the sound of both Police Constable Swift's typewriter and his whistling had suddenly stopped. Black stood, joints cracking, and went into the other room.

Swift was standing in front of the mapboard. On it he'd pinned a large sheet of paper on which he'd laboriously copied out the Malmstrom message, each number a full inch high.

78124117
25134349
66483274
83496965
96207461
93421907
02993002

The round-faced policeman turned, hearing Black come into the room. "I've just been thinking, sir."

"About that?" said Black, pointing at the large-scale copy on the wall.

"Yes, sir." Swift cleared his throat. "I'm not much at this sort of thing, sir, I mean I was never very good at the crosswords or the puzzle page, but something did occur to me." The policeman hesitated, frowning.

"Go on." Black drew up a chair and sat down, relieved at any distraction from the dreadful list.

"Well, sir," Swift continued, clearing his throat again, "Captain Liddell and yourself both mentioned that this kind of code usually needs a key—the same thing at both ends so you can unscramble it, so to speak."

"That's right." Black nodded. "Liddell calls it a one-time pad, I think. You transpose your message using a random alphabet printed on a pad used by both sender and receiver. Each letter in your message corresponds to a letter on the pad."

"Yes, but it doesn't really have to be a pad though, does it, sir? It can be something else?"

"Liddell says he's seen books used as one-time pads. It would work as long as you both had identical copies. Instead of a random alphabet you code the message using page, paragraph, line, and word references."

"A magazine, sir? Could it be a magazine?" Swift's voice was rising with enthusiasm. Black shrugged. "I suppose so. I'm not sure I see what you're driving at, Swift."

"Well, sir, it made me think. The message comes from Germany and gets decoded in England. What could you have in both places? It couldn't be a German book because that would arouse suspicion, and if you wanted to change the code from time to time, which seems likely, you'd have the devil of a time getting copies of the same one in both countries, don't you think?"

"Reasonable enough." Black sat back in his chair, beginning to get a glimmer of his assistant's train of thought. "Carry on."

"Well, sir, I thought, what sort of thing would it be reasonable to have both here in England and over there in Germany? It couldn't be a German magazine for the same reason it couldn't be a German book, and it couldn't be a British magazine because you wouldn't be able to get one over there."

"American."

"Yes, sir, that's the conclusion I came to."

"There must be hundreds of magazines published every month in the United States. It hardly narrows things down."

"Yes, sir." Swift nodded. "But there aren't many magazines you can get easily in both places—England and Germany that is."

"I suppose that's true."

"I've come up with five possibilities," said Swift. "*Newsweek* magazine—that comes out every week—*Time* and *Life,* also weeklies, and *Fortune* magazine and the *National Geographic,* which are monthlies. I checked with Smith's, sir. They get them all regularly except for the *National Geographic.* You can only get it by subscription."

"Interesting."

"Yes, sir, that's what I thought." Swift nodded eagerly. "If you used one of the weeklies, you could change the code anytime you wanted. The message is divided up into eight-number lines, but I don't think that means very much. The first number could be for the page, the second for the paragraph, the third for the line in that paragraph, and the fourth number could represent the right word on that line. There's fifty-six numbers in the whole message, four numbers for each word, fourteen words in all." The policeman beamed triumphantly.

"I don't think it would be one of the weekly magazines. Overseas mail isn't what it once was. One of the monthlies might be a possibility, though." Black thought for a moment. "And your number count would only work if just the first nine pages were used, anything more and you get into double digits."

"I hadn't thought of that." Swift's face had fallen along with his theory.

"Good try, Swift," said Black, standing up. He patted his crestfallen assistant on the shoulder. "Keep at it. You may be on the right track." He smiled. "Maybe we can show the boffins up for once."

"Yes, sir. Thank you." Black took a last look at the message on the wall and went back to his office. A few moments later Swift's whistling began again; this time it was Elgar's *Pomp and Circumstance*. Black groaned quietly and went back to the list.

After two weeks of nightly raids, Air Raid Precaution Warden Leslie Blythe had begun to consider himself something of an expert on the strategy and tactics of the Luftwaffe and a well-informed critic of the local anti-aircraft batteries in his particular patch, which happened to be the hem of Belgravia's skirt from the police station on Gerald Row, up and over the coal-smutty bridge that crossed the dozen or so lines running into the massive iron caverns of Victoria Station, round about the maze of little streets feeding into Grosvenor Place and the Vauxhall Bridge Road, then back down Ebury Street and home again to a nice spot of tea in the café of the big new motor-coach terminal on Buckingham Palace Road.

A liberal education it was, prowling about that part of the city, night after night. Prossies offering knee-tremblers and God knows what else to soldiers on leave under the arches of Elizabeth Bridge, doe-eyed queers skulking about in the trees around the statue of Marshal Foch in the little park across the road from the station, the occasional Rolls or Bentley streaming up to the palace, only a skip away beyond Lower Grosvenor Place. You had it all here, rich and poor, young and old, some coming, others going, even in the middle of a raid.

It was exciting, especially when you spent the daylight hours punching tickets on an omnibus as he did, or boning about on a bicycle with a sign round your neck saying "Take Cover" like his pal Police Constable Mickelthwaite. The blackout and the nightly raids brought out the best in people, just as they said on the wireless and in the papers, but it bloody well brought out the worst as well—he could attest to that easily enough.

His particular favorites were the groups of roving "shelter crawlers," roving bands of lathered-up toffs from the West End clubs with nothing better to do than go from shelter to shelter, drunk as lords, which some of them no doubt were or would be, seeing what life below ground had to offer and making a general nuisance of themselves. He'd had a few of them on report over the last fortnight, and no doubt there'd be more in the future.

If he were running things, by God, they'd all be branded for the white-feather conchies they really were and packed off to an internment camp with all the other ragtag Jews and

Gypsies Hitler had managed to sweep out of Europe. Bloody good-for-nothings, the lot of them.

For the last few nights Leslie Blythe had noticed a distinct weakening of intensity by the Luftwaffe, and he wondered if Goering's flyboys weren't coming to the end of their rope.

The afternoon raid had been light, and even though the sky overhead was clear tonight, there seemed to be fewer bombers. It was fully dark now, and the alert had been on since dusk, but it had been close to ten o'clock before he'd heard the first, distant droning of the Heinkels and Dorniers, and when they did come, it seemed to Blythe that they were spread thinly and flying at much higher altitudes than before. The big searchlight batteries in Belgrave Square, a dozen blocks to the north, didn't seem to be picking up anything either, and the ack-ack boys massed in Hyde Park were firing at shadows, the ratcheting cough of the big guns audible for miles around, the pink and yellow blossoms of the exploding shells turning the night sky into a gigantic fireworks display easily visible even at this distance.

Making his rounds the last hour or so, he'd also noticed that the bombers seemed to be flying in widening, searching circles rather than making a straight-on approach to specific targets. Fewer bombers, fewer bombs; there was no doubt about it: Fat Hermann was losing steam. Which was just fine as far as Leslie Blythe was concerned; he liked the extra money he received for his ARP duties, but he wouldn't mind getting a leg over with the Mrs. once in a while, not to mention a decent night's sleep.

Listening to the crumpled thump of the bombs ripping up the East End and the harsher moan of the sirens around Victoria Station, Blythe poked about among the trees in the triangular park around Grosvenor Gardens, then turned west onto Lower Belgrave Street. He checked his watch with the hooded light of his ARP-issue torch. Almost midnight. He went on, then paused again at the corner of Ebury Street to check the empty yard of the dark brick council school.

Hearing footsteps, he turned and watched as the uni-formed figure of a woman crossed to his corner. A Wren, in her early twenties from the look of it, her cardboard gas mask hanging from its shoulder strap along with a plain black leather purse. He put up a hand to stop her, more for the sake of having someone to talk to than any worry that she was up to no good.

"Identity card, please, miss," he said. A looker, this one, he thought as the woman sighed and began rummaging around in her purse. Short, dark hair peeking out from under her cap and a pixie face with a sprinkle of freckles across a nicely turned little nose. Not much in the chest, but good legs and a nice turn of ankle despite the heavy, square-heeled uniform shoes. Probably wearing those awful woolen knickers under her dark blue skirt.

She handed him her National Registration Card and he shone the torch on it briefly. Jane Julia Luffington, a Wren with Motor Transport. According to the card, she lived at 18 Palace Gate in Bayswater.

"Long way from home then, aren't we?"

She shrugged. "I was on my way to the underground."

"Visiting the boyfriend?" Blythe grinned.

"I don't see that it's any of your business," she answered coldly. She took back the NR card and stuffed it back into her purse. "Anything else, Warden?"

"Not a thing." He shone the torch into her face just long enough to make her eyes squeeze shut. Then he snapped it off. "Best be on your way then, miss."

"Thank you."

Blythe watched her go, admiring her walk for a moment. A long way from Edith, his wife of these last, long eighteen years. Even at twenty-two Edith hadn't walked like that. If he was ten years younger, he might have jotted down her address, just in case, but as it was, he simply sighed and turned away, continuing his patrol. Edith would have to do.

Had he kept his eyes on her, he might have seen Jane Luffington pause beside a dull gray Austin van parked at the curb less than fifty yards up the street. He might have seen her nod, then climb into the van, and he might have noticed the Government Post Office markings on the side panels of the vehicle. If he'd been suspicious enough, he might even have attempted to jot down the license plate number. But his back was turned and he did none of these things.

Twenty minutes later he was drinking a mug of hot, sweet tea with his friend PC Arnold Mickelthwaite. He mentioned his encounter and described the woman, but by morning he'd forgotten her completely.

At 7:15 A.M. the naked corpse of Jane Luffington was discovered halfway across the city in the middle of a bomb site in Broad Street, not far from the East End's Liverpool Street Station. Her hands and face had been badly burned in the blast and fire, making identification almost impossible.

The body was initially taken to a makeshift morgue in the basement of a church on Whitsun Street only a few blocks from where she was found, and then, after she remained unclaimed, she was transferred to the Coroner's Office in St. Pancras in the hope that she would eventually be identified.

CHAPTER FOURTEEN

Monday, November 11, 1940
11:30 A.M., Greenwich Mean Time

SEPTEMBER CAME TO AN END, and with its passing, the threat of possible invasion diminished. Indian summer was replaced by a gray, wet October, and the worsening weather on the English Channel was like a slowly closing door on Hitler's hopes for a quick and easy victory in England.

Sea Lion, the Nazi invasion plan, was postponed, then postponed again. Finally it was abandoned altogether except as a diversion for Stalin's benefit, and the Luftwaffe, with no four-engined bomber to cut deeply into the heart of the nation, was forced by necessity to concentrate on targets within the range of its available aircraft.

Most of its efforts were focused on London, and through October and the first part of November thousands of individual sorties were mounted and hundreds of tons of bombs were dropped onto the city each night. The Battle of Britain was over, at least for the moment, with no clear victor or vanquished. The Siege of London had begun. By November a large proportion of the city lay in ruins. An average of 170 people were dying during each night's raid, and 200 were serious-

219

ly wounded. Whole neighborhoods in the East End had been totally destroyed. Sixty thousand homes had been made unlivable, sixteen thousand had been completely destroyed, and each night more than twenty-five thousand Londoners were on the streets, desperately seeking shelter from the nightly, droning horror.

Looting became a serious problem. The newspapers ran interminable stories about "plucky East-Enders" and endless photographs of witty slogans and bombed-out shop fronts, but they failed to mention the growing numbers of "spotters" on the darkened streets who reported back to their gangs, pinpointing likely properties. People returning to blocks of shops and houses often found that they hadn't been touched by the Luftwaffe, but had been cleaned out by thieves, who'd removed everything, from clothes and food to razor blades and cigarette lighters. A special plainclothes anti-looting squad was established, using radio-equipped cars to track down their quarry.

Throughout this period there were no reports at all of any deaths that might have been laid at Queer Jack's door, and the murders of Rudelski, Talbot, Eddings, and Dranie remained unsolved. Despite the best efforts of all concerned no new clues were forthcoming in the case of the two men murdered in the WC at the London Zoological Gardens.

On November 5, Franklin Delano Roosevelt was elected by a landslide for an unprecedented third term, and within hours there were rumors circulating in London that Ambassador Kennedy was being pressured to resign. The most likely choice for his successor appeared to be John Gilbert Winant, the dreamy Lincoln look-alike and ex-governor of New Hampshire. On November 9, two years after the fateful Munich Agreement and his famous "peace for our time" speech, Neville Chamberlain died of throat cancer.

Since the unmarked death of Jane Luffington on the night of September 20, Detective Inspector Morris Black and his assistant, Police Constable Swift, had spent most of their time methodically interviewing the long list of people provided by Guy Liddell and assembling an ever-growing number of dockets that now filled eight file cabinets in the little offices on Kensington Park Gardens.

Liddell seemed absorbed in other projects and rarely visited Black, contenting himself with the occasional telephone call to check on progress or the lack of it. For the most part, the detective and his assistant were left entirely to themselves, and for the last fortnight Black had begun to wonder if he wasn't becoming something of an embarrassment to the tweedy, pipe-smoking intelligence officer.

Seated behind the wheel, Police Constable Swift drove tight-lipped along the highway toward Canterbury, peering through the inverted fan of clear windscreen created by the single thumping wiper. It had been raining since early morning, gray sheets of it obscuring the rolling hills of Kent and any view of the open sea beyond the widening mouth of the Thames at Sheerness. The water seemed to hang suspended in the air, turning the forests and the fields a brilliant, almost livid green against the dull pewter sky.

The Alvis that Swift had managed to cadge from the impound yard had long ago been replaced by a wretched little Austin Ruby with barely enough room for the two men to sit side by side and a canvas sunroof that leaked along the doorposts whenever it rained, leaving musty little puddles on the floor matting that filled the interior with the sweet-rot odor of mildew.

They had been traveling for more than an hour, and glancing out through the rain-streaked side window, Morris Black could make out the dark line of the railway cutting on his left and the dim, ghostly shape of the Isle of Sheppey lying a mile or so beyond. They had just driven through the old town of Sittingbourne, forty miles east of London; ahead lay Faversham and the southern secondary road leading to the rising, inland hill country.

"If he's dead, sir, I wonder why we're carrying on with all of this." Swift frowned and Black smiled, glancing at his assistant. He hadn't said a word for the past twenty minutes, and the question was obviously the result of a long, silent train of thought.

"Queer Jack?"

"Yes, sir." Swift nodded, keeping his eyes on the road. They reached the bottom of a low hill, and Black waited until the ritual gnashing of the gears had been completed before he answered.

"Why do you assume that he's dead?"

"It's been seven weeks since the last killing, sir. Not a whisper since that one in Southampton. Dranie."

"The last one we know about, Swift. There've been five or six thousand bombing deaths since then; easy to have overlooked any number of them."

"Yes, sir. I thought of that."

"And?"

"I checked with Central Records and the Register of Deaths. Since September twenty-first there've been two hundred bodies initially unidentified and fifty-one people reported missing. There's only six unidentified bodies left, and eight of the missing. Of the six corpses, three are women and two are children under the age of ten. Cause of death on the only adult man is listed as decapitation."

"The missing ones?"

"A brother and sister, eleven and fourteen, from Birmingham, three men from the Stoke Newington shelter bombing, two married women thought to have run away from their husbands, and a seventy-five-year-old man from Godalming with a history of wandering off." Swift paused, frowning. "None of them seem to fit, do they, sir?"

"No, I suppose not." Black lit a cigarette and wound down his window half an inch to let the smoke out. Looking through the spattered windscreen, he could see the distant spire of St. Mary's church in Faversham. A moment later, Swift wrestled with the gearshift once again and they turned off the main highway onto the narrower Ashford Road. As they began their climb into the hills, the engine noise steadily became more labored. Behind them the lowland marshes vanished, hidden behind the grizzled veils of rain.

"He's still alive," said Black. "I'm positive of that."

"I'm not sure Captain Liddell is quite so convinced." Swift lifted one hand off the steering wheel and flicked the leaking sunroof with an irritated thumb and forefinger. "What with his sending back the Alvis and giving us this." Swift made a small, throat-clearing sound. "Not what you might call a vote of confidence, sir."

"Liddell has other concerns," said Black, trying to be diplomatic.

Swift snorted under his breath. "Like keeping his clappers out of a vise," he muttered.

"Now now," Black chided with a smile. "Mustn't be disrespectful, Constable Swift. That's no way to get a detective's gong."

"I just don't want to see you caught in the middle, sir, that's all. I'm not completely in the picture, but I've seen enough to know that you'll take the blame if this all comes to nothing. There's police work, sir, and then there's politics, and the two don't mix." Swift paused. "And if you don't mind me saying so, sir, after what I've seen these last weeks, I'm not sure I'd want a detective's badge."

"I appreciate your concern, but I can take care of myself, Swift. Queer Jack's still out there, and we're going to find him eventually, never fear." It sounded weak, even to Black's ears. Swift was right. If something didn't happen soon, there was a good chance Liddell and all the rest of them would cut their losses. It would be his clappers in the vise, not Liddell's or anyone else's. He was beginning to think it had been planned that way from the beginning. He had no particular connections at the Yard, no powerful friends, and he was a Jew. What better sacrificial lamb or Judas goat?

They drove on in silence, engine rattling alarmingly, rain tapping on the canvas roof like old bones. Black stared out the window at the forested hills rising around them. His assistant was right. Traveling south they sputtered through the little village of Sheldwich, with its ancient slate-roofed houses, then Budlesmere, and finally the crossroads at Challock Lees. Following the directions they'd been given, they turned onto a roadway that was little more than a deeply rutted path and began climbing through the dense forests of King's Wood.

Half a mile later the trees began to thin, and they came out onto a wide pasture at the summit of the hill. They went through an open gate and Swift brought the car to a halt, the engine rattling for almost half a minute after he'd withdrawn the key. Directly in front of them was an assembly of barns and outbuildings surrounding a large brick and half-timbered farmhouse. To the right the hill dropped away in a long, sloping meadow, broken here and there with dark hedgerows and the tumbled remains of old stone walls.

In the distance, at the bottom of the valley and almost invisible in the rain, was the darker smudge that marked the tiny village of Bilting, its dozen shops and houses strung out along the narrow road leading northeast to Canterbury, ten miles away.

Black ducked out of the Austin and pulled up the collar of his mackintosh as the rain slashed coldly against his cheek. With Swift on his heels he trudged across the muddy yard and then hammered on the door of the farmhouse. It swung open a few seconds later, and Black found himself staring into the grinning face of a sandy-haired man wearing a worn, moth-eaten Navy pullover and a mud-clotted pair of gum boots. He was holding something that looked remarkably like a grenade in his left hand.

"Fleming?" asked Black. The burly man wasn't what he'd been expecting at all.

"No. I'm Calvert. His Lordship's inside. Who're you, pray tell?"

"Inspector Morris Black. CID. This is my assistant, PC Swift."

"Good Christ! The Yard!" Calvert looked back over his shoulder. "Burn the evidence, lads! We've been nicked!" He turned back to Black smiling broadly. "Bit of a joke. Welcome to the Garth." He used his free hand and gripped Black by the elbow, steering him into the house. Swift followed, closing the door behind him.

Once upon a time the large room had been two-storied, but someone had removed the first floor, planking, joists, and all, turning it into a high, arch-roofed enclosure that had the look and feel of a slightly impoverished chapel. A fuming inglenook fireplace stood at the far end of the room where an altar might have been, and rows of wooden packing cases littered everywhere could have passed for pews. The room was lit by two rows of grimy, rain-streaked lead-glass windows.

Off to one side several men dressed in the same style as Calvert were prying open crates with pinch bars. Littered around them were more crates piled with grenades, rifles, saucer-shaped land mines, and oil-paper packets of explosives. They were being overseen by a tall, slender man with dark hair wearing tightly fitted jodhpurs and a pair of highly polished riding boots.

"It looks like a bloody IRA camp," Swift whispered. Calvert clapped him on the back, laughing. "Not far off, Constable." He turned away and bellowed down the room. "Fleming! You have guests!"

The dark-haired man nodded to his men, then came

toward Black. Unlike Calvert, he was partially in uniform; his dark green sweater had captain's boards on the shoulders. Black frowned; according to his information Fleming was a lieutenant commander in the Royal Navy Volunteer Reserve. This man was wearing the pips of a Guards captain. Black groaned inwardly, wondering if he'd spent the last hour in a leaking Austin for no reason.

"Lieutenant Commander Fleming?" he asked as the man approached.

"That's Ian, my younger brother," said the man. "I'm Peter."

"I'm Inspector Morris Black. I was supposed to meet with your brother here this morning. Perhaps there's been some mistake?"

"No mistake," said Peter Fleming, shaking his head. "Ian's in the other wing." He smiled. "Still sleeping, I'm afraid." He gestured. "Follow me. You can wait in the kitchen while I knock him up."

Leaving Calvert behind, Peter Fleming took Black and Police Constable Swift across the large room and through a door leading into another, newer part of the house. They went down a narrow, freshly painted central hall, finally reaching a large, well-appointed kitchen.

There was a huge, oak monk's table with benches capable of seating at least a dozen people in the center of the room, two refrigerators, and an enormous stove that could have come out of a restaurant kitchen. A tall, bald man, dressed like Calvert but with the addition of a flowered apron, was chopping vegetables at a massive butcher's block in one corner.

"Hop it, Max," ordered Fleming. The bald man nodded, gave Black and Swift one brief appraising look, then left the room, wiping his hands on the apron. "Half a minute," said Fleming, flashing a quick smile. He turned away and disappeared up a back stairway. Black went to the windows over a pair of large stoneware sinks. The windows looked out over the valley and down to the village. From what he could see, no road or path led up from that direction. The only approach was up the track through King's Wood.

"They've got the high ground," commented Swift, clearly thinking along the same lines. He sat down on one of the benches. "Must be some sort of commando outfit. Cloak-and-dagger stuff."

"Yes," Black agreed. It stood to reason, given Fleming's position as assistant to Godfrey, the head of Naval Intelligence. Or something a little less optimistic, he thought to himself. Early preparations for an official but clandestine resistance movement if the Germans invaded.

After waiting for another five minutes, Black heard the sound of shuffling footsteps coming down the back stairs. A dark-haired man appeared, wearing bedroom slippers and a long silk dressing gown, black with a twisting pattern of snarling red dragons. The man was heavier set and an inch or so shorter than his brother, but the family resemblance was obvious.

"Shit," said Ian Fleming, looking blearily around the kitchen. "I've gone and missed bloody breakfast." He glanced at Black and Police Constable Swift with very little interest. "G'morning."

"Lieutenant Commander Fleming?"

"Not today," he answered, shuffling across to the stove. A tin pot was on the warming plate. He found a mug on the counter, inspected its interior, then poured himself coffee. Bringing the mug to the table, he sat down across from Black and sighed. "You're Black, I suppose?" He glanced down the table. "And this would be Constable Swift, Watson to your Holmes."

"That's right."

"I don't suppose you've got a cigarette on you?"

"Certainly." Black took out his Gems and tossed them over the table to Fleming. The younger man shook one out of the packet and lit it using a box of Swan Vestas from the pocket of his dressing gown. He blew out a long plume of smoke, then settled back in his chair.

"Turkish blend is better, you know," he said, looking critically at the cigarette in his hand. "Smoother than pure Virginia. Easier on the lungs. Better aroma."

Black shrugged. "It's all the same to me." Fleming was one step away from being a character out of a P. G. Wodehouse farce. If it hadn't been for the tense line of jaw and a hidden, flinty look in the man's eyes, he would have been ridiculous with his silk dressing gown and his tobacco.

"You've come a long way to see me. Perhaps you should get on with it." Fleming flashed a quick smile. "Peter's got something on for this afternoon. Bombs in butter churns or some such. I'm to join in."

"I won't keep you for very long."

"They rang me from the office. Said I should cooperate fully with your investigation." Fleming paused. "You're with Liddell's mob, aren't you?"

Black nodded. "For the moment. I'm looking into the possibility that information has leaked out concerning the Ultra decrypts."

"Good Christ. You're sure?"

"Not entirely."

Fleming held up a defensive palm. To Black it seemed an oddly feminine gesture. "I haven't said anything."

"I'm sure not. But we have to check."

"Surely there can't be that many who know." Once again Fleming looked in Swift's direction. The balding police constable had his pad out now and was making notes. "Admiral Godfrey had to move heaven and earth to get me clearance and I'm his personal assistant."

"My list has thirty names on it, including yours. There are eighty-seven others who come into physical contact with the material on a day-to-day basis. There are twelve copies of the decrypts made each day." Black looked down the table. "Swift?"

"Yes, sir." The constable consulted his notebook. "Bletchley Park keeps a check copy and there's another made for the radio operators who send the material out into the field. Then there is the one used by the Teletype operators. Colonel Masterman gets a copy and so does Menzies at MI6 and Harper at MI5."

Fleming looked surprised. "That many?"

"There's more," said Black.

Swift continued his litany. "Air Intelligence has its own as does Military Intelligence at Whitehall and Naval Intelligence at the Admiralty, that's Lieutenant Commander Fleming's copy. There is another copy made and taken to Oxford University each day for safekeeping, one for the prime minister's office, and a last copy which is taken to the Public Records Office."

Fleming nodded, sadness clouding his face briefly. "I knew about that one."

Black was suddenly interested. "Yes?"

"That was Jane's job. I don't suppose she had any real idea what she was carrying, but I did."

"Jane?"

"Jane Luffington. A Wren I was seeing for a time."

Black looked down the table at Swift.

The police constable flipped through the pages of his notebook, then nodded. "Yes, sir. She's on the list. Motor Transport Division. A motorcycle courier."

"She took the file copy to the PRO every day," said Fleming. "Bored her to tears. Trotting baskets of paper about wasn't her idea of fighting a war." He scratched his jaw sleepily. "Nor mine for that matter."

"You said you saw her for a time. You're not together anymore?"

"She's dead," Fleming answered bluntly. "Killed in a raid."

"When?"

The dark-haired young man thought for a moment. "It's been almost two months. Towards the end of September." His expression darkened. "She was badly burned; it took almost a week for her to be identified. I'm not sure exactly when she died. It was her days off, so they didn't miss her at work." He shrugged. "Between the twentieth and the twenty-fourth I suppose."

"Had you known her very long?"

"Not quite a year."

"You never discussed Ultra with her?"

"Certainly not."

"With anyone?"

"No. I've already told you that."

"Not even with your brother?"

"No."

There was a slight hesitation in the man's voice, but Black decided not to pursue it for the moment; he was far more interested in Fleming's girlfriend.

"Did Miss Luffington have any family in London?"

"Yes. Her mother runs a local in The City. A widow."

"Do you know the name of the local?"

"The Rising Sun, in Burgon Street."

"Did Miss Luffington live with her mother?"

"No. She shared a flat with three other girls."

"Did you know them?"

"No."

"The mother?"

"I met her once or twice."

"Did Miss Luffington see her mother often?"

"Every day. It was her big secret."

"Perhaps you could explain that."

"She popped in for lunch. To save money."

"While she was working?"

"Yes. She only took a few minutes."

"I see." Black paused for a moment, thinking. "What happens to the DNI copy of the decrypts once they've been analyzed?"

"They're burned."

"By whom?"

"Me," Fleming answered curtly. "There's a large fireplace in the office. Quite convenient, actually. Keeps the chill off."

"Umm." From his other interviews Black had learned that Air Intelligence used a modified confetti-making machine to destroy their copies, Military Intelligence used a Whitehall incinerator, and Bletchley disposed of theirs on a weekly basis using the furnace in the main building. From what Black could tell, all the departments kept their decrypts in locked and secure containers while not in use.

Still, keeping the material safe from prying eyes was a daunting task, with lots of room for error and oversight. At least a hundred separate flimsies were in each packet of decrypts, which amounted to thousands of copies flitting about from hand to hand.

Since the real flow of information had only begun a few months ago, it wasn't surprising that no one system of security had been established, but the various methods of transmittal—by hand, radio, and via Teletype—added to the confusion and increased the possibility of the information's leaking.

Even the supposedly secure Teletype line that now ran directly from Bletchley to Menzies at 55 Broadway was no guarantee of absolute privacy; Liddell himself had admitted that he and his people were monitoring telephone conversations at several embassies. If they could cut into telephone and Teletype lines, so could someone else. Unlikely perhaps, but not impossible by any means.

Morris Black thanked Fleming for his cooperation, and a few minutes later Black and Swift were back in the rain, trudging across the muddy yard toward the Austin.

"Worth the trip, sir?" asked Swift as they let themselves back into the car. The constable fitted his key into the ignition and pressed the starter button. The engine coughed, complained, then caught. He struggled with the gears.

Black nodded. "Yes, it was worth the trip." Looking out through the windscreen, he could make out the two figures of Ian Fleming and his brother, watching them from the doorway of the house. Swift jerked the Ruby into reverse, turned it around in the yard, then shifted into bottom gear and headed down the track leading to the gate. They passed through, and a few seconds later they were surrounded by the trees of King's Wood once again.

Black stared out through the windscreen. "I'm afraid we'll have to disturb Wren Luffington's eternal rest." He grimaced. "We'll need an exhumation order from Purchase, I suppose."

"Sir?"

"I'm not absolutely sure, but I think Queer Jack has changed his tune, Swift. The only way we're going to know for certain is by examining her remains." Black looked across at his companion "Ready for a bit of Burke and Hare, Constable?"

"Whatever you say, Inspector." Swift crashed through the gears again and they continued down the hill. "It is a bit of a coincidence about the lieutenant commander and the girl. Knowing each other, that is."

"Yes," said Black thoughtfully. The rain rattled angrily on the canvas roof and the windscreen wiper squeaked and thumped. "A bit of a coincidence."

Katherine Copeland crossed the empty expanse of the foyer in the Savoy Hotel and went through the open doors into the restaurant. When the first heavy raids began, the huge dining room had been closed down except for luncheon, and now, in mid-afternoon, it was almost empty. She found Bingham seated at a table overlooking the Embankment.

"Not very cloak-and-dagger, Larry," she said, sitting down across from him. "Aren't you afraid of being seen?"

"You're a society reporter, aren't you?" He shrugged. "I'm society. You could be grilling me about Winant and the embassy two-step for all anyone would know." He paused. "Or care, for that matter."

"I'm glad to see you're being your normal sour self." A waiter in an ankle-length apron appeared, took Katherine's drink order, and retreated.

"It's been a while," said Bingham.

"I was surprised when you called. I thought you'd forgotten all about me."

The waiter delivered Katherine's Scotch and withdrew again. She took a small sip from the drink, sat back in her chair, and lit a cigarette. Bingham hadn't asked her here to chat.

"So tell me, Larry, why have I been summoned into the presence?"

"You're being taken off the Morris Black operation." Katherine was stunned by the pronouncement. She'd come to the meeting prepared to defend herself, but she hadn't counted on this. "Whose idea was that, Larry? Yours or Donovan's?"

"It was a mutual decision."

"Based on your recommendation."

"It's been weeks, Katherine. You haven't accomplished very much."

"You mean I haven't gone to bed with him," she said flatly.

"I mean you haven't found out what the man is doing about the murders." Bingham shook his head wearily. "Everybody in the goddamn world is in on this thing except us, Katherine. It's getting to be an embarrassment."

"Everybody in the world?"

Bingham sighed. "We've just had word from the embassy in Berlin. Our contact on the Tirpitz Ufer says they're all atwitter. Schellenberg met with someone in Stockholm; we think it was their agent-in-place here. Even Gorsky at the Russian embassy is nosing around. With you involved we were supposed to be closer than anyone. It hasn't turned out that way." He paused. "Donovan isn't pleased. A lot of people are getting nervous."

"First it's everybody in the world, now it's a lot of people. Just who are we talking about, Larry? And why are they so nervous?"

"Who it is doesn't matter. The point is there've been some rumors. New ones."

"About the killings?"

"About Churchill's ability to survive. Things are coming to a head. Lend-Lease is just the beginning. Churchill wants us in the war. We have to have answers. Now, before an invasion."

"There isn't going to be an invasion."

"Not right this minute. But spring isn't far off." Bingham paused. "Black's investigation is still ongoing. We've also had some rumors from that end. They're more worried than ever about a security breach. So is Donovan."

"What does that have to do with me?"

"Nothing. Apparently. All your reports have been vague. You're no closer to him now than you were six weeks ago."

"I've got a lead on that photograph he was so interested in. I'm following up on it."

"No, you're not. I told you, Donovan is pulling you off the case."

"Just like that?"

"Just like that."

Katherine stabbed her cigarette out in the ashtray on the table. "Christ, you people are amazing." She shook her head. "I'm supposed to do a bump and grind for the limey policeman and then he tells me everything. Life isn't like that, Larry."

"How would you know?" Bingham responded coldly. "You haven't been trying very hard."

"Fuck you, Bingham."

"No." The diplomat didn't seem even mildly shocked at her use of the expletive. "Fuck Morris Black."

"He doesn't want to. Not me, not anyone else."

"What's the matter with him? Does he like boys or something?"

"He's a human being, Larry. Something you obviously don't know very much about." Katherine paused. "He's a Jew, did you know that, Larry?"

"Of course I knew it. So what?" He shrugged. "The world's full of them."

"Not so many as there used to be. Hitler is killing them like a scythe though a wheat field."

"There's no proof of that. Just a lot of talk."

"I think Black is worried that it could happen here. He's ready to throw in the towel." She paused. "It wouldn't surprise me if he quit the Yard and left the country."

"This doesn't have anything to do with the killings. Or you."

"No. It has to do with Morris Black. It has to do with the fact that he's lonely, because he loved his wife and now she's dead, and he's worried about a war that looks like it might swallow him up, and most of all it has to do with the fact that he's a nice man, Larry. Something else you wouldn't know anything about."

"I'm not here to be nice, Katherine. I'm here to do a job. So were you."

"You're right." She nodded. "It was a job I thought I could do. But I can't. I'm not who I thought I was. I'm not who Donovan thought I was."

Bingham stared at her thoughtfully. "You've fallen for him, haven't you?"

"He hasn't fallen for me, that's more to the point."

"That wasn't the question. You let yourself get personally involved, didn't you?"

"Jealous?"

"Of Black?"

"No, jealous of the fact that he still has a soul."

Bingham sighed. "There's no reason to continue with this, Katherine, it's a moot point. From what you say you don't want the job, and we don't want you doing it. As of now you are not to have any contact at all with Morris Black, nor are you to pursue any matters relating to the killings." He paused. "Eventually an assignment will be found for you that is less…taxing on your morality. Until then you will continue working at the newspaper." He stood up. "Goodbye, Katherine. I'll be in touch." He turned away and walked across the restaurant. Katherine watched him go.

"No, you won't," she whispered.

First Lieutenant Gustav Claus, twenty-two years old and *Staffelkapitän* in the First Wing of 51 Fighter *Gruppe* based in St.-Omer, sat slumped in the back of the rattletrap Austin Commercial lorry, trying without success to be philosophical about his sudden reversal of fortune. He shifted his feet, trying to get into a more comfortable position on the hard wooden bench. His leg shackles dragged depressingly over the floorboards of the truck, and he let out a long, heartfelt sigh; this was not the way things were supposed to work out.

For the last five months he'd been stationed in St.-Omer, escorting bombers in their sorties over southern RAF bases, doing convoy duty along the English Channel, and enjoying the occasional *Frei-Jagd*, or "free hunt," when time and fuel permitted. In the air he was at one with his Emile, a Messerschmitt Bf 109E, and had managed to bag nineteen kills, all

Hurricanes and Spitfires. One more and he would have achieved ace status and the coveted Knight's Cross. Yesterday it had been his lust for a twentieth kill that proved to be his undoing. Like some wet-behind-the-ears novice he'd spent too much time chasing his quarry and he'd run out of fuel over the Thames Estuary. He'd ditched, inflated his one-man dinghy, and an hour later he'd drifted into shore on the tide. A patrol picked him up only minutes after that.

This morning, after a surprisingly hearty breakfast of tea and piping hot oatmeal at the local constabulary, he'd been shackled, then unceremoniously dumped into the rear of the Austin lorry. The drumming of the rain on the lorry roof, the dank cold, and the raw itch of his salt-caked skin combined to suit his mood exactly. One day the *Ritterkreuz* was within his grasp, the next day it was gone, replaced by the ashes of defeat.

Worse than the chains around his ankles were the shackles of failure that bound him to the ground. He'd lived to fly, and now that life was over. As the lorry bounced and rattled along the north road into London, he felt the bitter taste of bile rise in the back of his throat. Gustav Claus, fighter pilot, was no more. He was Claus the POW now.

The truck reached the eastern edge of the city, found its way onto the North Circular Road, then edged off into the suburbs of Enfield at Palmer's Green, heading more directly north. Claus didn't have the slightest idea of where he was, and he was so exhausted by his recent ordeal that he barely cared. Even so he slid down the long bench to the rear of the truck and peeked out through a small opening in the canvas flap.

The lorry turned, then turned again, and suddenly both sides of the road were bounded by a low stone wall. Beyond that were dense trees. A forest of some kind, or a park. A moment later the vehicle slowed, then jerked to a stop. He could hear the driver talking and then they moved off again but much more slowly. Looking out, Claus saw that they had passed through a high stone gate secured by at least four guards. More trees but the stone wall had been replaced by a high barbed-wire fence. Even through the slanting rain Claus could make out the white porcelain knobs of electric insulators. What kind of prison camp was this?

They drove on for another half mile, then paused again. More conversation, none of which he was able to decipher. Another fence, also electrified, a wood and barbed-wire gate, more guards, and then they stopped again. The engine died. He had arrived. He slid back down the bench and waited. A few seconds later the canvas flap was thrown back and the RAF noncom who'd accompanied the driver from South Benfleet gestured at him with the barrel of the ugly little automatic weapon he carried.

"Come along then, Fritz. End of the line."

The only word Claus understood was the name Fritz. He shrugged his shoulders. "*Nicht verstehe*...I am not—"

"Get out of the fucking lorry, mate." The guard jerked his weapon again. This time the meaning was clear. Claus stood up groggily, ducked his head, and shuffled down to the rear of the truck. The driver appeared and helped him down. Stepping away from the lorry with the armed guard behind him, Claus saw that he was at one end of a huge stone mansion built around three sides of a square. It was surrounded by a double fence of barbed wire, and guards were everywhere, batlike in sodden dark blue rain capes that scraped over the muddy ground as they patrolled.

An Army sergeant wearing a beret topped with a bright red pompom came up out of a basement side entrance and took a large envelope from the driver. The driver then bent down and unlocked the shackles around the prisoner's ankles. He stepped back and the sergeant took over. He too was armed, this time with an enormous revolver. He waved it toward Claus.

Claus moved toward the side entrance, then down a short flight of steps to an open doorway. "In you go, mate," his keeper grinned. "Don't be shy."

The sergeant and his prisoner went down a long corridor, the ceiling a snaking maze of pipes. Claus wrinkled his nose. The passageway smelled like the stokehold of a ship: wet coke and warm ash. Another smell was in the air as well. Medicinal. Ether? Surgical spirits?

It reminded him of his uncle Otto's office. Uncle Otto the dentist. Claus shivered, suddenly feeling uneasy. What kind of prisoner-of-war camp was it that had no prisoners walking the grounds, even in the rain? Why was he in the basement of this place, and God help him, what was the meaning of that smell?

They reached a door and stopped. The sergeant knocked, then opened it. Claus found himself stepping into a small, brilliantly lit room, painted a glaring white. A bald man in a white lab coat was sorting through a tray of gleaming surgical instruments. He looked up as Claus and the sergeant came into the room.

"Right, Sergeant. Outside please."

"Yessir." The sergeant snapped a salute and withdrew. The bald man stared at Claus.

"Oberleutnant Gustav Claus?"

"Jawohl, Herr Doktor." Thank Christ for that, Claus thought, at least he speaks German, even if he does have a horrible accent.

"Strip." The doctor made an unbuttoning gesture. "Take all your clothes off, *verstanden*?"

"Jawohl, Herr Doktor!" Claus eyed the tray of surgical instruments. He'd heard rumors about what went on in the basement of Gestapo headquarters in Berlin, and he'd listened to the stories about German airmen being tortured in England. He noticed a large hypodermic syringe on the table beside the tray of instruments. Better perhaps to drown in the Channel than go through this. He began taking off his clothes.

Half an hour later his physical examination was over. The sergeant took the much relieved pilot along another corridor to the supply room, where he was issued a collarless flannel shirt, long woolen underwear, a pair of thick woolen socks, toilet articles, and a gas mask in a cardboard box. He was relieved of his flight boots and his leather jacket. Everything else he was allowed to keep. He was told, once again in terrible German, that as an *Oberleutnant* with equivalent rank to an RAF flying officer, he was entitled to three pounds pocket money a month, paid in tokens or credits.

Following the kitting-out, he was taken along more corridors, up several flights of stairs, and through four separate iron gates, each one manned with an armed guard. So far he had seen no sign of any other prisoners. At last he reached the third and top floor of the large building. The sergeant fitted a brass key into the lock and stepped aside. Carrying his newly issued clothes, Claus entered the room. The door closed behind him and he heard the clicking sound of the key being turned in the lock.

The room was large, high ceilinged, and gloomy, the only light coming from a narrow, wire-netted window. The four iron beds in the room were each piled with three striped mattress "biscuits." Two khaki blankets were folded neatly at the end of each bed. There was a table, metal lockers, four grubby chairs, and coconut matting laid out on the hardwood floor in strips.

To one side of the window a man wearing a light brown flight suit exactly like Claus's was washing socks in a small porcelain sink. He turned and smiled as Claus came into the room.

"Company at last," the man said. His German was excellent, with a faint hint of Austria—Vienna or Linz, perhaps. Definitely *hochdeutsch*. Like Claus, this man had the single bar and propeller of an *Oberleutnant* on the sleeve of his flight suit. Claus dropped his kit on the nearest bed.

"My name is Claus. Gustav Claus."

"Jurgen Volk. Pardon me if I don't shake hands, but I really do have to wash out these socks. They got terribly muddy when I crashed."

"You were shot down?"

Volk nodded. "Yesterday." Claus stared at him. Volk seemed to be a little old for a pilot. He was on the short side, dark haired and dark eyed. Good with women from the looks of him. Claus remembered being briefed by a Luftwaffe intelligence officer shortly after arriving in France.

He and the rest of the men in his *Staffel* had been warned about "cuckoos," RAF intelligence officers planted in POW camps as agents provocateurs to gather information. He sat down on the end of the bed. Volk half turned so his back wouldn't be to the new arrival. He continued to rinse out his socks.

"Where did you fly out of?" asked Claus.

"Cherbourg—9JG53."

"*Totenkopf?*" said Claus mildly.

Volk shook his head. "You know better than that, Claus. Death's Head doesn't fly out of Cherbourg. I'm *Pik As*, the renowned Ace of Spades *Geschwader*."

"Your commander?"

"Hauptmann Winterer."

"The name of the airbase?"

"Marquise. Satisfied?"

Claus had spent a fortnight in Cherbourg before being transferred to St.-Omer. So far Volk had answered correctly. He had one more question.

"Do you like the food at the Beausejour?" he said quietly.

Volk's smile turned into a broad grin. "You should have gone into the Gestapo, Claus, you're quite good at this."

"Just answer the question."

"All right. The answer is no, I don't like the food at the Beausejour."

"Why not?"

"Because there isn't any. The Beausejour Hotel doesn't have a restaurant. I eat at the Tourville just like everyone else." Volk cocked an eyebrow. "Can we stop the silly questions now? I can assure you that I'm not a spy."

"Where were you shot down?"

"Isle of Wight."

"Bad?"

"Bad enough." The man laughed and draped his socks over the edge of the sink. "At least I didn't get wet." He motioned with his chin. "Your flight suit could use an ironing."

"Do you have any idea where we are?"

"They call it Trent Park. A place called Cockfosters."

"It's not a real camp, is it?"

"I don't think so," said Volk, shaking his head. He sat down on the bed across from Claus and reached into the pocket of his flight suit. He brought out a packet of cigarettes. Player's. Both men lit up. There was a long silence, broken only by the tapping rain on the window above them.

"You haven't asked me any questions," said Claus finally.

"Why should I?"

"I could be the spy, you know."

Volk shook his head. "You're not. And even if you were, I couldn't tell you anything you wanted to know."

"No, I suppose not," sighed Claus. He smoked and looked up at the window. The other man was right. They were just a couple of pilots unlucky enough to have been in the wrong place at the wrong time.

"Shit," said Volk after another silence.

"Um," agreed Claus.

Volk got up and went to the sink. He checked his socks with a thumb and forefinger. "Still damp," he grunted. "I hate damp socks."

"Me too." If Claus had been alone, he might have cried. As it was, he stared at the floor. Idiotically he found himself thinking about a girl he knew in Neukolln, on Burkner Strasse. Her name was Lena and she'd been the first girl to let him do it to her. All he could remember about her now was the smell of the peppermint schnapps he'd used to get her drunk. He wondered how long it was going to be before he had either a woman or peppermint schnapps again. He let out a long fluttering sigh, then cleared his throat, embarrassed.

"Don't worry." Volk stubbed out his cigarette into the ashtray on the table, then crossed to where Claus was sitting. He patted him on the shoulder. "I know exactly how you feel." He sat down on the bed beside his new friend. "The worst of it is, I was looking forward to playing a little night music on Thursday."

"Were you part of *Mondscheinsonate*?" asked Claus, interested. Moonlight Sonata was the code name for the biggest operation to be mounted since the first London bombings in September.

Volk nodded. "Yes. We were going to be the escort for KG100. It would have been exciting."

"Which target do you think is going to be first?"

"*Regenschirm*. Birmingham is the most important target."

"I thought it might be *Korn*. Coventry's not as big, but the Cornercraft Works is making the new Spitfire engines; at least that's what they told us at the briefing."

"Maybe." Volk shrugged. "Not that it makes any difference to you or me anymore."

"No, I suppose not. We're out of it now. Shit." Claus took a last pull on his cigarette, then put it out. "I wonder what happens next?"

"An interrogation. Then off to a proper camp, I guess." Volk let out a long, shuddering yawn. "I think I'm going to sleep now if you don't mind. I'm still pretty slagged from yesterday."

"Good idea."

The two men spent a few minutes arranging their bunks,

then lay down, listening to the rain. Before he knew it, Gustav Claus was asleep. An hour later he was roused by the sound of footsteps outside the door to their room and then the rattling of a key in the lock.

The sergeant in the beret appeared, roused Oberleutnant Volk, and marched him off. Claus tried to stay awake until his friend returned, but his eyes closed of their own accord a few moments later, and then he was asleep again, dreaming of Lena on Burkner Strasse, and peppermint schnapps.

"Bloody marvelous!" gloated Col. John Masterman. The uniformed ex-Oxford don was sitting behind a cluttered desk in a dimly lit office on the main floor of the Trent Park "Cage." On the desk in front of him there were piles of prisoner dossiers, several gray *Flugbuch* flight logs, and a special Air Ministry edition of the 1939 Michelin Guide for France. Across from Masterman, Dr. Charles Tennant was sprawled in a leather-covered armchair, smoking a cigarette and taking occasional sips from the steaming mug of tea resting on the edge of the desk.

The psychiatrist was still wearing the Luftwaffe flight suit he'd worn while playing the role of Oberleutnant Volk, a real ME 109 pilot who'd been shot down the day before and who was now occupying a room three doors down from Gustav Claus on the third floor of the Cockfosters mansion. According to Masterman, the two men would be taken from their cells separately, then sent on to different camps. Claus would go to Grizdale Hall in Lancashire, while the real Jurgen Volk would be interned at the Hayes, a converted resort hotel in Staffordshire.

"Frankly, I was scared out of my wits," said Tennant, his voice weary. "He was very suspicious. He almost caught me with that question about the Beausejour." The psychiatrist glanced at the Michelin Guide. "I didn't have much time to bone up on things, and I also thought my German might be a bit rusty."

"You did a wonderful job, Tennant, and on very short notice. I'm very grateful, old man. That bit about the damp socks was a stroke of genius, and your idea of the preliminary physical examination was bang on."

"It's a variation on a very old theme. Frighten the subject, then quickly put him at his ease. Make him feel safe and you gain his confidence. Basic Pavlovian technique."

"Um, of course. Whatever the case, it seems to do the trick. We'll have to do it again."

"You'll have to find another actor." Tennant smiled. "I don't think I could do it very often."

"Don't be so bloody self-effacing, man. You could have a career on the stage. He swallowed it hook, line, and sinker."

"An interesting experiment." Tennant shrugged. "I'm not sure how valuable it might be in the long run."

"Valuable enough, long run or not. As it is, our friend Claus has given us confirmation of their big Moonlight Sonata raid."

"So that's what you meant when you mentioned 'a little night music.' I was wondering about that. You told me what to say, but I didn't understand it." The psychiatrist paused. "Confirmation?"

"Um." Masterman nodded. He began gathering up bundles of dossiers. "Always nice to have a second source." He made a little grunting noise under his breath and scowled. "Should get up their noses a bit in B Department. One nose in particular." He looked up at Tennant briefly, light from the gooseneck lamp on the desk reflecting off his glasses. "I really shouldn't say too much. Telling tales out of school and all that."

There was a knock at the door, and an Army corporal entered. He saluted Masterman, placed three spools of recording wire on the desk, and left the room.

Reaching down behind the desk, Masterman brought up a fat War Office-issue briefcase and began filling it with the files and dossiers. He topped it off with the spools of wire, then snapped the satchel shut.

"You will be discreet about this, won't you, Doctor?" There was a faint note of anxiety in the older man's voice. "It was very short notice. I suppose I should have gone through channels but…"

"Don't worry, Colonel." Tennant waved a hand. "My lips are sealed."

"Good show," said Masterman, relieved. He brightened. "Can I give you a lift somewhere?"

"Yes, thanks. As soon as I change out of these damp socks." Tennant smiled, and then both men laughed.

CHAPTER FIFTEEN

Tuesday, November 12, 1940
9:30 P.M., Greenwich Mean Time

KATHERINE COPELAND CLIMBED UP out of the Oxford Circus tube station and took a deep, shuddering breath as she stepped into the night. The station below was a pesthole of foul, barely ventilated air, and even this early the platforms were already awash in excrement. The newly installed bunks were filled to overflowing, and hundreds more shelters were crowded onto the stalled escalator steps.

The noise level was appalling: mothers calling to children, screaming babies, the screech of arriving and departing trains, whistles being blown, cries, moans, hysterical laughter, layer upon layer and underneath it all a steady muttering, mindless chatter like some mythical slumber beast beneath the ground.

Certainly not the stuff of Priestley's regular radio "chats" with his "indomitable cockney cheerfuless" and his "getting on with it," his grinning omnibus driver with a "Morning, gov-'nor," and the pudgy writer's relentless stouthearted optimism.

Instead of sitting in his cozy BBC studio, maybe he could try "chatting" from one of the makeshift toilets in the Oxford Circus underground, Katherine thought, or attempt to interview a cheerful cockney who'd just seen his wife and children blown to bits in front of his eyes. It grated on her nerves; they were already trying to make the war into a myth of good and evil.

People like Priestley were casting the British people as St. George, and Hitler and his Luftwaffe as the fire-breathing dragon. White would triumph over black, fairies wouldn't die if you clapped hard enough, and if we were all good and true, King Arthur might just come back, wielding Excalibur against the jackboot swarms.

And it just wasn't true. This war was about people cowering in the shit-stink of subway stations, waiting for their lives to be snuffed out in the blink of an eye, not knights in shining armor. It was about people like Larry Bingham and Wild Bill Donovan.

"To hell with them," Katherine said quietly. She'd been taken off the case and that was just fine with her. If Larry Bingham didn't want her services, perhaps Morris Black would. So a peace offering was in order, and hence her late-night visit to George Buckman at the BBC.

She found him on the roof of the pale, art deco building. Partially hidden by a set of large, softly moaning blowers, Buckman, a tall, totally bald man in a tweed suit, was holding a large microphone out over the bars of the safety railing that ran around the edge of the building. Several boxes of equipment were at his feet. From that distance, silhouetted against the flashing, fire-lit sky, he seemed to have a pair of enormous teacups over his ears, but as she edged around the blowers and approached him, Katherine realized that he was wearing headphones.

Sensing her presence behind him, the tall man turned slightly and held a finger to his lips, gesturing for silence. He went back to what he was doing, his arm extended over the railing, gripping the microphone. Katherine tiptoed to the edge of the roof, joining him. She looked out, trying to orient herself.

They were standing at the southwest corner of the building, overlooking the squat clock tower and one of the soaring transmission masts, looking like a Texas oil derrick that had somehow found its way to the top of the building. On the rounded balcony two floors below was the canvas-shrouded bulk of the giant loudspeaker that transmitted the natural-strength sounding of Big Ben once a day.

To her right, on the far side of Portland Place, was the dark, châteaulike rectangle of the Langham Hotel, while to her left, partially screened by the transmission mast, was the spire of All Souls. A little farther east, vanishing and reappearing in the cloud-reflected flashes of the ack-ack guns, was the oblong dome of Queen's Hall with Bloomsbury and Clerkenwell beyond, a jagged sea of rooftops and chimney pots, black, spiked shadows flaring in the pink and yellow hell-fire sky.

The air was filled with the moaning of the sirens, the banshee wail of falling bombs, the rip and tear of the pounding ack-ack, and the shrill clatter of racing fire engines and ambulances on the streets below as they rushed wildly toward the spreading threads of brilliant white that marked each new fire. It was a scene from Dante. Staring, Katherine Copeland felt her mouth go dry and her heart begin to pound as she tried to take in the terrible sights and sounds of a city being destroyed before her very eyes.

From somewhere in the distance on her right, far away to the southwest, there was a sudden, incredibly brilliant flash of light followed by a massive explosion so powerful she felt it shudder up through the building beneath her feet. It felt as though a dozen bombs had detonated together on a single target, and the rising multicolored mushroom of roiling smoke and flame was so intense that she could make out the hulking rectangle of Victoria Station, more than a mile and a half away.

"Jesus!" she whispered, then realized what she had done. The man next to her turned slightly, shook his head, and pulled the headphones off his ears, letting them dangle around his neck. He bent down and switched off the wire recorder at his feet. Unhooking the microphone, he placed it carefully in its own box and stood up, looking in the direction of the stunning explosion.

"Gas main. Maybe two," he said firmly, lifting his voice above the surrounding din. "Can't mistake it. Bombs go, 'Whiiizzzzzz! Thump! Kabang!' Gas main goes, 'Ker-rack! Whoomph!' " He squinted into the darkness. "Looks nasty." Turning back to Katherine, he smiled pleasantly. "You'd be Miss Copeland, I expect." He held out a small, delicate hand.

"And you're George Buckman."

"That's right. If you'll give me a hand with this equipment, we can go down to my office for a chat."

Buckman's office turned out to be a small room on the seventh floor of the building, just down the hall from the two-storied sound effects studio in the central core. Not only was the entire core soundproofed, it was also insulated by the out-lying offices, meeting areas, and conference chambers that ringed the various studios, totally isolating it from the outside world.

Buckman's room was lined floor to ceiling with steel shelving enameled in a revolting apple green that was probably supposed to be cheerful. The shelves were choked with hundreds of objects, some obviously musical instruments, others less recognizable: strips of wood studded with small nails, a tin can filled with pebbles, sandpaper glued to table tennis paddles, thin metal disks threaded with lengths of string, bunches of keys, an assortment of megaphones, balled-up sheets of cellophane, a metal throat-lozenge box filled with odd coins. A junk collector's dream and a housewife's nightmare, Katherine thought.

There were two chairs in the room, both of the wooden swivel type, no desk, and a small pass-through window with a glass slider that looked into another room, brightly lit, lined with fiber batts that looked like the inside of an egg contained and fitted out with half a dozen microphones mounted on metal brackets that looked like kitchen lazy tongs.

"The sound effects studio," Buckman explained, seeing Katherine peering through the little window. "I call it my laboratory." He put his boxes of recording equipment on the floor and dropped into one of the chairs. Katherine took the other.

"I'm sorry if I caused you any problem on the roof," she apologized.

Buckman shrugged. "Not to worry. Just gathering a bit of wild sound. Comes in handy."

"Bombs exploding?"

"The correspondents seem to like it. Especially your American colleagues. Gives their broadcasts a bit of verisimilitude. A bomb in the background now and again fleshes out their reports." Buckman smiled and ran one hand over his bald scalp. "But I gather you're not interested in sound effects, exploding bombs or otherwise."

"I was talking to a friend of mine at the newspaper. He said you were the local expert on rural Germany. He thought you could help me."

"Bit of an overstatement, calling me an expert." Buckman cleared his throat and Katherine smiled, trying not to laugh. The man was blushing, the pink flush running right up to the top of his head. She'd never seen anything like it. "I'm really just an amateur rambler."

According to Katherine's colleague, Buckman was indeed a rambler, but far from an amateur. As well as being a recording engineer for the BBC, he was also past president of the British Federation of Rambling Clubs, chairman of the Continental Ramblers Association, and an associate member of something called the Commons, Open Spaces, and Footpaths Preservation Society. Under the pseudonym of Walker Miles he had authored more than a dozen rambling guides including *More Rambles for Londoners, Rambling Through*

Bavaria, and *Shanks Mare: The Compleat European Rambler*. Apparently, given a pair of stout boots and a rucksack, George Buckman would, and did, walk anywhere.

Katherine opened her bag and took out an eight-by-ten enlargement of the photograph Morris Black had taken from the wall of Ivor Dranie's house in Southampton. She'd had the darkroom technician at the newspaper blow it up, concentrating on the central portion of the picture, keeping the foreground figures in focus and making the sign on the building behind them legible. She handed the photograph to Buckman.

"I don't suppose you know where this is, do you?"

Buckman held the photograph close to his face, examining it carefully. He nodded, then handed it back to her. "The Gasthaus Strobeck. They do a lovely schnitzel as I recall."

"You've been there?" said Katherine, astounded.

"'Thirty-six and again in 'thirty-eight." Buckman nodded again. "Dull little place, actually. In the Harz Mountains, near Halberstadt, between Berlin and Weimar. Not much to recommend it really, except for the chess."

"Chess?"

"Oh, yes. I thought that's what you were interested in."

"I don't understand."

"Look at the photograph. The figures in the foreground."

"They look as though they're going to some kind of costume party."

"They're going to a chess tournament. The woman in the front is the black queen, and the man beside her is the king. The fellow in the tall square hat with the spear in his hand is a rook—castle I think you call it in America. The one with the horse headpiece is a knight, and so on...pawns, bishops, another knight."

"My God," Katherine whispered, looking down at the picture. "You're right." It was so obvious she'd completely overlooked it.

"From what I can remember, they're quite mad about the game in the town. There's some legend about its being the first place chess was played in Europe. Teaching it is even part of the school curriculum. They had a thirteen-year-old grandmaster at the Stockholm Chess Olympiad in 1936. Every year they have a festival with games played using human pieces like the ones in your picture. Bit of a tourist attraction, I suppose, but they take it all quite seriously."

"And you say there's nothing else of any special interest in the town? Nothing else important?"

"Not really. It's a bit off the beaten track except for people like me." Buckman flushed again.

Katherine looked down at the photograph. "So there's no other reason for someone to hang this picture in his parlor except for its connection to the game?"

Buckman shook his head. "I shouldn't think so. Anyone displaying that photograph would almost certainly be a chess player. And probably a bit of a fanatic at that."

Katherine stared at the picture. If Dranie was a chess fanatic, did that mean his killer was one as well? What was the connection?

Police Constable Swift turned the Austin Ruby toward the curb and switched off the engine. Seated beside him, Morris Black glanced out the window. They were parked in front of the windowless brick façade of the Westminster Baths at 88 Buckingham Palace Road. On the opposite side of the empty street the sooty iron wall of the Victoria Station train shed stretched for a hundred yards up to Grosvenor Gardens and Victoria Street.

It was almost midnight but the sky in front of them was bright as dawn, lit by a hundred Docklands fires and the pulsing glow of the antiaircraft guns in St. James's Park. The distant air was filled with their steady, pounding bark and the rolling thunder of the bombs, but somehow this dark corner of the city seemed removed from it all, a shadowed, somber limbo in the midst of chaos where the dead and those attending them were safe from further harm.

Several gray-painted vans were parked in front of the Ruby, one with its wheels drawn up onto the pavement. An exhausted ARP worker stood slumped against the wing of the nearest ambulance, smoking a cigarette and watching as a crew of morgue attendants dressed in boilersuits came down the steps, each one carrying an empty canvas stretcher.

The Westminster Baths, as well as most of the other municipal swimming facilities in London, had been taken over as temporary mortuaries more than a year before, the pools emptied, covered, and equipped to handle several hundred fresh corpses every night. The tile floors and powerful ventilation equipment used for the baths were also ideally suited for mortuary duty.

Swift stayed behind the wheel of the little car, staring blankly ahead, both hands gripping the wheel, his eyes fixed on the blazing skyline, a small muscle in his jaw twitching slightly. To Black, his companion looked anxious, almost on the verge of panic.

"Come along, Swift, they'll probably have a mug of tea for you inside."

"No thank you, sir. I'll stay here if it's all the same to you."

"There's a raid on, man, don't be an ass."

"I'll stay here, sir, with the car," Swift answered firmly. Black looked at his assistant, then imagined what the inside of the baths would be like. Fresh corpses, the reek of blood and excrement. Too much like the beaches of Dunkirk and whatever other horrors Swift had lived through before that.

Black nodded. "All right. Stay with the car."

"Thank you, sir." There was obvious relief in Swift's voice.

"If it gets worse, I want you to come inside."

"Of course, sir."

Black let himself out of the car and went up the steps to the main doors. The imagined interior of a few moments before didn't even approach the terrible reality confronting the detective as he entered the building.

He found himself in a small vestibule, lit only by a single shaded lamp on a rudely constructed table made with planks set across a pair of sawhorses. Behind the table a gray-faced man in an Auxiliary Pioneer Corps uniform was matching "Death Due to War Operations" dockets to names on the local voters' list. The marble floor was slick with blood and other fluids, and the air was perfumed with a ghastly, pungent reek of charred wood and half-cooked meat.

Black showed his warrant card to the Pioneer Corps guard. The man nodded silently, then offered him something that looked like a flat tin of shoe polish. Black twisted the lid off. The tin was filled with a thick, white cream that smelled heavily of concentrated mothballs.

"Camphor ointment," said the guard. He shook his head wearily. "Bloody awful in there. The Sloan Square underground. Bomb and gas main. Twenty dead and more coming." He nodded at the tin in Black's hand. "Put a fingerful up each nostril and try and breathe through your mouth." Black did as he was told, then handed back the tin. Leaving the guard, he walked down the wide hallway beyond, then pushed through a pair of swinging doors that led into the baths themselves.

The high-ceilinged chamber was a hundred feet long and half as wide. The pool had been drained, filled with a framework of scaffolding, then covered with sheets of bile green marine plywood. At least fifty makeshift autopsy tables had been spread out over the new surface, and ranged around the perimeter of the covered pool were ranks of sawhorses, half of them set with loaded stretchers, their contents covered with everything from ragged blankets to newspaper. Only a very few of the remains had been put into rubberized shrouds like the one Stanislaw Rudelski had been found in.

Every one of the autopsy tables was in use, a dozen white-coated attendants moving up and down the rows, checking and tagging each body, followed by uniformed Civil Defense workers carrying wire baskets and harvesting personal effects. All of this was lit by a score of pan-lights dangling low over the tables on lengths of flex, the bright pools alive with a strange chalky haze of floating dust.

Squinting, Black spotted Spilsbury and Liddell in the far corner, standing over a standard-issue fiberboard casket raised on sawhorses. Spilsbury, his dark suit covered by a white lab coat, was watching as an attendant unscrewed the coffin lid. Liddell, in tweeds as usual, was standing to one side, smoking his pipe and staring upward.

Black stepped out onto the pool platform, his footsteps echoing dully. He made his way between the rows of tables, trying not to look at the displays of carnage to left and right, but betrayed by his peripheral vision.

A frail woman with a mass of snow-white hair and wearing a red cardigan, apparently uninjured but with bulging eyes that Black knew were the sign of death by massive compression shock.

The head of a man, covered in plaster dust and streaked with blood. Below the head a filthy, bloodstained shirt ending abruptly at the hips and below that nothing but a ghastly mess of white bone, torn flesh, and entrails.

The calm face of a sleeping girl, seventeen or so, lying on her side, but with her legs flat on the table, a hole in her chest so large that the glistening, bloody sheath covering her heart was visible.

Three infants sharing a single table, so mutilated as to be unrecognizable. A large man on his stomach, wearing the remains of a long nightshirt, head crushed almost flat, the flailed flesh of his back exposing the entire length of his spine.

A dust-covered bowler, half its brim torn away beside a large parcel bound in twine and leaking onto the table.

Black kept his eyes on the two figures ahead, breathing through his mouth in quick, short pants, feeling the cold sweat breaking out on his brow and refusing to give in to a growing feeling of reeling vertigo that was turning his legs to rubber and lead. This was no mortuary; this was a human abattoir. Gritting his teeth, he kept on.

He reached Spilsbury and Liddell just as the attendant removed the last screw in the lid of the plain gray coffin. The attendant stepped back and lifted up the wire and gauze mask that hung around his neck on a narrow rubber strap. Spilsbury and Liddell followed suit.

"Just in time," said Liddell, handing Black a mask of his own. Spilsbury turned to the detective, his eyes cold above the white gauze covering the lower half of his face.

"This is most irregular, Inspector Black. I've read over the records pertaining to this case. There is no doubt that the woman died of blast injuries and fire. A waste of valuable time." The pathologist waited for a response, but Black said nothing. He'd already spent hours convincing Liddell that the exhumation had been necessary, and he wasn't about to go over it again. He was already in a precarious position; in a few moments he would either be vindicated or proved utterly wrong. The detective put on the mask he'd been given by Liddell, and even through the cloying scent of the ointment in his nostrils, he could smell the sour-sweet odor of Dettol disinfectant.

Spilsbury waited for another long moment, then turned to the attendant and nodded. The man stepped forward and slid the top off the coffin, propping it against the nearest sawhorse. Spilsbury picked up a pair of surgical gloves from the table beside the coffin and snapped them on. Using a thumb and forefinger, he tipped his glasses up onto his forehead and leaned over the coffin, breathing deeply. Black saw that the pathologist had no telltale trace of white ointment around his nostrils.

Without turning, Spilsbury lifted one hand and gestured for Black and Liddell to join him. Black did so reluctantly, Liddell beside him. Knowing what he was about to see, the detective swallowed hard and forced his mind to become completely blank. He looked down into the narrow box containing the exhumed remains of the late Jane Luffington.

After being claimed by her mother, Jane Luffington's body had been taken to a funeral parlor and prepared for burial by way of a few simple procedures. The body was laid out, stripped, then washed with a mild water-and-alcohol solution. Following this, two long trocar needles were inserted in a parallel pair of veins and arteries in the groin, while a third needle was inserted into the umbilicus, piercing the stomach wall. Tubes were then attached to the needles, and a vacuum pump drained the body of blood and the contents of the abdominal cavity.

Since the coffin was to be closed during the burial ceremony, no attempt was made to enlarge the sunken eyesockets in the charred, ruined face, but in an effort to prevent too much gaseous odor from escaping, the mouth was filled with a plaster and linen plug, then stitched shut. The rectum and vagina were also sealed to prevent gas from seeping out, as well as any remaining body fluids.

After six weeks of decomposition, the body of Jane Luffington was covered with adipocere, a paraffin-like substance with the consistency of wet cheese and an unmistakable rancid odor. Huge speckled slabs of it were layered onto the remains of her face like lumps of clay, her breasts bloated with it, sagging off to either side like melted mutton fat, joining the multiple strata of maggot castings and insect husks on the bottom of the casket. Her legs had become immense tubes of the soaplike stuff, joined to a huge curving belly that had taken on the mocking appearance of pregnancy, the vaginal plug forced hermaphroditically out between her legs by the growing gases in her rotting gut.

The feet were blue-green sweetbreads; the hands, almost carbonized at the time of death, were nothing more than blackened claws. Here and there along the body, bone showed through; the cartilage at the joints was a jaundiced yellow, the bones themselves a grayish green beginning to turn brown. The only thing about the body that was even remotely human was the teeth, two perfect rows of them showing whitely, grinning up out of the burnt and blackened parody of her face, clamped down on the plaster and linen plug pushed into her mouth by the undertaker, the broken strands of cotton suture standing like catfish whiskers around the purpled, rotting orifice.

"Good Christ!" Liddell whispered from behind his mask. Beside him Morris Black said nothing.

"Normal rate of decay considering the length of time involved," Spilsbury murmured to himself. He glanced up at Black. "I gather that you think she was killed in the same way as the men I looked at."

"Yes, sir." Black nodded, his mouth unpleasantly full of saliva. He swallowed, lifting one hand to press the fabric of the mask against his nose, breathing in as much of the Dettol smell as he could stand. Fay had turned to this before she turned to dust and bones. For an instant he thought he was going to vomit.

"I'll have to turn her head." Spilsbury reached into the coffin, placed a gloved hand under each side of the jaw and twisted slowly. There was a damp, rotted sound, like old splitting cloth. Black closed his eyes for a moment and swallowed again.

Spilsbury leaned even farther forward, his spectacles threatening to drop off his forehead and into the casket. "Interesting," he said quietly.

Liddell cleared his throat weakly and then spoke. "You've found something, Sir Bernard?"

"Yes. A ligature mark." He raised a hand and waggled his fingers for the attendant. "The long forceps," he ordered. The man reached into the bag resting on the floor beside the pathologist and removed the gleaming tool. He put it into Spilsbury's upraised hand and stepped back again. Using the forceps, Spilsbury poked under the chin and jaw of the woman's head, digging deeply into the layers of the brownish, greasy adipocere. He twisted, then retracted the instrument, drawing up a long, thick, wormlike strand of fabric.

"What is it?" asked Black, his nausea overtaken by a growing fascination. The object in the casket was no longer human. It was evidence that might take him one step closer to Queer Jack.

"A length of fabric, twisted tightly into a rope. Silk. A scarf perhaps." Spilsbury held it up in the light. "Quite an odd knot."

"What do you mean?" Black asked.

"Some sort of complicated hitch with two running loops. I've never seen anything quite like it."

"A seaman? Someone in the Navy?" Liddell offered.

"Or a Boy Scout," Spilsbury said dryly. "A model-maker, even an electrician. Still it's odd. He could just as well have used a bowline, any sort of slipknot."

"Proud of his expertise?" said Black thoughtfully. "Could he be showing off?"

"I suppose that's possible."

"So she was strangled?" said Liddell.

"Not necessarily," Spilsbury replied. "The noose might have been used as a restraint."

"The other?" asked Black.

Spilsbury nodded, his interest piqued now, his irritation gone. "Just a moment." He put the forceps and the twisted length of silk down on the table and went back to the waxy remains in the coffin. He eased the head sharply to one side with his left hand firmly on the jaw, then reached under the neck with his right hand, searching blindly for the top of the spine with a long index finger. Finding it, he pushed into the transformed flesh, digging cautiously between the easily separated vertebrae.

"Anything?" said Black.

"Wait...there. Yes!" Spilsbury withdrew his hand from under the woman's neck. Using a pair of long tweezers, he poked into the hole, then withdrew the delicate tool. It now held a tiny, multiple-vaned object. Identical to the ones that had killed all four other victims.

"Well, I'm damned," said Liddell, staring at the vicious little instrument.

"I must apologize, Inspector," said Spilsbury, bowing slightly toward Morris Black. "You were quite right after all. She was murdered, just like the others."

The Number stood in the deeper pools of darkness offered by the spreading branches of the trees in St. Michael's Yard and watched the moon rise over the soaring spire of the cathedral. His first sight of it in the last of the daylight only a few hours before had been an epiphany, a moment of the purest truth, the completion of every anguished thought and moment that had brought him here. All fears and doubts had vanished in that instant. This was the hub of the wheel, a spike of holy stone at the center of the center, a dark sword uplifted to pierce the heavens.

He'd known the numbers would be perfect even before he bought the little shilling pamphlet from the hawker on Bayley Lane. Three hundred and one feet high from base to tip, the foot of the tower thirty-one feet on a side.

Staring up at it now, beams of light from the moon raking down through the thin, scudding clouds and cutting through the arched rows of windows, turning them to gold. The

Number could feel his heart expanding and the blood scouring through his veins like liquid fire.

Two months ago, after the Wren courier had discovered him pawing through her motorcycle panniers, he'd felt sure that his power had been taken from him. Her death and the false ritual of her sacrifice that had followed were nothing more than a mark of his failure—a humiliating mockery. Now he knew that it had been only an obstacle presented to test his determination and his resolve, a final skirmish before the real battle was finally joined.

It had been difficult, and more than once during the last eight weeks he'd thought of abandoning the task, admitting to the depth of his weakness and forfeiting himself to his demons, but in the end he had triumphed and found another path. This was his reward. The blinding truth that had eluded him for so long: his perfection would come only out of chaos, and from that chaos the partial would become complete.

He watched the moon, his guide and mirror. Like him, it lacked only a final sliver of light to become whole. Soon now the last would be revealed and he would know. All the world would know and he would find his perfect peace.

No detail had been overlooked. He'd arrived early that morning and gone to the proper address on Cherry Street in Radford, not far from the gasworks. He'd identified his quarry, then followed him to work on foot and by tram. He waited patiently until the day was over, then followed him home again, keeping a careful distance as they went along the ancient medieval streets and narrow byways.

In the early evening his chosen victim left the cramped little cottage on Cherry Street and went into the city once again, pausing briefly at a public house on Pond Street, then continuing on to the Gaumont Cinema.

They were showing the new American film *Gone With the Wind,* and sitting in the darkness, only two rows back from the man he would soon murder, The Number was astounded by the irony of it all as Atlanta burned, the leaping Technicolor flames destroying that earlier plague of sin and pestilence. Another omen, another subtle guide, telling him that his course was true.

By the time the film ended it was fully dark, but the depth of night and the blackout were overshadowed by the brilliant moon, and he'd had no difficulty following the man to the cathedral. More than an hour had passed since then, and it had taken all his strength to keep from following the man inside, to watch him as he practiced, or perhaps even to have introduced himself as a member of the Society, but that would have been a foolish risk.

Instead he stood beneath the trees, waiting, watching the moon and the low, scudding clouds, counting the ticking, turning moments, seeing the coming terrors in his mind's eye, knowing that each thing was as it should be, and knowing too that he was the linchpin of it all.

He brought out The Book, slipped the postcard out from between the leaves, compared it to the image confronting him, and smiled.

CHAPTER SIXTEEN

Wednesday, November 13, 1940
10:30 A.M., Greenwich Mean Time

WERNER STEINMAUR SAT RIGIDLY in the straight-backed chair and waited for the tribunal to begin. He was alone in the large room except for his escort, a uniformed corporal of the Royal Welsh Fusiliers seated by the door. The only other furniture consisted of a long wooden table and three office chairs with arms. A row of rain-streaked windows on the left looked out over Harris Promenade and Douglas Bay to the open Irish Sea. The Isle of Man. The camps.

They weren't camps at all, of course, not like the ones in Germany. Hotels and boardinghouses in the Manx towns of Douglas, Peel, and Ramsay had simply been expropriated for the duration, much to the delight of their owners, who'd depended on the tourist trade before the war and faced ruin without it. The food was good enough, better than he'd been able to get in Berlin, and later in France, and the company was stimulating, but one could attend only so many lectures, take only so many walks, before boredom set it. He shook his head; the British were a strange race. The internment camps were supposedly for "enemy aliens" of one kind or another—fifth

264

columnists who might sabotage Britain's war effort from within. In Hitler's Germany they would have starved and tortured such people—here they simply bored you to distraction.

He heard the muffled chattering of voices and then the door behind him opened. Footsteps creaked over the narrow-planked hardwood floor. For an instant he wondered if he was supposed to stand, but then it was too late. Two men and a woman took their places behind the table, barely glancing in his direction.

He realized how ridiculous he looked in his cheap blue suit: a narrow-shouldered man at the end of his youth, dark hair thinning away in a widow's peak, bony and pale, raw-knuckled hands gripping the arms of his chair nervously. Alien even to himself. What had happened to his life? What terrible joke had brought him here to this room in the Douglas Court House?

The woman, in her fifties, wore a long, dark blue skirt, a fitted jacket to match, and heavy-heeled black shoes. Her gray hair was pulled back tightly in a bun, and she wore dark-framed eyeglasses perched on her too large nose. Even from his position ten feet away, Steinmaur could see that her cheeks and chin were covered with fine downy hair.

The taller of the two men was also older, just short of retirement age. He was slim, clean-shaven, and hollow-cheeked with thick, heavily pomaded hair that was suspiciously dark for a man of his age. He had bushy eyebrows in need of trimming, and a straight-stemmed pipe was clamped between his teeth. The man had the hooded eyes of a predatory bird and long, thin-fingered hands. He was wearing a heavy tweed suit, a white shirt, and a dark green bow tie.

The other man was in his mid-thirties and wore a major's uniform without service insignia of any kind. He had a thin, neat mustache and carried a short leather riding crop in one hand, a swollen government-issue briefcase in the other. When he sat down, he placed his cap down on the table in front of him and laid the crop across it at an angle as though he were posing for a formal photograph.

The older man took the central position with the uniformed officer on his left and the woman on his right. The major leaned over and whispered something in the woman's ear. She nodded and then smiled politely, revealing two rows of very small teeth. Then the older man removed the pipe from his mouth and set it onto the heavy glass ashtray in front of him. The major leaned down, took out a thin file folder from his briefcase, and slid his cap and crop to one side. He flipped open the folder, examined the contents for a moment, then looked up at Steinmaur.

"My name is Major Hoyt. This is Inspector Cuthbert of Special Branch, and Mrs. Baldwin from the Prison Board. You are Werner Erich Steinmaur?"

"Yes."

"Age?"

"Thirty-two."

"You were born in Berlin?"

"Yes"

"You are a Jew?"

"My mother was a Jew. My father was Catholic. In Germany that makes you a Jew."

"According to our information, in 1932 you were a student at Freidrich-Wilhelm University."

"Yes. The Veterinary School on Luisenstrasse."

"You were training to be a veterinarian?"

"Yes."

"Is that where you learned your English?"

"Yes."

"You resigned from the school before graduation."

"I was a Jew. I was asked to leave."

"You went to work at St. Joseph's-Heilanstalt Lunatic Asylum?"

"Yes. In October 1934."

"What did you do there?"

"I was an orderly. It was the only work available to me. Mostly I cleaned toilets. Sometimes I would help with the inmates."

"Help?" asked the woman from the Prison Board.

"Many of them were incontinent. I sometimes helped to clean them up."

"I see," said the woman. Steinmaur doubted that very much. It was unlikely that she'd ever wiped the arse of a drooling, pissing woman in her seventies or stripped the reeking sheets from a score of beds each morning in the catatonic ward. He said nothing. The major took up the questioning again.

"How long did you work there?"

"Until September of the following year—1935."

"And then?"

"I left the country."

"Why?"

"My sister was raped by a group of *Jungbann*."

"*Jungbann*?"

"Boys between the ages of ten and fourteen. Too old to be *Pimpf*, too young to be *Hitler Jugend*."

"Ten-year-olds raped your sister?" asked Mrs. Baldwin. She didn't sound convinced.

"Yes. Seven of them. She was thirteen. When they were finished, they urinated and defecated on her. They wrote the words *Jiddische Sau* on her stomach in shit."

"*Jiddische Sau*?" asked Major Hoyt.

"Jewish pig."

"This caused you to leave the country?"

"After she was raped my sister committed suicide. My mother died less than a month later. I had no one left. I saw no reason to stay."

"Your father was already dead?"

"Yes. Several years before. He was gassed in the First War."

"We didn't use gas in the First War."

"The wind changed."

"Bad luck," said the major dryly.

"Yes."

"How did you leave Germany?"

"I purchased forged papers."

"Where did you go?"

"First to Switzerland, then France."

"You worked in France?"

"Yes. In Paris. I was a waiter at the Hotel Meurice for some time, then I worked on a farm outside of St.-Omer."

"Then you came to England?"

"Yes."

"You were sponsored by Dr. Franz Zimmerman of St. George's Hospital."

"Yes."

"How did you come to know Dr. Zimmerman?"

"He was a guest at the Meurice on several occasions. He took an interest in me. My situation. I wrote to him. He offered to sponsor me through the Refugee Association."

"He got you a job at the hospital."

"Yes. As an orderly."

"With your petition for release you included several other letters of recommendation."

"Yes."

"Miss Alice Derwent of the Red Cross Society, Dr. Menzer of the Jewish Refugees Society, Joan Rosenstock of the Association of Jewish Refugees in Britain."

"Yes."

"These are friends?"

"They are people I have written to." Steinmaur learned long ago that friendship was bought and sold like bread. The word meant nothing to him now.

"I see." The major plucked a pen from the breast pocket of his jacket and jotted something down on the file in front of him. Cuthbert, the Special Branch official, spoke for the first time.

"Herr Steinmaur?"

"Yes."

"Do you still consider yourself a German?"

"The Germany I knew no longer exists."

"Surely you don't consider yourself to be English," broke in Mrs. Baldwin from the Prison Board. She seemed appalled at the thought.

"I don't consider myself to be anything. At this point I have no country, no nationality." Steinmaur smiled. "Perhaps if the war goes on for long enough, I'll become a citizen of the Isle of Man by default." The members of the tribunal didn't seem amused.

"But you are still a Jew," said Cuthbert.

Steinmaur shrugged. "I suppose."

"You don't sound very sure," said Mrs. Baldwin.

Steinmaur thought for a long moment, wondering what the correct answer was. Presumably there was some right thing for him to say, but in the end he decided to tell the truth.

"Once I was very proud to be a Jew," he said slowly. "Then I was humiliated by my Jewishness. By the time I left Germany I was frightened of it."

"And now?" asked Cuthbert.

"Now I am tired of it. It is a burden I no longer wish to carry." There was a long silence. Finally the policeman spoke again.

"If your petition was granted, would you have any difficulty doing war work? Work which might harm people in your native country?"

"I would have no difficulty, no."

"You seem very sure."

"It was a question I knew would be asked. I've thought about it a great deal."

"What about the Auxiliary Military Pioneer Corps?" asked

the major. The AMPC was a revised version of the First World War Labor Corps. The Corps was made up of young, physically fit aliens willing to do noncombative work.

"I wouldn't make a very good soldier, I'm afraid."

"Farm work?" asked Cuthbert.

"I'd be better suited to it. Or to my old job at the hospital."

Major Hoyt closed his file folder and glanced at Cuthbert. The Special Branch officer nodded. Hoyt turned back to Steinmaur. "That will be all."

"When will I know about my petition?"

"In due time," the major answered. The tribunal was over.

Half an hour later Werner Steinmaur stood at the fence that ran along the promenade and stared out through the wire. Directly in front of him, just beyond the fence, was the tall, stone-block spike of the World War One Memorial. Beyond that, in the center of Douglas Bay and half-hidden by the squalling rain and mist, was Coniston Rock and the old tower lighthouse. After the rock there was only the sea and, somewhere in the distance, England.

Twenty feet behind him was the stone-porticoed entrance to the Flora, one of a score of private hotels that ran along the oceanfront in a single, unbroken row. It contained thirty rooms on five floors, each room curtained off into four cubicles smaller than the average prison cell.

Two of the other men who shared his fourth-floor room were smokers, and Shulman, the elderly Potsdamer who had operated a greengrocers in Birmingham until the internment, had terrible gas. Everything in Steinmaur's cubicle reeked of cabbage farts and tobacco. He preferred the promenade, even in the rain.

Standing at the fence with its high, inward-slanting shelf of barbed wire, Steinmaur watched the pewter-tinted sea and sky and wondered if his petition would be granted. Four hours away by ferry there was freedom, or something approximating it. He would take the train from Liverpool back to

London, find himself rooms, then begin his search for the right person to tell what he knew, to trade his secret knowledge for a future.

It certainly wasn't Cuthbert from Special Branch or Major Hoyt or the hairy-faced Mrs. Baldwin. They were nothing more than guardians at the gate. He needed someone with far more power and influence than they had to offer.

He thought about the face that haunted him. Steinmaur, no longer able to continue his studies, had been working at the Berlin Asylum when he'd first seen the man. Handsome, dark-haired, large hazel eyes ringed with gold. Seven years ago; a lifetime. He'd been wearing a doctor's white coat and he'd been speaking perfect, Austrian-accented German to his two companions. Steinmaur knew him only as *Der Wahlmann*, The Chooser, the man who selected the victims for Hoche's experiments.

Herr Doktor Alfred Hoche was the second man in the group he'd seen that day, a consulting psychiatrist at the asylum and author of *The Granting of Permission for the Destruction of Worthless Life, Its Extent and Form*. That vile little document was Hoche's vicious credo, a justification for the murder and sterilization of anyone he, or the Reich, deemed unfit to join in the Fuhrer's thousand-year experiment.

The other man with Hoche and The Chooser was equally recognizable: Reinhard Heydrich, the young, hawk-faced, newly appointed leader of the SD, the National Socialist Party's Secret Service, Himmler's *Wenig-Schatz*, his Little Pet.

Pushing gray water across the floor with his mop, Steinmaur had done his best to make himself invisible to the small group of men, but he couldn't help picking up smatterings of their conversation as they strolled slowly past. From what Steinmaur could tell, the three men were discussing a technological breakthrough in the business of extermination. One of Heydrich's people had come up with a plan to use carbon monoxide gas chambers for the disposal of Hoche's "worthless lives." A prototype gas chamber was to be set up at the asylum. Head bent over his mop, Steinmaur had felt the bile rise in his throat as they discussed the gas chamber's hypothetical efficiency rate. They might just as well have been talking about garbage.

The Chooser had made several comments about the proposed gas chamber and even brought up the possibility of making the devices mobile. Heydrich had been intrigued by the idea. Then the three had gone out of earshot. A week later Steinmaur had been transferred to the crematorium adjacent to the asylum; he never saw The Chooser again.

Until four months ago, as he rotted away in the filth at the Huyton Camp on the outskirts of Liverpool.

At first he didn't believe it. The Chooser was in British uniform now, one of a dozen in a party of officials on a tour of the facilities. Keeping his distance, Steinmaur had followed the group as they meandered through the camp, watching the uniformed man. After half an hour there was no doubt in his mind—it was the same man. A little older now, traces of gray at the temples, the features harder with the passing of time, but the same.

A handsome man in a white coat blandly discussing methods of mass murder with a high-ranking Nazi seven years before suddenly appears in the uniform of a Royal Medical Corps captain, taking a tour of an English internment camp. It didn't seem possible, but it was true.

Instead of going to the authorities at Huyton, Steinmaur decided to hold his tongue. Who was going to listen to the absurd suspicions of an interned Jew? Better to bide his time until he had formulated some reasonable plan of action.

In the end, of course, it all depended on the right explanation. Over the last few months he'd come up with half a dozen, none of which really fit the facts. It was barely possible that the man he'd seen at the asylum was a doppelganger mirror image of the medical officer at Huyton, or that he was some sort of agent sent to Berlin by British intelligence years before the war, but both ideas were far-fetched.

Even in fiction doppelgangers rarely shared the same profession, and it was hard to believe the British had been so farsighted about world events that they'd inserted a spy into the Nazi medical-military establishment almost a decade ago.

Steinmaur eventually came to the conclusion that the simplest explanation was probably the most likely. Heydrich was now head of Nazi intelligence, a spymaster in the business of employing spies. Hoche was a psychiatrist and clearly a friend of Heydrich's. The third man seemed to know both of the others well. Ergo, the third man, now wearing the uniform of a British medical officer, was both a psychiatrist and a spy. At the very least he was a doctor with a highly questionable past.

It was madness of course, a nightmarish conundrum: he was an interned German Jew, officially under suspicion, and by decree a man not to be trusted. Who would believe his story about an English psychiatrist being a Nazi spy? No one, of course. Not unless he had proof, or a sympathetic ear.

Werner Steinmaur put his hands up onto the cold wire of the fence, running them along it until they touched the sharp, rusted barbs. He pushed the tip of his left index finger against one of the twisted hooks and watched as a small crimson bead of blood appeared, bright against the monochrome background of the sea and sky.

He felt the sting of salt spray bite into the tiny wound, and he brought the finger to his mouth, sucking on it thoughtfully. He still had that small truth, even here in this godforsaken hole in the universe; Jew, German, or internee, when pricked, he bled like any other man. He was alive, but that wasn't enough. He wouldn't wait for the tribunal to decide his fate. It was time to act.

Police Constable Swift found a tiny parking spot between two cars on Grafton Street and deftly inserted the Ruby into the narrow gap. Yawning, Morris Black climbed out of the Austin and stood waiting on the pavement while his assistant locked up the vehicle. It was strangely quiet. The detective frowned, then suddenly realized what was wrong—for the first time in weeks the sirens were quiet; there was no alert. The weather was damply cold and the sky was overcast, but that wouldn't stop the bombers. Perhaps they'd run out of ammunition.

Black yawned again, hearing his jawbone crack. He hadn't finished at Westminster Baths until the small hours of the morning, and even then he'd found it difficult to sleep, his mind filled with morbid images of Jane Luffington's waxy, disintegrating corpse, his nostrils filled with the reek of camphor. He'd had other thoughts as well, of Fay, of Katherine Copeland. Of the past and the future, the pointlessness of a life he knew was only half-lived. He'd even considered leaving the Yard, but only briefly. Right now it was the only thing that seemed to give him purpose. Perhaps that was more than he had any right to hope for in a world being torn apart by war.

Leaving his flat shortly after eight o'clock this morning, he'd gone to a prearranged meeting with Liddell at the MI5 offices located midway between Boodles and Whites on St. James's Street only a few blocks away, just south of Piccadilly.

The conference had been a short one and consisted of a single order from the head of B Division: although the exhumation and autopsy of the Wren motorcycle courier had revealed the first direct connection between Queer Jack and Ultra, Black was to ignore this and concentrate solely on Liddell's phantom agent-in-place, presumably the man responsible for the two deaths at the Zoological Gardens. Liddell gruffly explained the abrupt change in assignment by telling Black that he was being pressured by Sir David Petrie, the newly appointed director general of MI5 and his hired "efficiency expert," the ubiquitous Mr. Horrocks, who was making life miserable for everyone.

If Black wasn't able to resolve the case in the very near future, the special investigative unit would be dissolved and the Scotland Yard detective would find himself in professional limbo, unable to return to his old job for security reasons, yet barred from continuing his investigation of the Queer Jack murders for want of authority and budget.

Adding depressing insult to an already grievous injury, Black had been confronted by a message from Katherine Copeland when he finally reached his attic office on Kensington Park Gardens. She had some new information about the photograph and wanted to discuss it with him. She would be waiting for him at her flat. If he didn't show up, she would assume that he wasn't interested and she would then make public use of the information, presumably in her newspaper. The detective was furious; the message was almost a threat of blackmail.

The only bright spot in the day had come from Police Constable Swift. At long last he'd managed to track down the only London merchant dealing in Rodolpho Verlicchi pen nibs—Asprey's on Old Bond Street. Black grasped at the small, floating shard of information like a drowning man.

"Strewth!" Swift whispered, eyes widening as they entered the lavish store. "Not half-posh then, is it, sir?" The man's usual military aplomb had vanished under the onslaught of Asprey's decor and contents. The shop, if it could reasonably be called a shop at all, was long and narrow, stretching from Grafton Street halfway down the block toward Stafford Street. The carpeting beneath their feet was a deep, rich green, the walls half-paneled in ancient oak, heavily varnished. The lighting was bright and welcoming, which was necessary since the natural light from the display windows was blocked by a series of heavy wooden shutters.

Rows of mahogany and glass cabinets marched around the perimeter and down the center of the main hall, each apparently given over to its own theme. Trinkets in gold and silver, Rolex, Piaget, and Patek Philippe wristwatches, antique clocks, traveling clocks, grandfather clocks, clocks in bell jars, and clocks chiming everything from Big Ben to the "Wedding March."

Candlesticks, tea and coffee services, salvers, bowls, and table decorations for pheasant and partridge. A veritable menagerie of creatures in crystal, gold, silver, and ceramic: lions, tigers, cheetahs, leopards, elephants, and giraffes. Birds carved from crystal malachite and amethyst. Kingfishers with ruby eyes hovering over agate ponds with sheet gold lilies.

Shelves of picnic ware, more shelves of silver-backed hair-brushes, crocodile toilet cases, ostrich-skin wallets, decanters, wineglasses, silver goblets, chessboards made from jade and ebony, gameboards of every kind, bone-handled umbrellas, silver-tipped walking sticks...all of it watched over by slow-stepping gentlemen in morning suits, one of whom approached them seconds after they stepped in through the door.

He spoke directly to Morris Black. "May I be of service?" Police Constable Swift, dressed in his usual badly fitted suit, was ignored entirely.

"Pens," said Black. The sheer volume of the goods in the store was giving him a headache. It seemed absurd; butter, cheese, and eggs were under ration, but at Asprey's there seemed to be no shortage of cabochon sapphire money clips or solid-gold cigar cutters. It was the sort of place that would have turned Dick Capstick apoplectic with the fury of a long-time Labour Party convert. Black smiled at the thought; given enough time and a few traumatic visits to Asprey's, Capstick might even become a Communist.

"Do you mean writing instruments?" asked the gray-haired attendant. The man had the look of a mortician and a strained vocabulary that went along with his adopted public-school accent.

Black nodded. He let himself fall into the flat, classless monotone of the working policeman. After the night he'd had, the detective was in no mood for this. "That's it," he said bluntly.

"Was there any sort of instrument you were particularly interested in?"

"Ones with Rodolpho Verlicchi nibs."

"In gold or silver, sir?" Not so much as an arched eyebrow.

"Gold."

"Ah." The attendant nodded. "If you'd be so good as to follow me, sir." The man bowed slightly, then turned away, leading Black and Police Constable Swift down to a large display cabinet along the far wall. Black bent over the case. A hundred different fountain pens were laid out on a spotlessly clean field of purple velvet. "As you can see," said the attendant, "we have quite a varied selection: H. A. Smith pearl and abalone, Aiken-Lambert repoussé, Waterman sterling, Crocker, Carey, Montblanc, Cross."

"Which ones use the Verlicci nibs?"

"None of them," the attendant answered blandly. "The Verlicchi nibs are only used in Penna Nettuno."

"Do you have any in stock?"

"I'm afraid not." The attendant cleared his throat. "Nettuno is an Italian company. Under the present circumstances we are not in a position to offer them for sale." He frowned at the effrontery of it; how dare Il Duce interfere with Asprey's sources of supply.

"The nibs?"

"We have some, yes."

"For previous customers."

"Quite so."

"Show them to me."

"For which Nettuno pen?"

"I'm not sure."

"There are several different types. If I knew which pen the nib was for..."

"Let's cut to the chase shall we?" Black turned to his assistant. "Swift?"

"Yes, sir."

"The nib."

"Yes, sir." Swift reached into the pocket of his suit coat and took out a small glass specimen jar. Inside the packet was the pen nib that had been removed from the Swedish courier's cerebral cortex. The end of the nib was bent and separated, and small pieces of human tissue were still clotted in the narrow slot. Swift gave the bottle to Black, who then placed it carefully on the glass top of the display case.

"Dear me," the attendant murmured, staring warily at the bottle. "May I ask..."

"It's evidence," Black explained flatly. "In a murder investigation. The murder weapon, as a matter of fact. The gray bits of meat are from the dead man's brains. Might be a bit of his eyeball floating about in there as well."

The attendant's eyes bulged and his pale cheeks flushed with sudden color. "You're with the police?"

"That's right." Black took out his warrant card and showed it to the man. The attendant nodded nervously and stared down at the bottle again. Black picked it up, holding the container to the light. "Familiar?"

The attendant swallowed. "Penna Nettuno makes several models of the fountain pen. The Nettuno a Serbatoio, an early eyedropper fill, the Nettuno Superba, and most recently the Nettuno Docet."

"Which would this fit?" asked Black, extending the hand holding the bottle. The attendant took a step backward, almost overturning a display of custom-made golf trophies.

"The Serbatoio used German findings," said the frightened man. "Nibs, guilloches, clips. And the nibs were retractable." He cleared his throat. Black put the bottle down on the counter and the man relaxed visibly. "The Docet probably uses a Verlicchi, but I can't be certain. It most probably came from a Superba."

"How many does Asprey's sell in a year?"

"I couldn't say positively. Twenty or so."

"Pricey are they?"

"They are quite expensive, yes."

"How many in the last five years?"

"Sixty. Perhaps a hundred."

"And they would all use Verlicchi nibs like the one in the bottle?"

"Yes."

"How long does a nib like this last?"

"With normal usage"—the attendant looked quickly down at the bottle and then back at Black—"several years at least."

"If someone wanted to replace the nib, he'd have to purchase it here, is that correct?"

"Yes." The attendant cleared his throat again and looked out over Black's shoulder, perhaps vainly searching for some sort of relief from his interrogation. "But I can see from your...specimen, that part of the barrel has broken off with the nib. The entire pen would have to be replaced."

Black nodded again and allowed himself a momentary smile. The man's obvious discomfort was acting like a tonic on his headache. Cruel and childish perhaps, but true nonetheless. "Do you have a list of customers for the Superba?" he asked finally.

"Certainly," the attendant said proudly. "We have an index of all our clients and their requirements."

"Good. I'd like to see it."

"I'm afraid that would be impossible."

"Oh? And why is that?"

"Customer information is strictly confidential."

"Not in this case."

"The index is classified by name, not item," insisted the attendant weakly. "To find out the names of our customers who have purchased a Nettuno Superba would require going through the entire list."

"A long list, is it?"

"Some two thousand names."

"Then we'd best get at it then, don't you think?" Beside Black, Police Constable Swift let out an expressive sigh of resignation. He knew perfectly well there would be no "we" about going through the list.

"I'll have to consult Mr. Asprey about this," the attendant muttered gloomily. Presumably Mr. Asprey would not be pleased at the intrusion into his affairs and those of his clientele.

Black smiled pleasantly. "By all means. Consult away." A quarter of an hour later, Swift, the attendant, and a score of large, leather-bound ledgers had been installed in a small office on the second floor of Asprey's, and Morris Black was making his way down to the Bond Street underground station on Piccadilly. He'd kept his promise to Liddell; now it was time to turn his attention elsewhere.

CHAPTER SEVENTEEN

Wednesday, November 13, 1940
7:00 P.M., Greenwich Mean Time

TIMING HIS ARRIVAL TO COINCIDE with the evening shift change, The Number made his way along the gloomy length of Little Britain, concentrating on his counted footsteps and the job ahead, ignoring the gritty Italianate and neo-Gothic façades of the buildings close around him, his fingers tightly gripping the satchel-like briefcase. The street was almost empty; work in The City was over for the day, and there would be no deliveries to the Smithfield markets until dawn.

Laggards from Olney-Amsden, the haberdashers, and nurses from the blue-curtained confines of St. Mary's Nursing Home were probably enjoying a pint or two in places like the White Horse at Cross Keys Square, celebrating the surprising lack of raids during the day and wondering if the night would be equally free of them as well.

In the dying light it could have been the London of Dickens or Conan Doyle: Wren's soaring spires looking down on the slate roofs and crumbling chimney pots of soot-stained, crowded offices; Tiny Tim hopping on his crutch down winding alleys that dated back to Roman times with Bob Cratchit at his side; Holmes and Watson on this very street, solving the problem of the Red-Headed League, Moriarty's minions lurking in every shadowed doorway.

The Number saw none of this, felt nothing of the history. To him the narrow byways and broader avenues were the veins and arteries of the beast that had to be vanquished at any price, the filthy pathways leading to the creature's terrible beating heart, its very soul.

Reaching the bleak Esterman and Eggington warehouse, he turned onto the broader reaches of King Edward Street. Ahead, a massive shadow in the dusky light, was the dome of St. Paul's, barely visible beyond the imposing Portland stone cliffs of the General Post Office headquarters. Heart pounding, The Number kept his eyes downcast and continued on.

He turned in at the main entrance of the GPO and went through the heavy doors. After showing his Standard Telephone and Cables identification to the dozing commissionaire at the receiving desk, he crossed the echoing, marble-floored lobby and made his way through the forest of soaring columns to the service lifts, joining the throngs of postal workers from the lower sorting halls who had just completed their shifts, mingling easily with the new shift coming on.

He rode down through half a dozen levels, eventually arriving at the maintenance floor above the huge shafts leading down to the platform of the automatic railway. Ignoring the frighteningly small cages of the open shaft elevators, he took the spiral, wrought-iron staircase bolted to the exterior of the auxiliary shaft and clattered even deeper below the ground. Through the sheet-metal walls of the shaft he could hear the thumping sounds of the heavy mailbags tumbling down the delivery chute.

Finally reaching the bottom of the staircase, he stepped out onto the brightly lit platform. A score of workers dressed in GPO coveralls were busy loading bags from the chutes onto a waiting train. The electrified trains, drawn by a small, remotely operated engine standing about five feet high, consisted of two and sometimes three cars, each one carrying four dustbinlike mail containers capable of holding fifteen bags of letter mail or six bags of parcels.

Waiting in the shadows of the stairway entrance, The Number watched as the train was loaded. When the loading was almost finished, he stepped forward, waved casually at no one in particular, and stepped onto a small metal platform at the end of the last car.

According to postal regulations, workers weren't supposed to ride the trains, but everyone did it and no one paid him any attention. A few seconds later the train jerked and then drew away from the loading platform smoothly, heading into the dark, low-ceilinged tunnel, gradually gathering speed until it was moving through the blackness at almost forty miles per hour.

The Postal Railway, the only one of its kind in the world, connected London's main postal stations and carried thirty thousand mailbags on forty of the little trains through more than six miles of tunnels.

Of the eight "stations" on the miniature line, three were key—King Edward Street, Mount Pleasant, and Paddington Station. From the GPO headquarters the subterranean conduit led north under Farringdon Road, split at Mount Pleasant to service Euston Station, St. Pancras Station, and the Northern District, with a secondary line tunneling south to the West Central District Post Office at High Holborn and Oxford Street and continuing to the South Western District Office at Victoria Station. The tunnels and platforms also provided a routing for the GPO's system of telephone, teleprinter, and telegraph cables, which were carried in thick, paper-wrapped bundles that dangled from the ceiling directly over The Number's head.

It took less than five minutes for him to go the distance from King Edward Street to High Holborn. Here he climbed off and made his way into the maze of crossovers, dead-ended "stabling tunnels" for unused cars, repair workshops, and tightly curved turnarounds. Once again he was completely ignored; the Standard Telephone and Cables uniform was both a passport and a cloak of invisibility.

As well as being a stop on the Postal Railway, High Holborn was also the junction of the cable network servicing Whitehall's Federal, or 333 Exchange, bringing together the telephone, telegraph, and teleprinter circuits of every government department, linking them by a single cable conduit to the Faraday International Exchange located in one of the GPO buildings at King Edward Street and St. Martin's-le-Grand.

The teleprinter cables, all of the new "coaxial" type, were color-coded: blue for Admiralty, green for War Office, white for the Air Ministry. Secure cables for each of the main ministries were red, with an identifying color band every few yards along the way.

"Secure" was a misnomer, the security of the cable coming only from its exclusivity. Most cable lines carried from eighteen to forty signals, but the red conduits carried only one signal, protected from potential "cross-talk" by two concentric conductors insulated by layers of acetylated cotton yarn. Theoretically this provided absolute security from either signal interference or eavesdropping.

There was nothing really secure about the cables at all, of course, since it was a simple enough task to break into the line at any point and add a secondary outlet in series with the main cable to pirate the signal. This caused a slight drop in current along the line, but it was easy enough to disguise by using a compensating resistor on the secondary outlet and adding a small dry-cell battery to boost the current on the output end of the corrupted circuit.

The Number had done just that. Two weeks before, he had traced the Air Ministry cable leading into the conduit connected to the Faraday Exchange. He'd cut into the line, added his own cable, and threaded it into an ordinary bundle of telephone cables using the same narrow passageway, then run it back to a small, low-ceilinged storage shed built into a niche along the tunnel wall.

The shed, secured with a large brass Post Office lock, appeared not to have been used for several years, and he assumed that it was a leftover from the construction of the Holborn-Faraday link several years before. He removed the padlock with a hacksaw, replaced it with a lock of his own, and began transporting his equipment to the shed over a period of several days.

Pausing at the entrance to the cable tunnel, he looked back the way he'd come but saw nothing but the receding line of lights strung at intervals from the ceiling. Distantly he could hear the humming whine of the railway engines, but there was nothing else; he was alone.

He ducked low and went down the tunnel, edging between the metal-strapped bundles of cable suspended from the walls. Time was already taking its toll here; damp, calcified stalactites were beginning to form in the curving concrete ceiling overhead, building drop by drop from the beads of mineral-rich moisture squeezing through the tunnel seams and joints. In fifty years the passageway would be impassable.

Pausing for a moment, he reached out one hand and pushed it in between the cable bundles until his splayed fingers touched the rough wall of the tunnel. He closed his eyes, listening to the count of his heart, whispering the numbers, feeling the deep, rhythmic pulse of the earth itself, groaning under the catastrophic weight of the city overhead. Soon there would be release.

He continued down the tunnel until he reached the storage shed. Unlocking it, he stepped inside, squeezing around the rudely organized equipment. Reaching upward, he found the battery-operated railway lamp he'd hung from the roof and switched it on, flooding the coffinlike chamber with light.

The Number squinted, checking the small ammeter he'd wired into the cable circuit, and nodded to himself. The impedance on the cable shunt from the Air Ministry tele-printer was being matched exactly; as far as anyone else was concerned, the circuit was unbroken, stretching virginally from the Ultra cryptanalysts at Bletchley Hall, sixty miles away, to Air Ministry Communications Headquarters, deep beneath Horse Guards Avenue in Whitehall.

The device filling up the tiny room was an altered Stearns differential duplex telegraph system modified to combine with a standard government teleprinter and brought in piece by piece over a period of many days. The modified Stearns sys-tem employed a relay wound with two sets of coils, which allowed current flow in opposite directions.

Combined as it was with an ordinary telegraphic repeater, the machine stole the Bletchley signal, shunted it onto the secondary length of coaxial cable, and ran it through the teleprinter, simultaneously printing out the messages and re-peating the signal, sending it back down the same cable and into the main circuit after a slight current boost to match the signal strength. In essence the system was the telegraphic ver-sion of a telephone extension set. A variation of the same device had been developed at Dollis Hill some time before and was now being used by Special Branch to tap into a selection of diplomatic telephone lines in London, including those of the Soviet embassy.

The hopper under the teleprinter unit was filled almost to overflowing, but The Number wasted no time reading through the day's accumulation of signals. Counting anx-iously under his breath, he tore the upper end of the paper roll across the serrated blade behind the teleprinter platen, gathered up the signals, and stuffed them into his satchel. He reset the paper, threading it under the blade and down to the hopper, checked the ammeter again, then straightened. By his perfect count he had less than three minutes to get back to the Holborn platform and catch the next train on its return circuit to King Edward Street.

If he missed it, there would be a seven-minute wait—much too long to spend on the Holborn platform, which was half the size of the one at GPO headquarters. Missing the train would also constitute an unacceptable failure in his calculations, and the thought of it made small beads of sweat spring up at his forehead and along his jaw.

Even such a small mistake meant punishment, and that was almost too terrible to think about. In his mind's eye he could see the waiting, locked, blank door leading to the third-floor rooms of his mother's house, and he made a small mewling sound as he fumbled with the satchel catch.

Securing it at last, he turned out the battery light, backed out of the enclosure, and locked the door behind him. Counting carefully, fear-flecks of spittle gathering at the corners of his mouth, he scuttled quickly down the passage, back the way he'd come.

Number 5 Bentinck Street in Bloomsbury was a five-story Queen Anne town house identical to its neighbors. Visibly, the block-long street connecting Marylebone Lane to Welbeck Street had changed little in two hundred years. By all appearances it was still very much an enclave of the wealthy, the brickwork scrubbed each year, wrought-iron fences painted black, brass bell pushes on white doorframes brightly polished

Time had taken its toll, however; the houses, once the private London pieds-à-terre of the ruling class, had long ago been broken into flats for civil servants and BBC employees, who liked them for their convenient location only a dozen blocks or so south of Broadcasting House. Marylebone Lane, once the winding main street of the original parish, had been almost totally rebuilt since the previous war and was now home to dozens of family shops and a seemingly endless supply of Italian restaurants.

Number 5 Bentinck Street, which housed the offices of the *London Practitioner* magazine on its upper floors, had been purchased only the year before by Lord Victor Rothschild, supposedly as an investment. Rothschild, a Cambridge graduate in sciences, had given over his mansion off Park Lane for government use at the beginning of the war and now lived with his wife and children at the Dorchester Hotel, but according to one of Charles Tennant's patients, the real reason Rothschild had purchased the house had been to house his mistress, Theresa Major, in the basement flat along with her old school friend, Patricia Rawdon-Smith, who, it seemed, was also amorously involved with a member of the peerage.

Standing in a far corner of the living room in the large, low-ceilinged apartment, Tennant now knew what his talkative patient had meant when he described the Bentinck Street flat as a high-class male brothel.

Guy Burgess, from whom Tennant had managed to cadge an invitation, was seated at the grand piano in the opposite corner of the room, dressed in a pale green silk dressing gown over matching pajamas, plump fingers giving a tinkling accompaniment to Perry Como singing "Prisoner of Love" on the phonograph. Seated beside him, but facing into the room, was a very young man with long blond hair dressed in a cream-colored suit and expensive-looking Italian shoes in dark blue leather.

To the right of the piano, seated in a grouping of astonishingly ornate Napoleon III carved, gilt-wood chairs, were three men, all in their late twenties or early thirties, dressed in evening clothes, talking earnestly together. From where he was standing it looked to Tennant as though the chairs were upholstered in some sort of hideous Aubusson tapestry in shades of red, green, pink, and beige.

Another man, his back to Tennant, was standing at a row of bookcases behind the Aubusson chairs, leafing through a slim, leather-bound volume and smoking a cigarette in a long ebony holder. Every few seconds he tossed his head elegantly, then looked around the room to see if anyone was watching.

A dozen other men and women, almost all of them young and dressed stylishly, were milling about in the center of the room, chattering brightly, drinking, laughing loudly, and striking an ever-shifting assortment of poses ranging from Isadora Duncans languorously holding on to the pale pink marble fireplace mantel to latter-day Oscar Wildes like the one at the bookcase.

Across from the fireplace, against the far wall, another half dozen guests were seated on a matched set of Biedermeier sofas upholstered in yellow shot silk, while others lounged on luxurious chairs of high historical pedigree. An absurd youth with obviously dyed, carrot-colored hair, wearing a short, black cloak. A tiny man with thinning dark hair, half-hidden by a huge potted plant, watching the partygoers with large, wary eyes. A man in wrinkled seersucker, mouse-brown hair sweat-plastered across his forehead, asleep, mouth gaping, thick spectacles balanced on the oily red tip of his bulbous nose.

A variety of foods, mostly cakes of one sort or another, were laid out on a long dining table next to Tennant, and drinks were being served from the shelf of an enormous 16th-century burled-mahogany secretaire on the far side of the fireplace.

Sipping his small sherry, Tennant felt the beginnings of a splitting headache begin to clamp like a spring-steel band around his temples. The overall effect of the room was grotesque, the voices and the laughter tinged with the hysteria of an asylum. He'd hoped to meet Liddell here tonight, or at least see him, but the cello-playing MI5 man hadn't made an appearance. It was time to go. Coming here had been an utter waste of time.

On the far side of the room dimly seen through the smoke haze, Burgess had begun to sing along with the gramophone record, his heavy tenor washing over the recording as he edged along the piano bench, his broad, fleshy buttocks in the silk robe pressing against the thigh of his much younger seatmate. In the middle of the song, Burgess, smiling dreamily, turned on the bench, leaned to one side, and pressed his lips into the curve of the young man's neck. Sighing, Tennant put his glass down on the table to his left and prepared to leave. He'd had more than enough of 5 Bentinck Street and its decadent, dandified troglodytes.

He had a brief, surreal vision of Heydrich standing in the center of the room and almost burst out laughing. Heydrich, the imperious Spartan, psychopathic demigod of a new race, the quintessence of the *Übermensch,* versus Guy Burgess, Etonian mud lark, Milquetoast booby squatting in this millionaire's nest, leader of an army of peroxide street pickups, pimps, and ponces. There was no doubt who the victor would be.

A woman standing at the table was looking at him very directly. She took a sliver of cake from a silver tray on the table and popped it into her mouth, still staring. She looked to be about twenty-one or two, not pretty, but attractive, high-cheeked, strong-chinned, and broad-mouthed. The large, staring eyes were hazel, the bobbed, slightly waved hair a glorious, coppery auburn that seemed to be natural. She was the same height as Tennant, slim and small-breasted, wearing a black velvet skirt and a white silk blouse. At least a dozen Gypsy bangles were on her narrow wrists. Long legs ended in small feet enclosed prettily in black patent Lilywhites with velvet bows and high, block heels.

"You don't look as though you belong," she said, speaking around the cake. She swallowed, then licked her fingers delicately.

Tennant shrugged. "I don't feel as though I belong."

"Then why are you here?"

"I was invited."

"One doesn't necessarily go where one is invited." The accent was somewhere out of London, but educated.

"I was curious."

"We all know what that did to pussy," she said coyly.

"I'm not pussy."

"So who are you then?"

"My name is Tennant. Charles Tennant."

"Caroline Pope-Hennessy. My friends call me Poppet. What do your friends call you?"

"Charles." He smiled.

"Well, Charles, which of them invited you, Guy or Tony?"

"Burgess. I don't even know who Tony is."

"Tony Blunt," Poppet said, nodding toward the small group in the chairs by the bookcase. "He's the horsey-faced one with his hands on Donald's knee. Trying to get him into bed again by the looks of it. Keeps on telling him he's the reborn essence of the Pre-Raphaelites or some such nonsense. Good bloody luck to him!" Tennant nodded; he remembered Maclean now—a "promising" man at the Foreign Office he'd been introduced to once at Whites.

Beside him the young woman frowned. "Close friend of Guy's, are you?"

"Not really. We've met once or twice."

"Oh, good." Poppet sounded relieved.

"You don't like him?"

"I think he's a dear, but if you're a friend of Guy's, that probably means you don't like girls very much, which means I shan't be able to go to bed with you."

"I see." Tennant smiled. She was trying very hard to shock.

"You're not a Jew are you?"

"No, why?"

"I've never been to bed with a Jew. I've thought about going to bed with Victor, but he's not here, and anyway, he's all in a dither about Tess, so I suppose I should just forget about it. Mind you, I've never been to bed with a black man either. Perhaps I should try that."

"Sorry to disappoint you. On both counts."

"If you're not a Jew, then what are you?"

"Church of England, if I'm anything at all."

Poppet shook her head. She swayed slightly, clearly a little drunk. "No, I mean what is it that you do? Everyone else here is either an unemployed actor or works with the rest of us at the Circus."

"The Circus?"

"BSS, MI5, whatever you like."

"You're a spy?"

"Secretary, actually. I model at Harrods at the weekends, though. Ladies' wear and undergarments."

"Ah."

"You still haven't answered my question."

"I'm a psychiatrist. From time to time I vet new applicants for the Circus as you call it."

"Freud was a psychiatrist wasn't he?" Poppet blinked.

"Yes."

"And a Jew as well."

"Yes. But it's not a prerequisite to join the profession."

"It doesn't matter." She smiled brightly. "I've never gone to bed with a psychiatrist either." There was a loud piano flourish from the far side of the room, and Burgess began to sing again. "Oh, Christ!" Poppet groaned. "It's drinking songs now! Next it'll be limericks."

"I really should be going," said Tennant. Burgess hooted on, describing Abdul A-Bul-Bul's confrontation with Ivan Skivinsky Skavar and his Muscovite maid. By the time he'd reached the next verse, the rest of the room had taken up the chorus.

"I think I'll come along," said Poppet, slipping her arm under Tennant's. "All the singing is going to wake up Muggeridge, and Tony will get into another of his arguments with him about why sweet little Kenny Clark is National Gallery director and he isn't. Puts me right to sleep. All Malcolm wants to do is feel superior." She looked brightly up at Tennant. "Where shall we go, then?"

They took a cab through the empty streets to Piccadilly and the Ritz Hotel, Poppet commenting on how quiet it was without the ack-ack pounding away, and how dark without the twisting, brilliant beams of the searchlight batteries next door in Green Park. The bar at the hotel was almost empty at that time of night, even without the threat of a raid.

"Do you do dreams?" asked Poppet, one long nail tracing a line of condensation down the glass holding her gimlet. "Interpret them, I mean?"

"I have done," Tennant admitted. "I'm not sure I give them as much importance as Dr. Freud, though."

"I have one quite often."

"The same one?"

"Umm." She nodded, sipping her drink. "I'm being followed about in the garden of my parents' house by a dead male torso. Nude, I'm afraid, all waxy. The head is on, but I can't tell who it is. It stumps about on its knees because the legs are all folded up behind."

"Is that the extent of it?"

"No. After a bit I notice that I'm stumbling over things in the grass as I go along, and then I realize that I'm tripping on bits and pieces of the dead body. It's rotting away you see, shedding like a snake, ears, fingers, nose. The worst is when the cock falls off. Rather a large one and very pink. That's when I scream and wake up."

"It doesn't sound much like a woman's dream."

"Well, no," Poppet agreed, her expression serious. "That's what bothers me. I mean, I don't have a cock to worry about falling off, do I?"

"Perhaps it's the company you keep." Tennant smiled.

"The boys?" she said. Tennant nodded. "They're not so bad." She took another sip of her drink. "Guy's a bit aggressive in his affections and he drinks too much, but they all mean well. It's very hard for them, you know."

"What? The war?"

"No, not that," she said, shaking her head. "It's the way things have turned out. Guy's father and stepfather were both Navy types, Donald's father was an MP, Tony's father is a vicar and the King's cousin..."

"A privileged lot, then."

She shrugged. "It's not that. Well, I suppose it *is* that, but it's more the fact that when they were at school, they all knew exactly where they were going, don't you see? They were the avant-garde. The great la-de-da. It was going to be a brand-new world and they were going to be the ones at the helm."

"And now that's all changed."

"Umm. Donald goes on about it all the time."

"Donald? You mean Maclean?"

"That's right. The one in the natty suit Tony was seducing in the corner." She swallowed the last of her gimlet. "He says it's as though the lot of them are back at Eton in the lower school wearing straw boaters and playing at games. It's all prefects and masters and fagging. They're forever the lower-form boys trapped in their youth."

"And railing against it," said Tennant, nodding. The analogy was probably quite astute. Boys repressed by their fathers, unable to take their places in the world, venting their frustrations through outrageous behavior. "How does Liddell fit into the pattern?" he asked, casting a tentative line into the pool. Poppet looked a little surprised at hearing the name.

"You know Captain Liddell?"

"Only through Burgess."

"He doesn't fit at all, I suppose. I mean, other than the fact that Tony works for him. So do I for that matter."

"Oh?"

"Well, he is head of B, after all. Tony's his assistant and I work in the typing pool."

"So Liddell is the grand old man, then?"

"The other way round, actually. He comes round to the flat now and again to play his cello and for drinks, but I think he likes being with them because they're young and angry. I think that part of him has faded away. He's at least ten years older than the rest of them."

"I wonder what they'd think if they knew you were telling tales about them out of school."

"I doubt if they'd think about it at all."

"You never know." The psychiatrist smiled, raising an eyebrow. "I might be a Nazi spy."

"You could be Hermann Goering on a milk float for all they'd mind." She laughed. "No one pays much attention to security." She made a snorting sound and twiddled with the stem of her glass. "Half our documentation has been moved to Blenheim Palace for the duration, and whenever we need something they bring it down by motorcycle driver. Sometimes the panniers aren't tied down properly and we've got secret documents blowing about in the street. We once had a dossier on German war production handed in to us by a streetsweeper. The clippie on the omnibus calls out the Blenheim stop as, 'All change for MI5.' It's a bit of a joke really."

Tennant smiled. "What about you? Do you think it's a joke?"

"I think it's a job. My bit for the war. Daddy's a lord and does something in the War Office, and Mummy breeds hydrangeas and rolls bandages. If it wasn't for working, I'd be married off to some third-rate baronet from Shropshire by now, breeding like mad."

"Hydrangeas?" Tennant smiled. Left on her own the woman was probably capable of talking endlessly to a blank wall. The flower of British womanhood.

"And children. Tiny little baronets and baronesses getting filthy and stealing my cosmetics. Not to mention ruining my figure." She sighed at the empty vision. Tennant wondered if working as a secretary for Liddell and attending decadent soirées at Bentinck Street was very much better. Much more likely that this was her way of giving herself a past, knowing that there was very little for her in the future. Hydrangeas and filthy children.

"Would you like another drink?"

She shook her head. "If I drink any more, I shan't be able to feel anything when you make love to me."

Tennant would gladly have paid for a cab, but the young woman insisted on taking the underground. Since Morrison had taken over the job of managing the shelter program, the subterranean platforms had taken on a look of squalid propriety. Rows of bunks tiered up to the ceiling had replaced benches for passengers, and places on the platform itself were neatly outlined in white-painted rectangles. The shelters still smelled frightful, though, the torpid air thick with the stench of body odor and excrement; Tennant was relieved when they reached Notting Hill Station and climbed up into the darkness once again.

Poppet lived in Chepstow Villas, a broad street in the middle of Bayswater, bracketed on the west and east by the working-class slums of Notting Hill and the mean streets and rookeries around Paddington Station. To the north there were more slums around the railyards at Royal Oak, and to the south there was Bayswater itself and Kensington Gardens.

Poppet's flat was on the third floor of the Chepstow Villas house, two rooms with incredibly high ceilings tucked in beside the lavatory. A tiny bedsitter with a view of a shabby back garden. A neatly made-up folding bed was open in the front room, along with a single, and obviously expensive, leather club chair. A freestanding wardrobe loomed over the bed, and there was also a large desk with a matching chair. The second room contained a sliver of kitchen with a small dining table tweaked in between the refrigerator and the sink.

Within seconds of entering the flat and without turning on the light, Poppet gently pushed Tennant onto the bed, then dropped down on her knees in front of him. She opened his flies expertly and took him into her mouth, sucking noisily and working his organ with her hand like a baker kneading dough until he was fully erect. It was obviously something she was familiar with. After a few moments she removed her mouth with a loud plopping noise and looked up at him.

"Is that nice?"

"Very."

"Guy says that learning the art of fellatio is the only real benefit of a classical education."

"Liddell?"

"Good God no, Burgess." Poppet laughed.

She stood up and began quickly removing her clothes, dropping them to the floor. She was slim, with narrow hips and small, boyish buttocks. Her skin was almost translucent in the faint light from the window.

"You don't have to do anything to me if you don't want to," she said, pulling back the quilt and climbing into bed. "I'm always ready."

Tennant removed his own clothes and joined her on the narrow mattress. He turned on his side and tried to kiss her, but she pulled him urgently on top of her, one hand moving down between their bodies, gripping him and guiding him inside her. He entered her fully in a single stroke and she sighed with contentment. She hadn't lied; she was slick with fluid and very smooth. He felt himself swelling even larger within her.

"I like this the best of all," she said sleepily. "Do you like to do it slowly or would you prefer it to be quick?"

"That depends," Tennant answered, bemused by the whole thing.

"Yes, I suppose it does." Poppet brought her hands up, laying them flat on Tennant's chest. He began to move slowly, bringing himself almost fully out, then sliding in again. As he moved, the young woman began to talk.

It was an extraordinary experience; for the next quarter hour Caroline Pope-Hennessy kept up an uninterrupted monologue, her subject matter ranging freely from her past life (St. Mary's Convent in Folkestone; an uncle who'd rummaged about under her nightdress and offered her sweets if she didn't tell), her lovers (an impotent cousin named Charles, now fighting in India; assorted writers and artists; several people she knew from Bentinck Street, including Donald Maclean; an attempt to seduce Cecil Beaton, the society photographer), the war (her mother was sure it was the Jews and the dagos, but since Victor Rothschild was a Jew and he was off defusing bombs for king and country or something else equally heroic, that didn't make any sense, although she wasn't sure about the dagos except for the uncle who was partly Spanish), and her job (the difficulty of getting fresh typewriter ribbons; her training as a cipher clerk; her fondness for Liddell and his present difficulties justifying the special unit investigating a number of suspicious deaths, including the murders at the zoo).

At the mention of the zoo killings Tennant almost lost his erection, but he managed to continue, astounded by the woman's constant flow of conversation in the midst of the sex act. He'd never experienced or even read about anything quite like it in the clinical literature.

It seemed as though her body and her mind were completely divorced from each other, separate entities capable of utterly independent action, her panting breath and bucking hips, the arching spine and pulsing, clutching vagina, at odds with the flat banality of her voice.

Eventually, of course, there had to be a resolution. She moved her hands from his chest, reached back, and dug her fingers into his buttocks, pulling him deeper down between her uplifted thighs. She grimaced as his pace increased and her words came in short, shuddering bursts, panting as she neared the finish line of her strange, sexual foot race.

"I think I'd like to...I think I'd like to finish please." She paused, taking in a long whispered breath. "Very hard please. I like it that way."

He did as she instructed, thrusting in rapid, arrhythmic bursts, feeling his pubic bone grinding hard against her own, the steel springs of the folding bed voicing squeaky, rusty objections, their perspiration-drenched flesh slapping together wetly.

She moved her arms, holding her hand up against the pillow at her head, her ankles crossing over the small of his back. "Hold my hands please. Please."

He shifted, gripping her hands tightly, forcing her arms back, letting his movements become much harsher. She began to grunt in unison with each downstroke, her heels pummeling his buttocks as she struggled beneath him.

"Come off now please, Charles...hard as you can. Now!"

He exploded within her, gasping, and she let out a small, mewling groan, her face completely collapsing in on itself as though she were drawing his passion and her own down to a strange, invisible vanishing point deep inside some unshared sector of her mind. He dropped down onto her small chest, breathing hard, then rolled off, gasping for breath. They stayed that way silently for a moment, then she spoke again.

"Would you like a cup of tea?" She paused. "Then perhaps we could do it again if you'd like."

"That would be nice. You can tell me more about your work and Captain Liddell."

She sat up in bed, running one finger through the sheen of perspiration above her breasts, and looked down at him.

"You're *not* a Nazi spy, are you?"

He smiled and shook his head. "Of course not."

"I didn't really think so, but loose lips sink ships and all that, you know." She frowned. "You don't mind the asking, do you?"

"Don't be silly."

"I'm glad." Poppet reached over, patted his now shriveled organ with a possessive smile, and then got up to make the tea. Within an hour or so Tennant had convinced the impressionable young woman that his work vetting personnel for MI5 would be considerably easier if he had more information about the internal workings of the organization. He was continually being faced with the problem of a multilayered bureaucracy that spent much of its time going around in circles, and having someone on the inside would be a great help. Poppet had agreed almost immediately; they were, after all, on the same side, and it wasn't as though she would be divulging any earthshaking secrets. Their pact was sealed with another conversational bout on the narrow little bed and Tennant's promise that he would give her as much psychotherapy as he thought she needed, free of charge.

Morris Black reached Katherine Copeland's flat shortly before midnight. The front room overlooking the street was heavy with cigarette smoke, and an empty glass and a half-filled bottle of Scotch were on her desk. Katherine offered him a chair and he sat down, still wearing his tan, belted raincoat.

Katherine looked nervous. Her cheeks were faintly flushed and her eyes had a strange, almost feverish brightness. "Can I get you something?" she asked.

Black shook his head. "No thank you." He cleared his throat. "Your message said something about the photograph I gave you. Some new information."

Katherine smiled and shook her head. "We're all business, are we?"

Her words were faintly slurred; Black suddenly realized that she was quite drunk.

"What else would we be?" he asked.

She dropped down into the chair across from him. "Friends."

"It's late. Your message said it was urgent."

Katherine gave him a long appraising look. "You're really quite good-looking in a sensible sort of way." She frowned. "I suppose that's why Bingham thought it would be so easy."

"Bingham?"

"Fellow I worked for. At the embassy."

"I'm afraid I don't understand."

"He wanted me to sleep with you. Screw all your secrets out of you. Find out why everyone's so worried about these killings. The leak."

"Leak?"

"Bingham says there's some big secret Churchill's keeping from us. The Americans, that is. Something to do with your murderer. Very hush-hush."

Black stared at her as the truth dawned on him. "You're a spy," he said quietly.

"Not a very good one. Not according to Bingham."

"You weren't on the train to Cambridge by accident, were you?"

"Or in the restaurant."

"Christ," he muttered wearily. He looked across at her. "Why are you telling me this?"

"Because I'm goddamn well drunk and I've been trying to work up the courage to tell you for the last six or seven hours, Morris by God Black from Scotland Yard. Because I don't like what they tried to do to me. What they wanted me to do to you. I don't like any of it." She was on the verge of tears.

"They?"

"Bingham and his friends."

"How much do they know?"

"Not as much as they want." She shook her head. "Jesus, I must be crazy, telling you now."

"You said you worked for Bingham. Past tense."

"He took me off the case."

"Why?"

"Because I wasn't getting anywhere. He said things were coming to a head. It was too late."

"Just exactly who is this fellow Bingham?"

"First secretary at the embassy. He's also in charge of intelligence."

"Who else knows about this?"

Katherine laughed. "According to him, just about everyone. The Germans in Berlin, the Russians. I think he's worried about some of our own people too. He and Kennedy didn't get along."

Black closed his eyes for a moment. The mire he'd been traversing so carefully had been dangerous enough; now it was a minefield of hidden agendas more complex than he could ever have believed. He glanced at Katherine again, trying to judge the true level of her intoxication. She sounded sincere enough, but there was no real way of telling whether or not she was playing a part. Confession as a method of gaining his trust? He squeezed his eyes shut again, feeling the beginnings of a searing headache as he tried to concentrate on the matter at hand.

"You said you wanted to talk to me about the photograph."

"It's a village in Germany. A place called Strobeck. There's a legend that it's the first place in Europe where chess was played. They even teach it in school there."

"Chess." The checkerboard in Rudelski's footlocker. The chessboard table in the Soho drinking club where Talbot had last been seen. Gurney from the Stag garage, playing chess with Talbot. The photograph. "Dear Lord," he whispered aloud as the pieces of the puzzle came together in his mind. Why hadn't he seen it before?

"They even play chess by mail with people in other countries," said Katherine. "The games sometimes take months to play."

"What?" said Black, staring at her. "What did you say?"

"They write letters back and forth, making one move at a time."

In that instant he knew he had it. The last piece. Now he knew how Queer Jack was choosing his victims, and why. He cursed softly under his breath. He'd been a complete fool not to see it weeks ago. He stood. He had to call Swift immediately. "Do you have a telephone?"

"Through there." Katherine pointed toward the kitchen. Black nodded, crossed the room, and went into the kitchen, closing the door behind him. He reappeared a few minutes later, the tired expression on his face replaced with something else: excitement, even elation.

"I have to go."

"Is the photograph important?" Katherine asked, climbing to her feet.

He nodded. "Yes. Very important." He turned and headed for the door.

"Glad I could lend a hand," said Katherine wryly. She shrugged her shoulders. "But what's a little bit of treason between friends, right?"

Black stopped in midstride and turned. "I'm sorry."

"Sorry for what? I'm just the lying bitch who tried to spy on you, remember?"

Black took a step toward her, then stopped. "No. You're not that." He smiled. "You're really quite wonderful, as a matter of fact." He flushed hotly and then turned on his heel, moving toward the door. Reaching it, he turned again. "We'll talk again, I promise you. When I get back."

"Get back from where?" asked Katherine, but he was gone. "Jesus," she whispered, staring at the blank face of the door. "What have I done?"

She wandered into the kitchen. In his haste Black had left the telephone half out of the cradle and it was now buzzing angrily at her. She replaced it properly, then noticed that the small pad and pencil she kept beside the telephone was out of place. Black had used it, then torn off the top page of the pad. She stared blearily down at it. Standard stuff she'd learned at Donovan's silly little spy school in Washington's Foggy Bottom. Picking up the pencil, she held it sideways, rubbing the wide edge of the lead point over the pad. The ghostly impression left on the pad under the one Black had used stood out clearly. A single line.

Coventry. Bomber's moon.

Katherine turned and checked the small calendar taped to the front of her refrigerator. The full moon for the month of November was clearly indicated. The 14th.

Tomorrow night.

CHAPTER EIGHTEEN

Thursday, November 14, 1940
11:30 A.M., British Standard Time

"**N**O ONE'S NAME REALLY LEAPS from the page, does it?" said Anthony Blunt. The long-nosed and aristocratic young man was lounging in a leather-covered armchair in Guy Liddell's office on St. James's Street, leafing through the Asprey's list Police Constable Swift had brought over from Kensington Park Gardens earlier that morning.

"No," Liddell answered on the other side of the desk. He scratched at his temple with the dry stem of his pipe, frowning down at a copy of the list in front of him. From the Duke of Windsor to Joan Miller, Maxwell Knight's not-so-secret paramour. Now there was something to boggle the mind, he thought. Perhaps the Miller woman had given the pen to Knight as a gift and then he'd used it to skewer the brains of the man in the lavatory at the Zoological Gardens. Max Knight as double agent. Liddell smiled bleakly. Given Knight's odd habits, there was probably a case to be made.

"Rather like going through the latest edition of Burke's Peerage," Blunt commented. "All lords and ladies." There was a wistful note in his voice. "The pens must be frightfully expensive." He glanced up at Liddell. "What does your man Black have to say about it?"

"Nothing. Swift said he hadn't come in this morning."

"Dear me!" Blunt smiled. "Don't tell me the earnest Scotland Yard inspector is cutting class." He wagged a finger. "Not a good sign."

"No, it's not." Liddell's frown deepened and he found himself wishing that his assistant would shut up for a minute or two. Blunt must have read his mind because he stood up and waved the fluttering pages of the list.

"I suppose I'd better begin following this up," he said, standing in front of the desk. The tone was clear; he was asking for permission to hand the job off to a subordinate. Liddell sighed. Tony was a brilliant, fascinating person, especially when it came to art, but as far as the drudgery of day-to-day affairs at B were concerned, the man was a dead loss. Then again, it was early days; perhaps he'd learn. But not by letting other people do the work.

"Yes, follow up on it," Liddell said finally. "And do it yourself, Tony." He looked up at his assistant. "Lords and ladies, as you said. Calls for a bit of discretion, don't you think? Your sort of thing."

"Umm. I suppose so." He didn't seem pleased by the prospect. He nodded once, then left the office, still clutching the list. Liddell leaned back in his chair. He lit his pipe and puffed thoughtfully, staring up at the ceiling.

Eighty-one names were on the list Police Constable Swift had compiled at Asprey's and, as Blunt had observed, most were wealthy and titled. The only doctor on the list was Sir Hugh Rigsby, the King's surgeon, and setting aside his background and present position, it seemed unlikely that a 70-year-old man would be skulking about in public toilets poking pen nibs into people's eyes.

Still, a Penna Nettuno Superba with a Rover nib had been used as the murder weapon, and a pen like that could easily be stolen. All eighty-one names would have to be checked. Even if one of the pens had been stolen or lost, the name of the original owner was a place to start. At least Morris Black had finally come up with *something*.

Liddell slumped forward, pushed back his chair, and stood up. He went to the window and looked down onto the street. A very ordinary nightmare. A clear day in early winter, cabs tooting about in Clubland, lunatic killers wandering about anonymously carrying earth-shattering secrets, black-market filet steaks being offered with a wink and a nod at Whites, and tonight...

Tonight there was a full moon.

Black had called him just after midnight with his news. According to the policeman, Queer Jack had made a mistake at last. He'd be in Coventry today, stalking his next victim, and Morris Black was sure he knew how to track him down. He wouldn't say how.

Liddell had forbidden it, of course, without any explanation. What explanation could there be? Black certainly assumed there was going to be a raid—Queer Jack's supposed presence was proof enough of that—but dear God, Black had no idea what kind of raid it would be, and Liddell wasn't about to tell him; bad enough that he knew himself. Three days ago a series of Ultra messages had been decoded by the boffins at Bletchley Park. Under the overall code name of Moonlight Sonata, three possible targets had been chosen for a massive raid. Yesterday the final target had been chosen: Coventry, code-named Korn by the Luftwaffe, probably in reference to the huge Cornercraft Machine Works located in the center of the city. Hundreds of bombers, as many as the Luftwaffe could muster, and led by KG100s—incendiary pathfinders, known for their pinpoint accuracy—would seek out their target. By midnight Coventry would be a fuming torch. And the twenty or so people who knew just what sort of raid it would be had been sworn to secrecy.

Liddell could taste the sour bite of anxiety building in his gut. How would it look on the cover of *Life* magazine or *Newsweek,* or God help us all, the front page of the *Evening Standard*? A city in England's heartland offered up like a sacrificial lamb without so much as a whispered warning to local officials. Only a few weeks ago Coventry, a legitimate military target with a score of factories in military production, had been stripped of its antiaircraft defenses with most of the ack-ack batteries shifted to London.

From a public relations standpoint it would be catastrophic: Churchill portrayed as the arrogant warmonger, a coward surrounding himself with a wall of protective artillery while his innocent countrymen are left defenseless. It was just the sort of thing to make the American Congress hesitate. Fuel to feed the isolationist fires. A propaganda disaster. Hitler and his wretched crew would laugh themselves senseless, and here Liddell was caught in the middle of it all.

He swore under his breath. As director of B it was his job to ferret out the nation's enemies and bring them out into the light of day, but Ultra was forcing him to walk in Goebbels's dragging clubfoot steps and create yet another lie, cloaking the truth in darkness.

Even more horrifying was the cold calculation of people like Desmond Morton, Churchill's éminence grise—he saw the whole affair as an opportunity to capitalize on. Coventry would be bombed into martyrdom, the government would be officially outraged, and the city would become a veiled threat to the Americans—join us now or perhaps this will be the fate of your own cities. Christ! What kind of war was Liddell fighting?

He jammed his balled fists into the pockets of his trousers. There was no way around it; the Ultra secret had to be protected at any cost. If any move was made to evacuate Coventry, or even bring in additional fire-fighting equipment, Nazi intelligence might make the connection and assume that their coding system had been compromised. They'd stop using the Enigma encryption machine within hours, and Churchill would lose his precious intelligence source. Lunacy. The fate of an entire nation hanging on the thread of a mad killer's whim.

Liddell stared up into the sky, visible over the rooftop of the Carlton Club, directly across the way. Pale as watercolor and bloody well clear as Waterford crystal. No clouds and a full moon; no rain or snow to stop the Luftwaffe as they made their way across the Channel; bad weather wasn't about to ease his guilt.

He went back to his desk, and using the multiple tool he kept tucked into the watch pocket of his vest, he began reaming out his pipe, scraping the dottle into the large, brilliantly colored art deco ashtray Burgess had given him on his last birthday. It was a Noritake with a flamboyant leaf and flower motif, probably frightfully expensive if he knew Burgess. Puffing out his cheeks, Liddell blew into the stem to free the last bits of old tobacco, the tip of his tongue burning with the bitter taste of accumulated tar.

Burgess. Dear God, another secret he had to carry about, not to mention Blunt and all the rest. He'd vouched for all of them at one time or another, got them jobs, helped them avoid being conscripted, convinced himself and others that their vices could be tolerated for the greater good on the basis of enlightened liberalism. He frowned, took out his pouch, and began packing his pipe again.

Their homosexuality was one thing, but what about the rest? A decade ago he'd made his mark at Special Branch by infiltrating the Communist Party of Great Britain and bringing a dozen of its leaders to trial for sedition. Now here he was turning a blind eye to the political backgrounds of people like Blunt and Burgess and Maclean, all of whom had definite Communist affiliations during their student days. He'd managed to convince himself that it was nothing more than youthful idealism, but he was also aware that his connection to them was probably enough to have him pilloried.

He closed his eyes for a moment, trying to ward off a sudden wave of mental exhaustion. Was he really fool enough to risk being drummed out of public service simply for the sake of his loneliness? Apparently so. Between his friends, his enemies, and Morris Black, it looked to be a rocky road ahead. Sighing, he struck a match and lit his pipe again. How many secrets could one man keep before they drove him mad? He reached out, picked up the telephone on his desk, and dialed Tony Blunt's local.

"Forget about the list for now," he said when his assistant answered. "I want you to find out what's happened to Inspector Morris Bloody Black."

Morris Black, going directly against Liddell's orders, had taken the eleven o'clock train to Coventry, first telling Police Constable Swift that he wouldn't be in that day. There had been no raids on London the night before, but a few sorties had been made over outlying areas, and the London & North Western Line had been disrupted, forcing him to take the longer route from Paddington, traveling via Didcot, Oxford, and Birmingham. Instead of reaching Coventry shortly after one o'clock in the afternoon, he didn't arrive until almost four.

It was infuriating, since he could have driven the distance in a little more than two hours, but he hadn't wanted to involve Police Constable Swift, even though he was reasonably sure that his assistant knew what he was planning.

Black had never been to Coventry before, and entering the city by his circuitous northern route, it struck him that it had been built rather like an oyster, sprawling suburbs and industrial districts built up in rings around the perfectly preserved pearl of the walled medieval town, concrete and steel giving way to half-timbered Tudor.

Leaving the station, the detective asked a porter for directions, then took the tram up into the market center, getting off at the High Street near the old Corn Exchange. The roadway was thick with traffic, the pavement on either side filled with shoppers, dressed against the chill. Directly ahead of Black, rising above the low, surrounding buildings, was the majestic bulk of St. Michael's Cathedral, the gray needle spire jutting into the pale, clear sky, the image of Queer Jack's postcard come to life. A little farther on was the lesser spire of Trinity.

Ignoring them for the moment, he turned down the High Street and eventually found the number he was looking for, a small antique store at the entrance to a narrow cobbled alley.

The sign over the shop window said Garlinski's. A huge fat marmalade cat was curled up in one corner of the window display, as dusty as everything else, catching a sliver of sunlight. The rest of the goods cluttering the window were more old than antique—embroidered souvenir pillows from Edinburgh; a badly framed tintype of a sad-faced Victorian child posed kneeling on a grandfatherly chair; a Meccano set still in its box, the yellowing cellophane still wrapped around the neat rows of girder and plate; a glass globe etched with countries that no longer existed; a coronation biscuit tin commemorating the ascent of Edward VII to the throne. A small glass bowl containing a few shirt studs and a silver fob without a watch. The marmalade cat flicked its tail in a brief snakelike motion. Morris Black pushed open the door and went into the shop.

The interior was as cluttered as the window, hundreds of items, large and small, dimly lit clues to vanished lives and times. At the far end of the narrow, low-ceilinged room Black could see a glass-fronted counter, light pooling over it from a green-shaded lamp. An old man, wisps of snow-white hair circling the bald dome of his skull like a halo, was seated on a stool behind the counter, hunched over a chessboard. He wore an old-fashioned collarless white shirt and over it a shapeless gray cardigan. Steel-rimmed spectacles were balanced on his forehead.

He looked up as Black edged down the aisle and flipped the glasses down onto his broad, jutting nose. The man's face was seamed like shoe leather, lips thinned with age, cheeks hollowed, skin drawn over bones like parchment. He smiled, the pale blue eyes behind his glasses glinting with curiosity.

"You must be Inspector Black, the young man who telephoned me." Coming from the old, worn body, the man's voice was surprisingly rich and strong. A singer's timbre, trained and even, but still heavy with a middle-European accent.

"Hiram Garlinski?"

"Yes." The old man's smile widened. A pleasant face, full of years. "A rag and bone man in Warsawa, but here, an antique dealer."

"How did you know who I was?"

Garlinski shrugged. "You have the look of a policeman. A Jewish policeman, which makes you all the more interesting."

"What does a Jewish policeman look like?"

Garlinski smiled again. "Official, but nervous. An odd combination, don't you think?" He looked down at the chessboard in front of him, moved a piece, then looked up again. "Jews have been looking over their shoulders in this country since Cromwell allowed us to return. Policemen have knocked hard on the Jew's door for even longer. One in the same is a very rare thing. A little uncomfortable for you, *nu*?"

"Sometimes. A little."

"It's good for Jews to be nervous. A necessary instinct for survival. Especially now.

"You've had some trouble?"

"No. So far there has been no *Kristallnacht* in Coventry, but you never know. The English have a lot of German in them, and even more of the French. Not a healthy mix." Garlinski held out one rawboned hand above the chessboard and waggled it back and forth. "Being a Jew in these times is like balancing over a bottomless pit on a single strand of thread. The slightest change in the wind's direction and so it goes." He shrugged again. "But you know all this, don't you, Inspector?" Garlinski added softly.

"I didn't come here to discuss anti-Semitism."

"No. You came to talk to me about playing chess. Or so you said. What does a detective inspector from Scotland Yard want to know about the game of kings, and why does he want to know about it from someone like me?"

"I telephoned the British Chess Federation. They told me you were the local chairman of the Correspondence Chess Association in Coventry."

"That's true. I told you so when you called."

"They also said you were one of the coaches for the national team last year. That you are considered a grand-master."

"Buenos Aires." Garlinski nodded. "Alexander, Thomas, Milner-Barry, Golombek, and G. H. Wood." He said the names softly. "But I was never the official coach. I didn't go with them; Milner-Barry knew better than that. But I helped." He sighed wistfully. "It would have been a great thing to see. Capablanca played for Cuba. Of sixteen matches, there were seven won, nine drawn, and none lost. A great thing to see." He looked at Black. "There won't be another tournament like it, not in my lifetime, Inspector. Perhaps never."

Black reached into the inside pocket of his jacket and took out the postcards from David Talbot's rooms at Cambridge. He handed them to the old man. Garlinski examined the squares of cardboard carefully, then nodded.

"You know what the numbers mean?" Black asked.

"Certainly. They are chess moves."

"Could you explain?"

"Of course." Garlinski set the postcards aside and gestured toward the chessboard in front of him. "There are sixty-four squares on the board, thirty-two in the white field, thirty-two in the black. When playing correspondence chess, the squares are numbered, from the player's left to right. Numbers one through thirty-two are white, thirty-three to sixty-four are black. You understand me so far, Inspector?"

"Yes."

"Good." Garlinski nodded briefly, the scholar with his new pupil well in hand. "As well as representing a square, the first sixteen numbers in each field also represent a piece."

Black looked down at the board on the counter. "So the white queen is number four then."

"Quite so." Garlinski nodded, obviously pleased. "Throughout the game the piece's number never changes, only its location, identified by the second number for each move."

"I see. And the X you see on some of the moves means that one piece has taken another."

"*Ei gut!* You have it!" The old man lifted his shoulders. "Not very difficult really, only time-consuming. But that is part of the pleasure, really. The anticipation."

Black looked thoughtfully down at the board, then gathered up the postcards again. He leafed through them slowly. "I don't suppose these particular moves mean very much."

"Only that the player making them was very good."

"Why do you say that?"

"The level of play. The sophistication." Garlinski took the cards from Black and glanced at them, nodding, his thin lips pursed. "This comes from the Munich tournament in 1936. The Reti opening. Reti was a Hungarian who died ten or eleven years ago. A great master, but the opening is reasonably obscure. Keres, the Estonian, was the last to use it in international play."

"In Germany?"

"Yes."

"How many British chess players would know about the opening?"

"Thousands." Garlinski smiled. "But there can't be more than a few hundred who have the middle-game technique to use it."

"Would they be members of the British Chess Federation?"

"Presumably."

"And your organization?"

"The two groups are not mutually exclusive. The man who played this game may well belong to both."

"Are there any members of your association here in Coventry who could reasonably use the opening?"

"Other than myself?" Garlinski shook his head. "I would think not."

"Do you have a membership list?"

"Yes."

"Could I see it?"

"Of course." Garlinski stared at the detective. "But first perhaps you will tell me what this is about."

"I'm afraid I can't. Not at the moment."

"A question of security?"

"Something like that."

"I see." The old man got up from his stool, glanced briefly at Black again, then shuffled back through the rear of the shop, going through a doorway hung with a long, dark blue velvet curtain. Black could hear footsteps climbing stairs; presumably Garlinski lived above the shop.

He reappeared a few minutes later carrying a small wooden recipe box filled with neatly tabbed file cards. Shifting the chessboard to one side, he opened a drawer in the counter, took out a sheet of paper, and began transcribing names from the cards, using a pencil stub he took from the pocket of his sweater.

"How many members of the association live in Coventry?"

"A dozen or so," Garlinski answered, still writing. The

detective glanced at his watch. It was already past five in the afternoon, and outside, dark would be closing in. Within an hour or so, two at the most, it would be fully dark. There wasn't much time.

Garlinski spoke without looking up from his writing. "You are in a hurry, Inspector?"

"Yes."

"You won't have time to take tea with me then, I suppose?"

"No. I'm sorry."

"A disappointment. You seem to be an interesting young man."

"For a Jewish policeman?" Black smiled.

Garlinski laughed and continued writing. "An old man like me can't be choosy these days. I have been alone for too many years." He looked up at Black. "You are married?"

"My wife is dead."

"Then we are the same man, Inspector. Our hearts have been broken."

"Yes."

"I play chess to ease the loneliness, but you, Inspector, your game is much more dangerous. Chasing small criminals in the middle of a war."

"Or worse."

Garlinski finished his list and handed it to Black. He scanned it quickly: eleven names, eleven addresses. Six had telephone numbers. He could place calls from the nearest post office; the rest he would have to visit in person.

"Thank you," he said, folding the sheet of paper and slipping it into his pocket. He gathered up the postcards as well. "You've been a great help."

"A pleasure, Inspector. God should hear you and favor you." The same blessing Black's father had spoken the day he married Fay; words he hadn't heard in years. And no longer believed in.

"Thank you," he said again. He shook the old man's hand and turned away. He took a few steps toward the door, then paused. Garlinski had gone back to his chess problem, hunched over the board. Again Black heard the fear in Liddell's voice, forbidding him to come to Coventry. "*Zayde?*" he said, raising his voice slightly. Garlinski looked up from the board, surprised at Black's use of the familiar term.

"Yes?"

"*Zayde*, do you have friends, relatives in the country?"

"My granddaughter, in Nuneaton." Garlinski frowned. "Why do you ask?"

"Perhaps you should pay her a visit."

"You're not saying this idly, Inspector?"

"No."

"Am I in some danger from whoever it is you seek?"

"No. Much worse than that, I think."

"I see." Garlinski looked at Morris Black, searching the younger man's face. "And you think I should pay this visit soon?"

"Immediately. This afternoon. You must believe me."

Garlinski continued to stare at the detective. Finally he nodded. "Go with God, Inspector." He looked back to the chessboard.

"And you, *Zayde*." Black could feel the sting of salt in his eyes. He gritted his teeth, nodded once, then turned away at last and left the store.

Dr. Charles Tennant sat behind the desk in the small office off the main hall of Scotland Yard's Central Records Office, working his way slowly through the stacks of card file drawers on his left, occasionally making a note on the foolscap pad in front of him.

It was just after five-thirty, and outside the office he could hear the faint sounds of the Records staff as they prepared to leave for the day. He had been in the office since before noon, and he was still barely halfway through the card files he'd chosen to examine.

He yawned, jaw cracking, and lit another cigarette. He'd stayed with Poppet until almost dawn, and that, combined with six hours spent at Central Records, had made him bleary-eyed. Still, it was worth it, even considering the risks involved.

Poppet, regardless of her strange sexual proclivities, had been a gold mine of information. Through three separate acts of talk-filled intercourse and two long tea breaks in between, she had innocently, and effusively, told him everything she knew about the murder investigations that were causing so much concern to Guy Liddell and MI5.

Her information was remarkably complete, which wasn't so surprising when you considered that she was Liddell's favorite stenographer and had transcribed both the reports filed by Detective Inspector Morris Black as well as the original Scotland Yard case files concerning the first two murders.

Five deaths were under investigation: the four ritual slayings that seemed directly connected to night bombing raids in London, Portsmouth, and Southampton, and the fifth, apparently anomalous, murder of the Wren motorcycle courier, Jane Luffington.

He was particularly interested in the Luffington death, both because she was the only woman and because of her association with British intelligence.

According to Poppet, the Wren had two regular courier runs—one from Bletchley Park, a government installation outside London, to 55 Broadway Buildings, the headquarters of the Secret Intelligence Service; and a second route from SIS to the cavernous halls of the Public Records Office in The City. Almost as intriguing was her romantic relationship with a young lieutenant commander in naval intelligence, a man named Fleming.

A tangled web by the looks of it, and connected directly to the other four murders by modus operandi; according to the post-exhumation autopsy performed by Bernard Spilsbury, she, like the other four, had died as a result of having her spinal cord severed neatly by a small, machine-tooled projectile, probably delivered by a compressed-air or spring-loaded weapon. Three of the four previous victims, all males, had been mutilated; Jane Luffington, the only woman, had not.

An interesting enough case for any psychiatrist, but doubly so for Tennant. By itself, ritual and multiple murder in the style of Jack the Ripper was a fascinating subject, albeit one that had little value in "normal" psychiatric practice. As far as Tennant could tell from Poppet's information, the death of Jane Luffington was less anomalous than it was prophylactic.

Somewhere along the line the killer of the four previous victims had made a mistake that left him vulnerable to the Luffington woman. There was no doubt in Tennant's mind that she had been murdered for practical reasons and was not part of the killer's ritual.

To Tennant, it was her intelligence associations, and MI5's interest in the slayings, that were the most important. From what Poppet knew, Queer Jack, as he was being called, represented the distinct possibility of a major security leak.

Originally this worry had stemmed from the murderer's apparent powers of prophecy in predicting exactly when and where bombing raids would occur; this had now been reinforced by the death of Jane Luffington. Queer Jack obviously had some kind of access to extremely sensitive intelligence information.

By definition, the fact that he knew when raids would occur meant that British intelligence also knew—the "other source" referred to so casually by Masterman after Tennant's brief role as a captured Luftwaffe pilot. The obvious conclusion was that SIS had a highly placed agent somewhere in the German High Command who reported regularly on Luftwaffe bombing plans. Somehow Queer Jack not only knew who he was, but also had access to the information he was sending to British intelligence.

Tennant stubbed out his cigarette. Poppet, of course, had made none of these associations; she had neither the intelligence to do so nor the interest. But examined on a broader plane, it all fit very neatly, especially when you considered Jane Luffington's main route from Bletchley Park to SIS.

Bletchley, as virtually everyone knew, was the new headquarters of the Government Code and Cipher School and the central location for much of the British intelligence establishment's cover radio traffic. To Tennant it was obvious— the listeners at Bletchley were picking up the coded signals sent from their agent in Germany, decoding them, and sending them on to MI5. If Tennant could somehow find out who Queer Jack was, discover his source of information, and inform Schellenberg and Heydrich, the British war effort could be dealt a mortal blow before the almost inevitable entry of the United States into the war.

But how to do it, and do it before the ubiquitous Morris Black? Poppet seemed to think that the Jew's investigation was leading nowhere, but the psychiatrist wasn't so sure. A call to Smith, his contact in Special Branch, and a vague reference to an ongoing research project about the criminal mind had given him access to the Central Records Office Criminal Index, and even the most cursory examination of Black's arrest record over the years showed that he was far more successful than better known members of the force like Robert Fabian or Reginald Spooner. Given that record and his seniority, it appeared that his lack of political friends within the Metropolitan Force, together with his Jewishness, were the only things preventing his promotion to detective superintendent, or even deputy commissioner. Regardless of his rank and religion, Morris Black was relentless, stubborn, and extremely intelligent; Tennant had no intention of underrating his abilities.

Charting Black's career was only a minor part of the psychiatrist's presence at Scotland Yard that afternoon and evening. His convoluted conversations with Poppet, both in and out of bed, had given him the germ of an idea.

Morris Black's investigations were hamstrung by a century of firmly entrenched procedure and the narrow limits of the law. The rules and regulations governing his work were straightforward and inflexible, based on the Metropolitan Police Act and standard texts like Smith and Fidde's *Forensic Medicine* as well as dusty tomes like Gross, Adam, and Kendal's *Criminal Investigation*, which still contained serious warnings about Gypsy confidence tricksters. Tennant had no such restrictions, either on his thinking or his actions.

Years before, at the Institute in Vienna, the psychiatrist had run into a visiting American psychoanalyst named Walter Langer. At the time Langer had been convinced of the great value of hypothetical psychological case histories of important political figures as well as of criminal personality types. Hopefully a reasonably accurate "crystal ball" would be created to predict patterns of behavior and even identify criminals before their crimes were committed. Ironically, much of Langer's theorizing used Jack the Ripper as an example. The American had dubbed his scientifically dubious process "profiling."

The previous year Tennant had heard through the psychiatric grapevine that Langer, with the backing of the United States government, had embarked on a project to divine the inner thinking of Adolf Hitler, presumably so that Roosevelt would have some idea of which way the wind was blowing if he allied himself with the British cause.

Tennant had thought that the possibility of such predictive analysis was a trifle fanciful, but even then he had been interested in the possibilities. Much about what he remembered of Langer's theories he was now applying to Queer Jack. The initial results of his very preliminary thinking, combined with the small amount of information he had culled from the Central Records Office files, were intriguing, and a sketchy "profile" of the killer was now beginning to emerge.

Some elements were obvious: the multiple nature of the killings, the nudity of the victims, and the mutilations were almost a sure sign of sexual psychopathy. The fact that four out of the five were men pointed toward a homosexual nature. Tennant could also assume that the killings had been triggered by the first serious bombings of London and probably coincided with Queer Jack's first access to information concerning the raids.

These facts, combined with Tennant's readings of the clinical literature, his professional experience with the criminally insane at the Sheffield Lunatic Asylum, and the historical evidence contained in the Scotland Yard records led him to believe that he could safely guess Queer Jack's approximate age.

Of the cases he had examined in the CRO files, all had involved murderers between 30 and 55 years of age. This coincided with his own experience. In a normal man, frustration with his declining sexual abilities and increasing ennui with a marital partner might lead to the use of prostitutes, or possibly the favors of a younger mistress.

To a man consumed by the dual evidence of the psychopath and the homosexual, the use of prostitutes, male or female, would hardly be of value. Murder, often brutal and of a ritual nature, was often a solution. Thus he could reasonably conclude that Queer Jack had been born sometime between 1890 and 1910, with a median birthdate of 1900. The man's obvious freedom of movement also supported this and made it highly unlikely that he was a member of the military, which in turn meant he was over the age of conscription.

He could also assume that his quarry was not a professional. Psychopathic behavior seemed almost invariably to stem from frustration and a sense of failure, often compounded by an inability to get along with other people. Such behavior also tended to have a crippling mental effect, and of the cases he had examined today, almost all of the murderers had either shown signs of mental instability at a young age or had been previously confined to a mental institution of some kind.

This had also been one of Walter Langer's key points in describing the man most likely to have been Jack the Ripper. Of all the named suspects, Kosminski the Pole was by far the most likely. He had been incarcerated in an asylum prior to the Whitechapel murders, and the prostitute killings had come to an abrupt end immediately following his return there. It seemed obvious enough to conclude that a madman might commit mad acts.

On the other hand, it was also probable that Queer Jack was extremely intelligent, whatever the nature of his lunacy. The strange murder weapon was a clear indication of that; according to Poppet, the autopsy reports from Spilsbury's office referred to the small, barbed instruments as "brilliantly lethal." At the very least Queer Jack was familiar with sophisticated metal fabrication—a skilled technician or engineering assistant perhaps silently railing against the more educated men he worked for, his resentments growing, day by day, until they eventually exploded into violent life.

His year at the Sheffield Asylum had also taught Tennant that the majority of those deemed criminally insane seemed to come from large urban areas, most probably because early signs of deviant behavior would be much more visible in a rural setting; it was much easier for a madman to remain anonymous in a place like London than a small village or a town. Once again, the CRO files bore this out: of the cases he'd gone through, almost all had been centered in London or other large cities.

Although he had no sure evidence, Tennant was almost certain that the killings that had taken place in the last few months had come about as the result of a major trauma in the killer's past. He'd had half a dozen "lunatic killers" under his care at Sheffield, and from what he'd learned, their sudden, seemingly unprovoked acts of violence had their roots in the distant past, most often in early adolescence.

So there it was—his vague, still cloudy image of Queer Jack. A man in his mid-thirties to early forties, secretly homosexual, a lone wolf, socially inept, and perhaps painfully shy. A skilled man who took pride in his vicious but "brilliant" instruments of death, born in London and possibly having a history of mental illness, perhaps carrying the weight of some awful, traumatic secret from the past.

A man who saw the war, and the nightly visitations of the Luftwaffe bombers, as the perfect, insane environment in which to act out his monstrous rituals. And most bizarre of all, a man who had somehow come into possession of knowledge that had MI5 terribly worried.

Tennant nodded to himself, gathered up his notes, and stood up. Not very much. Not yet. But a beginning. He smiled. He'd have Queer Jack, and he'd have him before Detective Inspector Morris Black of Scotland Yard.

CHAPTER NINETEEN

Thursday, November 14, 1940
6:45 P.M., European Standard Time
5:45 P.M., British Standard Time

MORRIS BLACK EMERGED FROM THE glass-doored call box in the Coventry GPO office, grinning from ear to ear. By an astounding stroke of good fortune the first name on Garlinski's list had been the right one—Brian Trench, 24A Cherry Street, Radford. A few moments' conversation with Mildred Trench, his wife, had proved that he was the man Black was looking for. According to Mildred Trench, her husband was indeed a member of the Correspondence Chess Association and was due to meet with an out-of-town member that evening in one of the local pubs.

"God knows what it'll be after that. With my Brian it's always one thing or another. This chess business, the Society. You'd think he didn't have things to do here at home." If Black wanted to catch him beforehand, it was likely that he was still at work. Work, as it turned out, was Fry's Butcher Shop in the market off West Orchard Street.

The post office was located partway down Grey Friars Street, less than a block away from Garlinski's shop. Black walked quickly back to the blacked-out High Street and hailed a cab, but the driver told him that it wasn't worth the fare since the market and West Orchard Street was only a few hundred yards away. The cabbie gave Black directions, pointing him up Hertford Street.

A few minutes later the detective reached the small market square and found Trench, still dressed in a bloody apron, winding up the awning as he prepared to close up shop, whistling happily to himself in the darkness. It was Mozart, which seemed out of character for a butcher's assistant, but then again, so was correspondence chess.

"Mr. Trench?"

"Sorry, sir. We're closed, I'm afraid."

Black took out his warrant card and held it up. "I'm not here to buy anything, Mr. Trench."

"Scotland Yard?" Trench peered at the card, frowning.

"That's right."

"Bit far from home, aren't you?" Trench tied off the awning with a complicated knot looped over a wrought-iron cleat and turned to face Black fully.

"I'd like to ask you a few questions."

"Christ! Not another one of the black-market investigations!"

"No, nothing like that."

"What, then?"

Black told him, making it as vague as he dared. He was investigating a serious crime. Evidence pointed toward the man Trench was scheduled to meet at the pub. He would appreciate Trench's cooperation.

"What do you mean by cooperation?"

"Point out the man to me. I'll do the rest." It was insane, of course. What he should have been doing was bringing in the local Coventry constabulary, but he was afraid of scaring off his quarry.

"I can't point him out to you. I've never laid eyes on him."

"How were you to recognize him?"

"I was supposed to wait for him at the chessboard."

"Chessboard?"

"The one in the Stump."

"That's the name of the pub?"

"The Magpie and Stump is the proper name. We all call it the Stump."

"Where is the chessboard?"

"At the far end of the bar. Inlaid right into the wood." Black frowned, thinking hard, and then he had it. There'd been a table like that at the Mandrake in London. He could feel a tightening in his chest; it was all coming together now, down the sharp, gleaming point of a needle.

"Sounds like he knows the place," said Black.

Trench shrugged. "Maybe."

"Who suggested it as a place to meet?"

"He did, now that you mention it."

Black nodded to himself. Queer Jack had probably followed Trench on at least one occasion and knew that the Magpie and Stump was convenient. Knew about the chessboard table.

"He gave you no way to recognize him?"

"No. He said he'd find me."

"How did he introduce himself?"

"He said he was a member of the Society, like me, and that he thought we'd have a lot in common, considering our mutual interests. He said he was going to be in Coventry today on business and offered to buy me dinner. I said I'd give him the tour."

"You weren't suspicious?"

"No. Why should I be? It wouldn't be the first time something like that has happened."

"All right. What time were you supposed to meet him?"

"Six-thirty, spot on."

"Spot on?"

"He said he was a bit of a fiend about punctuality."

More than just a fiend for being on time. Black glanced at his watch. It was ten past six. "How far is the Stump from here?"

"Not very. Cope Street, just the other side of the cathedral." Trench reached back and began untying his apron. "Half a minute to change and we'll cut along."

"One more thing."

"Yes?"

"What name did he give you?"

"Exner. Bernard Timothy Exner."

The Stump turned out to be a narrow, half-timbered building in the shadow of the huge Triumph Cycle Works complex located just off Priory Street, only a block or so away from St. Michael's Cathedral. According to Trench, the faint smell of sewage wafting up to them on the night air came from the River Sherbourne, a sluggishly flowing ditch that wound snakelike through the old city, which the various Works operations used to dump effluent.

The interior of the public house was crowded with men and women from the nearby motorcycle factory, most still dressed in coveralls, the familiar Triumph lettering stenciled on the back. The long, L-shaped bar was jammed two deep, and the tables and booths around the perimeter of the main room were all filled. Through an open doorway at the far end of the bar, Black could see another group playing at darts in a small games room beyond.

The pub was noisy, alive with sounds of laughter and the clink and clatter of bottles and glasses. A haze of cigarette smoke hung like a fog from the dark rafters overhead. Two men wearing aprons and a middle-aged, blowsy woman with peroxide-blond hair were working hard behind the bar, while at least four waitresses carried huge trays loaded with drinks through the chattering throng, yelling new orders back to the barmen every few seconds. The room reeked of tobacco, hops, and human sweat.

Following the plan they'd discussed on the brief walk up the hill from the West Orchard Street market, Trench made his way down to the end of the room and took up his place at the inlaid chessboard close to the games room doorway. Elbowing his way through the crowd as politely as he could, Black found a spot midway down the long bar and ordered himself a pint. By craning his neck he could just see Trench, who was now setting up pieces on the chessboard.

The detective peered at his watch, blinking at the tobacco sting in his eyes. It was now almost exactly six-thirty. He could feel his heart pounding and he lit a cigarette of his own. If past experience was any gauge, the raid, if there was going to be one, would begin sometime between seven and eight o'clock, giving the guiding moon a chance to rise fully over the target.

If Queer Jack had any hope of escaping before the cataclysm began, he was cutting it very fine: ninety minutes, or perhaps even less, to meet with Trench, lure him to whatever out-of-the-way spot he'd chosen, do the deed, then vanish before the bombers came.

Standing there in the roiling currents of humanity around the bar, Black found it almost impossible to think clearly, but he clutched at that single thought—Queer Jack was cutting it very fine. The detective smiled, then took a long pull on his lukewarm drink, a hundred tiny details suddenly falling into place. He hadn't lost it after all, not yet. The Sight.

Of course Queer Jack was cutting it fine—"spot on," as Trench had said, an obsession with punctuality. For Black's quarry, timing and place would be everything. Whatever evil nest of vipers the man carried in his heart, the essence of him was logic, neatness, clarity. He knew his victim, knew the place where he would make his kill with the efficiency of a stalking huntsman. Would have the method of escape planned with meticulous care. You bastard, Black thought. You evil bloody bastard.

Black gestured to the blonde woman behind the bar, busy

swabbing out another tray of freshly washed glasses. "Would you happen to have a train schedule about anywhere?"

"Might," the woman grunted. She dropped her cloth down on the bar, then bent down and began rummaging below the counter. She resurfaced a moment later and slapped a damp folder down in front of the detective. "There you are, love." She went back to her duties and Black picked up the schedule, thinking hard.

Four trains were listed as departing Coventry between seven and eight. A local to Nuneaton, another to Rugby, and two express trains—one to London and the other to Birmingham. The London train was scheduled to leave at 7:20. The only train before it was the one to Nuneaton at 7:05. Assuming that Queer Jack would try to return to London, the 7:20 was the most likely. On the other hand, the line had been blocked earlier in the day. It had probably been repaired by now, but would Queer Jack take the chance or would he catch the Birmingham train at 7:45?

"How far is the railway station from here?" asked Black. The blonde woman looked up from her dish washing and frowned. "Down the way a bit. Ten minutes by tram. Longer in a taxi."

"On foot?"

"Depends on how you go. Fifteen minutes on the main streets, ten if you go through the back ways at Jordan's Well and Whitefriars Gate." Too long, Black thought, too much chance of error. Somehow it seemed unlikely that he would have hired a car so...

"Is there a bus terminal nearby?"

The blonde woman nodded. "Block away. Midland Red. Up Priory Street on the far side of Pool Meadow by the fire hall."

"You don't happen to have a schedule by any—"

"Don't need one. On the hour to Kenilworth and Rugby, on the quarter to Lichfield and Nuneaton, on the half to

Birmingham." Times and destinations Queer Jack would already know.

And once in Birmingham he'd have an almost infinite number of choices. Granting ten minutes after the commission of his crime to reach the bus terminal, Queer Jack had given himself less than an hour. Utterly self-assured, supremely arrogant. And with good reason, Black thought bitterly. He thought about the bodies of Talbot and Rudelski, Eddings and Dranie. The moldering waxy corpse of Jane Luffington. Five dead, and without the accident of the photograph in Dranie's house and Queer Jack's own taunting postcard left in Talbot's car, virtually nothing to go on. He'd almost managed it. But not quite.

Black leaned forward and looked down the length of the bar. Trench was hunched over the board, staring down at the pieces. The detective picked up his pint glass and turned around casually, letting his eyes drift over the crowd. Whom was he looking for? Someone anonymous, nondescript, and, according to Spilsbury, someone with strong hands. No one stood out as far as the detective could see. No one sat alone. The blackout curtains over the door hung heavy and unmoving. He looked at his watch again. Twenty to seven. Queer Jack was late.

Or was he? Black felt a terrible chill run down his spine. He put his glass carefully down on the bar. Queer Jack lived by the force of time and logic; by his own admission to Brian Trench he was obsessed with punctuality. Which meant the man was here, had been here before they arrived, waiting, assessing, watching. The detective closed his eyes for a moment and tried to breathe evenly. Thank God he and Trench had come into the Stump separately.

He glanced toward the curtain-covered front door again. He'd noticed a call box outside, a few steps from the entrance, the small light in the cubicle painted dark blue. How long would it take to reach the local police, explain to them who he was and why he was here? Too long. Too bloody long. It was insanity. Without taking even the most rudimentary precautions he'd put Trench at terrible risk, all for his own desire to catch Queer Jack. To prove himself to Liddell and God knows whom else. To be Morris Black, perfect detective, perfect Jew. Bloody, bloody hell!

He took a deep breath and let it out slowly. No matter what the consequences, the only thing he could do now was to stop the process before it was too late. If Queer Jack was already in the Stump, he'd see Trench being approached and slip away, unnoticed. If the murderer really was late, he'd arrive at the pub and find his victim in Black's company. It was the only way to keep Trench safe from possible harm.

Black turned, edging away from the bar, and began to work his way back toward the rear of the room. Then he froze, horrified. Through the crowd he could just make out Trench. The butcher's assistant had turned away from the chessboard and was talking to someone who had his back to Morris Black. All the detective could make out was a figure in a dark trilby hat and a fawn-colored raincoat. Not a large man, but not small either. Nondescript. Where in hell had he come from?

It was too late to think about that now. Black gritted his teeth and moved on, pressing through the crowded room. At least the man had his back to him. He hesitated. Through the din he was sure he'd heard someone call his name, but that was ridiculous of course, since no one in Coventry—

"Morris!" A woman's voice, calling him. Oh, dear God! Who? He looked around wildly, and then the voice came again, much more loudly, pitched against the noise in the room. Almost laughing. "Detective Inspector Morris Black!"

For a single, nightmarish instant it seemed to the detective that time had been suspended. Thirty feet away he saw Trench's surprised face looking desperately in his direction over the shoulder of his companion. Beyond them, framed in the doorway leading to the games room, Katherine Copeland stood smiling, one hand lifted, waving at him.

The man with Trench turned slightly, and Black had the brief sight of a thin, terribly pale face, eyes hidden behind the lenses of wire-rimmed spectacles. Then the face turned away. A hand, gray-gloved, came up carrying something dark and rectangular and thrust it in Trench's direction. The butcher's assistant's eyes bulged enormously and his hand came up, gripping his throat. He dropped back onto his seat at the chessboard and disappeared from view. When Black looked again, Queer Jack was almost gone, pushing past Katherine Copeland, who was still standing in the doorway leading to the games room, a bewildered half-smile on her face, her wide eyes confused.

Black rushed forward, his hopes of surprise dashed with the sound of Katherine's voice. He bludgeoned through the crowd, pushing people out of his way with one hand, the other reaching into his jacket and puffing out his warrant card. "Police! Clear the way!"

He barely paused when he reached the end of the bar, his eyes sweeping quickly over the slumped figure of poor Brian Trench, the front of his crisp, white shirt now flooded with blood from the gaping faucet of his torn throat, his eyes rolled back in their sockets, his mouth sagging. People were already crowding around the dying man; if there was any help for him, someone else would have to give it.

The detective reached the games room door, pushed Katherine aside without a word, and kept on, waving the warrant card, his other arm sweeping people out of the way. Black saw his mistake now; another doorway led to a small dining room and beyond that a rear entrance to the Magpie and Stump. Running now, stumbling as his hip smashed into a table, overturning it, he raced for the door, watching as it swung shut behind his elusive quarry. Sensing someone behind him, he wasted another precious second, half-turning, spotting Katherine behind him.

"Keep the bloody hell away!" he yelled. He rushed for the door, pushed it open, and ran out into the darkness. A laneway, cobbled, stones pale in the cool, bright light of the fully risen moon. Fifty feet away a racing shadow and the sound of running footsteps.

He rushed on, vaguely hearing the sound of a slamming door and other footsteps. The Copeland woman, following him. Ignoring her, he pelted down the lane after Queer Jack, desperately trying to orient himself as he ran. The rear of the Stump would face north, so he was moving east now, the blank, windowless walls on his left the back of the Triumph Works. Which way would the bastard go?

The barmaid said that the bus terminal was no more than a block away, up the hill on Priory Street. But they were moving downhill. The wrong direction. Christ! What was Queer Jack doing?

The lane ended at the entrance to Dale Street. Peering to the left, Black saw the high, locked main gates of the Works complex. No sign of Jack. He turned right. Behind him he heard Katherine calling his name, pleading for him to stop, but once again he ignored her. Fifty feet farther on and still no sign of his man. He was back on Cope Street, the front entrance to the Stump dimly visible on his right. Across the street the pitch-dark gloom of another lane. He threw himself forward, his breath ragged now, lungs burning.

Reaching the entrance to the lane, he paused for a split second, listening. He was facing south now, away from the bus terminal. He heard the barmaid's voice again—Jordan's Well and Whitefriars Gate. The train station. A fallback. He headed into the dark mouth of the alley, moving more slowly now, but still running. Would Queer Jack wait? Lurk in some shaded doorway? Strike again the way he'd struck at Trench? In his mind's eye, Black saw the man's drenched, scarlet shirtfront, and he groaned helplessly, increasing the pace.

The alley twisted and turned, following a downhill path

between the backs of office buildings and shops. Far ahead he heard the sudden tinny smash of a dustbin overturning and then the yowling screech of a cat. Queer Jack was still ahead. A minute later, passing the scattered litter from the dustbin, he came out onto New Street and paused again. A block away on his left he could see the tower of St. Michael's Cathedral rising above the screening back of trees around it, the four flying buttresses like huge stone needles at the tower's square summit, supporting the massive, soaring spire. The lead roof of the cathedral was lightly coated with early-evening frost, turning it a ghostly silver that would be visible from miles away in the all-revealing light of the fat full moon.

Black could barely breathe now, and he was forced to pause again, bending, hands on his knees as he fought to take in huge breaths of the cool night air. Suddenly he felt a hand on his shoulder and he straightened, whirling in panic-stricken terror, his fist cocked back, ready to strike.

"Morris! No! It's me!"

Katherine. "Oh, Jesus! I told you to bloody well stay away!" he gasped. Her face was pale and frightened in the faint cold light.

"Morris! God damn it! What the hell is going on?"

"No time. He's getting away!" He shook off her hand and stumbled forward again, weaving across the street. There was no sign of Queer Jack. No sound. Directly ahead of him the entrance to yet another alleyway. Oh, God! He thought. So close, so bloody close! He moved off again, ignoring the tearing pain in his lungs and the sound of Katherine's running steps echoing behind. He came out into the open briefly, the melancholy vista of the old bishop's graveyard sloping away on his right. Above him the huge circle of the pitiless full moon glowed like a treacherous searchlight in the dark night sky. Black ran on.

Halfway down an alley to the south of Jordan's Well, the detective paused again, his frosty breath coming in long panting gasps. On his left was the high, windowless brick wall of a cinema, on his right, the hoardings surrounding the Lea Francis Cycle Works. It was pitch-dark here, the path between the buildings so narrow that even a full moon could shed no light.

Directly ahead of him the alley split like the frayed end of a rope, going off in all directions. Black, totally unfamiliar with his surroundings, was lost within the complex maze of mews and lanes in the center of the old, closely built domestic and factory district crowded into a six-hundred- by four-hundred-foot area between Little Park Street, Earl Street, and Much Park Street. Queer Jack had vanished into this ancient, dingy rabbit warren, and with a sinking heart Morris Black knew that he didn't have the faintest chance of finding him.

"Morris?" It was Katherine, catching up with him at last. He turned angrily. She was standing a few feet away, hair madly tousled by the chase, eyes wide. Somewhere along the way she'd managed to tear away the sleeve of her short, dark-blue coat, and one of her shoes was missing.

"The bastard's gone," said Black. "The bloody bastard's gone!" He suddenly felt a tearing, burning sensation in his side, and for a mad instant he wanted to reach out and smack the woman in the face. It was her fault! All her fault! He bent over, ears ringing, ashen-faced at the tearing pain from the muscle spasm. Katherine took a step forward, then stopped, her head jerking upward, the anguish on her face changing instantly to fear.

"Morris!"

"Shut up!" he groaned. "Just shut up, can't you!" If it hadn't been for the wretched woman's sudden appearance...Still a chance though. He could get to the train station and then...

She stepped forward again, grasping his arm. "Morris! Listen!" Sirens. The sickly, undulating moan of an alert.

"It's starting!" he whispered, looking up at the sliver of sky over their heads.

The high-pitched siren's wail began to fade, and then, for one long moment, there was absolute silence. Finally, out of the distance, both Black and Katherine heard the sound of the approaching bombers, a low, growling mutter that grew with each passing second. Not the threaded string of a London raid—this was something different, a solid wall of sound.

Black looked around wildly. Behind them, up the hill, was St. Michael's and the center of the city; in front, a score of twisting paths that might lead to safety or just as easily to a dead end without any kind of shelter. A single high-explosive bomb on the cinema beside them would bring the looming brick wall down on their heads; an incendiary in the yard of the Cycle Works would see them incinerated.

They'd managed to survive the single bomb that struck the Burlington Arcade by merest chance; chance would not be part of anyone's equation tonight. Ignoring the white-hot sear of pain in his side, Black grabbed Katherine's hand.

"Run!" he yelled.

They had gone less than fifty yards when a new sound was added to the bombers' thunder. A faint, hissing sound, like a nest of dozing snakes disturbed in some dark hole, or the first rush of a rain squall on the flat, oily surface of a dead calm sea an instant before the breaking of the storm. There was a brilliant flash high overhead, and looking up, still running, Black could see the retina-burning splash of a parachute flare igniting. Far in the distance, the few antiaircraft batteries still in place around Coventry began to snort and bang, and then the rain sound was all around them.

Black heard a sharp, smacking noise directly in front of them as the first incendiaries reached the ground. There was a burst of light and then a shower of sparks twenty feet ahead, and Black threw himself to the ground, dragging Katherine with him.

A split second later the small thermite charge lodged in the core of the magnesium exploded with a shattering roar, sending bits of white-hot shrapnel flying in all directions. Within an instant, a dozen fires were burning in the once dark alleyway.

They stumbled to their feet and ran on, swinging around the small crater where the incendiary had exploded, ducking past a sheet of flame as it began to suck up the plank wall of a small millwright's shop. Almost unbelievably, they managed to slip by and ran on into the safety of the darkness beyond.

There were no single sounds now, only an ever-growing hell of a hundred different noises; the steady thunder of the bombers, the coughing chatter of the ack-ack, the swish and roar and Roman-candle hiss of the incendiaries; and now, like the hammering of mad kettledrums, there was the new sound of the larger high-explosive bombs, some no more than a screaming whistle followed by a ground-shaking thump, but others so massive Black could feel the huge pressure waves smashing into his chest, threatening to knock them over.

Behind them the small incendiaries fell in a steady, horrifying shower, banishing the evening chill with the steadily rising heat from the combining fires as a hundred buildings began to burn. To Black it seemed almost as though the fire were a living thing, trying to seek them out, following them as they raced onward. Without some kind of shelter soon, they would be turned to cinder.

A huge, unbelievably loud explosion came from directly behind them as a five-hundred-kilogram *Flammenbombe* oil canister detonated, sending out a whirling, searching fireball of flaming kerosene and bunker oil, but they turned a corner in the lane before it reached them.

Even so, Black could feel the air being sucked out of his lungs, and he was vaguely aware of a searing wave of heat blistering the skin on the back of his neck. Beside him, Katherine's hair began to curl and frizzle, and the back of her short coat was actually smoking. Another explosion like that in front of them and they would be trapped.

Abruptly the alley ended and they found themselves standing on the pavement of Much Park Street. They stopped dead, frozen by the terrible spectacle before their eyes. An entire block was engulfed in flames.

One of the huge, buff-colored AB1000 incendiary containers had failed to split and open at the preset altitude, and all 610 of its two-pound incendiary bomblets had been released less than thirty feet above the ground, spewing hundreds of the two-foot-long magnesium tubes into the walls and windows of the surrounding factories and commercial buildings as well as turning the street itself into a fuming mass of puddling, liquefied macadam that was now rolling like flaming lava down the gutters, then cascading into the storm sewers.

More incendiaries had fired the roof of the Lea Francis Cycle Works, which fronted onto Much Park Street, and several 250-kilogram high-explosive bombs had turned the narrow façade of the old Midlands Brewing Company into a pile of flaming rubble that blocked the roadway to the south.

In the midst of it all an abandoned trolley car was burning like a huge torch, while closer to them the skeletal remains of a motorcycle were literally melting into the pavement, its rider reduced to a charred and blackened stick figure hunched horribly over the handlebars.

"Sweet mother of Christ!" whispered Katherine, looking out into the raging hell of Much Park Street. As she spoke, there was another explosion in the alley as the fires started by the thousand-pound oil bomb reached the preservative storage sheds of the Providence Milling Company.

Above them the night sky was hidden now, masked by a roiling, impenetrable cloud of oily smoke and brightly spinning sparks. Invisibly the bombers continued their onslaught, one after the other in a never-ending wave, their bombs released in screaming, whistling streams, hurtling through the smoke, down to join the boiling cauldron of flame below.

"Morris! We're trapped!" Gasping in the terrible heat, Katherine wrenched off the smoking remains of her jacket and threw it aside. Her throat was seared, and no matter how hard she tried there seemed to be no way to take enough air into her lungs.

"No! There!" Black pointed across the roadway, and without another word he dragged her forward. Both her shoes were gone now and she screamed as her bare feet touched the glutinous, superheated tar of the roadway. Black ignored her and pressed on, eventually bringing them both to the far side of the street.

Directly in front of them a wrought-iron enclosure protected three sides of a basement entrance. They staggered down the short flight of steps, ducking as the main doorway above them and to their left suddenly burst into flame, its frame collapsing in a deadly shower of flaming splinters. Black smashed into the basement door with his shoulder, then struck again. The door flew open and they burst into the dark interior of the basement.

With a terrible cracking sound directly over their heads, the entire front of the building collapsed with an earsplitting roar, fifty tons of brick and timber filling the entranceway behind them, sealing them underground.

Still gripping Katherine's hand, Black plunged forward in the darkness. Above them the sounds of the exploding bombs and the raging fires had dulled, but the detective was only too aware of the deadly creaking of the floorboards and joists above their heads. His free hand, outstretched, smashed into a thick metal supporting column, and he breathed a sigh of relief. At some point the owners of the building had reinforced the foundations with steel beams. For the moment at least, they were safe.

Loosening his grip on Katherine's hand, he began rummaging through the pockets of his coat and then began to laugh.

'What's so goddamn funny?" asked Katherine out of the darkness.

"The whole city is going up in flames outside, and here I am looking for a bloody match to see my way."

"Here." Black heard a faint sound beside him, and then Katherine's Ronson flared, offering up a tiny, weak halo of light. She lifted her hand and swung around slowly. "Where are we?"

"The basement of a funeral establishment by the looks of it."

Neatly stacked piles of caskets were all around them, each coffin separated from its neighbor with wooden planks. If the fires over their heads managed to burn through the floorboards, the place would go up like a spark in a tinderbox. A crematorium. Beside Black, Katherine shivered.

"Morris, I don't want to die in a place like this," she whispered.

He put one hand on her shoulder and squeezed gently, his earlier anger gone in the face of their present danger. "Don't worry, I won't let that happen." He took the lighter from her and stepped forward cautiously, glancing toward the joists above them every few seconds. Katherine followed.

Beyond the rows of coffins they found a doorway, the closure sprung and twisted, a cracked joist above it. Squeezing through the opening they found themselves in what could only have been the body-preparation room. It looked like one of Spilsbury's mortuaries.

Half a dozen metal tables were in a row, glass-fronted cabinets along one wall and a line of metal drawers along the other. The body of an elderly woman was laid out on the table closest to them. She was naked, thick tubes running from groin and flabby abdomen, draining into a large metal canister at the foot of the table. Another tube ran into her chest, connected to some sort of pump on a counter behind the table.

Someone had already been working on the woman's face; the mouth, still open, was stuffed with cotton, and a heavy curved needle dangled from her lower lip, probably left there at the first sounding of the sirens. Her cheeks were rouged and her hair was neatly curled. A row of small glass cosmetic pots were lined up on the table beside her head. The eyes, wide, dry, and blind, stared upward toward the unseen inferno blazing only a few feet above.

"God, Morris, get me out of here," moaned Katherine, staring down at the corpse. An edge of panic was creeping into her voice, and Black felt it rising in himself as well. The heat from the lighter was becoming unbearably hot and he loosened his cramped finger on it. The light snuffed out, leaving them in utter darkness. Overhead they could hear the blast-furnace roar of flames, and beyond, muffled by debris and distance, the steady thumping detonations of more bombs. Switching hands, he flicked on the lighter again, revealing the unmoving corpse of the old woman.

"Over there," said Black, moving the lighter to his right. Another door, large and metal-clad. They made their way between the tables, crossing to the far side of the room. Black tentatively reached out with his free hand, pressing his palm against the green-painted tin covering the door. The metal was relatively cool; no fire was burning beyond. He pushed down on the handle and dragged the door back on its hinges. Stepping through the doorway, he raised his arm.

They were in a sub-basement of some kind, standing on a rough wooden landing with a flight of steps leading down to a stained cement floor with a large, grille-covered drain in the center. Looking upward, Black saw that the roof was very old, the beams and joists nothing more than crudely squared tree trunks.

Rows of shelves were built against the stone walls, filled with large, wicker-covered flasks and an assortment of tins and boxes. He sniffed. No smoke, but a biting stink of chemicals and the sick-sweet stench of human excrement. Somewhere a sewer pipe had ruptured and gas was backing up into the smaller drains like the one in the floor.

Against the far right wall Black could see several heavy lead pipes running from side to side, sloping from floor to ceiling. Water and sewage. He closed the door carefully behind them. From what the detective could see in the faint light cast by the lighter, the door was the only way in or out of the room.

"We'll be safe enough here," he said, not really believing it. "Come on." They went down the steps, Black holding up the lighter. As he reached the bottom and turned slightly to say something reassuring to Katherine, there were two massive explosions, less than a second apart.

The first came from an externally carried thousand-kilogram parachute mine that detonated in the rear yard of the Charlesworth Motor Body Works, which was located midway between Much Park Street and Little Park Street, connected to both by a narrow lane used both by the Motor Body Works and the MacMillan Funeral Parlour.

The second explosion was caused by a smaller, yellow-striped SC 500 bomb that cut through the flaming roof of MacMillan's, smashing through the ceiling of the main viewing salon before it detonated. By an odd stroke of luck the blast and pressure wave from this second explosion snuffed out the blossoming fire that was threatening to burn through the floor over the body-preparation room and the sub-basement storage area.

It also brought down the already weakened walls of the narrow, brick building, burying Morris Black and Katherine Copeland under twenty tons of rubble and insulating them from the other fires consuming the larger, wood-framed buildings on either side of the funeral parlor.

However, the shock wave from the explosion in the Charlesworth yard was so severe that it completely destroyed the large water and sewage mains running from Earl Street to

Whitefriars Lane as well as rupturing the narrower conduits that actually ran through the sub-basement of MacMillan's. Both Morris Black and his companion had been knocked unconscious by the force of the explosions, and neither of them was aware that their dark, solidly sealed bolt hole was now a catch basin for water from the ruptured mains and sewer waste bubbling up through the central drain. When it filled, they would drown.

CHAPTER TWENTY

Saturday, November 23, 1940
10:30 A.M., British Standard Time

MORRIS BLACK LAY IN THE DIMLY LIT ROOM, his plaster-covered right leg elevated on a canvas-sling-and-chain arrangement fitted to a metal cage over the lower end of the hospital bed. His left eye was still covered by a gauze patch, and both hands were swathed in bandages. When he first began swimming up out of unconsciousness, he'd been sure that he was blind, but this morning a doctor had removed the patch on his right eye and informed him that the left patch would be removed in a day or two. Now at least he could see, even if it was only partially.

By turning his head slightly he could make out the narrow window on his left. The blackout curtains were drawn back, letting in the weak November sunshine. Midday or later by the looks of it. He could still smell the hot-ash reek of the fires in his nostrils, but through it he could also smell the familiar odors of ointment and disinfectant.

He moved his head on the pillows propped up behind him, wincing at the shooting pain in his neck, and glanced at Guy Liddell, seated in a large, comfortable-looking chair to the right of his bed, a cup of tea perched on one padded arm.

"You still haven't told me exactly where I am," Black croaked. His throat burned and his mouth felt thick as glue, his tongue a swollen obstacle that made swallowing an effort. More than once since regaining consciousness he'd seriously wondered if he wouldn't be better off dead.

"The Queen Victoria Hospital in East Grinstead." Liddell leaned forward and put the teacup on the enameled table at the head of the bed. "Quite new, all mod cons. The RAF uses it now. So do we. Excellent facilities for people who've been burned, and it's discreet."

"I spoke with a doctor today. He wouldn't tell me anything except that there wouldn't be any permanent damage."

"Curt fellow with horn-rims?"

"Yes."

"McIndoe. They call him the Maestro."

"Was he telling the truth?"

"I believe so. You were extremely lucky, Black, I hope you're aware of that."

"What about Katherine? No one seems to know anything about her."

"She got off a sight better than you, old man. Superficial burns, singed hair, some cuts and bruises."

"Is she here as well?"

"She was. She was released some time ago. Back in London by now, I presume."

"I've been here nine days?"

"That's right. It's Saturday, the twenty-third. You were unconscious for three days and then you started coming out of it. The doctors kept you under with morphia until you were a bit further along. Standard procedure, as I understand it." Liddell paused. "How much do you remember about what happened?"

"Nothing at all after the explosion."

"Miss Copeland saved your life. A water main burst and started filling up the room you were in. She managed to drag you up onto some sort of landing; kept you from drowning until the ARP lads dug you out the next day. Quite a feat, I gather. She must be strong as an ox."

There was a long silence. "I almost had him," Black whispered finally.

Liddell sighed. "So I'm given to understand by Miss Copeland." He smiled thinly. "She takes full responsibility, by the way. She said if it hadn't been for her barging in on things, you would have nicked him."

"No. My fault," said Black weakly. "I should have—"

"You should have done what you were told," said Liddell flatly. "And you were told not to go to Coventry under any circumstances."

"Queer Jack knew there was going to be a raid." Black stared at the intelligence officer. "A major one. So did you."

"Obviously."

"There was no warning."

"No."

"Who else knew?"

"A number of people. People who had to know."

"Your bloody Magic Circle. Ultra."

"Yes."

"You could have issued a warning, done something."

"It was decided that nothing could be done. Not without prejudicing Ultra."

Black was silent for a long moment. Martyr a city and save the winning of the war. "How bad was it in the end?"

"Very. The entire center of the old city was burned to the ground. The cathedral was gutted. You were lucky to escape."

"How many dead?"

"Five hundred."

"My God." Black let his head fall back against the pillows.

He thought of Garlinski, and of Trench. "There's going to be hell to pay when word of this gets out."

"It won't get out. That's been attended to. We had to keep Ultra safe."

"'We'? Does that include Churchill?"

"There was no need for him to know. It was decided to keep the information from him until it was too late to do anything about the situation. A fait accompli. The prime minister has enough to deal with as it is. There was no time for moral handkerchief wringing. A decision had to be made. It was. Any problems down the road will be dealt with."

"You're all mad," Black said quietly. He couldn't bring himself to look at Liddell. He turned away and stared up at the shadowed ceiling. "I've had enough of you, Liddell. The whole bloody crew."

"You're hardly in a position to cast aspersions, Inspector. You have your own cross to bear, I'm afraid. You involved an innocent party in your little scheme and he died for his efforts."

"Trench." That great stain of blood down the front of his shirt, the look in his eyes. Another link in his chain of guilt.

"Yes. Mr. Brian Trench. We found his name in your little book. The rest we put together after interviewing Miss Copeland." Liddell took out his pipe and began to rub the bowl with the thumb and forefinger of one hand. "Fortunately the evidence of your blunder has been destroyed; at least we don't have that to worry about. Nor do you, except for the occasional pang of conscience I suppose."

"What do you mean?"

"The public house—the Stump I believe it was called?"

"The Magpie and Stump."

"It no longer exists. Neither does Mr. Trench nor anyone else who was there at the time. The Triumph Motor Cycle Works was hit by several large, high-explosive bombs as well as a score of incendiaries. From what I understand the site is still too hot to investigate."

"He was married. His wife will want to know what happened to her husband."

"Dead as well," Liddell answered briefly. "We checked on that. They lived in a house on Cherry Street. She went to her Anderson Shelter when the alert came. The house was less than fifty yards away from the old gasworks on Abbot's Lane. Went up like a Roman candle. The entire street was demolished." Liddell put the pipe back into the pocket of his jacket. "Saves us a bit of trouble, actually."

"Queer Jack?" asked Black after a moment.

"For the time being we're assuming that he perished in the raid. A nameless victim." Liddell paused. "There were enough of them," he added dryly.

"You don't really believe that. He was well away from things when the alert came," said Black, remembering. "He'd planned for the raid. I'm sure he survived."

"What you're sure of is irrelevant, Inspector. As far as any official record is concerned, the man you were after is dead."

"And when he kills again?"

"So far that hasn't happened."

"It will."

"Perhaps not."

Morris Black stared unbelievingly at the intelligence officer. "My God, it's all being swept under the carpet."

"I'm afraid so, yes."

"And I'm to be swept under the carpet along with everything else?"

"Yes. Your secondment to my department has been terminated. You are, however, still bound by the Official Secrets Act."

"Swift?"

"He has been assigned to other duties for the time being. A transfer to sunnier climes. Palestine, as I recall."

Black let out a long breath, trying to ignore the throbbing pain in his hands and the ache in his neck. It was madness, and it made no sense. Liddell knew that Queer Jack represented a potentially disastrous security leak, yet he was collapsing the investigation. Something had frightened him off. "And the other man? The one you call The Doctor?"

"We are pursuing other lines of inquiry," Liddell answered stiffly. He stood up, patted his pockets, and glanced down at Black.

"So that's the end of it?"

The MI5 officer nodded. "As far as you're concerned, yes. You will remain here for the next few weeks until you're quite recovered from your injuries. After that there will be another debriefing and that will be that."

"I go back to the Yard a sadder and wiser man," said Black, his tone bitter.

Liddell raised an eyebrow. "I think not, Inspector."

"What precisely is that supposed to mean?"

"It means that as a result of your injuries you will no longer be deemed fit to act as a police officer. You will be offered the opportunity to retire on a full disability pension."

Black stared, unbelieving. Liddell was dismantling his world, brick by brick.

"And if I refuse?"

"You will be asked to undergo a physical examination, which you will fail. You will then be asked to resign your commission in the Metropolitan Police Force."

Black knew the answer but asked the question anyway. "And if I don't resign?"

There was a hint of sadness in Liddell's voice. "Then you will be fired, Morris. There is also the possibility that you could be tried under the Treachery Act for divulging secret information to an agent of a foreign power."

"You can't mean Katherine."

"That's exactly who I mean."

"She's a reporter, Liddell, not a spy," Black lied.

Liddell smiled and shook his head. "I may be insane, Morris, but I'm not naive. Miss Copeland told me who her recent employers had been. She also told me that she discussed the matter with you the night before Coventry."

"She was drunk. I didn't think she was telling me the truth."

"Bollocks." Liddell smiled.

"I want to see her."

"I'm afraid that won't be possible. You're not to be allowed any visitors."

"A telephone then."

"No."

"Then I'm a prisoner here?"

Liddell said nothing; instead he reached out and laid a hand on Black's shoulder for a moment. "I'll see you again in a few weeks, Inspector. We'll have another chat then." He smiled, squeezed Black's shoulder, then turned and left the room, closing the door softly behind him. Listening, Morris Black was quite sure he heard the sound of a lock being turned.

Katherine Copeland climbed out of her cab, paid the driver, then checked the address on the small card she'd been sent by Larry Bingham: 23 Tedworth Square on the edge of Pimlico, not far from the Embankment and the Thames. She clenched the collar of her coat tightly around her neck against the cold and went up the short flight of steps to the front door, still limping slightly. The burns she'd sustained in Coventry had been superficial, but somewhere along the way she'd managed to severely tear the Achilles tendon of her left foot. A small enough price to pay, all things considered.

Pressing the small buzzer, she waited on the top step, wondering why Bingham had asked her to meet him in such an out-of-the-way spot, or anywhere at all for that matter, especially in broad daylight. After a moment the door was opened by a young, dark-haired woman, who smiled and ushered her inside. Katherine found herself in a small, tile-floored foyer. Directly in front of her was a long flight of stairs with an ornate, heavily varnished banister.

"They're waiting for you in the projection room," said the woman. She took Katherine's coat, hung it up on a rather plain-looking stand, and led the way up the stairs. Reaching the landing, the woman went down a short, dim hallway, opened a door, and stood aside. Katherine stepped into the room and the woman closed the door behind her.

The room was large and high-ceilinged, heavy blackout curtains drawn over the tall bay window looking out over the square. In front of the curtains a pull-down screen on a tripod had been set up. The only furniture was a small table holding a motion-picture projector and half a dozen wooden folding chairs. The only light came from a bare-bulb fixture in the ceiling.

"Hello, Kat." Lawrence Bingham unfurled himself from one of the chairs and crossed the room to her. "Good to see you again. Wounds healing all right?" His voice was solicitous.

"Well enough," she said. Lying bastard, she thought. Someone else had been seated with Bingham, and he was now standing, waiting to be introduced. He was short with dark, thinning hair and a hawk nose that belonged to an entirely different face. He was wearing a British Army uniform without any sort of insignia.

Bingham took Katherine by the elbow and brought her across the room. The man in the Army uniform extended a hand and Katherine took it. The man's fingers gripped hers loosely and then withdrew. It was like shaking hands with a dead fish, and Katherine found herself recoiling slightly.

"Maxwell Knight," he said. The voice was soft and well educated. "I'm very glad you could attend at such short notice." He gestured to one of the folding chairs and Katherine seated herself, throwing Bingham a fast, quizzical look.

"Major Knight is a member of the British security service," said Bingham, still standing.

"MI5," said Katherine.

Knight smiled. "If you wish." There was as much humor in his expression as a waiting vulture. What in God's name was Larry Bingham doing with a man like this? For that matter, what was she doing here?

"Major Knight was the man who uncovered the Tyler Kent affair," said Bingham. Katherine nodded. Now she was beginning to understand. Larry had been the U.S. diplomatic representative when the embassy clerk was arrested. It still didn't explain what the two men were doing together now though, or the reason for her own presence.

"Since you're so intimately involved with our present situation, I thought you should be here today," said Knight, his voice smooth. "Mr. Bingham concurred."

"What situation would that be?" asked Katherine warily. This was Larry's game and now the devious bastard was drawing her into it. For some reason she was a useful commodity again.

"The situation regarding Detective Inspector Black and your mutual adventure in Coventry," Knight answered.

"I don't think I'm really in a position to say anything about that." Katherine gave Bingham another look, but he just smiled and shrugged his shoulders. "From what I've been given to understand, there's a chance I might still be arrested as a spy. Or tried for treason."

"I rather doubt that," said Knight, his voice dry.

"He's in on the whole thing, Kat," said Bingham. "All of it."

"I think someone should explain just what the hell is going on."

"Of course." Knight threaded his way through the double row of folding chairs, went to the screen, and turned, hands clasped behind his back. "Let me begin by saying that I am aware of Mr. Bingham's function at your embassy." Knight smiled bleakly. "The corollary to this, of course, is that I am also aware of your relationship with Mr. Bingham."

"I don't have a relationship with Larry," said Katherine, not seeing at all. All she knew for sure was that Bingham was playing fast and loose with security.

"Consider yourself reinstated, Kat, at least for the time being."

Knight spoke again. "My department is also aware of your...friendship with Morris Black."

Katherine turned to Bingham, shocked at the disclosure. "Larry, what—"

"Let him talk."

"Your job was to find out why Inspector Black was so interested in a series of murders which have occurred since early September, and what connection those murders had with my department. Over the course of the last two and a half months neither you nor Inspector Black was able to discover very much about the so-called Queer Jack murders." Knight paused.

"Until ten days ago. At that time, with your help, Inspector Black established a connection between Queer Jack and the British Correspondence Chess Association. Apparently this is how the killer was choosing his victims. More importantly, you were also aware that Queer Jack possessed information about when and where Luftwaffe bombing raids were to occur. This, of course, is the basis of our interest in the murders. The killer did, and perhaps still does, represent a serious leakage of strategically important knowledge. Inspector Black's primary objective, apart from tracking down the killer, was to ascertain how the murderer was getting this information."

"This is all history," Katherine interrupted. "Why don't you get to the point, Major Knight." She could still feel the man's weak, sexless handshake. There was something almost spooky about his flat, emotionless discourse, and she knew intuitively that Knight was a dangerous man.

"History is important, Miss Copeland. I believe it was one of your own philosophers who said that 'those who cannot remember the past are condemned to repeat it.'"

"George Santayana."

The short man in the anonymous uniform smiled, nodding. "Quite so, Miss Copeland. But Mr. Santayana also observed that 'history is always written wrong, that is why it is always necessary to rewrite it.'"

"We've established your knowledge of American philosophy," said Katherine. "As well as letting me know how good a snoop you are. But you still haven't made your point, and I still don't know why I'm here."

"Please, Miss Copeland." Knight held up one placating hand. "We're on the same side."

"Really?"

"Mr. Bingham was instrumental in our arrest of the spy Tyler Kent. With Kennedy as ambassador, trapping the embassy code clerk might well have been a very sticky situation. Mr. Bingham smoothed the way considerably. It is now time for the favor to be returned. Quid pro quo."

"Not without some benefit to you, I'm sure. Tit for tat."

"Of course not." Knight smiled. "One hand does wash the other, after all, since we seem to be exchanging homilies." He paused again, the smile fading. After a long moment he spoke again. "Miss Copeland, what conclusions have you and Mr. Bingham reached about Inspector Black's investigations?"

Once again she turned to Bingham. Which came first, the tit or the tat, the quid or the quo? The first secretary nodded silently. Katherine took a deep breath, then let it out.

"We assume that you have a highly placed agent who is giving you accurate and regular information about Nazi bombing raids. Maybe other things. Somehow Queer Jack has access to the same information, probably here at the receiving end. The fact that you let the Germans firebomb Coventry into ashes proves just how important this agent is. Up until now you've been playing it pretty close to the chest. How's that?"

Knight nodded. "Good enough. Although not entirely accurate. The fact is, there is no such 'highly placed agent' as you describe. On the other hand our people have managed to break the main codes used by the German General Staff. We have a copy of their Enigma encoding device and a high-speed method of decoding their signals."

"Jesus Christ!" Bingham muttered. He stared at Knight, astounded.

"Umm," said the intelligence officer. "Without Ultra, as we call it, the German Air Force would almost certainly have destroyed the RAF within a few weeks. We were able to husband our meager resources and put them where they could do the most damage. Had the Luftwaffe succeeded, England would have been invaded long ago. It was a near enough thing as it turned out. Even closer than your ambassador suspects, or President Roosevelt."

"Why are you telling us about this?" asked Bingham. "And on whose authority?"

"You are being told this because we are now faced with a crisis even more acute than the Nazis."

"Such as?" Bingham asked, ignoring Knight's melodramatic pause.

"Treason. The possibility of civil war." The small man's voice was toneless; he might have been repeating a recipe for meat loaf.

"You'll have to explain that one," said Katherine. "And you still haven't told us whose authority you're acting on." Bingham nodded his agreement; it was obviously worrying him as well. A few moments ago Knight had blandly divulged something that was obviously in the top-secret category. The last thing they needed now was to find themselves embroiled

in some sort of internecine battle between government bureaucracies. Roosevelt would have both their heads on a platter if they did anything to upset the delicate balance of neutrality. She glanced at Bingham covertly. If they were smart,
they'd cover their ears and get the hell out of here. The first
secretary ignored her look and sat beside her, stone-faced,
waiting for Knight to answer. He did.

"I am acting under no authority except my own. Frankly,
there are few people I can trust, even among my own staff.
Loyalty to one's country seems to be getting short shrift of late."

"So you come to us?" asked Bingham. Katherine felt her
stomach twist. Every instinct was telling her to leave the room
before anything more was said. The man was clearly a paranoid. She glanced over her shoulder at the projector on the
table behind them.

It suddenly occurred to her that Knight might well have
them under surveillance. Wouldn't that look lovely on *News of
the World*. The first secretary of the U.S. embassy in London
and herself palling around with MI5. What kind of hole had
Larry dropped them into?

"We need your help, and your cooperation," said Knight.
"Quite frankly, we had no one else to turn to. It is key that the
American security authorities understand exactly what is
going on."

"'We'?" asked Bingham pointedly.

"I'll get to that." Knight went behind them to the projector, flicked it on, then crossed the door and switched off the
overhead light, plunging the room into darkness. A bright,
flickering square appeared on the screen in front of them.
Knight went back to the projector.

"What are we looking at?" asked Bingham. The blank
square resolved itself into a fuzzy black-and-white image. A
large country house, partially surrounded by a stand of trees.
Bright sunlight and a sky full of fluffy clouds. The frame
jumped and flickered. The image was suddenly much larger,

focusing in on a wide, stone terrace flanked by two wings of the house. The film steadied.

Knight's voice came to them out of the darkness. "This is Priory Close, a country estate in Kent about twenty-five miles from London. The house is owned by Sir Alexander Walker."

"The distillery millionaire?" asked Bingham. Katherine stared at the screen. She drank the man's whiskey; she'd been pissed to the gills on it when she confessed all to Morris that evening in her flat.

"Yes."

"Friend of Kennedy's," murmured the first secretary. "Been doing business for years. Kennedy is the American agent for Hiram Walker."

"And Sir Alexander is chairman of the board," put in Knight.

"When was this film taken?" asked Katherine.

"In late summer," said Knight, "before the Blitz began." The film jumped again, went out of focus, then steadied again.

On the screen a figure appeared, coming through the French doors of the wing on the left. "It's Joe Kennedy," said Bingham, identifying the tall, bald man with his trademark spectacles.

"Quite so," said Knight. "Apparently Sir Alexander gave your ambassador use of the house for this meeting, although he wasn't in attendance himself."

A number of other men followed Kennedy out onto the terrace, most of them drifting toward a buffet table that had been set up close to the doors leading to the opposite wing of the house. Including Kennedy, nine men were now on the terrace; there were no servants.

"Lord Halifax," said Bingham, picking out the bald, formally dressed British foreign secretary. "The chubby one with him is R. A. Butler, his undersecretary. His friends, such as they are, call him Rab." The silent film spooled on, the projector clattering behind them as the film on the screen moved slowly back and forth over the assembled group on the terrace. "I'll be damned," said Bingham.

"That's Lord Wellington standing by the table. The weasel-faced one with the mustache is Carmel Office, Bullitt's assistant in Paris. Amazing!"

"Indeed," said Knight.

"I don't recognize any of the others," Bingham murmured.

"The heavyset man beside the Duke of Wellington is James Mooney," Knight explained. "Vice president of your General Motors. Wellington sits on the board of Vauxhall, one of their British subsidiaries." Knight coughed politely. "Mooney is also in charge of the General Motors interests in Germany, specifically the Opel Werks." He paused again, then went on. "The rosy-cheeked man with the white hair speaking to Kennedy is James P. McKittrick, also a fellow countryman of yours."

"I've seen him at a few embassy parties." Bingham nodded. "Here and in Washington. A banker isn't he?"

"Quite so. At the moment Mr. McKittrick, among other things, is chairman of the Bank for International Settlements in Switzerland."

"I thought BIS was run by the Nazis," said Bingham.

"It is," said Knight calmly. "The shorter man in the shooting jacket on the ambassador's left is Paul Koch de Gooryend, also a banker, also with connections to BIS, and a personal adviser to Menzies."

"Stewart Menzies, your SIS head, MI6?"

"I'm afraid so." Another sigh.

"What about the one in the tweeds?" asked Katherine. The man was standing alone close to the doors on the left, his face partially in shadow.

"Charles Bedeaux. Another American, although he rarely goes there anymore."

"Time and motion studies." Bingham nodded. "Calls himself an efficiency expert. He's on Hoover's list. Friend of Goering's."

"And also of the Duke and Duchess of Windsor," said Knight. "He is, in fact, at this meeting representing their interests, as is Mr. Office. He has, um, rather a close relationship with the Duchess as we understand it."

A tenth man stepped out into the sunlight and paused, bending slightly to speak with Bedeaux. He was in his fifties, balding and wearing a baggy, three-piece suit with a watch chain across his thickening stomach. Katherine recognized the figure immediately.

"Anderson, the home secretary!"

"Quite correct," said Knight coldly. "The man in charge of Scotland Yard and Civil Defense among other things."

They continued to watch as the men on the screen moved around the terrace, choosing food and drink from the buffet table on the right.

"Quite the little party," said Bingham eventually. "Two cabinet ministers, the U.S. ambassador, some international bankers, and a smattering of Nazi sympathizers." He lit a cigarette, lighter blazing in the gloom. "Too bad we can't hear what they're saying."

"We can. You can listen to the recordings later if you wish."

"You eavesdropped as well?"

"We had some prior notice of the meeting. Walker was in Scotland shooting grouse. Tucked a few listening devices here and there among the potted plants. Surprisingly easy." Knight smiled. "The same sort of procedure you had in place when Mr. Kennedy was ambassador."

"You bugged Joe Kennedy's telephone?" asked Katherine, turning to Bingham. He ignored her and turned to Knight.

"So you know what the meeting was about?"

"Yes, I'm afraid I do."

"You mentioned the word *treason*," said Katherine bluntly. "Then you show us newsreels of our ambassador consorting with some pro-Germans and a pair of Churchill's ministers. Presumably this is all leading somewhere."

The film came to an end, the celluloid tail snapping off the reel and flapping angrily for a few seconds. Knight switched off the projector, turned on the lights, and sat down with Katherine and Bingham, turning one of the folding chairs to face them.

"Both Anderson and Halifax are remnants of Chamberlain's government," said Knight. "Of the two, Halifax was the most certain that peace with Hitler could be negotiated. He still feels that way. When Churchill took over as PM, he became a leader without a party. Halifax was the King's choice as well as Chamberlain's. If Churchill hadn't kept His Lordship on as foreign secretary, he would have had a political mutiny on his hands. He wouldn't have been able to function. Blackmail of a sort, or expediency, take your choice."

"Is that what the meeting was about?" asked Katherine.

"In part. McKittrick from BIS and this Koch de Gooryend fellow had been putting pressure on Kennedy. McKittrick had also been feeding the ambassador some highly sensitive information regarding stock prices."

"British stocks?" asked Bingham.

"Yes." Knight nodded. "Among others."

"That's illegal," said Bingham. "Foreign diplomats aren't allowed to trade in the country they're posted to."

"Nevertheless, that is what he was doing. From what I gather, Mr. Kennedy has become quite wealthy trading on Europe's present misfortunes."

"The ambassador has been involved in some questionable business dealings before this," put in Katherine. "You don't have to convince us of that."

"You said that Kennedy was only part of it," Bingham interjected.

"A small part," Knight answered, nodding. "As I mentioned, Anderson, Halifax, and Butler were very much for appeasement. Anderson and Halifax because they are essentially weak men, Butler because he has the mind of a Machiavelli and an eye to the main chance. The man is an immoral swine." Katherine couldn't help smiling; it was the first sign of emotion she'd seen from the uniformed man.

"Go on," Bingham prompted.

"Immediately following Churchill's appointment in May, there was a serious attempt to come to a negotiated peace. Overtly the offer was made through Swedish diplomatic channels. In fact the offer came from Hess and Goering. The conditions included a large loan, which was to be made to BIS, and a transfer of gold bullion. Ambassador Kennedy was involved, but backed out at the last minute. Churchill refused to have anything to do with it. Needless to say, neither Halifax nor Anderson were, or are, aware of the situation regarding Ultra."

"If Churchill had gone for a negotiated peace, his career as prime minister would have fizzled out like a wet firecracker," said Bingham. "Chamberlain would have been back in a minute."

"Halifax more likely; he was the chosen successor after Chamberlain's cancer was diagnosed. Whatever the case, the prime minister's position is still insecure, especially after the debacle in Dunkirk and the bombings here."

"And now Coventry," said Katherine.

"And now Coventry," Knight agreed.

"You're saying that Halifax and the others are going to take another stab at it?" asked Bingham, nodding his chin toward the film screen.

"Beyond that, I'm afraid. It goes much farther than Halifax. When Anderson invoked the 18B Internment regulation, he neglected to intern quite a number of questionable people, including several members of Parliament for a start. And various pro-Nazi business interests—powerful ones."

"Vauxhall?" Bingham suggested. "Hiram Walker?"

"Yes. You could add a number of others." Knight shook his head wearily. "It really is quite awful, you know. There's even some evidence that Montagu Norman at the Bank of England is involved, and McGowan."

"Who is McGowan?" Katherine asked.

"Sir Harold McGowan. Chairman of Imperial Chemical Industries. Neville Chamberlain was a major shareholder."

"A tangled web," said Bingham.

Knight nodded. "Very. ICI had a dozen agreements with German companies before the war, mostly with I. G. Farben. They're still in place, handled by McKittrick at BIS and one of the Nazi board members, Hermann Schmitz, who also happens to be on the board of I. G. Farben."

"So all these men at the meeting are part of some plot to make peace with Hitler?" asked Katherine. "Can they really do it? Get around Churchill, I mean?"

"Yes, almost certainly," said Knight. "With the help of people like McKittrick and Mooney. You'd be surprised at how much sympathy these people have. To them the real enemy is Stalin, not Hitler. As far as they're concerned, even wholesale murder by the Nazis is better than Communism. Unless Churchill manages to get Roosevelt into the war, England is doomed. Take away Ultra and the advantage it gives us and you simply speed up the process. According to our sources, Hitler has only postponed the invasion until spring. He'll bleed us, bomb us, and starve us to death.

"Capitulation or disintegration, that's how Kennedy described it. They'll make their separate peace and force Churchill out. If they don't manage it, you'll see Hitler crossing the Channel on the May tides, that's the implied threat that runs under all of this; if that comes to pass, Halifax will probably greet him on bended knee." Knight scowled. "I wouldn't be surprised if they gave Butler the bloody Knight's Cross with Oak Leaves for his efforts." Katherine glanced at Bingham; it was all he'd said to her before, and much more.

"And Bedeaux?" she asked, slightly bewildered. "The Duke and Duchess? Where do they fit into this?"

Knight shrugged. "King Across the Water and all that," he said. "Halifax stood against the Simpson marriage. From what we can tell he's done a complete about-face on that score. If the Germans do invade—"

"Edward takes the throne again. A puppet for Hitler," said Bingham. "Christ, it's diabolical."

"It would probably be somewhat more sophisticated than that," said Knight. "The country couldn't stand another abdication. More likely that Halifax would force the King to step down. Elizabeth would be crowned queen with the Duke of Windsor as prince regent until she came of age. It would work constitutionally—Bedeaux goes on about it at length during the meeting."

"So what we're really looking at here is a palace coup," said Katherine. "Banks and industry throwing their lot behind Hitler."

"In simple terms, yes. You Yanks stay out of the war, cut off any support to England, and we become a Nazi fiefdom. Scotland Yard becomes Gestapo headquarters, and Buckingham Palace is turned into a hunting lodge for Goering." Knight made a derisive, snorting noise. "Goebbels as editor of the *London Times*."

"Jesus," Bingham whispered.

"It's all insane of course," Knight commented blandly. "None of these men knows the first thing about war and less about Hitler. If he invades, England will be thrown back into the Dark Ages, or worse. And he won't stop in England long; America will be next. You don't appease a rabid dog, you shoot it. They don't seem to understand that." He paused. "Mad or not, the effect would be catastrophic."

"Who'll give our little group of traitors the Ultra secret?" asked Bingham. "Koch de Gooryend?"

"Even Menzies isn't that much of a fool. He won't have told him. But Koch de Gooryend is bright. All the recent interest in Liddell's investigations will have made him suspicious. There's some talk of it on the wire recordings we made."

Knight looked at Katherine. "He knows about Miss Copeland, for instance. Her escapade in Coventry with Inspector Black will simply make things worse." He shook his head. "There's already evidence of that. There was a direct order from the Home Office yesterday, from Anderson himself, ordering Liddell to stop the investigation forthwith. Black is being forced to resign. Liddell has problems of his own; his credibility has been seriously prejudiced, I'm afraid. Among other things, his ex-wife is the daughter of one of the conspirators."

"For a bunch of lunatics they seem to have covered all the bases," said Katherine. "And with this kind of evidence I don't know why you haven't arrested them all."

Knight sighed. "Sadly, things aren't quite that simple. There are...political considerations."

"I'm not quite sure that there's very much we can do to help," Bingham commented. "Not without jeopardizing our own position."

"You can protect Ultra, at least for the moment. Buy us some time."

"How are we supposed to do that?" asked Katherine.

"You can find this murderer Black was looking for, and the agent Liddell refers to as The Doctor."

"The Doctor?" asked Katherine.

"A German agent operating out of London," explained Bingham. "We've known about him since the Tyler Kent thing. At first we thought it might even be Kennedy himself, but the two men who were killed at the zoo put the kibosh on that theory."

"I didn't know about any of this," said Katherine, looking at Bingham coldly.

The first secretary shrugged. "You didn't have to know." He glanced across to Knight. "If you want our help, there will have to be some kind of arrangement. Quid pro quo, remember?"

"What did you have in mind?"

"The wire recordings. I'll need to have full transcripts."

"Easier to have copies made of the recordings themselves. The fewer people who know about this, the better."

"Fine," said Bingham grimly. "The president can listen to Kennedy's own voice. Hear it from the traitorous bastard's own mouth."

"You want Roosevelt to know about this?"

"All of it. It's the only way. If the Nazis can be kept in the dark about Ultra until Beaverbrook gets your war production back on its feet, then there's a chance. If they change the codes, the British war effort will collapse. Simple as that. But the president will have to know. He's already concerned." He shrugged. "Not to mention the political bonus for him. Kennedy is already on his way out the door. This will keep him there. The same with Mooney and McKittrick. Threaten them with God knows what. The others are your concern, though. No promises, but give me the recordings and I'll see what I can do."

Knight thought for a long moment, then nodded. He stood up. "Fair enough," he said quietly. "You'll have copies by tomorrow."

Five minutes later Katherine Copeland and Lawrence Bingham were standing on the windy pavement in front of 23 Tedworth Suare. It was only mid-afternoon, but already the sky overhead was darkening to tarnished silver. In France and Belgium the Luftwaffe would be preparing for yet another raid on London. Katherine looked upward nervously. They went on and on, as though intent on destroying the city stone by stone. No matter what the headlines touted, it was having much the same effect on the people; suddenly the plot being concocted by the men she'd just seen on the film didn't seem so far-fetched after all.

"Can I give you a ride anywhere?" asked Bingham. "My car's just around the corner."

"No thanks," said Katherine, turning up her collar. "I think I'll walk. The doctors said I should exercise my ankle." She looked at Bingham. "How much of that did you believe?"

"Most of it. I think our friend Knight is skating on pretty thin ice. By telling us about Ultra he committed an act of treason himself. Even so, I don't think he told us the whole story."

"That's what I thought." She frowned. "He's using us."

"And we're using him. For the moment."

"Quid pro quo."

"That's how wars are fought these days, Kat," said Bingham, smiling thinly. "Boardrooms, not battlefields. Or haven't you figured that out yet?"

Naked, filthy, cold, The Number lay curled on the small landing, the locked door only inches from the pink-white soles of his bare feet. He had soiled himself more than once since coming to the landing and the door, but he made no attempt to clean up after himself since he knew very well that it was part of the penalty he would have to pay.

From time to time he would look up, see the door, and cower down again, small sounds escaping from his dry, cracked lips. He'd had neither food nor water for almost five days now, and he was beginning to hallucinate. The sounds had come first—the telltale creaking from behind the door, the whispered voices of his sacrifices, some old and faint like the first, whose remains were now buried, strewn across the Heath, but others were louder, especially the soft, wet mewlings of the Luffington woman; the dry whistling of air as the loop went round her neck, choking her life away. Or the single rising gasp of the last one as the razor vanes sliced through his heart. His own terrible failure, his weakness, perhaps even the forfeiture of his power.

He prayed for that power's return, his cracked lips whispering on the landing, down the stairwell, into the empty rooms. But even as he prayed, he knew that he had yet to pay the price that lay waiting for him behind the door. He must pay it, he knew, and would, but not yet, not yet.

After the sounds came the desperate memories from his childhood, and in some ways they were even worse. The giant, twist-limbed yew in the garden of the rectory, purple-black in the moonlight as he crept so quietly across the rooftop of Big Dorm and down to it. The fleeting glint of moon on blade as he sliced away the perfect length, sneaking back to his bed beneath the window, slipping the heavy, exquisitely balanced limb between the spring and mattress, leaving it there to cure. The guilt of his transgression, the fear of capture and revelation. The long, waiting silence of the room and all the sleeping boys.

Going Home Day. The cabs, horses plodding invisibly behind the low brick wall and trees, appearing finally on the drive. A line of them wheeling around the ilex tree and pausing before the door. The red-cheeked cabmen waiting. The flick of the whips and then the line moving off, leaving him, alone with no home to go to, watching from the upstairs window as the procession finally moves off, reaches the lane, and wends across the countryside like a line of marching ants, vanishing into the distance.

Worst of all, another window, this one at Cane Hill in winter. He would press his cheek and ear against the cold glass, listening to the chapel bells at Earlwood House, echoes joining to produce the complex tangles he had learned by heart, tumbled single notes and far-ranging courses that spoke so clearly to him and told him what he must do. The will of God, the crack of doom, the handwriting on the wall.

Finally, the landing and its bolted, fourfold door—waiting. The Door of Sighs. The Door of Despair. The Door of Penitence. The Door of Paradise Regained. The Door, and what lay behind it.

CHAPTER TWENTY-ONE

Monday, December 23, 1940
3:00 P.M., British Standard Time

Capt. Guy Liddell took a taxi from his St. James's Street office to Whitehall, telling the driver to let him off at the sandbagged entrance to Downing Street. It was cold, with a light snow falling from a leaden sky, and the Royal Navy warrant officer on duty at the barricaded street corner was dressed in full foul-weather gear, complete with a cozy-looking khaki-colored balaclava that hid his entire face except for eyes and mouth.

The guard examined the intelligence officer's pass, nodded, and pulled open the barbed-wire gate in the wall of sandbags. He let Liddell pass through, then closed the gate behind him and went back to stamping his booted feet, blowing out great clouds of steamy breath into the mid-afternoon air.

Liddell walked quickly down the narrow street, clasping his briefcase tightly in his right hand. Twenty yards beyond the plain black door of Number 10, he turned into the Foreign Office courtyard and showed his pass to yet another guard before he was allowed into the bleak, Italianate building.

A few moments later he was shown into the undersecretary's waiting room, a large, gloomy apartment fitted out like the old first-class departure hall at Victoria Station: hard chairs, more potted plants, and bad copies of pictures of royalty round the walls, Edward VIII conspicuous by his absence, while Victoria, Edward's great-grandmother, gazed down sternly from her position over the cold hearth of the ornate fireplace. The formalization of deceit; as far as Liddell knew, there wasn't an official portrait anywhere that showed the dour old monarch with her withered arm, a birth defect that was common knowledge but never revealed in public.

The only literature provided for visitors consisted of back copies of the *Herald* and *Telegraph*, an atlas long out of date, a book of photographs published by the *Studio Magazine* entitled *This Is England*, and a book of photographs from the 1910 International Horse Show.

Sighing, Liddell lowered himself into one of the chairs and took out his pipe. This was England indeed—resolutely lodged in the past and refusing to admit to a future where Britannia might not rule the waves, or anything else for that matter.

Twenty minutes later Butler's parliamentary private secretary appeared. Henry "Chips" Channon, forty-three, was an American by birth, but with strong connections to the old boys' network in England. Educated at Christ Church Oxford, he'd married Lady Honor Guinness, the earl of Iveagh's eldest and plainest daughter, purchased a safe Conservative seat in Southend-on-Sea, and then did enough favors to gain a position for himself as Butler's private secretary.

"Hallo, Guy," he said, grinning broadly as he entered the waiting room. "You're looking well."

Not as well as Channon. Liddell was aware of the man's legendary status among the clothiers of Bond Street and Savile Row. It was said that Chips Channon couldn't step out of his garishly furnished flat on Belgrave Square without spending several hundred pounds. Today he was dressed in a dark blue, beautifully cut suit, creamy white silk shirt, and a maroon tie discreetly dotted with the Iveagh crest.

"Channon." Liddell nodded politely.

"Here to see Rab are we?"

"If it's not too much trouble."

"Well, we are extremely busy." Channon offered up a well-practiced frown of concern. "This Dutch situation is causing a great deal of trouble."

Liddell smiled; he'd only just heard about it himself. Somehow the entire Dutch Navy had managed to sneak away from the German Navy and the Luftwaffe, then put into port at Hull the day before, complete with a cargo ship full of German prisoners. "I only need a few moments."

"I'll see what I can do." Channon gave a little bow and then vanished. He returned almost immediately and led Liddell into his office, a dark-paneled room that connected to the undersecretary's chamber. "Go right in." Channon seated himself behind his desk, watching as Liddell went through to Butler's office, paying particular attention to the briefcase in the intelligence officer's hand.

Butler was standing behind his heavy partner's desk, examining a wall map of Europe. He turned as Liddell came into the room. "See to the door, will you?"

Liddell did as he was told. Butler motioned to a carved, Spanish-style chair upholstered in red leather and sat down behind his desk. Liddell sat down, the briefcase on his lap, and examined Butler. He'd seen photographs of the undersecretary in the newspapers, but he was still surprised at the man's unfavorable first appearance.

In the first place he looked at least ten years older than his actual age of thirty-seven. He had an unhealthy pallor, sallow skin, and dark, puffy bags under his pale gray eyes. The broadly cut pinstripe suit in dark brown had obviously been tailored to hide a spreading belly. If Liddell hadn't known who Butler was, he'd have taken the man for a Mayfair pub crawler, or worse.

"I presume you're here with your report on Inspector Black," said Butler, his pudgy hands tented together under his chin, small mouth pursed.

"In part."

"He's been released from Queen Victoria?"

"Yesterday. He's back in London."

"But not at work."

"No."

"Good." Butler nodded. "You've spoken to him?"

"Yes."

"He'll resign then?"

"If necessary."

"I assure you, Captain, it is necessary." Butler frowned. "Presumably you're keeping him under surveillance until we've ascertained his loyalties in this matter."

"For the time being." Liddell nodded. "Although I don't think his loyalties are at question."

"He is a Jew, as I recall."

"That is correct, yes."

"His people haven't been in this country long from what I gather. German extraction, yes? Schwartz or some such is his real name?"

"His name is Black," said Liddell tightly. "His grandfather came to London in 1846. His father was born here, as was Black himself."

"Nevertheless," murmured Butler. "You can never tell about these people."

"These people?"

"Foreign Jews."

"I've been a policeman for a long time, Mr. Butler. In my experience you can never tell about anyone, Jew or...parliamentary secretaries."

Butler ignored the comment. "Still, we'll keep a watch on him just in case, shall we?"

"That's one of the things I've come here to discuss."

"It's not a matter for discussion, Captain. I believe you've had a direct order to that effect from the Home Office."

"From Mr. Anderson, yes."

"And presumably you will follow those orders."

"Under normal circumstances I would, yes."

"I don't have time for opaque comments from somewhat less than senior civil servants, Liddell. There are matters involved which you know nothing about."

"Perhaps." Liddell shrugged. He took out his pipe.

Butler frowned. "I'd rather you didn't light that."

"Of course." Liddell put the pipe away and undid the snap on the briefcase in his lap. "According to Inspector Black, he is preparing to leave for Wales in the morning. Holyhead, to be precise. He tells me that he intends to stay there for the holidays."

"I really don't have the slightest interest in what Mr. Black's plans are for the Christmas season."

"Nor do I," Liddell said, smiling briefly. "In light of which I thought you would like to know that I intend to withdraw our surveillance of him as of today. Our manpower capabilities are already stretched to the limit. I see no purpose in continuing a useless watch on the man."

"I thought we had established that you are not the arbiter of what should or should not be done vis-à-vis this situation. It has been taken out of your hands, Liddell."

"And I'm taking it back again."

"You're being insolent." Butler was going red in the face. The tented hands were now flat on the green leather desktop, the knuckles whitening. "I am aware of your—"

"Do you have any idea how Channon got his nickname?" said Liddell, enjoying the moment.

"What on earth are you talking about?"

"Your secretary, Mr. Channon. His nickname is Chips, were you aware of that?"

"I don't see what—"

"He was given the nickname because of his passionate affections for a young man at Oxford named Charles Herring. Herring, fish. Fish, 'chips.' I'm sure you can see the connection."

"This is preposterous!"

"I'm afraid not. In fact it's all rather well documented. As are his connections with a number of other people whose—how did you put it?—'loyalties have not been ascertained'?" Liddell reached into the briefcase and drew out a single typewritten page. "They include the late Sir Phillip Sassoon, who had, as I believe you yourself once said, 'a prolonged and hazardous relationship with the Duke of Windsor,' Lady Diana Cooper, also a friend of the Duke and Duchess, and an assortment of Guardsmen and rather unseemly types from the Fitzroy and the Marquess of Granby." Liddell paused and extended the sheet of paper toward Butler. "I have the names if you'd like to read them yourself." He waited for a moment. "Including that of Mr. Margesson."

Butler paled. Margesson had been Conservative whip in the House of Commons for the past eight years and was directly responsible for Channon's elevation to the rank of parliamentary secretary. As well, it was rumored that the florid young man's personal expenses were being paid by the outrageously anti-Semitic Lord Bearsted, and there was also the more serious question of his relationship with Archibald Ramsay, the pro-Nazi MP who had been interned in May. "Mr. Channon's private life is none of my concern, Liddell, and none of yours," Butler muttered finally.

Liddell made his tone purposely harsh as he replied, "Sodomy is a crime, Mr. Butler. And it *is* my concern when it involves a man in Mr. Channon's position." He paused again, took a deep breath, and then went on, "There is also the question of your own situation, sir."

"You're on very dangerous ground, Liddell." Butler's face was now as mottled as a piece of old cheese. "I'm not at all sure I like the direction you're headed in."

Liddell raised an eyebrow. "No, I don't suppose you do."

"Perhaps you should leave, Captain Liddell, before this goes too far." Butler paused. "For your own sake."

"It's already gone too far, Mr. Butler." Liddell watched the man carefully. Knight had told him to tread with extreme care; they were dealing with an extremely powerful group of men, and of them all, Butler was almost certainly the most dangerous. "I don't suppose you know what a 'Pig and Eye' is, do you, sir?"

"No." Butler's voice was cold as ice.

"It stands for 'personal investigation' file. We've been keeping a number of them for some years now."

"I'm not sure I understand."

"Pig and Eyes are kept on anyone in government or industry who occupies a sensitive position." Liddell looked at Butler directly. "Someone like yourself, for instance. A man occupying a position of authority who might be unduly influenced if certain...pressures were brought to bear."

"And what exactly do you keep in these files?" Butler's tone was flat and the gray eyes had turned to flint.

"Details concerning sexual proclivities and peccadilloes, financial transactions that might be misinterpreted should they be made public, membership in various organizations, illicit or questionable friendships and liaisons." Liddell stared blandly at the man on the other side of the desk. "That sort of thing."

"You have a file like this on Channon, is that what you're saying?"

"Yes. Quite a large one as a matter of fact."

"This is dangerously close to blackmail, Liddell."

"On the contrary, Mr. Butler. The files are for the protection of the people involved." Liddell smiled thinly. "We wouldn't want this sort of thing to fall into the wrong hands, would we?"

"Am I to assume that you have such a file on me?"

"Yes. I was just getting to that, as a matter of fact." Liddell opened the briefcase again, took out a thin folder, and stood up, placing the briefcase on the floor beside his chair. He put the file on Butler's desk, then sat down again. It contained one thing—a blowup of a single frame from the damning film of the conspirators taken by Knight at the Walker estate. With the recordings that went along with it, the picture was ample evidence of treason. The undersecretary stared at the plain folder as though it were a coiled snake. He looked across the desk at Liddell but made no move to open the file. "What you have is an extract, of course; the entire file is a good deal larger."

"Who put you up to this, Liddell? Morton?"

"I'm afraid I don't know who you mean." He did, of course, know precisely whom Butler was referring to—Desmond Morton, Churchill's very private assistant. God, he thought, if only it were true!

"You're saying that you're acting on your own authority? If that is the case, then—"

Liddell interrupted before the man could say anything more. "I'm not saying anything at all, sir. I'm merely bringing the file to your attention and also informing you that, contrary to instructions from the home secretary, I am suspending surveillance on Inspector Black."

Butler still refused to open the file in front of him, but Liddell saw that one hand had moved slightly, the fingers just brushing the edges of the folder.

"You have copies of this?" Butler asked finally.

"Of course." Liddell picked up his briefcase, snapped it shut, and stood up. "I've taken up enough of your time. According to Mr. Channon, you're having some trouble with the Dutch Navy at the moment."

Without waiting for a reply he turned on his heel and left the office. Three minutes later he was standing in the Foreign Office courtyard, taking in deep grateful breaths of the icy air.

Tucking his briefcase under his arm, he crossed the snow-covered garden to Downing Street. Instead of going back to Whitehall he turned in the opposite direction and made his way toward St. James's Park. A brisk walk to Whites would do him good, and a treble gin would be better still.

Reaching the Guards Memorial, he paused to light his pipe, then continued on into the park. He'd done all he could; now Black was on his own.

Following the instructions contained in the obscure telegram he'd received from Liddell that morning, Morris Black left his flat in Shepherd's Market shortly after two o'clock and proceeded on foot to the underground station at Green Park.

The fracture in his leg was almost completely healed, but he still used the cane he'd been given at the hospital in East Grinstead. He also continued to wear a patch over his eye; his sight had returned two weeks before, but the minor skin graft above the lid was still angrily inflamed.

Going down to the platform, he lowered himself gingerly onto one of the benches to wait for his train, acutely aware of the looks he was getting from other travelers, most of whom presumably assumed he was a wounded soldier home on recuperative leave and not a policeman who'd almost got himself killed for his stupidity.

The day before, he'd gone to the cemetery at Golders Green and stood by Fay's grave. It was foolish, of course; he needed the answers to a thousand questions and absolution for a thousand sins, none of which were to be had in Golders Green. Fay was dead, he might as well be, and only old men and fools conversed with headstones. Somehow, though, the quiet moment seemed to help. Perhaps there was no peace for him alive, but inevitably, at least, there was this final end to pain and sorrow: a small plot, a plain marker, and the endless wheel of infinite seasons turning overhead.

A westbound train whistled noisily into the station and he boarded it, taking the Piccadilly Line to South Kensington, then doubling back on the District Line to Victoria. Still following instructions, he took the lift up to the main railroad terminus and stopped for a moment to buy a copy of the *Times* at the W. H. Smith kiosk. Limping across the bustling concourse to the far side of the station, he went out through the exit into Hobson's Place, an ancient, cobbled, and little-used dead-end passage tucked in against the south-facing wall of the station.

He lit a cigarette, leaned on his cane, and waited, completely alone on the pavement of the narrow little side street. A full five minutes went by, the bitterly cold wind flapping the tails of his overcoat and pinching at his nostrils, making him wish he'd thrown the telegram into the wastebasket as he'd initially intended. Suddenly he felt a light hand on his elbow.

"Hello, Morris." He turned, surprised. It was Katherine Copeland. Before he had time to react further, he heard the powerful growling of an automobile engine, and a massive, dark green Bentley Tourer, canvas top raised, edged around the corner, pulling to a halt in front of them.

Katherine stepped forward, pulled open the door, and gently prodded Black into the passenger seat. She squeezed in beside him and the huge automobile moved off, turning around at the end of the snow-covered cul-de-sac and moving back toward Wilton Street and the main entrance to the station. Black turned and stared at the handsome, dark-haired man behind the wheel. On the single occasion they'd met previously the man had been half-asleep, wearing a dressing gown and slippers, but Black recognized him instantly.

"Good Lord, it's you."

Ian Fleming smiled. "I'm afraid so." The young naval intelligence officer shifted gears, spun the wheel tightly as they reached Buckingham Palace Road, and began driving north. The Bentley only had two seats, and Black was uncomfortably aware of Katherine's body pressed against his side. He could smell the faint perfume of her hair, and for a single jarring moment his mind filled with images of the explosion at the Burlington Arcade and the fiery death of Coventry. He shifted slightly in the seat, trying to keep his cane from becoming entangled with the Bentley's gearshift.

"Is this someone's idea of a joke?" he asked finally.

"Certainly not," said Fleming, glancing quickly in his direction and offering up a broad grin. "Just a bit of judicious subterfuge, old man." As they slid by the Palace and rounded the Victoria Memorial, Fleming dug into the inside pocket of his coat and pulled out his cigarette case and lighter. He handed them to Black. "Light one for me, would you? Have one yourself if you like."

Black lit two cigarettes and handed one to Fleming along with the case and lighter. Beside the detective, Katherine Copeland squirmed awkwardly and managed to roll down the side window, letting in a blast of cold air. Black drew in a lungful of smoke and recognized the sweet tang of expensive Turkish tobacco.

"Well," said Black, "if this isn't a joke, then perhaps one of you would be kind enough to tell me just what the bloody hell is going on. I'm really not up to playing at Mata Hari and the Scarlet Pimpernel."

"All right," said Katherine. She spent the next quarter hour telling him everything she knew, including what she'd learned from Maxwell Knight. By then they were beyond Maida Vale and Belsize Road, still moving steadily northward. Black stared forward through the windshield, barely aware of his surroundings. What Katherine had told him was utter madness, but it also had the ring of truth to it.

"Plot within plot, conspiracy on top of conspiracy," she said. "And now we have to wage a private war all our own."

"And Fleming? Where does he fit into all of this?" The detective glanced at the man beside him.

"I've known Knight for quite some time," Fleming said, speaking for himself. "We've worked together before. He asked me if I could help out. I agreed." He frowned. "Not to mention that I have my own interest in this whole affair."

"The Luffington girl?"

"Yes."

"This is insane! You're attached to Admiralty and Naval Intelligence. Katherine is an admitted foreign agent, and I've been stripped of any authority in this case. Liddell made it quite clear: either I resign or face possible charges. On top of that, from what you tell me, I'm probably under some sort of surveillance."

"What Liddell told you and what he's actually done aren't necessarily the same thing," said Katherine, close beside him.

"Meaning?"

"Liddell's being pressured to stop the investigation into the Queer Jack killings and the man called The Doctor. He can't help, at least not directly, but we're his only chance now."

"But he won't hinder, either," put in Fleming. "It's a lot of silly bureaucratic mumbo jumbo, really, but there's nothing to stop you from investigating on your own. Officially you're on Christmas leave; by this evening the watchers will be removed, and hey, presto! Morris Black is no longer a consideration. It was the best that he could do." The young naval officer turned the wheel, guiding the Bentley onto West End Lane.

"Queer Jack is the key to all of this," said Katherine. "Queer Jack and Liddell's German." She paused. "But we don't have much time left."

They were in Hampstead now, moving toward the Heath. Behind and far below the city was lost behind the veil of lightly falling snow. On either side of them the suburban row houses crouched depressingly, faint wisps of smoke rising almost invisibly from the chimney pots, blank windows already curtained and shuttered against whatever the coming night would bring.

Skirting the High Street they took Branch Hill to Whitestone Pond, dropped down along the East Heath Road, then turned into the Heath itself, swerving abruptly into a small enclave of attached houses.

"Where exactly are we?" Black had been to Hampstead often enough, but he never knew this street existed, hidden as it was so far off the beaten track.

"Byron Villas," said Fleming, pulling the automobile to a stop. Black peered through the windscreen. On their left was a short row of twin-storied houses, brick-walled, slate-roofed, and iron-gated. A stained and crumbling concrete wall ran the length of the row, topped with empty wooden planters half-filled with snow.

Just beyond the end of the row, right on the edge of the open Heath, there was a large crater protected by a makeshift wooden barrier. The last two houses closest to the crater had been severely blast-damaged. Windows were shattered, doors hung drunkenly open, and a section of roof was burnt down to the rafters, open to the sky.

"Inviting," Black commented dryly. "Jolly nice spot for the holidays."

"Better digs than mine," said Fleming. "I was bombed out of house and home last week." He switched off the engine. "This was Knight's idea. Street's been abandoned for the duration. No one will bother you here." He turned and smiled. "Quite a famous spot, actually. This is where D. H. Lawrence wrote *The Rainbow*."

"Oh, well," said Black sourly. "That changes everything, doesn't it?" He sighed. "This is all fine and good, but how am I supposed to do anything without my files and notes?"

"Been taken care of," said Katherine, opening the door. "Your assistant was transferred God only knows where, but he managed to duplicate everything before the files were seized by Butler. Knight sent one of his people round and whisked it all away."

"You must be congratulating yourselves. You've thought of just about everything."

"Just about," said Fleming. "Your assistant, Swift?"

"Yes?"

Fleming smiled wolfishly. "He outdid the boffins at Bletchley Park. Managed to figure out the message from the Swede. The key was the *National Geographic* magazine. I'm going through their subscription list now, looking for a possible connection."

Black spoke wearily. "Did it ever occur to you that I was bloody sick and tired of the whole thing? That I might not want to join in on this little lark?"

"Not for a minute," said Katherine, smiling sweetly. "After all, Morris, you're a cop, aren't you?"

Dr. Charles Tennant sat in the newspaper room of the Brighton Library, leafing through the bound volumes of the *Sussex Daily News* and the *Brighton Argus* for the year 1914. Caidin, the headmaster at Wick Hall School, had been totally uncooperative from the moment he discovered Tennant's purpose, but the yellowed newspapers in front of him told the story well enough.

Poppet, in her empty-headed way, had been kind enough to give him the details of Morris Black's unfortunate trip to Coventry within a few days of the ill-timed event. It had, she said, got the wind up in just about everyone, and Liddell was apparently making life miserable for the entire staff of B Division, herself included. Utter security was now the order of the day, and scrupulous attention to the details of day-to-day work. No more short days and long lunches for her.

Poppet, in the throes of her own particular brand of passion, had also been kind enough to tell Tennant the name Queer Jack had used in Coventry and which Trench had passed along to Black—Bernard Timothy Exner. She didn't have the slightest qualm about giving her new lover the name, since a thorough search of the records showed that no such person existed, or at least no one presently carrying a National Registration Card.

The name, however, had planted its seed in Tennant's mind, and a week or so later the psychiatrist had managed another session at the Scotland Yard Central Records Office. There he discovered the reason for the elusive Exner's nonappearance. Bernard Timothy Exner, born in Nottingham, August 11, 1903, was dead. Murdered in the vicinity of Cold Dean, Sussex, on September 23, 1914.

Tennant had spent a great deal of time since his first visit to the Yard expanding and refining his "profile" on Queer Jack, and he knew instantly that Exner's neatly inscribed name on the buff-colored file card was the final proof of his theory.

Queer Jack hadn't given Trench the name of Bernard Timothy Exner without reason. There had to be a link between the boy murdered thirty-six years ago and the present-day Blitz killer. But what? Tennant was no detective, and his search required some discretion, but eventually he traced Exner to a second-rate public school a few miles north of the city of Brighton: Wick Hall School.

He wrote to the headmaster with a general inquiry about the possibility of enrolling a nonexistent child, then followed it up with a request for a tour. He'd been given a date for that readily enough—there weren't many parents these days willing to put their child into a school standing directly in the way of a Nazi invasion—but today, when Caidin discovered Tennant's interest in the almost forgotten murder, he'd quickly been shown the door. His visit to the library on Church Street had followed, but not before he'd managed to slip a copy of the 1914 *Wick Hall Annual* into his briefcase.

In September and October of 1914, the London newspapers would have been filled with nothing but news of the stalemate on the Marne, or the first zeppelin raids, but in Brighton the leading story was that of Bernard Timothy Exner, barely eleven, at first simply missing, then discovered some days later in nearby Stanmer Park, savagely tortured, violated, and then murdered.

According to the reports, Bernard had been well-liked at Wick Hall School, even though, as Oswald Freeman, headmaster at the time, suggested, the Exner family was "in trade" and not of the titled aristocracy; to wit, Bernard's father manufactured bicycles, the Exner Flight being his best-known product, several hundred of which he had donated to the Royal Army Signal Corps for use in France against the Kaiser.

Various other masters at the school had commented that young Bernard had been a bright boy, particularly in maths, and from what they knew, he had no real enemies. Given the savagery of the attack, the details of which were not included in the newspaper stories, the local police quickly came to the conclusion that the murderer was a vagrant, or perhaps an escapee from an asylum. Presumably the man had managed to lure the Exner boy away from the school grounds, and then, possibly after holding him against his will for some time, murdered him.

The newspaper stories contained only the vaguest allusions to what had been done to the child, but the clear inference was that he had been grossly sexually molested before finally being asphyxiated.

The story kept its grip on the local imagination for the better part of a fortnight, and then, with the police unable to report any progress, it faded and eventually died. The coroner's report, filed in a back-page squib under legal notices during the third week of October, concluded that Bernard Timothy Exner had died as the result of foul play committed by a person or persons unknown. The child's remains had long before been taken back to Nottingham for burial. Like Bernard, the story was laid to rest. Until now.

Tennant set the bound volume aside, opened his briefcase, and took out the buckram-covered annual he'd managed to steal from the school library before he'd been evicted by the headmaster. Sitting alone in the newspaper room, he turned the pages slowly, eventually discovering Bernard Exner in a photograph of the assembled lower school.

The boy stared out of the photograph, a small, fixed grin on his innocent face. Very blond, dressed in uniform cap, jacket, and flannel shorts. His right stocking was sagging slightly, and a scab was visible on his knee. A score of other boys looked up at Tennant from the page, all with identical, vacant looks. He scanned the faces slowly, hoping for some sign, but there was nothing.

Bernard Exner appeared four more times: once in a group photograph of the lower-school cricket team for 1913, listed as being a member of both the junior and school chess clubs, and listed as captain of the junior maths club. According to the notes, Exner had placed second in his division during the National Boys' Chess Tournament in the spring, and sixth overall.

Tennant paused, looking up from the volume. Chess. According to Poppet, that was the clue that had sent Morris Black to Coventry. Queer Jack had been choosing his victims from the membership list of the Correspondence Chess Association. He flipped back and forth through the pages, comparing the names on the lists of the junior, senior, and school chess clubs as well as the maths club list. Other than Exner there were only three names that reoccurred: one boy with the unlikely name of George Le Fanu Gurney, Raymond Loudermilk, and John Pastermagent. Gurney was a member of the junior chess club and the maths club, and Loudermilk and Pastermagent—obviously both upper-school boys—were members of the maths club and the senior chess club.

Pastermagent was also a member of the school chess club, which probably meant he'd gone off on the National Chess Tournament with Exner that spring. It made sudden, terrible sense. According to his "profile," the trauma endured by Queer Jack had most probably occurred during early adolescence—when he was twelve or perhaps thirteen. He'd be in the upper school, not the lower, his victim younger and more vulnerable. Which probably ruled out Gurney.

Acting on a hunch, Tennant went off in search of a local directory for the Brighton area, found it, then returned to the newspaper room. He looked up the remaining two names. There were no Loudermilks of any kind, but there was a J. Pastermagent, listed as being resident in Hove, a suburb on the western end of Brighton, and also listed with a business address: J. Pastermagent, rug merchant, 21 The Lanes, Brighton.

"Good Lord," Tennant whispered softly, staring down at the notation. "It can't be that simple."

There was only one way to find out. He jotted down the address in his notebook, stuffed the school magazine back into his briefcase, and glanced at his Rolex. Just past five. If he was lucky, the premises of J. Pastermagent, rug merchant, would still be open for business.

The Lanes proved to be a narrow network of alleyways just off East Street only a few blocks away, still busy even at the end of the working day. A blustery snowfall blew up from the Marine Parade and the Pier as Tennant approached.

Pastermagent's shop was tiny, crouched in the shadow of Harrington's, a gigantic department store that spanned both sides of The Lanes and spread out, multistoried, down two blocks of East Street. A war was on, but it was also Christmas, and shoppers were everywhere, bundled up against the cold, scurrying along the pavement, puffing up great gusts of steamy breath as they hurried home in time to beat the black-out curfew.

Pastermagent's already had its heavy felt curtains in place, and for a moment Tennant thought he was too late, but the door opened at his hand, a tinkling bell announcing his arrival. He closed the door behind him and looked around at the walls of the narrow shop, lined with hanging rugs of every description, silk and wool, ornate and primitive, Chinese, Persian, and Turkish.

Hundreds more were stacked waist high across the floor, laid out in staggered rows. At the end of the brightly lit room there was another pile, pushed up like a multicolored snow-drift in one corner, and beside it a delicately made desk of some dark wood, scrolled, carved, and inlaid with strips of ebony and mother-of-pearl.

Behind the desk, a broad-shouldered, youthful-looking man with jet-black hair was scowling down at the cumber-some-looking adding machine in front of him, working the crank with one hand and bashing at the keys with the other. He glanced up as Tennant approached.

"Thing's bloody useless," he muttered. "An abacus was good enough for my father, but I'm stuck with this lot." The scowl vanished, replaced instantly with a broad smile as the man stood up and came around the desk. "Sorry. Mustn't be a Scrooge." He laughed. "Mind you, Christmas is a retail event, I suppose." He paused and shook his head. "Sorry," he repeated. The man's dark complexion was clearly foreign, but his speech was educated and without any discernible accent.

"Mr. Pastermagent?"

"Quite right." The man nodded. "Except you don't pro-nounce the *T* on the end. Pastermagen'." He laughed again. "Mind you, everyone does, so I suppose I shouldn't mind." He extended a hand and Tennant shook it. The grip was firm and dry. If this was Queer Jack, he was flying in the face of the psychiatrist's theory.

"My name is Tennant. Dr. Charles Tennant. I'm a psychiatrist."

"Well, that's a first. I don't suppose you're here to buy a rug?" he added wistfully.

"No."

"I didn't think so. You don't have the look." Pastermagent shrugged his shoulders and raised his hands in an expression of sadness. "Not many do these days, I'm afraid." The man's mood changed yet again, the brilliant smile returning. "Would you like some coffee?"

"That would be nice," Tennant answered politely. Pastermagent went behind the desk again. He poured two small cups from a large samovar standing on its own table, stirred in several spoonfuls of sugar, and came around the desk again. He handed a cup to Tennant and motioned him toward the pile of carpets in the corner.

Pastermagent dropped down onto the pile and Tennant joined him, balancing the minuscule cup and saucer awkwardly. Seated, he took a small sip of the steaming brew. It was incredibly strong and sweet as treacle. He tasted grit in his mouth and peered into the cup. It appeared to be half-full of dark, sludgelike sand.

"Hideous stuff, isn't it?" Pastermagent smiled. He took a swallow from his own cup and smacked his lips. "An acquired taste, but I'm afraid it's all I've got on hand. Grows on you after a bit. Quite addictive, really. My father used to say that the grounds cleaned out your bowels like a scouring pad." He laughed yet again. "Must have known what he was talking about, he was a hundred and two when he died." Another mood change. The smile slid away, replaced by a quick, analytical glance. "You're from London, I take it?"

"Yes."

"And why is a London psychiatrist sitting about in an Armenian rug shop in Brighton?"

"You went to Wick Hall School, I believe."

The Armenian nodded. "Guilty as charged, Doctor. Worst seven years of my life. My father wanted me to be an English gentleman. He was also a bit of a nose-tweaker, my dad. Liked nothing better than putting the cat among the pigeons."

"I don't understand."

"I was a wog," Pastermagent explained without a trace of anger. "Touch of the tar brush and all that. Drove the head quite mad, but he couldn't do anything about it. My father kept on endowing the place with all sorts of things—cricket balls, books for the library, two or three scholarships, that sort of rot. The trustees loved him, but The Owl couldn't stand the sight of him, or me for that matter."

"The Owl?"

"Freeman, the head. Spectacles thick as the bottom of a bottle. They gave him a gong not long before he handed in his lunch pail. Sir Oswald Freeman, OBE. I hope he's in his grave, spinning like a gyroscope. Sadistic old bugger."

"You knew a young boy, I believe. Bernard Exner," said Tennant slowly, watching the man's reaction to the name. Pastermagent's eyes widened. "Good Lord, I haven't thought about him in ages. 'X-marks-the-spot' Exner." He shook his head. "Poor little sod."

"He was murdered."

"That's right."

"And they never found the man who did it."

"No." Pastermagent shook his head again. "Must be twenty-five years now."

"Twenty-six."

"Right." Pastermagent nodded. "I'm thirty-nine now so I would've been…"

"Thirteen."

"That sounds about right. I was in upper school that year,

fifth form. Exner was lower third, I think. We were on the school chess team. Went to the National Tournament the term before he was killed."

"So I understand."

"He had a wizard end game," said Pastermagent, remembering. "Alphabet used to call him the Thinking Machine after that detective in the Jacques Futrelle stories."

Tennant blinked. He couldn't understand a word the man was saying. "Alphabet?"

The Armenian laughed. "Sorry. You've taken me back through the mists of time, I'm afraid. Alphabet was Crawley. Alfred Benjamin Crawley. We made his initials into a nickname: A.B.C.—Alphabet. We had names for everyone. Mine was Beater, as in carpet beater." He sighed and took another sip of coffee. "This certainly does take me back, Doctor."

"Did you ever wonder who might have killed him?"

"Not for years."

"But at the time?"

Pastermagent frowned and set his cup aside on a flat area on the pile of rugs. "I had some theories, yes," he said finally. "A few of us did."

"Did you come to any conclusions?"

"Can I ask what your interest in this is?" asked the dark-haired man. "I really don't like the idea of telling tales out of school."

"It has to do with another investigation."

"You work for the police?"

"From time to time." Not quite a lie.

"Well, I suppose it's all right then." Pastermagent thought for a moment. "None of us really thought it was a stranger, I remember that Exner was young, but he wasn't stupid. We were fairly sure no one lured him off with a licorice whip and a stick of Brighton Rock."

"A teacher?"

"Good Lord no!" Pastermagent said, laughing loudly.

"Milquetoasts, the lot of them. Most were trying to avoid conscription, if you ask me. They wouldn't have dared." He thought for a moment. "There was also the matter of the bow and arrow."

"I don't know anything about it."

"No, it wasn't in the newspapers as I recall." Pastermagent paused again. "When they found Exner, it was discovered that he'd been shot."

"With a bow and arrow, you mean?"

"That's right. Gray goose feather and all that. We all made them. The boys, I mean. Straight out of Sir Walter Scott." Pastermagent smiled. "These days I suppose it would be Errol Flynn. At any rate, some of us stole yew branches from the tree outside the rectory, but mostly we used ash from the end of the drive. You didn't have to waste time letting it cure. We used them to knock chestnuts out of the trees. A few of us actually made proper arrowheads from tins."

Tennant nodded to himself. The weapon used by Queer Jack supposedly resembled a sophisticated arrowhead. "Young Exner was wounded by one of them?"

"Umm. In the thigh. Enough to have brought him up short if he'd been trying to run away. Not a lot of Gypsies and transients wandering about fixed up like Red Indians."

"So you think it was another boy, then?"

Pastermagent hesitated for a moment. "Perhaps," he said finally.

"Likely suspects?"

"Loudermilk," said the rug dealer flatly. There was no hesitation in his voice now. He hadn't even paused to think about it.

"Raymond Loudermilk? Chess team and maths club?"

Pastermagent's expression darkened. "That's the one."

"You seem very sure."

"Yes."

"Why?"

"I don't know, really," said the rug dealer, scratching the dark line of his jaw. He stood and made his way to the desk. Opening a drawer, he brought out a flat, white-labeled tin and a small tinplate ashtray. He returned to the pile of rugs and sat down again, offering the box to Tennant. They were Abdullah's. "Bit of an affectation. I'd just as soon smoke Player's, but people have their expectations." Pastermagent snorted. "My father used to smoke Senior Service through a hookah. Customers thought it was terribly exotic." He grinned broadly. "Crafty bugger, my old dad. Had a thousand little tricks."

Tennant took a cigarette from the box and Pastermagent joined him. The Armenian looked up at the ceiling.

"Raymond Loudermilk," the psychiatrist said, prompting gently.

"Umm. Just thinking."

"Did you know him well?"

"No. I doubt anyone did."

"He was a member of the school chess club. The maths club as well. Sounds sociable enough."

"Not really. If you were good at something, The Owl insisted you join the appropriate club. My friend Crawley was an absolute layabout, but he could run like the wind, so he was on the track-and-field team. Hated it, as I recall."

"Loudermilk was good at maths?"

"Close to brilliant, I'd say. Especially when it came to the practical end of things. Trigonometry, mechanical applications. Made wonderful things in shops. Not terribly imaginative, though. The same with chess."

"A good player?"

"I wouldn't say good. It was something more than that. Mechanical, but incredibly accurate. I think they have a name for people like that."

"A savant?"

"That's it." Pastermagent nodded. "He could remember

every move made in a masters tournament, but he could never think for himself, make up his own moves. Not like Exner."

"Did they get along?"

"I never noticed."

"What else do you remember about Loudermilk?"

"Lonely. Never said much. Brooded a lot. I think his father was in the Army. A chaplain?" Pastermagent shrugged. "I have some vague memory of his having been in India." The rug merchant puffed on his cigarette. "It's just that he was so...different. Not like the rest of us. Alphabet Crawley was the son of a lord and my father sold Persian carpets, but we were the best of friends. I suspect it was because we had a common enemy."

"The Owl?"

"All the masters. The school, our parents. Us against them."

"And Loudermilk?"

"He didn't seem to have friends or enemies. As though he lived in a different world. Do you understand?"

"I think so." Tennant paused. "Do you have any idea what happened to him?"

"Not the foggiest. He wasn't there the following year. I remember some rumor about his father being killed in France or Belgium. Probably couldn't afford the place after that." Pastermagent sighed again. "He wasn't the only one. Same thing happened to Fanny." He grinned. "George Gurney. Riches to rags overnight. He was taken out in the middle of term. Sad. The whole world changed during the war. I suppose it's about to change again." He smiled bleakly. "Already has as far as the rug trade is concerned."

"I'm still not quite sure why you were so quick to mention Loudermilk."

"You went to a public school, presumably?"

"Eton."

"Well, then, you know, don't you? A public school is nothing more than a jungle for well-groomed savages."

"A fair enough assessment." Tennant smiled.

"One learns to live by instinct in a place like Eton or Wick Hall, not intellect. Some things you simply feel. Survival of the fittest. I can remember that about Loudermilk."

"Remember what?"

Pastermagent's voice was soft and a distant look was in his eyes. "It really only occurred to me after he was gone. Perhaps it had something to do with poor Exner as well. Crawley felt it too."

"Felt what?"

"That we'd been invaded. I can remember being terribly relieved when we found out that he wasn't coming back. We'd been an innocent flock of sheep with a wolf in our midst and we'd never known."

"Loudermilk being the wolf?"

"Oh, yes," said Pastermagent firmly. "A wolf in sheep's clothing. Or worse."

"Worse?"

"Umm." Pastermagent paused, frowning, lost in the past. Suddenly he nodded. "I've just remembered," he said quietly. "About the nicknames."

"Loudermilk's?"

"Well, that's just the point, you see…he was the only boy at Wick Hall who didn't have one."

CHAPTER TWENTY-TWO

Tuesday, December 24, 1940
11:30 A.M., British Standard Time

DR. CHARLES TENNANT SAT IN ONE of the gloomy cubicles at the Somerset House Births and Deaths Registry working his way through a pile of dusty ledgers covering deaths under LO to LU from 1914 to 1925. He'd been at it for the better part of two hours and had only just discovered the entry he'd been after. There were two Loudermilks listed during the period: William Cornwallis Loudermilk, forty-nine, captain, Royal Army Chaplains Corps, who died on September 15, 1914; and Emily Marguerite Loudermilk, née Bambridge, forty-one, who died October 17, 1923.

There was a Ministry of War notation beside the entry for William Loudermilk, and, given the date, he'd probably been killed during the Battle of the Marne. The entry for Emily stated that she'd died accidentally as the result of a fall. There was no place-of-burial entry for the captain, but Mrs. Loudermilk had been interred at St. John's Cemetery, Church Row, Hampstead. A ray of hope there; the parish records might have some information Tennant could use.

With the correct dates now in hand, it took him almost no time at all to find Raymond Loudermilk's birth record.

Tennant discovered his quarry in the listings for September 1901. Capt. William Loudermilk and his wife, Emily, were indeed Raymond Loudermilk's parents. By a macabre and ironic twist, it appeared that the child had been born on September 15—the date of his father's death thirteen years later. The place of birth was listed as Chitradurga, Karnataka Province, India.

As interesting as the birth date was the prior notation of the parents' marriage: April 21 of the same year at Jamnagar in the Rann of Kutch. By all indications, the thirty-six-year-old Scots Presbyterian chaplain William Loudermilk and the nineteen-year-old Miss Emily Bambridge had sinned grievously: Raymond Loudermilk had been conceived out of wedlock.

Tennant looked up from the ledger entry and stared thoughtfully into space. A young Calvinist minister gives in to temptation and impregnates a nineteen-year-old girl. Guilt-ridden and facing disgrace or even worse, he marries the girl to legitimize the birth.

What kind of relationship would he have with his near-bastard? Not a good one, certainly. Then and forever, Raymond Loudermilk would be nothing but a glaring, constant symbol of his fall from grace, the ever-present incarnation of his lust. During the child's early years he'd probably done everything possible to stay as far as he could from the object of his sin, eventually placing the child in a Brighton boarding school. The ultimate abandonment had come just as Raymond entered adolescence—in fact, on the boy's thirteenth birthday. A week later, Bernard Timothy Exner vanished from the grounds of Wick Hall.

Smiling, Tennant closed the ledger. Weeks ago the search for the mysterious Queer Jack had been a matter of intelligence gathering for Heydrich, a way to hasten the inevitable invasion and an end to war, consequently ensuring Tennant's position in the new order. Now it was something else, and sitting there, alone, surrounded by the stacks and cabinets full of moldering files and records, he knew what Morris Black must have felt so often in the past. The hunt was coming to a close. He had his man; all he had to do now was find him.

"I'm not sure this is such a good idea," said Katherine Copeland, seated behind the wheel of the hired car. "These are the golden boys. Ruffle their feathers and it's sure to get back to Liddell. He'll have to report it."

"I don't intend to ruffle any feathers," answered Morris Black. "I just have to ask a few questions."

"But why Bletchley? Can't you find out some other way?"

"No. There is no other way. And Bletchley fits."

Katherine slowed as they reached a sharp turn on the almost deserted road, fumbling the shift lever and swearing under her breath, still unfamiliar with driving on what she considered to be the wrong side of the road. They were twenty miles out of London, heading north toward Bedford on the A5 through low, undulating countryside still dusted with a light coating of snow from the day before. The sky above them was overcast and dark, heavy with the promise of another storm.

"Explain it to me again," said Katherine, straightening the wheel and relaxing slightly. "According to you, chess is the key to this whole thing, is that right?"

"It's the one thread that seems to run through it all. The single factor connecting the murders." The detective paused for a moment, looking out through the windscreen, marshaling the facts that had kept sleep at bay until the small hours of the morning. "When I first examined Rudelski's things, I noticed that he had a game board in his footlocker. I assumed it was draughts, checkers you call it. I was wrong. I looked again. It was a chessboard.

"We also know that young David Talbot was an avid chess player. He was a member of the Chess Society at Caius, and a member of the Correspondence Chess Association, which is how Queer Jack found him in the first place. He even played chess with that fellow running the garage—Gurney. Eddings, the man killed in Portsmouth, was also a member of the Association, and so was Dranie in Southampton. Trench as well." Black frowned at his own mention of the name.

"And from that you arrive at Bletchley? I don't see the connection."

"It was something Garlinski said. The old man in Coventry. He mentioned the name of the man who'd been the captain of the British chess team at the championship in Buenos Aires last year, just before war broke out. Stuart Milner-Barry. Milner-Barry is on the list Liddell gave me. He works for GC and CS at Bletchley Park. So does Hugh Alexander, and he was on the British team as well. Another man, Alan Turing, also works at Bletchley. He was a team alternate. Milner-Barry and Alexander were both British boy champions in their day, and they all went to Cambridge, just like Talbot."

"So did a lot of other people, Morris."

"I spoke with David Talbot's tutor. Talbot worked as an assistant at the Cambridge Engineering Laboratory and the Cavendish Laboratory last summer. The man he worked for was Alan Turing."

"Okay, I'm almost convinced."

"Jane Luffington," Black murmured. "Fleming's friend. A motorcycle courier who went back and forth between London and Bletchley Park every single day. Believe me, we'll find the answer there, or at least part of it."

At Morris Black's direction they turned off onto a narrower road that veered slightly to the west. In keeping with the invasion orders of a few months before, there were no road signs to indicate where they were going.

"Where exactly are we supposed to meet them?" Katherine asked.

"A little place called Fenny Stratford. It's not far from Bletchley."

The Buckinghamshire village turned out to be one street on a rising hill just across the River Lofeld. It had once been a coach stop on the road to Holyhead. Katherine drove the car across the narrow stone bridge and they began to climb the hill. They went past a pseudo-Gothic red-brick church with a stubby little clocktower, and then they were in the village, little more than a widening in the road lined with old, white-washed cottages and a few shops.

"Stop here," said Black, watching through the windscreen. Katherine did as she was told, halting beside a building slightly larger than its neighbors, an ancient inn sign swinging over the front door.

"The Cock," said Katherine, peering out. The sign showed a large, wide-eyed rooster, sharp-looking spurs fitted to its aggressively raised foot.

They crossed the roadway and entered the inn.

It was a comfortable enough place, low-ceilinged, with dark, rough-hewn beams low enough to cause a tall man trouble, plaster walls, and a wood floor gone dark as pitch over three or four centuries of constant use. Tables ran along the left wall and a bar ran along the right.

The room was empty except for two men seated at the farthest table. They were both dressed in tweeds, the taller of the two in a suit that seemed several sizes too large. The shorter man was drinking from a glass pint mug while his companion was working his way enthusiastically through a large meat pie. Both appeared to be in their early thirties.

"You must be Black," said the shorter man as they approached. "I'm Milner-Barry and Piglet at the trough is the inimitable Dr. Alexander."

"Hugh," said Alexander, speaking around a mouthful of food.

"And the lady?" asked Milner-Barry.

"Katherine Copeland."

"A Yank!" said Milner-Barry. Black noticed that he was a blinker, the eyes shuttering up and down nervously. Probably a reaction to members of the opposite sex. "The advance guard of Lend-Lease?"

"Not really." Katherine smiled. "I'm helping out Detective Inspector Black."

"Officially?" asked Milner-Barry.

"Yes," Black answered before she could say anything.

"Well, then," Milner-Barry said. "I suppose you should sit down." Black drew up chairs for himself and Katherine.

Alexander mopped up the last bit of pie with a morsel of bread and sat back in his chair, sighing. Black saw that he had a large inkblot on the pocket of his shirt. An old stain, faded by a number of washings. The collar of the shirt was frayed and so were the cuffs. Glancing down, Black saw that the man's right shoelace had come undone.

The innkeeper drifted over from the bar and Black asked for coffee. Katherine asked for the same. The man nodded and went back to the bar.

"I remember speaking to you some time ago. A murder investigation."

"That's right."

Milner-Barry glanced at Katherine. "Am I to presume that this young lady has some sort of security clearance?"

"She's here on my authority," Black answered, sidestepping the question.

"Well, then, I suppose it's all right then." Milner-Barry cleared his throat and looked briefly across the table at his friend. Alexander smiled beatifically and pulled a straight-stemmed pipe from the pocket of his jacket.

"I was checking a list given to me by Captain Liddell," said Black.

"Alibis." Alexander nodded. "I remember now. Skulduggery and jiggery-pokery. Cloaks and daggers everywhere."

"Presumably we're not suspects," said the shorter man.

"No," said Black. "You're not. However, it did occur to me that you could help in the investigation."

"Deputies," said Alexander. He lit the pipe and blew a cloud of sweet-smelling smoke toward the ceiling. "Two-Gun Milner-Barry; double-barreled by name, double-barreled by nature."

"Enough of that, Piglet," said Milner-Barry with mock sternness. The innkeeper returned with a coffee service, put it down on the table, and then withdrew again. Katherine poured for herself and Black. "What is it that you think we can help you with, Inspector?" Milner-Barry glanced at his wristwatch, realized he wasn't wearing one, and pulled a pocket watch out of his vest. "It is Christmas, after all."

"Trees to trim, stockings to fill," murmured Alexander. He seemed to be enjoying the conversation immensely, especially his own contributions. Black sighed inwardly. Interviewing the two men was difficult enough; working with them on a daily basis would require the patience of Job.

"Chess seems to be the linking factor in a series of murders," he said bluntly. "That and an association with the work being done at Bletchley Park and perhaps Cambridge University. Both of you are chess masters, both of you work at Bletchley Park, and both of you went to Cambridge. An associate of yours had one of the murder victims as his assistant last year."

Milner-Barry smiled weakly. "Well, that's succinct enough at any rate. Proper scientific method."

"How exactly can we assist you?" asked Alexander, sitting forward in his chair.

Black shrugged his shoulders and took a sip of his coffee. "I'm not quite sure. I'm simply flailing about at this point."

"We do quite a bit of that ourselves," said Alexander.

"You said that chess was a linking factor," said Milner-Barry, ignoring his companion. "How is that?"

"The murderer chose his victims from the membership list of the British Correspondence Chess Association."

"Good Lord," said Alexander, taking the pipe from his mouth. "We both belong." He glanced at Milner-Barry. "So does Turing, for that matter."

"As do eleven hundred and twenty-six others," said Black. "It's a long list."

"Do we presume that the man in question is a player?" Alexander asked.

"Yes. A knowledgeable one. One of the matches he played by mail used something called the Reti opening."

"Munich." Alexander nodded. "In 'thirty-five."

"'Thirty-six," corrected Milner-Barry.

"As you say," Alexander murmured, giving his friend a nasty look. "Munich, 1936."

"Anyone using the Reti would shorten your list considerably, I should think," said Milner-Barry, his voice serious. "It's something you'd expect to see from a master, not the average player."

"How many masters are there?" asked Katherine.

"In this country?" said Alexander. "Perhaps a hundred. Fewer now, with the war."

"How many of them do you know?" asked Black.

"Most," Alexander answered.

Milner-Barry nodded. "Between us we probably know all of them."

"Not really the types you'd expect to go around killing people," said Alexander. "Academics mostly, like MB and myself. The odd solicitor, the occasional anomalous one from the House of Lords."

"As well as being a chess player, the man seems to have considerable mechanical skills," said Black. He thought of the vicious little instrument he'd seen in Spilsbury's laboratory and the grisly artifact the pathologist had dug out of Jane Luffington's spine. Master chess player, master craftsman, master killer.

Milner-Barry shrugged. "Not an impossible combination. Chess and mathematics have a lot in common. Music as well, come to think of it. Was your man a musician by any chance?"

"Not that I'm aware of. Was there anyone at Cambridge who had those sorts of skills? Mechanical aptitude and chess?"

Alexander thought for a moment. "Not that I can recall. Mind you, I didn't have much contact with the engineering types," he said finally.

"Nor I," added Milner-Barry, shaking his head. He thought for a moment, then frowned. Suddenly his eyebrows rose. "Winkle!"

Alexander nodded. "That's right. I'd forgotten about him."

"Who is this man Winkle?"

"A technician at the Cavendish and the Engineering Laboratory," Milner-Barry explained. "Good God! Winkle!" He glanced at Alexander quickly. "He did some work for Turing too," he said quietly. "At Dollis Hill."

"I don't understand," said Black. "Dollis Hill?" What did Turing have to do with a north London suburb?

"Nor should you," said Alexander quietly. "Very hush-hush, I'm afraid." The two men glanced at each other covertly.

Black sighed. Another secret. "Forget that for the moment. What can you tell me about him, this Winkle?"

"He was a technician, just as MB mentioned," said Alexander. "A machinist, electrician, general technical dogsbody. Quite a wizard when it came to following a diagram. Build anything you asked for."

"Did he play chess?" asked Black.

Milner-Barry laughed explosively. "Dear me, yes! That's what made me think of him." He paused. "Actually, he didn't so much play chess as remember it."

"I believe you'd call him an idiot savant," said Alexander. "I think that's the proper term. He could recall games played twenty or thirty years ago, move for move."

"We made a bit of a game out of it," put in the shorter man. "You'd call out something like, um, 'Maroczy-Vukovic, London, 1927, Alekhine defense,' and he'd trot out the whole thing, either on a board, or straight out of his head. Quite extraordinary."

"Useless as a player of course," said Alexander. "Had no style of his own. A mimic. A mirror, that's all."

"Would he have known the Reti opening?"

"Without a doubt," said Milner-Barry. "No one in his right mind would actually use it, of course; the defense is far too well known except for the London System Variation." The mathematician smiled. "The game can become quite independent after the second or third move. It's a transpositional."

Black looked at the man blankly. "I'll have to take your word for it."

"Generally it results in a loss or resignation in twenty-five moves," said Alexander. "The London System is even chances."

"Ah," said Black. The two men at the table seemed to live in an entirely different universe from his own.

"You call him Winkle," said Katherine.

"A nickname. Never knew his real one." Alexander frowned. "Never thought to ask him, come to think of it."

"Is he still at Cambridge?" Black asked.

"No," said Milner-Barry. "As we said, he was working at Dollis Hill, but that all came to a bad end, I think."

"What do you mean?"

"Alan told us about it. Turing, that is. Winkle was never, um, what one might call a social lion. Kept very much to himself. One day he simply went off the deep end, so to speak. Ran about muttering all sorts of odd things, smashing instruments. Had to be let go."

"There'd be a record of his employment surely?"

Alexander shrugged. "Presumably. I don't think there's much chance of putting your hands on it. Not on Christmas Eve."

"Would he have been attached to the Ministry of Works? Or hired directly by the university, or this place at Dollis Hill?"

Milner-Barry laughed again. "We're boffins, Inspector Black, not bureaucrats. Why on earth would we know something like that?"

"You could ask Charlie Snow, I suppose," Alexander suggested. "I imagine he'd know, and if he didn't, he could find out."

"Snow." Milner-Barry nodded. "The very man."

"Who is he?"

"Read physics. King's, I think. A little before our time. Made him a fellow and then he went off to the city. Funny little gnome of a man with tiny little feet and an enormous bald head. I believe he does something obscure now, like writing novels. Boring ones. Uses his initials like that fellow Priestley on the wireless. C. P. Snow he calls himself."

"I'd call him a pompous ass," put in Alexander. He smiled. "Merely my own, uninformed opinion, of course."

"Why would he know anything about Winkle?" asked Black.

"Well, because it's his job," said Milner-Barry. "His bit for the war and all that."

"Writing novels?" asked Katherine.

"No, dear heart," said Milner-Barry, blinking at her sweetly. "I'd venture to say that writing novels and waging war are mutually exclusive. Charlie does the hiring and firing of all the scientific types. DSP. One of those obscure offices connected to the War Ministry. Department of Scientific Personnel."

With the interview complete, Morris Black and Katherine

Copeland thanked the two men for their help, then left the inn. It was mid-afternoon and it was snowing again. They stepped out into the cold air, snowflakes whirling erratically in the gusting wind. They reached the parked car and Black went around to the passenger side. Katherine pulled open the driver's door, pausing before she got in behind the wheel.

The detective stood for a moment, watching the blowing snow as it dusted the young woman's hair, glistening jewel-like in the dusky, silver light. Tiny flakes of it were on her eyelashes, and the cold had put a flush of color on her cheeks as well. She was very beautiful.

"The one they call Winkle."

"What about him?"

"He's the one, isn't he?" Katherine said quietly, speaking to Black across the roof of the car.

"Yes." He nodded, feeling it for the first time. "He's the one."

Seated on the padded seat at the bow of the launch, Guy Liddell yawned and pulled the fur collar of his coat a little more tightly around his neck, shivering in the chill breeze blowing in from the Irish Sea. He'd been traveling since early morning, taking the train from Euston Station and arriving in Blackpool at four. Met there by the British Amphibious Air Lines bus, he'd been driven the few miles to the Flying Boat Terminal at Squires Gate. After collecting his ticket and handing his one small bag to the attendant, he'd been escorted to the small boat that would take him out to the aircraft.

Fifty yards ahead, tethered to its moorings like some gigantic, prehistoric flying whale, was a Short S23 Empire Flying Boat, tossing gently in the wind chop ruffling the waters of the shallow bay. From where he sat, Liddell could clearly make out the name on the bulbous nose of her fuselage: *Cathay*.

According to the ticket clerk, Liddell was lucky; the airline normally operated the route to the Isle of Man with much smaller Saunders-Roe Cutty Sark amphibians, but today the RAF was using *Cathay* to test its newly installed long-range fuel tanks.

The huge aircraft had been impressed at the beginning of the war and was eventually destined for use by Coastal Command, but it still had its original and quite luxurious Imperial Airways fittings. Even better, *Cathay* was much faster than the Saunders-Roe machines and could make the trip across the Irish Sea from Squires Gate to Douglas Bay or Ronaldsway in half the usual time. Liddell would be in the air for less than an hour.

The launch reached the tethered giant and swung around beneath one massive wing to the rear passenger door. Liddell climbed out of the boat, went up the short companionway ladder to the hatch, and stepped inside the aircraft.

The ticket clerk had told the truth. The main compartment on the passenger deck was more like the drawing room in a good-sized country house. Velvet curtains over the portholes, divans and couches instead of ordinary seats, soft lighting from recessed lamps, and thick carpeting everywhere.

The colors were all soft and easy on the eye, gentle shades of green and blue and tan. By the looks of it Liddell was the only passenger. He found a comfortable, upholstered club chair close to one of the windows and settled gratefully into it.

Almost instantly a white-jacketed steward appeared and Liddell ordered coffee. Before it arrived, the four cowled engines fitted on the wings began to fire, one after the other, and soon *Cathay* began to move off along the water, steadily gathering speed. After a brief sense of weightlessness, they were in the air and gaining altitude, swinging to the north and heading out to sea.

The steward appeared again, this time with a tray loaded down with an elegant silver coffee service. He unhinged a small hidden table in the bulkhead, set down the tray, and poured. Liddell thanked him briefly and the man withdrew. The intelligence officer took out his pipe, lit it, and stared out the window, allowing the coffee on the table in front of him to cool.

He was still astounded at how quickly things had changed; it seemed somehow to defy all the deeply entrenched and glacial laws of bureaucratic entropy. He'd given the Pig and Eye information on Chips Channon, Butler, and the others to Desmond Morton on Friday the twentieth. Within hours of Liddell's leaving Rab Butler's office on the twenty-third, yesterday, Churchill announced a surprise cabinet shuffle.

Halifax was out, banished to the ambassador's post in Washington, and Eden was the new foreign secretary. God knows what had happened to Channon and Butler as a result. Margesson had survived the purge, though, Churchill having "promoted" him to the position of war minister. It was a promotion in name only, of course, given Churchill's iron grip on all the services.

The cabinet changes offered a ray of hope, but at the root Liddell knew that little had really been altered, at least as far as he was concerned. It appeared that the possibility of Maxwell Knight's bloodless coup d'état in the name of negotiated peace had been staved off, at least for the moment, but the threat was still there. The men listed in Liddell's confidential report to Morton weren't the only ones who saw position and advantage in a new and firmer order.

And now there was this new question to consider, the strange series of events that had led him to a comfortable seat in the broad, metal-clad belly of *Cathay*. The German Jew internee, Werner Steinmaur, and his bizarre allegations.

The man's letter, and its incredible contents, had gone through a complicated game of leapfrog that had seen it shuffled from office to office, eventually reaching Liddell six weeks after it had been sent. Attached to the letter and its translation was a brief, unsigned note on 10 Downing Street stationery informing Liddell that he had full authority to use whatever means necessary to establish Steinmaur's astonishing claim as quickly as possible.

According to the letter, Steinmaur, an orderly in a Berlin asylum prior to the war, had once seen a man he assumed to be a German or Austrian doctor in conversation with Reinhard Heydrich. Years later he swore he'd seen the same man, dressed in a British Medical Corps uniform, touring the Huyton internment camp in Liverpool.

The claim was reiterated several times within the letter, and Steinmaur was more than willing to prove his assertion by identifying the doctor, either in person or through photographs. This he would do in exchange for an unconditional release from the Manx camps. Other than that there were no conditions or demands. All he wanted was his freedom.

At first Liddell assumed that Steinmaur's incredible assertions were nothing more than the last desperate act of a desperate man, but his constant referral to "the doctor" was too much of a coincidence for Liddell to dismiss out of hand. Eventually he decided to follow it up. Now here he was.

Half an hour into the flight his musings about Steinmaur's allegations were interrupted by a visitor. A uniformed officer came through the forward door of the passenger compartment and approached the intelligence officer.

"Captain Liddell?"

"Yes."

"Bit of trouble with the weather, I'm afraid, sir."

"Oh?" Liddell glanced out the window. Beyond the end of the wing there was nothing to see but a blank wall of falling snow.

"Yes, sir. I know you were planning on going back with us at midnight, but I don't think that's going to be possible. There's a storm closing in behind us and another coming down from Islay."

"We're not turning back, are we?"

"No, sir, but Captain Store says we'll have to stay over in Douglas tonight. Perhaps longer if things get worse."

"Aren't there ferries?"

"I very much doubt it, sir, not in this weather. It looks like we'll all be spending Christmas on the Isle of Man. Sorry."

Liddell sighed. This was the last thing he needed. "So am I." He reached out and touched the coffee cup on the little table in front of him. It had gone cold long ago. He sighed again. "Perhaps you could have the steward bring me a brandy."

The uniformed man nodded. "Certainly, sir."

"A large one."

Katherine Copeland and Morris Black reached the down-at-the-heels house in the Vale of Heath just after dark. Both of them had been lost in thought since leaving Fenny Stratford, and neither one had said a word in the last quarter hour.

Drawing up in front of the house, Katherine switched off the engine and stared out through the windscreen. It was still snowing, and at the end of the street beyond the ruins of the last house, the bleak, deserted reaches of Hampstead Heath were lost in utter blackness.

"What will you do now?" the young woman asked.

"Very little, at least for the moment," answered Black. "This man Snow won't be in his office until after Boxing Day. I'll just have to wait."

"I didn't mean that. I meant Christmas."

"I don't keep Christmas. Not really. Nor Hanukkah, for that matter."

"No family?"

"My father's dead. My mother has been staying with her sister in Devon since the spring. I don't have anyone else."

"No brothers or sisters?"

"My younger brother, Jacob, died when I was fifteen. In a zeppelin raid, as a matter of fact."

"I'm sorry. I didn't know."

Black shrugged. "There's nothing to be sorry about. He was only five; I barely knew him. It was all a very long time ago." He looked across at her. "What about you?"

Katherine spoke out of the darkness. "My family is all back in the States. This is the first Christmas I've ever spent away from home. Quent Reynolds is having a lunch tomorrow in his flat at Landsdowne House. I suppose I'll go to that."

"And tonight?"

"Nothing. Home and sleep, I guess. Everyone says there's some sort of unspoken truce so there won't be any raids for the next few nights." She paused. "Do you think that's true?"

"Probably." There was a short silence. "Would you like to come in?" he said quietly. "You and Fleming seemed to have stocked the larder rather well. I can offer you a drink at least."

"I'd like that."

No. 2 Byron Villas was typical of middle-class housing built in London at the close of the last century. A drawing room, dining room, and kitchen were on the ground floor, with three small bedrooms and a bath above, the two narrow levels joined by a simple staircase that ran up the adjoining wall.

The house had been let empty, and Knight's people had only furnished it with the necessities. The floors were wood or linoleum, uncovered except for a threadbare Axminster in the drawing room, and there was minimal furniture.

Two well-worn upholstered chairs in front of the electric fire in the drawing room, table and four chairs in the dining room, folding table and two chairs in the kitchen. The rest of the furniture and decorations were shades from previous owners: an elongated area of unfaded wallpaper in the dining room where a sideboard might have stood, similar patches on the walls marking framed prints or paintings long since removed.

Nail holes above each doorway in the house, vague indicators of crucifixes and Catholic ownership. A dark stain on the battleship linoleum in front of the grumbling old refrigerator, sign of a forgotten kitchen accident.

Morris Black could read the domestic runes as easily as printed words on paper; his own flat was a journal of such marks and jottings, each one telling a tale about the life he'd lived with Fay.

He found a bottle of brandy in the cupboard above the sink, poured two glasses, and brought them to the drawing room. Katherine had pushed back the blackout curtains and switched off the lights. She was standing at the small bay window, looking out into the night. Black handed her a glass.

"*A gesund dir in pupik,*" he said, raising his glass.

"Is that a toast?" Katherine asked, standing beside him.

"Not really," Black answered, smiling and remembering. "It's something my father used to say."

"What does it mean?"

"Literally? 'Good health to your navel.' The proper toast in Yiddish is *l'chayim,* 'to life,' or you could say *sholem aleichem,* 'peace be unto you.'"

"Is there a response?"

"*Aleichem sholem.* 'To you be peace.'"

"*Sholem aleichem,* Morris Black."

"*Aleichem sholem,* Katherine Copeland."

They touched glasses and drank, looking out at the gently falling snow. After a moment Katherine put her glass down on the windowsill, half turned, and put one hand on Black's shoulder. Rising slightly, she kissed him softly on the lips.

"Teach me to say something in Yiddish, Morris. A question," she whispered.

"What question?"

"How do you say, 'Will you make love to me?'"

"No."

"Is that an answer to the question or just that you won't teach me how to say it?"

"Both."

"Why?" she asked quietly. "Why won't you let me give you this, Morris? I know you'd never ask me on your own. Why?"

Black sighed. He'd known it would come to this, felt it again after leaving the two men from Bletchley. Known what needed to be said. "Trust. You lied to me, Katherine. About who you were and what you were doing."

"I didn't have any choice."

"There's always a choice."

"When it was important, I told you the truth. Jesus, Morris, doesn't what we've been through mean anything? Don't you think you can trust me now?"

"I don't know who to trust."

"Me. Believe that, Morris, please."

"I don't know what to believe, either. About anything."

"Is that the only reason you won't make love to me?"

"No."

"Is it because of your wife?"

"Yes."

"She's dead, Morris. You're still alive."

"That doesn't mean I love her any less."

"I asked you to make love to me, Morris." Katherine stepped away from him. Releasing him. "And now you're turning it into something awful."

"I'm sorry," he answered, knowing that what she said was true. He knew that it wasn't lack of desire stopping him; it was guilt, a feeling that he would be betraying memory. He smiled to himself, remembering Fay, wondering how she would have dealt with his problem. Probably tell him to stop being a fool and get on with it. Always so wise, and relentlessly practical in the face of logic.

Katherine spoke quietly in the gathering darkness. "Do you have to love the person you make love with?"

"I always thought so."

"So did I. Once. Now I'm not so sure. All I'm certain about right this minute is that I want to go to bed with you. Is that wrong?"

"No," he said after a moment. She kissed him again, pressing against his chest. He felt himself respond this time, the hard ache in his heart he'd kept so long suddenly changing, almost melting with the warmth of her body so close to his. But he pushed her away. Gently. Dear God in heaven. Forgive me, Fay, he thought. No. Forgive yourself.

"What now?" she murmured, refusing to take her hands away from his shoulders this time.

"I'm making a moral judgment."

"On me, or you?"

"Neither. Both. The world."

Katherine moved one hand down from his shoulder and laid it flat against his chest. With her other hand she took his and brought it up to cup her breast and shivered at the feel of it.

"You're not responsible for the morality of the world, Morris. And you don't have to forget the past, you just have to make peace with it." There was another silence. Under her hand Katherine could feel the steady pulse of his beating heart and knew that she could feel hers as well.

"What about the future?"

"It doesn't exist, Morris. Not tonight."

Outside, in the darkness, the snow continued to fall. Not very far away it would be whispering over the cold earth of the cemetery in Golders Green, lying over it like a blanket, warming Fay as she slept. Imagining it, he smiled, then looked down into Katherine's waiting eyes.

"*Vilstu schlofen mit mir?*" he said, asking and answering the question at last.

"Yes."

CHAPTER TWENTY-THREE

Friday, December 27, 1940
10:00 A.M., British Standard Time

BY TEN O'CLOCK IN THE MORNING Dr. Tennant was driving his Bentley south on the Streatham High Road heading for Smithabottom, Coulsdon, and the Cane Hill Mental Hospital. Behind him the city was enjoying its brief respite from the raids, locked in a rolling yellow fog that had come down from the marshes the night before to melt the last of the newly fallen snow. He almost had his quarry now and he drove quickly, eager to ring down the final curtain.

Even on Christmas Eve, his attempts to trace Raymond Loudermilk's movements after leaving Wick Hall School had proved remarkably easy. Acting on the assumption that Loudermilk had almost certainly come in contact with the law sometime between 1914 and the present, Tennant placed a call to Nosey Smith at Special Branch and was once again given access to the wealth of information in the Central Records Office. Thankfully, Scotland Yard, like the criminals it pursued, took no holidays.

Searching through the index under the letter *L*, the psychiatrist wasn't particularly surprised to find that Loudermilk indeed had a card made out in his name. The surprising thing was that it contained only one conviction. In July 1917, Loudermilk, then fifteen, had been arrested for violently assaulting a boy three years his junior at a funfair in the south London district of Battersea.

After a magistrate's hearing held under Section 11 of the Prevention of Crime Act, Loudermilk was given a two-year sentence and sent to a Borstal institution for training. Three months later, after a series of violent incidents, his Borstal license was revoked and he was reassigned to the Boys' Wing of Wandsworth Prison. Six weeks after that, there was another violent altercation, this time with a warder, followed by two suicide attempts.

It was concluded that Loudermilk could not be kept within the general prison population, even after a long period of confinement in a straitjacket. After examination by the Wandsworth medical officer, Dr. Allan Pearson, Raymond Loudermilk was remanded to the Cane Hill Mental Hospital for a period of four years under authority of the Mental Deficiency Act. His release date was not on file. Although Loudermilk had been a minor at the time of his arrest, he was listed as having no fixed address and no next of kin.

Dr. Richard Hillman, the director of Cane Hill, had already left for the holidays when Tennant called, but the administrative assistant who answered the phone made an appointment for the morning after Boxing Day. Frustrated by having to wait for almost three days, Tennant had spent Christmas alone in his Cheyne Walk Mews office, assembling his notes.

Enjoying the feel of the Bentley's wheel beneath his hands, Tennant continued his southward journey. From Tooting Bec to Croydon and even beyond to Purley and Riddle's Down, the road was relentlessly suburban, the old villages and the newer, gray-faced "garden cities" melding into a long, bleak unbroken wall, but at Smithabottom, just past the Coulsdon railway halt, the landscape suddenly became more rural. Open country replaced the cloying lines of pseudo-cottages, rolling chalk hills and gentle downs marking the farthest limits of the city.

Following the directions in his RAC guide, Tennant turned off the main road onto a narrower track; ancient hedgerows, deep woods, and downland farms ranged on either side, overseen by a long high ridge that ran away at an angle to the west. Half a mile later he turned again, swinging between the high stone gates that marked the entrance to Cane Hill, then climbed along the winding drive between the trees, eventually reaching the asylum itself.

It was monstrous, of course, places like Cane Hill always were. The asylum was a featureless pile of brick built by prison labor at the turn of the century, identical to the other institutions of its type that seemed to have chosen this particular part of the countryside. As well as Cane Hill there was Netherne Mental Hospital, no more than three miles away below Farthing Downs, and Caterham Asylum to the east. Between Caterham and Reigate there were half a dozen smaller clinics for those who could afford their special care.

Cane Hill was made up of a central block, two sprawling wings jutting out from it to the north and south, and two minor wings at the rear. Every window on every floor was glassed, wire-meshed, and barred. The grounds were sodded in short, mean-spirited turf gone brown with winter. The bleakness of the place was made even worse by the heavy fog, great trails and wisps of it caught against the damp, dark brickwork like the remnants of a rotted shroud.

Hillman was seated behind his large, utilitarian metal desk when Tennant was ushered into his office. The asylum director was in his late fifties, slim, his close-cropped hair and the sides of the second and third fingers of his left hand the same nicotine shade.

He had a thin, clean-shaven, foxlike face with prominent cheekbones and a knife-edged Adam's apple that bobbed up and down between his navy blue bow tie and his small, pointed chin. A pair of circular, wire-framed glasses perched on a hooked, wide-nostriled nose. He was wearing a plain, blue suit and a white shirt.

The desk in front of him was almost bare. To the left there was a single black telephone, to the right a simple wooden letter box. Between them was a large unframed sheet of dark green blotting paper. At the edge of the blotter on the bottom left corner was a row of sharpened Eagle pencils in a perfectly straight line. In the upper right corner three identical fountain pens waited to be used.

To the ordinary eye the desk would be taken as an orderly reflection of the man who sat behind it. To Tennant the surface of the desk marked the overt expression of an obsessive-compulsive neurotic. Dr. Richard Hillman was half as mad as the inmates he controlled.

"Dr. Tennant." The voice was flat, almost metallic.

"Dr. Hillman."

The Cane Hill psychiatrist nodded in the direction of a padded chair. Tennant seated himself. Another nod and the secretary withdrew, closing the door behind her. In the distance, muffled by the thick glass of the office windows and the sound deadening of the bricks, Tennant could hear the grumbling of aircraft engines. Spitfires at Kenley revving up for a practice sortie in the fog.

"According to my secretary, you appear to have some interest in one of our ex-patients." As Hillman spoke, he used his left hand to disturb the row of pencils, then rearrange them again.

Tennant nodded. "Raymond Loudermilk. He was sent here in 1918, remanded from Wandsworth."

"Yes." The pencils askew, the pencils aligned. The movement of Hillman's hand kept distracting Tennant, and he suddenly realized that the man didn't have the slightest idea of what the hand was doing.

"Were you director of Cane Hill at that time?"

"No."

"Did you know Loudermilk?"

"Yes." The pencils moved, then returned to their position. "I was on staff here. An interesting case."

"How so?"

"Perhaps I should know why you've taken an interest in him first."

"His name came up in connection with a patient."

"I see." Hillman didn't sound convinced. The pencils moved magically under his twitching fingers.

"My patient and Loudermilk would seem to have a great deal in common," said Tennant, lying easily. "It occurred to me that I might publish."

"Ah." Hillman nodded. This was something that he could understand. He frowned, then the small mouth opened as though he were about to speak. The fingers moved. Tennant knew what he was going to say and spoke first.

"Of course, I'd be more than happy to share credit with you in the article." Tennant paused. "If I do publish, that is." He paused again. "I suppose that would depend on what I could find out about Loudermilk," he added, smiling. The request made and the payment arranged.

Hillman smiled briefly and nodded. The fingers stopped moving for a moment. Tennant's transparent blandishment had done its job. Hillman sat back in his chair.

"Yes." He nodded, tenting his hands over a nonexistent stomach. "It might be useful. Loudermilk was quite an exceptional case."

"How was he diagnosed?"

"Restricted ego, substitutive, totemic."

"Not psychotic?"

Hillman smiled condescendingly. "Dear me, no, Dr. Tennant."

"But he was violent. Extremely so."

"Only in terms of his substitutive neuroses," Hillman pontificated. "His anger was aimed at inducing his substituted mother-image to accomplish his wishes. He had no mother; ergo, he transferred those frustrations onto society in general. Thus, violent expression."

Tennant nodded. Hillman was clearly one of the new post-Freudians. The words he had spoken were a perfect parroting of Ian Suttie's *The Origins of Love and Hate.* Suttie was one of the typically British School who would rather deal with the esoteric nuances of love than the raw realities of sex.

"You mentioned totemism?"

"Yes. By far the most interesting feature of the case." Hillman offered the bland smile again. "Were you aware of Loudermilk's obsession with the works of John Martin?"

"The painter?" Tennant could vaguely remember seeing some of the nineteenth-century religious artist's gigantic canvases on display at the Tate. Huge, melodramatic evocations of biblical catastrophe and cataclysm. "No, I wasn't aware of that."

"He was fascinated by the man; compulsively so. Here, let me show you something." The asylum director rose from his chair and went to the row of filing cabinets on his left. He found the right drawer, opened it, and withdrew a large manila folder. Returning to his chair, he turned the file around on the desk blotter and opened it. Tennant moved his chair forward and began leafing through the pages contained in the folder.

It was like staring into a neatly organized vision of hell. Dozens of carefully executed pencil drawings showed various scenes from the Bible and Milton's *Paradise Lost*, each one with a neatly inscribed notation in the lower left-hand corner giving date and source. *Pandemonium, The Bridge of Chaos, The Conflict Between Satan and Death, Satan on the Burning Lake, The Destruction of Sodom, The Opening of the Seventh Seal, The Deluge, The Great Day of His Wrath.* There were also a series of draw-

ings with a single repetitive image: *The Last Judgment.* In these
the scene was always the same. Hillman read Loudermilk's
own title aloud:

*"God, seated on his Heavenly Throne, flanked by A Gathering of
Saints, Sternly watching the Avenging Angel bringing the fiery Spear
of God to the Damned assembled in the Valley of Jehoshaphat below."*

The largest of the drawings, folded over twice in the file,
had been done on translucent vellum and had obviously been
traced. There were literally hundreds of tiny figures in the
drawing, each one numbered, faint lines joining one to the
other, and all to the tip of the flaming spear.

"There's another file as thick as this one," said Hillman as
Tennant went through the drawings. "Drawings based on
Martin's plans for...what was it now?" He paused for a
moment and thought. "Ah, yes, *Plan for Improving the Air and
Water of the Metropolis.* Quite astounding for the times. Aque-
ducts, cambered rail lines, bridges. Martin was something of
an engineer as well as a painter."

"You sound as though you learned a great deal about him
yourself." Perhaps even shared in Raymond Loudermilk's
obsession.

"Part of the therapeutic process." Hillman shrugged. "He
never stated it explicitly, but Raymond suffered under the
delusion that he was Martin's reincarnation. Chess was another example."

"Martin was a chess player?" asked Tennant, startled at
the connection.

"Oh, yes." Hillman nodded firmly. His hand had gone
back to the pencils again. "One of the great ones of his time.
He had weekly gatherings at his studio. Played with people like
Sir Robert Peel, Constable, Turner, even Brunel, the fellow
who engineered the Suez Canal."

Tennant closed the file in front of him. His mental image
of Raymond Loudermilk was complete. It was time to move
on to more practical considerations.

"How long was Loudermilk a patient here?"

"A little short of three years."

"Do you recall exactly when he was released?"

"He wasn't," said Hillman, frowning.

"I beg your pardon?"

"I assumed that you knew." The pencils stood in a perfect line. The fingers moved toward the pens. "Raymond Loudermilk was never released from Cane Hill. He committed suicide twenty years ago. He's dead."

Charlie Snow's office was located in Golden Cross House, a modern, six-story Portland-stone block only a year or so old, which had replaced the ancient hotel of the same name. The building was roughly triangular, filling the island site formed at Trafalgar Square by the convergence of Duncannon Street, Charing Cross Road, and the entrance to the Strand.

Officially, Snow was assistant deputy director of the Directorate of Scientific Research's Department of Scientific Personnel Technical Division, reporting directly to the War Office. Or, as the cardboard placard on his door described him: *A.D.Dir/DSR/Dep't Sci. Per. (Tech Div.)-WO.*

"My God!" Katherine whispered as Black rapped on the door. "And I thought Foggy Bottom was bad!"

"Foggy Bottom?" Black frowned.

"Forget it."

A mild voice came from behind the door. "Enter!" They did so. The top-floor office was tiny, no more than twelve feet on a side, with a single window looking down over the grimy façade of Charing Cross Station and the delicate miniature spire of Charing Cross itself, which stood in the station's forecourt. The replica of the thirteenth-century monument laid down by Edward I on the occasion of his wife's funeral was the official point from which all distances were measured on

Ordnance Survey maps and was almost certainly the X marking the spot on Luftwaffe bombing charts.

"One assumes that Jerry is incapable of hitting the bull's-eye spot on," said Snow, reading Morris Black's brief glance. "Statistically it's probably the safest place in London." Snow came out from around his heavily varnished desk, beaming brightly and adjusting the vest of his blue suit across a beach-ball stomach. He looked to be a well-nourished thirty-five or so. "You must be Inspector Black, and this would be Miss Copeland."

They shook hands and Snow returned to his desk. Black and Katherine seated themselves in two plain wooden chairs across from him. Behind Snow, pinned to the wall, was a gigantic chart filled with names, squares, and squiggles that dwarfed the little man below it.

Snow was small, built like a heavy-chested sparrow, large, intelligent eyes made larger by the thick, perfectly round spectacles perched on his small, beaklike nose. His head was perfectly round, the large dome of his skull feathered by a tonsure of dark hair. He had a full, almost feminine mouth and a soft, rounded chin.

"Have a good holiday, then?" he asked.

Black threw Katherine a quick, embarrassed look, then turned his attention back to Snow. "Yes. Quite."

"Good. Good." Snow nodded, the large head bobbing up and down. Black smiled, suddenly realized why the man looked so familiar. He looked exactly like Mole in the illustrated *Wind in the Willows* he'd read as a child. "Worked all through, myself. First a blizzard and then this hideous fog. Marooned at the Oxford and Cambridge Club for three days." He blinked happily behind the glasses. "I suppose that illiterate wretch Alexander told you that I'm actually a novelist." Black almost laughed. The war at home was apparently being run by a hodgepodge assembly of mystery writers, mathematicians, and Oxford dons playing at espionage.

Black answered Snow diplomatically. "He mentioned something about it."

"God knows what sort of vile aspersions he was casting in my direction. I should have the little rotter sacked." Snow smiled again. "I could, you know. Apparently that's the sort of thing I've been hired on to do." He shook his head. "Extraordinary way to spend the war. Much rather be in the field. Rather a good shot in my time, even if I do say so myself."

Black tried to imagine the portly figure carrying a Lee-Enfield or wearing a tin hat and manning an antiaircraft gun. The image failed to materialize.

"Alexander and Milner-Barry said that you might be able to help us."

"Yes, so you said on the telephone." Snow nodded, then pulled out the central drawer in his desk. "I've done my home-work on your request already, as a matter of fact. Got it out of the way first thing."

"Thank you."

Snow found what he was looking for—a single sheet of lined paper. He laid it flat on the desk in front of him, frowning. "Wilkes."

"That's the man's name?" said Black. He looked over at Katherine; she'd already taken a stenographer's notebook from her bag and had it on her lap.

"Yes. Arthur Sidney Wilkes." Snow spelled it out slowly and Katherine jotted it down in the book. "Odd sort of fellow by the looks of it."

"He worked at the Cavendish Laboratory?"

"Among other institutions." Snow looked up from the sheet of paper and beamed again. "Can't tell you all the names, I'm afraid. Top secret and all that."

"I understand."

"I can tell you that he seems to have been employed as a technician of one sort or another for a number of years. According to the record, he was with Standard Telegraph and

Cable for a time, and before that he was with the Government Post Office. That was before coming to Cambridge."

"Can you tell me when that was exactly?"

"Cambridge? Nineteen thirty-eight. March."

"What about his education?"

"None to speak of. He seems mostly to have been hired on previous experience. Not so uncommon these days."

"When was he let go?"

"Five months ago," Snow answered promptly. "July twenty-eighth to be precise."

Black nodded to himself. Six weeks for the anger to grow. Six weeks to first put his terrible plan into place and then into action.

"Do you have his National Registration Card number?"

"Certainly." Snow read it off and Katherine wrote in her notebook once again.

"What about an address or a telephone number?"

"No telephone. And the only address I have here is a postal box number."

"Which district?"

"NW3."

Katherine looked up from her notebook. "Where's that?"

Black's voice went cold. "Hampstead."

Wexfordian was a roller. The eight-hundred-ton coastal steamer twisted like a corkscrew with each passing wave, and Guy Liddell's stomach twisted with it. It was late afternoon now, and somewhere the sun was setting, but the intelligence officer hadn't seen even the vaguest sign of it since they'd left Douglas Bay three hours before. According to the latest Met report, the fog that covered half of southern England was also covering most of the Irish Sea from Drogheda to Caernarvon.

Liddell couldn't have cared less; as he sat on a bench bolted to the bulkhead of the topside stem cabin, every ounce of his concentration was fixed on the Wexford Steamship Co. pennant fluttering on its lanyard over the stern. Above him, at his back, *Wexfordian*'s foghorn sounded a single, doom-filled note.

Somehow he had convinced himself that if he focused on the little striped flag, he wouldn't be sick again. Unbelievably, the ghastly, Gravol-resistant motion of the coastal steamer didn't seem to be having any effect at all on Steinmaur. The last Liddell had seen of him he was sleeping comfortably in the day cabin they'd been offered as quarters for their passage.

Liddell lifted his wrist and glanced at his watch. Time seemed to be standing still, and time, it seemed, had now become his greatest opponent. Steinmaur had positively identified the man he'd seen at the Liverpool internment camp, and Liddell had no way of acting on the information. The undersea telephone cable had been out even before he arrived on the Isle of Man, and there was no way that he was going to trust the incredible news to a wireless transmission.

All through Christmas and Boxing Day the storms sweeping down from the north had made flying out of Douglas impossible, and then the fog had appeared like some creeping nemesis sent by something Dennis Wheatley or one of Maxwell Knight's other spiritualist friends might have dreamed up.

Wexfordian had been the first ship out of Douglas, and Liddell, almost frantic with frustration, had booked passage for himself and the little German. He'd regretted his decision from the first minute past the end of Victoria Pier. And there was worse to come.

As well as carrying coal and mixed cargo, *Wexfordian* also carried mail. She would put in at Wicklow and her home port of Wexford on the Irish coast, then cross to Cardigan and Pembroke before finally docking at Cardiff sometime late tomorrow. That is unless they were interrupted by a passing

U-boat off to deliver more Special Branch fifth columnists to the Irish coast.

If by some lucky twist of fate they arrived at Cardiff intact, he and Steinmaur would catch a connecting train to London, but the earliest they could arrive would be close to midnight. Sadly, Dr. Charles Tennant, captain in the Royal Army Medical Corps and suspected Nazi spy for Reinhard Heydrich, would have to wait one more day for his just deserts.

Steinmaur's immediate and unequivocal identification of the psychiatrist still astounded Liddell. There had been seven members of the medical committee on the tour of the Liverpool internment camp, all in uniform. Of them, Charles Tennant was the last one Liddell would have suspected. With hindsight he was the obvious man, of course, at least as far as his usefulness to Heydrich was concerned.

The implications of the man's treachery were mind-boggling. Charles Tennant was an adviser to Masterman and the Double X Committee, one of several psychiatric advisers to the Home Security Office on matters pertaining to mental health and morale, and he sat on the Air Ministry Fitness Evaluation Board. Even worse than his official status was the man's private practice.

Liddell had only the vaguest notion of the psychiatrist's social and professional contacts, but even so, he was aware of Tennant's reputation. From what he knew the bulk of Tennant's practice was made up of ministerial wives, ministerial mistresses, and the ministers themselves. God only knew what deep dark secrets they'd divulged in confidence, and God only knew what damage the man had done by passing those secrets along to the Nazis.

The intelligence officer stared numbly out at the seething, porridge-gray surface of the water running out from beneath the low, rounded stem of *Wexfordian*. He shivered in the damp, foggy air. The whole idea of it was as brilliant as it was grotesque.

A psychiatrist to the gentry, privy to every sin and cause for shame offered up to him freely and in total confidence, or so the gentry imagined. What better way to wheedle out the grubby horrors burrowed so securely in the woodwork along the corridors of power?

The Pig and Eyes on Halifax, Channon, and the esteemed Rab Butler had been responsible, at least in part, for the downfall of the Peace at Any Price cabal. What could Tennant accomplish with the information contained in *his* files?

Liddell was also well aware that far more was at risk here than just the nation's secrets. If news of Charles Tennant's role as a spy got out, there'd be skeletons rattling from Buckingham Palace to Whitehall, not to mention Secret Intelligence and MI5. He only knew the names of a few of Tennant's patients, but for the seasick intelligence officer it was more than enough.

The present wife of Stewart Menzies, head of SIS, had been under the psychiatrist's care for a variety of eating disorders, and Menzies's first wife, a member of the ubiquitous Sackville clan, was also his patient. What tattle were they whispering in Tennant's ear?

Worse yet, it was common knowledge that Princess Marina, the Duchess of Kent, was also seeing the psychiatrist on a regular basis, probably to complain about the questionable nocturnal activities of her husband, George, younger brother to the King. The royal family had always cast a blind and mildly affectionate eye over the homosexual proclivities of its kith and kin, but having details of the Duke of Kent's "entertainments" spread across the front pages of the German and American press was unlikely to do much for wartime morale.

Both Tony Blunt and Burgess had told Liddell stories about parties they'd attended themselves, and according to them the Duke's stamina was almost legendary. Prince George's coterie included a host of other Clubland figures like Dickie Mountbatten, Patrick, the seventh Baron Plunkett, and the almost absurdly foppish James Pope-Hennessy, now conveniently installed in a Foreign Office sinecure within cooing distance of none other than Chips Channon. Princess Marina, of course, would know them all, and well.

Thinking about Pope-Hennessy brought Liddell up short. The man's sister, Caroline, was a secretary in his own office. He moaned, wondering just how far Tennant had managed to spin his web. His stomach lurched violently at the thought of what that could mean.

He rose quickly, staggered to the portside rail, and vomited again. He had enough secrets of his own to keep and he knew that he wasn't alone. Above him, just forward of the tall, single-striped funnel, *Wexfordian*'s foghorn boomed out, shatteringly loud, the sound seeping into the mist, then fading without an echo into nothingness.

Liddell retched until he tasted bile, then stumbled back to the bench. Too many secrets to protect, too many lies to tell in order to keep them safe. There would be some judicious editing of Dr. Charles Tennant's records and case histories before they drifted too far beyond Liddell's reach. Vertigo and nausea returned as his train of thought plunged into a bottomless chasm of linked, accumulating disaster.

Gritting his teeth, he focused hard on the dangling pennant, silently cursing whatever convolution of fate had put him on this wretched lurching ship, tossed on this wretched, heaving sea.

CHAPTER TWENTY-FOUR

Saturday, December 28, 1940
11:00 A.M., British Standard Time

MORRIS BLACK WALKED UP East Finchley Road from the underground station and paused in front of the high wooden gate barring the entrance to the Stag Motor Garage. It seemed as though the world had changed in the span of a few short days, or at least his world. In Katherine's arms he'd felt a terrible burden of sadness lifted magically from his shoulders, and now he could feel the familiar, cold sense of elation that came with the Sight.

This, he thought, was how an actor must feel, reaching the penultimate dramatic speech in the final act of a play. It was as though the lines had already been written, needing only to be spoken for the climax to be reached.

There was always the chance that he was mistaken about Gurney, but he'd sensed something false in the man at their earlier meeting, and the fact that the Finchley Road garage stood on the border of Hampstead—the location of Wilkes's postal box—was an added incentive for returning to the Stag. He pushed open the small door set into the gate, entered the cluttered yard, and crossed to George Gurney's shop.

Sam the dog came out to meet him, fangs bared, growling low in his heavy chest, but this time Black ignored him. Inside the shop the Hispano Suiza had been replaced by a mundane Wolesley with a crumpled bonnet. Gurney, dressed in his oily boilersuit, was standing at his workbench when the detective entered. Turning, the tall, blond-haired man stared blankly for a moment, wiped his hands with a rag, then crossed the shop to where Black was standing.

"Inspector Black, isn't it?" The man was nervous, that was clear enough. The handshake was too easily offered, the voice artificially hearty.

"That's right."

"I didn't expect that I'd be seeing you again."

"I'm sure you didn't," Black answered, his voice purposely flat.

"Still investigating?" A quick smile that was almost a facial tic.

Black wasted no time with small talk. "You knew him, didn't you?"

"Talbot? I've already told you that." Gurney kept on wiping his hands on the rag. "I minded his car."

"I don't mean Talbot."

"I beg your pardon?"

"I meant the man who went away with him that day. The man you said must have come by train because he and Talbot went away in the Ford."

"I don't know what you're talking about."

"Oh, yes, you do, Mr. Gurney, oh, yes, you bloody well do." Black dropped any pretense of politeness. He was definitely taking a blindly aimed shot in the dark, and the only way to make Gurney crack was by intimidation.

Gurney took a step backward, startled. "You're being offensive, Detective Black."

"It's 'detective inspector.' And I get offended when I'm lied to."

"I think you should leave," Gurney answered stiffly. Sam the dog growled at his master's feet.

"Not until I have some answers." Black gave the dog one short glance. "If he comes any nearer, I'll boot his arse up through his fucking ears. Understand, Mr. Gurney?"

"Yes." He snapped his fingers, and the dog skulked away.

"Now tell me about Talbot."

"I've told you everything I know. David Talbot was a customer, that's all."

"I think he was more than that, Mr. Gurney. You chatted, told him your life story, listened to his. Played chess. Not a customer, Gurney. Something else."

"I'm not at all sure I like your tone, Detective Black." It was all there now, and in force. Plummy Oxford accent, Eton lurking close behind it. The crisp, down-the-nose tones of wealth and position.

"Don't bother playing the haughty lord with me, Gurney. It simply won't do, old fellow." Behind the man and to his left Black could see the framed photograph on the desk. Another shot in the dark, but not so blindly fired. "You lied to me about your wife and kids as well." He pushed brusquely past Gurney, went to the desk, and picked up the photograph.

Gurney followed. "I...," he began, and stopped.

"They didn't leave on the *Arandora Star*, did they, Gurney?" The blood had drained from the man's face and Black could see the muscles in his jaw working. The detective kept on, following the freshly opened crack in the façade. "I asked about. The *Arandora Star* didn't take regular passengers. Internees only." He stared at Gurney coldly. "She left you, didn't she? Took the children off with her. Perhaps she went abroad as you said, home to mother, but not on the *Arandora Star* and not because you were worried for her safety." He was playing the bastard copper to the hilt now, not enjoying it, but using deliberate crudeness to widen the cracks in Gurney's armor.

"Please, I don't..."

Don't let it go now, push hard, then harder still. "Was it because of David Talbot? Someone like him? Young. So handsome he was pretty? Did she find out and leave you?" There was a long silence. There were tears in Gurney's eyes now. Finally the blond man spoke again.

"Yes," he whispered, almost choking on the word. Black gave him a moment, turning to put the picture back on the desk.

"Tell me," Black said quietly. Gurney nodded and dropped heavily into the chair in front of the desk. "Tell me about David Talbot." The Scotland Yard detective stood above him, waiting.

"David and I were...friends, as you say."

Black pushed again, loathing himself for what he was doing, knowing that it had to be done and wondering what Katherine would say if she could hear him now. "Don't beat around the bush, man. You were arse-fucking the boy."

Gurney paled. "Oh, God, please, it wasn't like that."

"No, I'm sure not. Damon and Pythias. Bosom friends for life, I suppose. Pals all round." Black snorted. "Get on with it. Tell me about Arthur Sidney Wilkes."

Gurney paled at the name. "How did you find out about that?" *That,* not *him?* Black leaned forward. Something more here. Something deeper, darker than he'd expected.

"It doesn't matter. Just tell me what you know."

"Wilkes wasn't his real name. I don't know why he changed it."

"What was his proper name?"

There was a long, fragile silence; Black could see Gurney being torn apart by this, right before his eyes. "Loudermilk," Gurney whispered faintly.

"I didn't hear," snapped the detective. Push. Hard. Squeeze the bastard dry for everything he knew. It was all attack now, no quarter given.

"Raymond Loudermilk. I knew him. At school."

"Was he your bum boy as well?"

"Christ no!" Gurney breathed. "It was nothing like that. Not with him."

"This was at university?"

"Before that. Wick Hall."

"Where's that?"

"Cold Dean. Stanmer Park. A few miles from Brighton."

"A public school?"

"Yes."

"But you knew him after that as well?"

"Yes."

"Tell me." An order, harsh and direct.

Gurney flinched, then nodded. "I had to leave Wick Hall. There had been some financial reverses at home."

"In other words your family couldn't pay the fees."

"Yes."

"You lost track of Loudermilk."

"Yes."

"But he popped up again."

"Yes."

"When? Where?"

"The first time was at STC." Gurney saw Black's frown and explained. "Standard Telegraph and Cable. I was an engineer with them for a while."

"Why did he contact you?"

"He needed work."

"You found it for him?"

Gurney nodded. "Yes. I left STC shortly afterwards. It was several years before I saw him again."

"Where was that?"

"I was at the Post Office Research and Development Station at Dollis Hill. Loudermilk just appeared one day."

Black nodded thoughtfully. He had no idea what the Dollis Hill research facility did, but he remembered the name from the conversation with Hugh Alexander and Milner-Barry.

Turing, one of their colleagues, had worked there as well. Perhaps something to do with Ultra. Another connection.

"He needed employment again?" the detective asked.

"Yes."

"And you found it for him."

"Yes. A little while after that I decided to get out of the engineering profession entirely."

"Because of Loudermilk?"

"Yes. No. Partly. I was married to Karen. I..." He stopped.

Black pressed on. "You purchased this place?"

"Yes. I had a small inheritance."

"But he followed you here."

"Yes."

"He didn't want a job though, did he?"

"No. He'd come by from time to time. Sometimes he'd take things."

"What sort of things?"

"Machinery. Small motors. Tools and bits of wire. I didn't ask why."

"He saw you with Talbot, didn't he?"

"Yes. At the Mandrake. He followed me back here. He met David. Jumped to the obvious conclusion. I think he was jealous."

"Was he blackmailing you?"

"I suppose you'd call it that. He never asked for money."

"But he wanted David Talbot, didn't he?"

"Yes." Gurney lowered his head and brought his hands up to cover his face. "Oh, dear God!" he whispered, sobbing.

"When I came here, you thought that Loudermilk might have murdered David, didn't you?"

"Yes."

"But you said nothing."

"No."

"Why not? Sodomy is one thing, Gurney, murder is something else altogether."

The blond man looked up at Black. "I was afraid," he said quietly.

"Because of what Loudermilk would say? To your wife?"

"No. Karen had already gone by then." Gurney paused, a flush suddenly fevering his cheeks. "David wasn't the first." Here it was, Black thought. The source.

"Why did you keep silent?"

"Because of...the other thing."

"What other thing?"

"Exner."

"Who is Exner?"

"Bernard Timothy Exner. He and I were in lower third together at Wicks Hall. Loudermilk was in the fourth form."

"What happened?"

"Loudermilk...caught us."

"In flagrante?"

"Yes."

"His blackmail started that long ago?"

"Yes."

"But you were just boys. And probably not the only ones." Black remembered his own boarding school days; he knew the temptations and the frustrations well enough.

"It wasn't so much the...sex."

"Shame?"

"Yes. And fear."

"Of disclosure?"

"No. Worse." Gurney paused. "I thought Loudermilk would kill me."

"Why?"

"Because he was insane," said Gurney, looking up at Black again. "I knew that even then."

"How?" Another silence. Gurney looked as though his nerves were stretched to the limit. Black waited, then spoke again, softening his tone. "Tell me how you knew."

"Because he was the one who killed Bernard," the man answered finally, all emotion drained from him now.

"Bernard was killed?" Queer Jack's first victim, that long ago. Gurney had held the secret for half a lifetime.

"Yes. The police said it had been a stranger. A vagrant. I knew better."

"Why?"

"Because Loudermilk told me he'd done it. When Bernard vanished, the entire school went searching for him. Loudermilk took me to the spot. Showed me." Gurney's voice had begun to crack.

"The body?" said Black, speaking gently now.

"Yes." Gurney nodded. "It was Loudermilk's sacred place, or that's what he called it. He said that one day it would be famous once again."

"Where exactly was this 'sacred place'?"

"A thicket on the edge of Stanmer Wood, not far from the school. We used to go to the old chapel there on special days. It was beautiful, actually. He'd...he'd buried him just at a spot where you could see the spire rising up through the trees. I remember thinking that Bernard would be able to listen to the bells. He wouldn't be lonely."

"What did he mean when he said the place would be famous once again?"

"I don't know," sobbed Gurney. "I only know that he showed me the body and told me that he'd kill me if I said anything. He said he'd tell everyone that it was me." The tears began to roll down Gurney's face again and he was shaking. "Oh, God! He made me..."

"What?"

"He made me touch the body, touch Bernard's...Oh, Christ!" he moaned. "He said my fingerprints would prove that I'd been the one!"

Black reached out and gently laid one hand on the anguished man's shoulder. It wasn't true, of course. As a boy

Gurney's fingerprints wouldn't have been on file, and even if they'd been taken at the time, it wouldn't have mattered since the dead child's skin couldn't have held the prints.

A ten- or eleven-year-old child wouldn't have known that, though. Queer Jack had set the hook deeply and well, then left it there to grow and fester until he came again to pick at the wound and make Gurney bleed once more.

"You never said anything?" Black murmured.

Gurney shook his head. "Not until now."

"But you knew what he was capable of when he went off with David Talbot."

"Yes. God help me, I knew. But I was afraid. Terribly afraid."

Black left it there for the moment. "Do you know where Loudermilk was living?"

"No. He never said and I certainly never asked."

"Any idea?"

"Not really. At a guess I'd say nearby."

"What makes you think that?"

"One of the times he was here a chit dropped out of his trousers."

"What sort of chit?"

"It was a receipt. From the Hampstead Subscription Library."

Charles Tennant, closeted in the house on Cheyne Mews since his return from Cane Hill, paced back and forth across the large oriental carpet in his office, thinking hard. On his way back from the asylum he'd stopped in at several secondhand bookstores and gathered up what little information he could find on John Martin, including an illustrated catalog of his work originally published by the Tate. The pile of texts now stood on his desk, next to the overflowing ashtray that had remained unemptied since the night before.

After working his way through the books and taking down whatever morsels of information he thought might be useful in better understanding Loudermilk's character, he found himself returning to the question of the man's suicide. It seemed like an idiotic way to think, but by the evidence of the Queer Jack killings it seemed almost impossible that Raymond Loudermilk wasn't the killer.

Everything pointed to him as the logical suspect, from the Armenian's suspicions about the death of Bernard Exner to Loudermilk's obsession with the art and life of John Martin and the connection between both Martin and Exner and the game of chess.

A dozen times in the last few hours Tennant had returned to the annual he'd stolen from Wick Hall, poring over the lists of names and scanning the small faces in the photographs, searching for some clue. There was nothing, and it was telling that of all the pictures in the small volume, there was none that showed Loudermilk.

Ordinary shyness, or some deeply rooted fear? The primal instinct of a savage who felt his soul would be snatched away by the photographer? Or a boy acting on a different instinct entirely, somehow knowing that he shouldn't leave any passing images of himself behind?

Suddenly, midway across the floor he came to an abrupt halt. All the evidence led to Raymond Loudermilk, therefore it was logical to assume that Raymond Loudermilk was the killer, and the man who somehow knew the when and where of the Luftwaffe's most secret plans. On the other hand, according to the records at the Cane Hill Mental Hospital, Raymond Loudermilk had committed suicide almost two decades ago. One set of truths denied the other.

The answer, when it came, was absurdly simple, the sort of basic tenet favored by Sherlock Holmes: with the possible dismissed only the impossible remained. Either the evidence did not point to Loudermilk, or Loudermilk was not dead. Since the evidence most certainly did point to him, it followed that he had not committed suicide and was somehow still alive.

According to the records that Hillman had shown him the previous day, including a perfunctory coroner's report, Raymond Loudermilk had died as the result of self-immolation. Somehow the man had managed to find several gallons of flammable solvent used to clean the lavatories and had taken it to a small clearing beside the main building, screened from view by a dense stand of trees.

The fact that Loudermilk was out of the building apparently had little significance. He was ambulatory, not subject to fits of any sort, and had been a patient in the open wards for the previous year, rather than being kept in one of the euphemistically named, lower-level, high-security "confinement rooms."

According to Hillman, patients of this type were allowed regular periods outside since escape was highly unlikely. A high chain-link fence topped with barbed wire ran all around the grounds, discreetly hidden from the road; the main gate was watched from an observation tower atop the administration block, and the open heaths and valleys beyond Cane Hill were an added deterrent. The local constabularies were used to dealing with the occupants of places like Cane Hill, and the occasional escapee seldom remained at large for long.

None of which did anything to stop Raymond Loudermilk from killing himself. Once hidden from the main building he proceeded to douse himself with the cleaning solvent and set himself alight with a single match.

By the time the guard in the observation tower noticed the plume of greasy smoke rising from behind the trees, Loudermilk's corpse was little more than a charred stump. His remains had been identified by means of his clothing, several folded drawings, and an unintelligible note found several yards away, the tidy pile neatly topped by a heavy stone. The note made several references to "Martin's other self."

Hillman explained that the reference probably referred to one of Martin's brothers, who, for some strange reason, had been given the same name—the younger John Martin had been an infamous arsonist in his time and had spent most of his life in places just like Cane Hill.

Tennant went back to his desk and sat down. Arson. Fire. There had been a body burned at Cane Hill that day, but it wasn't Raymond Loudermilk's. He reached for the telephone and dialed the asylum. Hillman was away for the weekend, but the same administrative assistant who'd made his appointment on Christmas Eve was more than happy to help out Tennant now. He told the psychiatrist that he would go and fetch Loudermilk's file as well as the logbook entries for that particular day and then call him back. Less than fifteen minutes later the telephone rang.

"Was anyone released the day Loudermilk died?" asked Tennant.

"According to the logbook there were three releases that day."

"Who were they?"

"Ellis, Taplow, and Wilkes."

"I don't mean to be any trouble, but could you find their files for me as well? I'll wait."

"Certainly. Glad to be of assistance." The man at Cane Hill went away and then came back on the line three or four minutes later.

"You have them?"

"Yes. Right in front of me, Dr. Tennant. What would you like to know?"

"Ages first."

There was a short pause. "Ellis was fifty-six," said the assistant slowly, reading from the file. "Taplow is listed as unknown, but presumed to be in his seventies. Dementia praecox, it says here. He was taken away by his nephew." Both men were too old.

"Wilkes?"

"Twenty-four."

Much better, thought Tennant. "How tall was he?"

"Five feet seven and one-half inches," the assistant answered promptly.

"And Loudermilk?"

"Five foot six."

"What about his weight?"

"Nine stone four pounds when he arrived, ten stone exactly at his last physical examination."

"Wilkes?"

"Nine stone thirteen pounds when he was released."

Tennant nodded to himself. Loudermilk weighed one hundred and forty pounds and Wilkes weighed one pound less. Not enough to make a difference.

"Is there any reference in Loudermilk's file about particular friends he had while he was at the hospital?"

"Just a minute." Tennant could hear the distant, rustling sound of pages being turned. Finally the assistant came back on the line. "Yes. Here it is. Listed under social interactions."

"Well?" asked Tennant anxiously.

"You're quite right, Doctor. Loudermilk did work at the library with Wilkes—Arthur Sidney Wilkes." Tennant could almost see the man's eyebrows rising. "Now isn't that a coincidence?"

"Yes. Isn't it?" Tennant thanked the man and then rang off. Opening his desk drawer, he took out a sharpened pencil and a tablet of lined paper. In a swift, neat hand he wrote four names, putting them one atop the other:

John Martin
Raymond Loudermilk

Bernard Timothy Exner
Arthur Sidney Wilkes

Loudermilk was John Martin, brought back to life. Loudermilk murdered Bernard Exner and took his name. The final link in the chain was Arthur Sidney Wilkes. The last transmigration of Raymond Loudermilk's black, twisted soul. A journey begun so long ago in the desperately wounded heart of a lonely boy; a journey that was almost ended. Charles Tennant added a fifth name to the list:

Queer Jack

CHAPTER TWENTY-FIVE

Sunday, December 29, 1940
7:00 A.M., British Standard Time

MORRIS BLACK AWOKE TO THE SOFT breathing sounds of Katherine Copeland next to him on the narrow bed and the deep silence of the Heath beyond the bedroom window. In times past, before the war, before Fay had died, they would wake up on Sunday morning surrounded by the echoing peals from nearby St. George's Chapel and the distant rolling thunder striding magnificently out from St. Paul's and across the city. For Black the bells were pure, pleasant sound, inextricably entwined with the smell of freshly brewed coffee and the waking scent of frying bacon—the small, sinful secret he'd somehow managed to keep from his relentlessly kosher mother. Fay had always cooked him breakfast in bed on Sunday. But Fay was gone and he could let himself think about her now with only a fleeting pain in his heart.

He rolled over and stared at the woman in the bed beside him now. He'd loved his wife deeply, but she'd had little of the raw, lustful passion that Katherine had offered to him so freely over the last few days, and which he had gladly, then joyously accepted. Sex had been hard for Fay, something to be done in

444

whispers and in haste, not the spirited, bawdy pleasure that Kat made of it.

Black turned away again, slipping out of bed quietly. Taking his clothes from the back of a chair, he carried them out into the short hall above the stairs and dressed. He frowned, standing on one foot to pull on a sock. For some reason he'd found himself thinking of Trench, the chess-playing Coventry butcher, and from there his thoughts led him to Garlinski and finally to Queer Jack.

He went downstairs to the kitchen, quietly brewed himself a pot of tea, and took a steaming mug of it out through the scullery to the back garden. The fog had cleared and over the waist-high brick wall he could look across the ponds to the heath itself.

He put his mug down on the top of the wall and lit a cigarette. The sun was still little more than a brightening in the sky above the heath's low hills, but the air was clear and crisply cold. In other times the weather would have meant a pleasant winter's day; now it was the sure guarantee of a visit from the Luftwaffe. Tonight there'd be a raid.

But would the raid bring out Queer Jack? Maybe Liddell's rationale had merit. There was a chance that the man who called himself Arthur Sidney Wilkes had died in Coventry, burned to ashes in the storm of fire that had swept through the center of the city. Perhaps Trench had been the madman's final victim, and Black's search for the killer was now nothing more than an academic exercise.

Black sipped his tea and smoked his cigarette. Yesterday he'd left the broken figure of George Le Fanu Gurney behind him and returned to Hampstead, making his way to the Subscription Library. The address they had for Wilkes turned out to be an accommodation, a mailbox rented on a monthly basis from a tobacconist on the High Street.

From there Black had gone to Church Row and the parish office of St. John's Church. Several Wilkeses were buried in the adjoining churchyard, but according to the records, there hadn't been a Wilkes in the congregation for more than fifty years. The same was true of the Catholic church on Holly Walk. Nor were there any Raymond Loudermilks. If Wilkes lived in Hampstead, he wasn't using either name. Black hadn't mentioned any of this to Katherine or to Fleming. Not yet. Not until he was absolutely sure.

The detective stubbed out his cigarette on the brick wall and finished off the cooling dregs of his tea. In front of him the soft, velvet hills and vales of Hampstead Heath stretched out forever. With the exception of the dark scars marking the places where the ARP workers had scooped up the soil to fill their incendiary buckets and sandbags, the heath looked as it had a hundred thousand years ago and would look a hundred thousand years hence, long after Morris Black and Arthur Sidney Wilkes had gone to dust.

He sighed. It was all so bloody meaningless. What did Queer Jack matter in the unraveling skein of time that stretched infinitely back and forth from where he stood? He picked up his mug, preparing to go back into the house, and once again he thought of Trench. Why did the man keep coming back into his mind? He put down the mug, stared out at the heath again, listening to the silence.

That was it. He'd awakened and the first thing he'd thought of was the sound of churchbells in Mayfair. What on earth did that have to do with a butcher in Coventry? Black stood there, frozen, staring blindly at nothing, willing the association to come.

The Sight again, like the puddling of mercury from a broken fever thermometer, tiny silver beads of disparate facts drawn together by some unseen magnetic force. He waited for it, heart pounding, his growing despair vanishing in the moment. Something about the postcards of cathedrals? Trench? Chess? The sound of Milner-Barry's voice, the scientist from Bletchley?

"Was your man a musician by any chance?"

"Bells?" he whispered.

Something Trench's wife had said on the telephone, and something Trench himself had repeated. Mrs. Trench had mentioned that her husband was never home and said something about his work with the Society. Later, speaking with Trench directly, the butcher had said that he, like the man he was to meet that evening, was a member of the Society. Black had assumed that both Trench and his wife had been referring to chess, but it was the Correspondence Chess Association, not Society. What Society then?

Standing there rigidly, Morris Black had a sudden, vivid memory of Spilsbury bending over the fiberboard coffin that contained the liquefying, waxy thing that had once been Jane Luffington. He'd commented on the obscure knot tied in the length of cord that had strangled her. The same knot Black had seen Trench using to tie up the awning as he closed his shop. A knot with two closed loops, intricately twisted so that with a single pull on the free end the whole thing would come undone. Knots. Bells.

"My God!" whispered Morris Black, suddenly understanding. "Burlingame!" He turned and raced back toward the house.

"This," said Maxwell Knight, "is almost unbelievable." He sat on the edge of Dr. Charles Tennant's couch in Cheyne Walk Mews, still wearing his trench coat and his plain officer's cap, the exotic Chinese carpet ankle deep in strewn paper and file folders. Thumps and bangs could be heard from the floors above as Fleming and the others rooted through the psychiatrist's flat.

Guy Liddell sat behind Tennant's desk, going through the drawers, more files piled in front of him. An hour ago they'd found the hidden wire recorder, and great loops of flex now hung down from the ceiling, ending with the microphone hidden in the wall to one side of the patient's couch. So far they'd found no spools of recording wire that might have been used on the machine.

They had, however, cleared up the mystery of the Italian fountain pen. Liddell's idle fantasy about Joan Miller and Maxwell Knight hadn't been far wrong. The woman had bought the pen for her psychiatrist. Tennant had even made a note of the gift. Liddell hadn't mentioned his discovery to Knight, nor would he.

"Yes," Liddell said absently. "It's quite disturbing."

"Disturbing?" Knight crowed. "This is King Solomon's mines, Liddell." He glanced at one of the file folders in his hand. "Astounding. We've got half the bloody aristocracy having it off with the other half and more besides. The Duchess of Kent sobbing on about her husband and Noel Coward. Dear God, Liddell! Think of it!"

And Charles Henry Maxwell Knight having it off with his chauffeur, thought Liddell, closing the file folder on the desk in front of him. Joan Miller's file. Dear God indeed. After arriving at Cheyne Walk Mews and beginning their search, it quickly became clear to Liddell that they had fallen upon a powder keg, not a gold mine. At least a third of the patient records in Tennant's office were neatly cross-indexed with references to an entirely different set of files—files that they had yet to find.

Even without them the basic patient records would be enough to blot the escutcheons of a score of ancient and influential families, not to mention ruining the reputations of at least that many cabinet ministers, high-ranking bureaucrats, and intelligence officers. This was Pandora's box with all the plagues and furies about to be released.

Liddell had already found a file on Poppy Baring, his ex-wife's sister, which linked directly to the Duke of Kent and elsewhere, and another file on Diana Cooper, Duff Cooper's wife, listing both her lovers and her husband's mistresses as well as giving details of her various addictions to cocaine, morphine, and even chloroform.

Going through the vast assortment of files was like peeping through some all-encompassing social and political keyhole. What, for instance, would the world press do with the knowledge that the Duke of Windsor suffered from a bluntly self-descriptive medical condition called "micropenis" and at his wife's insistence was regularly taking a drug prescribed for him by Theodore Morrell, Adolf Hitler's personal physician? It was worse than anything Liddell could possibly have imagined.

"These will all have to be destroyed of course," he said. "You know that, don't you, Knight?"

"You must be mad. We can't do that!"

"I beg your pardon?" said Liddell stiffly. Maxwell Knight had influential connections within the intelligence establishment, but officially at least, Liddell was his superior. Apparently his longtime detachment to the small unit at Dolphin Square had given him airs.

"We have the makings of something here," the smaller man insisted, a handful of paper clutched in each hand. "You can't simply make it all just vanish."

The makings of what? thought Liddell—an empire of secrets, with Max Knight on the throne, bringing all the high and mighty to heel like so many baying hounds? A corrupt and evil man had gathered all this information together, and whoever used it would be equally corrupted. This kind of power could not be allowed to survive.

"Yes. We can make it all vanish. We have to."

"We'll have to evaluate it all first, you'll agree to that, certainly."

A conditional armistice. Without Knight's help there was no way that Liddell could keep the secret of Tennant's treachery. A word or two in the appropriate ear and Liddell would be swamped with calls from the man's patients, all of them desperate to retrieve their confessions.

"There'll have to be a time limit," Liddell murmured cautiously.

"It will take at least two months to go through all of this," said Knight, gazing around the littered room.

"Two weeks."

"Give me to the end of the month."

"All right. Then everything is destroyed. Agreed?"

"Agreed."

Knowing that Knight was watching him, Liddell opened the file in front of him again, withdrew the sheaf of papers, folded them lengthwise, and slipped them into the inside pocket of his jacket. Knight frowned but said nothing. Who shall watch the watchers? Liddell thought. If Knight went too far, there was enough information in the file he'd just taken to bring the man down to earth again. He rubbed a hand across his jaw and yawned. He was still recovering from his voyage across the Irish Sea and the long train trip that followed. With this job done and Steinmaur under guard and hidden away safely, all he wanted to do now was sleep. He knew that he wasn't likely to get the chance.

Flushed with exertion, Ian Fleming came into the room. He was dressed informally, wearing twill trousers, a navy roll-neck sweater, and smoking a cigarette. He was carrying a magazine.

"What did you find?" Liddell asked.

"*National Geographic,*" said the young man from naval intelligence. "Swift was right. A new key for the code with each month's issue."

"Do we have any indication of where Tennant might be?" asked Knight.

Fleming shrugged again. "It looks as though he has some country place along the Thames. Calls it Rooksnest, just below Dorney Village. There were some receipts in the desk in his bedroom for work he'd had done."

"Then we should cut along and find the bastard." Liddell frowned. "Pray God he hasn't already done a bunk." He turned to Knight. "Will you be coming with us?"

"I don't think so." Knight smiled thinly. "You take the kudos, old man. After all, you were the only one who really believed that he existed." He paused. "Plenty to do here. Cleaning up this lot."

"Where will you be taking it?"

"Not Dolphin Square," Knight answered. No indeed, thought Liddell. Not with Joan Miller so close at hand.

"The Pimlico address?"

"Yes, I think that would do well enough, at least for the time being."

"All right." Liddell nodded. "I'll see you there then. After we're done."

"Fair enough." Knight smiled again. "Good luck."

Charles Tennant was coming up the path from the river when he heard the ringing of the telephone. He frowned. No more than half a dozen people in London even knew that Rooksnest existed, let alone that it was equipped with a telephone. Probably a wrong number. Even so he quickened his pace, went in through the scullery door, and crossed the kitchen without taking off his Wellingtons. The ringing continued. He reached the small desk beside the stairs in the hall, hesitated, then picked up the telephone receiver.

"Yes?"

"Dr. Tennant?" The voice was flat and businesslike, the accent neither one thing nor the other. They had a name for it: mid-Atlantic?

"Yes." He knew the voice, had prayed that he would never hear it again. Coming now, it could only mean one thing.

"You know who this is?"

"Yes."

"They've identified you."

Tennant closed his eyes, squeezing them tightly shut. He could feel a rushing sound in his ears and his mouth was suddenly dry.

"How?"

"Something we couldn't have foreseen. They've already raided your house in Cheyne Walk Mews. They'll be coming there next."

"You're sure?"

"Of course. You're very lucky they didn't catch you." There was a crackling electronic pause. "We're all very lucky. We'd like that luck to continue, Dr. Tennant."

"I'm very close. Another few hours and I can—"

"That doesn't matter now. You'll have to leave."

"But—"

"There's too much at stake, Doctor. If you're captured and interrogated..."

"I understand."

"You know the procedure?"

"Yes."

"Good. Get out now. You'll have to hurry."

"All right."

"Good-bye, Doctor. Have a safe journey." There was a harsh click and then nothing. Tennant stood numbly, the receiver hanging limply from his hand. His world had been turned upside down in a single instant, and for a moment he didn't know what to do. Panic welled up in him and it was only through sheer force of will that he regained control of himself.

He'd been found out, but he hadn't been captured yet, and he had all the linking files and wire recordings here with him at Rooksnest. Hanging up the telephone, he went back into the kitchen, sat down at the table, and quickly examined his options.

As far as he could see, only two choices were left open to

him. He could either use the files and the recordings as a form of barter with the British authorities, or he could follow the procedure set down by Schellenberg after their last meeting.

The escape route was simple enough and as close to fool-proof as could be expected. He was to take *Sandpiper* to the mouth of the Thames, wait for nightfall, then sail directly out into the Channel. Once he reached one of the floating "rescue islands" set out by the German Navy for downed pilots, he would send out a prearranged radio signal, scuttle the little boat, and wait on the rescue platform for an E boat to pick him up.

Neither choice was particularly attractive. If he turned him-self over to the British authorities, there was no guarantee that he wouldn't be interrogated, then tried, convicted, and hung for what he was—a traitor and a spy. Even if he was simply imprisoned, he was fully aware that the forces represented by the man on the telephone could hardly let him survive for long.

On the other hand, what would happen to him if he es-caped and made his way to Germany? His usefulness was ended, now that he'd been discovered, and the information in the files and recordings wouldn't be enough to keep Heydrich and his people occupied for long.

Depending on the state of Heydrich's unpredictable mind, he might be pensioned off somewhere without anything like the advantages and perquisites he'd had here in England or, at worst, be put up against a basement wall in Prinz Albrecht Strasse and summarily shot. Unless...

Tennant glanced at the Rolex on his wrist, calculating quickly, trying to recall the basic tide tables at Sheerness. He nodded to himself and stood up, making his decision. If he hurried, there might still be a chance.

CHAPTER TWENTY-SIX

Sunday, December 29, 1940
4:00 P.M., British Standard Time

THE MAN WAS JUST WHERE Morris Black expected him to be, even on a Sunday morning in the middle of a war. During his waking hours Roger Burlingame was seldom, if ever, found far from his allotted place in the enormous, glass-domed Reading Room of the British Museum, usually with a tall stack of books at his elbow and his twin, rubber-tipped canes slung over the back of his chair.

The fact that much of the huge collection had been removed from the library for safekeeping was irrelevant to Burlingame; as long as there were any books at all still in the stacks, he would be there, compiling, collating, and updating his endless lists, somehow managing to relate bits of information on virtually any subject to the Burlingame family tree.

For almost as long as Black had known him, Roger had been writing the family's official history. A task that was necessary, according to Roger, since it was unlikely that anyone would ever write the unofficial version.

Black had known the crippled man since childhood. Burlingame, only son of a minor peer, born with withered legs, thin as sticks, had been the object of endless bullying at school, and Black, a Jew, had been equally sought out by the resident bullies. The two boys found common ground together, Black defending Burlingame with his fists and feet, his friend defending Black with his astounding intellect and a wit often crueler than any gibes either boy was given by their enemies.

Their friendship had continued, and Black often spent summers at the family estate in Staffordshire. Burlingame's father, a bluff, hearty man who was also the local magistrate, regularly took Black and his son on his official rounds and, just as regularly, interrupted them to show the boys something of interest on the way, especially if it had to do with birds and birds' eggs, Lord Burlingame's private passion. His Lordship had another vice as well: bells. According to Roger, his father was the preeminent bell-ringer in the county, and one of the ten best known in England.

"Hello, Roger," said Black, sitting down across the narrow table from his old friend.

Burlingame looked up from the enormous tome opened in front of him and blinked hard, the action detaching his spectacles from their resting position on his forehead. As the years had passed, it seemed to Black that his friend's body was becoming as wasted as his legs. He looked frightfully thin, and Black noticed now the trace of gray in his longish hair. They were both getting old.

"Oh, Morris, it's you. Been some time since I saw you last. Come down for some intellectual stimulation, have you?"

"Afraid not." Roger was right; they didn't see much of each other anymore, not since Fay had died. For a moment the observation shocked him. Fay's death seemed to have brought an end to a lot of things in his life. He wondered what would have happened if he hadn't met Katherine. Perhaps he would have withered up like Roger's legs.

"Dear me, not a professional visit?"

"I need your advice."

"My advice? What on earth could I know that would be of interest to you?"

"Can you tie a bell-ringers knot?" It seemed like a thousand years ago, two young boys watched Roger's father in the bell tower of a village church, tying off a bell rope after ringing a long, complicated course of notes.

"What an astounding question." Burlingame sat back in his chair and stared across the table at his friend.

"Can you?"

"I suppose so." The pale, thin man nodded, blinking in the pale light coming down from the green-shaded lamp above his work area. "Or I could if you had a bit of string lying about."

Black pushed back his chair, bent down, and untied one shoe. He slipped it off, then stripped out the lace, handing it across the table. Roger took it, the long, deft fingers of his hands a blurring contrast to his almost useless legs. He frowned, concentrating, then turned the final loop. He held up the completed knot.

"That's it," Black murmured.

"Of course that's it," Burlingame answered, slightly miffed.

"No, I mean, it's the same knot I saw."

"Saw where? Hanging about in belfries now, Morris?"

"Around a woman's neck," Black answered, staring at the innocent length of shoelace in his friend's hand. "And tying up a butcher's awning."

"Extraordinary. It's certainly not what it was intended for. The whole point of it is to keep the loose end of the bell pull out of the way when you're doing the ringing, and to keep the pull secure after you're done." Burlingame shook his head. "There's any number of knots you could use to strangle someone or tie back an awning."

"It's that rare?"

"Yes. Quite." Burlingame laughed, the sound more of a

cough. "There aren't that many bell-ringers about, you know. It's a fairly obscure occupation, especially these days. Not much call for it when you aren't allowed to ring church bells until the war's over or the Germans decide to drop in for a visit."

"Bell-ringers have a guild of sorts, don't they?"

"That's right." Burlingame nodded. "My father was chairman of the Staffordshire chapter for years. The Ancient Society of College Youths." He frowned. "I've no idea why it's called that. I suppose I'll look it up one day. Might be an interesting derivation. Surprised I don't know it actually."

"How many members all told?"

"In the entire country?"

"Yes."

"No more than two or three hundred."

"In London?"

"Fifty or so, perhaps. Maybe less. Being a member isn't a matter of age, you see, it's more of an aptitude, so some of the younger members may have been called up."

"What sort of aptitude?"

"Mathematical." Burlingame pursed his lips thoughtfully, then spoke again. "For instance, a full round of Kent Bob Majors runs to something like, um, fifteen thousand eight hundred and forty changes. Take you about nine hours to ring it in. I think that's the record. Or it was anyway."

"A lot of permutation?"

"Endless."

"Like chess?"

"Oh, much more complicated." A sad expression passed across Burlingame's face. "I rang the nine tailors for my father when he died, and that was difficult enough to remember."

"What are the nine tailors?"

"Tellers actually. I think it comes from the French originally, though they don't have the slightest facility with bells." Burlingame paused. "That Sayers woman wrote a book all about bell-ringing a few years back. Called it that. You ring the nine teller-strokes on the senior bell, three sets of three, or at least that's what it is for a man. Six tellers for a woman who's died. For Queen Victoria they did the Kent Treble Bob Majors, the six tailors, and then a toll for each year of her reign on the bells at St. Paul's. Apparently it went on forever."

"So you'd need a very good memory."

"Oh, yes. A bit excessive, really. I'm afraid my father was disappointed because I never really took to it. Not that I could have done what he did, not with my legs." Burlingame sighed wistfully. "I did his nine tailors sitting in a chair."

"How would I find out who the members are in London?"

"I'm not sure, really. It's not as though they keep office hours, Morris." Burlingame frowned, thinking again. "They used to have some sort of meeting room over a public house in The City."

"You wouldn't happen to know which one, I suppose?" There were dozens of pubs in The City, most of them with rooms above.

Roger Burlingame smiled. "Of course I know which one. The obvious one, Morris. In Wardrobe Place. The Bells."

Ian Fleming and Guy Liddell, together with a well-armed crew of watchers, reached Rooksnest shortly after noon. They parked at the gate and made their way down the narrow drive leading to the house, then took up positions at the edge of the dense woods, hoping to surprise the psychiatrist as he climbed into his waiting car. Eventually, after a cold and frustrating hour, Liddell ordered the watchers forward, but Rooksnest was empty; the bird had flown.

"Bloody hell," said Liddell, standing in the kitchen of the small house.

"He can't be far," said Fleming. "His car is still here."

"He's gone. I can feel it."

"You think someone warned him?"

"It's possible." In his mind's eye the intelligence officer saw the flood of files strewn across the man's office floor. A hundred names, and at least a dozen of them directly, or indirectly, connected to Whitehall and the War Office. Easy enough to blackmail one of them to be his informant. Or perhaps blackmail hadn't been necessary. He'd seen the film Knight had shown Bingham and the Copeland woman, and he'd read the transcripts. No, there'd be no lack of help for Tennant, under duress or freely given. These days treason was being traded as openly as a commodity on the stock market.

Fleming came back into the room. He had a small notepad in his hand.

"I've just been on to the telephone exchange," he said, looking at the notes he'd made. "Our man was rather busy right up until a few hours ago. He placed more than a dozen calls."

"Who to?"

"John Martin. All different ones, listings in the London directory."

"Who the bloody hell is John Martin?"

"There was a pile of books on his desk in town. They were all about someone named John Martin. An artist, turn of the century."

"Tennant's not ringing up dead artists," fumed Liddell. Another of the watchers appeared, coming in through the kitchen door. The cuffs of his trousers were splotched with mud.

"He had a boat, sir," the man said. "There's a dock. Bit of oil slick around the piers."

"That's it then." Liddell nodded. "He's on the river."

"Upstream or down, I wonder?" said Fleming. Upstream there was Oxford, downstream, Windsor and the city.

"Get your men together," Liddell ordered the watcher.

"Canvass every house for half a mile in either direction. See if you can find out what sort of boat he had, a name, and find out if anyone's seen it on the river in the last twenty-four hours. I want to know which way he was heading."

"Yes, sir," said the man, and vanished.

"This is a disaster," said Liddell. "There's a hundred places he could have gone to ground. And we don't know how long he's been gone."

"You really think he can escape?" said Fleming.

"Of course he can!" snapped Liddell. "The man's no fool. All he needs is a change of clothes and the price of a ticket to Ireland. Bloody, bloody hell!"

The younger man nodded toward the pad in Liddell's hand. "Maybe he's gone off to find Mr. Martin. Maybe we should do the same."

"I suppose we ought to have a fucking go at it," Liddell growled.

Fleming was momentarily startled by the profanity and then he smiled thinly. "I suppose you're right. It's all we've fucking got."

Charles Tennant's escape in *Sandpiper* was completely un-eventful. From Queen's Eyot to the serpentine curve of the Thames above Kew, he barely saw another soul except a series of bored, uninterested lockkeepers who took his fees and moved him on his way. It was too cold for punting and the season for day-trip steamers was long over.

For the first hour his nerves were wire taut, and he ex-pected to see waiting platoons of policemen at every bridge and lock, but as the miles went by, his tensions eased. After a time he even began to enjoy himself, faintly surprised that he was looking forward so eagerly to a confrontation with his quarry.

He watched, sitting in the stem as the river water changed from clear, cold crystal to the color of beer, filthy as he reached Richmond, carrying enough sediment to plant an allotment garden in, and full of the stink from the huge filter plant and sewage pools at Barnes, across from Fulham Cemetery.

It was mid-afternoon by the time he reached Hammersmith Bridge, the sun already lowering in a pale winter sky. A brisk wind was blowing upriver now, coming from the south in breezy gusts, and the tide was at half-ebb. Another hour and he would have been too late; as it was, there was less than a foot of freeboard by the time he swung in toward the pier.

He moored *Sandpiper*, slipping her discreetly between a coal barge and a small steamer, obviously docked now until the spring. There were at least fifty possible moorages on the Thames between Rooksnest and Hammersmith, and another hundred beyond from Hammersmith to the docks at Tilbury. If *Sandpiper* was being looked for at all, she'd be almost impossible to find. He was safe enough for now.

Climbing up to the wharf, he checked the daily tide table tacked up on the wharf hoarding. By six the tide would be fully ebbed, only the very center of the river carrying an appreciable flow. By ten it would be navigable once more. He'd be traveling against the current then, but at full speed he could make Canvey Island by three or four in the morning, then wait and ride the racing current into the Channel well before dawn.

He handed a ten-pound note to the wharfkeeper, asking him to put up some provisions in a basket for his return later that evening. After some coaxing and another ten-pound note, he also managed to hire the man's nondescript Fordson van. Telling the wharfkeeper that he would return for the van within an hour, he went up to the Dove, an old public house higher up the Embankment and supposedly the trysting place of Charles II and Nell Gwynne.

He used the call box to ask for a cab to be sent round, and

when it arrived, he told the driver to take him to Bruton Street and the premises of Holland and Holland, the gunsmiths and outfitters. Once there, he purchased several items of foul-weather gear, including a warm, fleece-lined jacket, a large clasp knife equipped with a sturdy marlinespike, and a civilian model of the standard Enfield service revolver, complete with cleaning kit and extra cartridges.

Taking another cab, he returned to Hammersmith Pier, changed clothes aboard *Sandpiper,* and then went to collect the Fordson. By four-fifteen, with full darkness approaching quickly, he was on the Hampstead Road, traveling north. As he drove, Tennant mentally retraced the investigation that had taken him here.

Finding out where Queer Jack actually lived had, in the end, been ludicrously simple. It was all a matter of identity. At some early point in his life the boy must have learned of his less than auspicious beginnings, and this lack of an "honest" name might well have been the start of his slide toward insanity. He had "adopted" Wilkes's name and identity and resurrected Bernard Exner's name to suit his needs as well.

Given Loudermilk's obsession with patterns, numbers, and rituals, it was also fascinating to note that Wilkes's name was as perfect a choice as his body measurements. Exner's initials, read aloud rather than spelled, were BTX. Wilkes's initials were ASW. It was a variation of a standard substitution code. B followed A, T followed S. W preceded X. There was an insane logic about it. A small point, perhaps, but for Raymond Loudermilk the pattern must have seemed like some sort of terrible omen—by his very name Arthur Sidney Wilkes was the perfect sacrifice.

It wasn't a great leap from that to assuming Loudermilk/Exner/Wilkes might have another ritual name, one kept pure and without any possible connection to the others: John Martin.

After his illuminating conversation with the administrative

assistant at Cane Hill, Tennant had gone to the Chelsea Library and consulted the most recent *Kelly's London Post Office Directory*. With either a name, postal address, or telephone number it was possible to find the other, missing elements. Within an hour he had what he needed. He drove directly to Rooksnest. When he was done, a transmission to Heydrich would be in order.

Forty-five John Martins had been listed in *Kelly's Directory*, and another sixty listed simply as J. Martin. Assuming that Loudermilk's passion and obsession with the artist would not allow him the use of an initial, Tennant ignored the J's and concentrated on the Johns. He began to call them one by one, and then stopped. Why would he need a telephone for an identity that only existed in his mind? Ruling out any listing in *Kelly's* with telephone service, only two names remained. One address was given as the Chelsea Hospital, which almost certainly made him some ancient veteran of an equally ancient war. The last was John Martin of 31 Mount Vernon Street, Hampstead. Then the telephone call had come and everything had changed. Without Queer Jack's secret he would be forced to face Heydrich empty-handed. It was that or hand himself over to Masterman and the others at MI5.

By the time Tennant reached Hampstead in the Fordson van, night had drawn in completely and the streets were dark, the blackout fully in effect. Slowed to a crawl, he piloted the rented vehicle through the tree-lined streets of the old village, turning past St. John's Church and the cemetery flanking Church Row, then climbing Holly Walk to the Catholic chapel. He parked the van beside the church and stepped out into the chilly air. Adjusting the padded Grenfell jacket he'd purchased at Holland and Holland, he climbed the rest of the way up the hill and turned onto Mount Vernon Street.

The twin rows of blank-faced houses marched down both sides of the street to the foot of Holly Hill, looming like silent witnesses to his passing. The winding road was bleak, without a single planted tree, the tall, plain stone houses built flush with the pavement without any room for front gardens. Like everywhere else in London at this hour, the windows all had their blackout curtains drawn. The street was blind.

Passing No. 31, Tennant gave it a casual sidelong glance but saw nothing to make the address stand out from its neighbors. He didn't notice the corner of the curtain lifted in the house next door and was unaware of Mrs. Monkman seated discreetly at her usual station by the front window of No. 33. By the same token Mrs. Monkman was just as unaware of Tennant reaching the end of the street and turning back up the narrow laneway that ran behind the houses, carefully counting chimney pots until he was sure that he stood at the rear of No. 31.

If anything, the rear elevation of the houses on Mt. Vernon Street was even bleaker than the front. A head-high wooden fence, slats gray with age, ran the length of the alley, each address having its own gated doorway, secured with a simple hook and eye.

Tennant let himself in through the rear gate, pausing for a moment, scanning the rear windows. The houses on either side of No. 31 had the usual drawn blackout drapes, but Martin's house had taken the regulations even further; even in the pitch darkness of the narrow little garden the psychiatrist could see by the lack of reflection that the man had painted out the windows entirely.

A path led up to a small raised stoop, and Tennant followed it, stepping carefully, climbing the rudely made stairs and keeping close to the wall in case of creaking boards. The rear door was plain wood, dark paint bubbled and crazed by decades of neglect. He tried the knob.

It was locked, but by the feel of it, not too securely. He brought out the clasp knife, snapped up the marlinespike, and dug into the crack between door and frame just below the lockplate. There was a brief resistance and then a short, snapping sound as the bolt released. Tennant pocketed the knife, undid his jacket, and pulled out his revolver, cocking the well-oiled Enfield mechanism. Taking a deep breath, he pushed the door open slowly and stepped inside.

Twenty minutes later, assuming that the first muffled screaming from the house next door was actually the well-known and profoundly irritating howling sound of cats mating in St. John's Cemetery, Mrs. Monkman lifted her tired bones from the chair by the window and turned her hearing aid off, disgusted with the blatant caterwauling. She fixed herself a nerve-soothing cocktail of Dr. J. Collis Browne's Chlorodyne mixture and scalded milk, drinking it down slowly, savoring each thick, hot swallow of the gluey concoction.

She enjoyed the strong taste, especially since she hadn't been able to smell or taste much of anything in years. First nose and taste buds, then the ears. Pretty soon it would be her eyes, and where would she be after that? Finishing her drink, she climbed the stairs wearily, grumbling to herself about the unfairness of it all. She spent a frustrating few minutes in the lavatory, then finally went to bed.

CHAPTER TWENTY-SEVEN

Sunday, December 29, 1940
5:00 P.M., British Standard Time

THE CITY WAS DARK AND SILENT as a crypt, empty and abandoned for Christmas-week Sunday. Taking the tube to Blackfriars, Morris Black made his way up the hill into St. Paul's Precinct, meandering through the maze of cobbled lanes and alleys until he found the half-hidden passage on Carter Lane that led into the enclosed courtyard of Wardrobe Place.

The Bells was shut, of course; without the steady flow of office workers and tradesmen who normally worked in The City, there was no reason for it to be open. Going out to Carter Lane and walking back to the corner of St. Andrew's Hill, Black found a small Italian café named Brogi's, which was still doing business, and from Antonio Brogi, the restaurant's owner, he learned that Mr. Sedgewick, chief bell-ringer at St. Paul's, regularly took his dinner there before proceeding on to the Bells, where he and other members of the Society practiced on hand-ringers for several hours at a time. Brogi had operated his café on the corner for the past twelve years, and in that time Sedgewick had rarely missed a day, invariably arriving at exactly 5 P.M. All Black had to do was wait.

True to the café owner's word, a tall, slightly stooped man with snow-white hair entered the restaurant on the stroke of five, seating himself at a corner table in the empty room. Brogi introduced Black, then brought the man his meal—a small plate of spaghetti, a small basket of bread, and a small glass of red wine. Sedgewick was in his late sixties or early seventies, thin-faced and pale. He ate like a bird, quickly, with short pecking jabs of his fork.

"You are interested in bell-ringing, Inspector Black?"

"The father of a close friend was a member of your Society."

"Ah, and who would that be?"

"Lord Burlingame."

Sedgewick smiled. "Toby Burlingame. Good man with a Treble Bob. Let him ring Great Paul once. Pleaded with me. Dead now, I suppose." Sedgewick flicked his fingernail against the side of his glass. It rang clearly, a single teller-stroke for a departed colleague. "Drank too much."

"He died several years ago."

"Too bad. Not many of us left." Sedgewick frowned. "Should have taken better care of himself." The old man ate a forkful of his dinner and then took a sip of wine. "How can I help you, Inspector?"

"If it's at all possible, I'd like to see a list of your members. You have one, I assume?"

"Of course." He took another sip of wine. "Might I ask why?"

"An investigation."

"Nothing more you can say?"

"Not at the moment."

"Does it involve the Society in any way?"

"Not directly, no."

"Well, that's something." Sedgewick paused and took a piece of bread out of the basket beside him and began to break it into smaller morsels. "No interest in bells yourself, I suppose? Good shoulders. We could use a man like you on the full peal. Takes good shoulders to ring the Tenor. Sixty-two hundredweight. B flat, *Domine, dirige nos.*"

"I'm afraid I was a complete failure at maths. Not much better at Latin."

"Well, that's no good then," Sedgewick sighed. "You really must have maths, or at least a very good memory for numbers. Concentration, dedication. I suppose you also have to be a little mad. Takes more than shoulders."

"So I understand." A little mad, he thought, a poor description of the man he was pursuing.

"Unique to England." Over Sedgewick's shoulder Black could see the grinning figure of Brogi, piloting a long-handled broom across the floor and watching them. The Italian had obviously been given any number of lectures about bells and bell-ringing in the past, and now he was enjoying the sight of someone else receiving the same education.

"I didn't know that," said Black politely, wishing the man would finish his meal.

"Oh, yes." Sedgewick nodded, eating a tiny fragment of bread and lifting another forkful of spaghetti. "No one else does it." He smiled proudly. "And no one else does it better than our little group at St. Paul's. The heaviest full peal of twelve in England."

"That's interesting."

"No need to humor me, Inspector. I'm quite sure that I'm boring you witless."

"Not at all."

"Of course I am. Everyone tells me I'm a bore." Sedgewick finished his wine, lifted his napkin from his lap, and patted his lips. "Bells are like anything else; utterly without interest except to bell-ringers. Come along, Inspector. I'll show you the list and then you can be on your way."

They went back to the Bells, and Sedgewick took Black up a dark, narrow flight of wooden steps that led to the meeting room. The room itself was spare as a monk's cell, a dozen wooden chairs arranged in a long rectangle, each with a small brass handbell waiting on the seat. The only other piece of furniture was a small desk beside the door.

"Before the war and the 'no bells' regulation, we used to send out little cards to all the members from time to time." Sedgewick rooted about in the desk drawer, searching for the list. "Advising them of upcoming peals around the country." He pulled a single, slightly yellowed sheet of paper from the drawer. "Here we are." He handed the list to Black. He counted. Thirty-four names, and of those half a dozen had inked asterisks beside them, and four were struck out completely.

"What do the asterisks mean?"

"Conscripted. The ones with lines through them have passed away." Of the twenty-four remaining names, only two had addresses in Hampstead.

"This man Stroud. Do you know him?"

"Certainly. Three of twelve. Ten hundredweight, By Faith I Obteigne. The Burdett-Coutts bell. Key of D. A policeman like yourself, Inspector."

"What sort of policeman?"

"A constable. Talks about his children a great deal."

"And John Martin?" The address was on Mount Vernon Street, no more than a quarter mile from the house in the Vale of Heath.

"Treble bell. Eight hundredweight. To God Only Belong Honour and Glory. Key of F."

"Anything memorable about him?"

"Nothing in particular. Quiet sort. Good hands. A lot stronger than you might think at first glance."

"Nothing else?"

"No. Except for the night I found him in the cathedral, long after service."

"What was he doing?"

"Do you know the cathedral at all, Inspector?"

"Not very well."

"The floor beneath the dome is decorated with an enormous compass design. Wren wanted to express the idea that St. Paul's represented the heart of English Christianity. In the exact center of the compass is a large, brass heat-transfer grate, and around that there is Wren's epitaph: *Si monumentum requiris circumspice* and all that. The circle with the epitaph is perfectly in line with the center of the dome, the tower, and the ball and cross above; you can actually see the epitaph from the porthole in the ball if you have a mind to climb all those stairs and ladders."

"Martin was in the middle of the compass?"

"Quite so. Pacing around the epitaph, over and over. I watched him at it for several minutes before I came forward. Very strange."

"Was he reading the epitaph?"

"No."

"What then?"

"He was counting."

"Numbers?"

"Precisely. At first I thought he was practicing courses for the peal, but that wasn't it. They were odd combinations, almost equations."

"How did he react when you interrupted him?"

"It was really quite extraordinary. He smiled and then he started singing."

"Singing?" Black stared.

"Umm," Sedgewick murmured. "It was one of those Army songs from the last war."

"Do you remember what it was?"

Sedgewick cleared his throat, then frowned as he tried to remember the words. "I believe it went something like this:

"O Death, where is thy sting-a-ling-a-ling
O grave, thy victory

The Bells of Hell go ting-a-ling-a-ling
For you, but not for me."

Guy Liddell stood on the roof of the block of flats beside the Dove at Hammersmith Pier, peering down at the dock through a pair of high-powered binoculars. All he could make out were rough patches of shadow marking the pier and the boats moored to it, all of them now mired drunkenly in the ebb-tide mudflats.

"I can't see a damn thing with these," he said, taking the binoculars away from his eyes. "It's too bloody dark."

"Not to worry," said Ian Fleming, standing beside him. "Capstick is watching from the car. He'll flash his lights when Tennant appears."

"Pray he doesn't run into a wandering ARP warden." Liddell glanced up at the night sky and then at the luminescent dial of his wristwatch. "The Luftwaffe will be here any minute now."

"Maybe there won't be a raid. Perhaps the Germans have run out of bombs."

"I wouldn't count on that if I were you, Fleming. It's early days yet."

"Not for Tennant." The young naval officer grinned.

"No, not for him."

The psychiatrist had severely underrated the abilities of the police. An hour after entering Rooksnest one of the watchers had discovered the name of the boat. By that time Tennant was just reaching Kew, but a radio report was quickly sent out and the River Police were alerted. With the tide ebbing it was assumed that *Sandpiper* would put in somewhere to keep from being trapped in the narrowing midstream, so three Flying Squad cars were also sent out to check the landing spots from Puddle Docks below St. Paul's to Putney Bridge.

By an odd coincidence Richard Capstick, Morris Black's longtime friend, was one of the Flying Squad detectives assigned to the task, and Capstick decided that perhaps *Sandpiper* might have put in earlier than expected. When nothing turned up within the limits of their search, he went a little farther west and found the boat sinking into the mud on the far side of Hammersmith Bridge. He questioned the wharfkeeper, found out about the van, then radioed Central from his car. Central in turn relayed the message to Liddell and Fleming, already on their way into town from Rooksnest. The two men had rendezvoused with Capstick at the Dove. That had been at five o'clock. It was now almost six.

"Where the hell is he?" said Liddell.

"He's sure to come back here," said Fleming. "I mean, he really doesn't have anywhere else to go."

"No word on the Fordson?"

"Nothing yet. They've put people at all the railway stations, and everyone is looking for the van just in case he tries to slip away by road." Fleming ducked down and lit a cigarette behind his cupped hand. "It's not as though they're running the boat train across the Channel, Liddell; he'll turn up eventually." The young Navy man shivered; the southeast wind was even stronger now, blowing steadily across the river and into their faces. "Damned cold," he grunted, puffing on his cigarette.

Liddell put the binoculars to his eyes for a moment, surveying the barren wharf where Capstick was on the watch. After a long silence he said, "The policeman who found the boat?"

"Capstick? What about him?"

"Friend of Black's, isn't he?"

"Who?" asked Fleming innocently.

"Oh, do us a bloody favor, won't you?" Liddell said dryly. "You're one of the people Morris interviewed, you're an associate of Maxwell Knight's and you're Godfrey's bloody assistant at Naval Intelligence. Knight brings you along to Tennant's office and you've been sticking to me like glue ever since. Let's pretend that we're all grown-up lads and not playing at sixes and sevens, shall we?"

"All right," Fleming agreed after a moment. "In that case, why don't you admit you know perfectly well Capstick and Black are friends?"

"I almost expected him to be here, or at Tennant's."

"Black?"

"Yes."

"Knight asked me to tell Black about Tennant. I couldn't reach him. Katherine is half out of her mind with worry."

"The American woman? The supposed journalist?"

"Yes. He wasn't there when she woke up, and she hasn't heard from him all day. She's frantic."

"She works for Bingham at the embassy, doesn't she?"

"My, we are well informed, Captain Liddell."

"Not as well as I'd like," he muttered. "I'll have to put a word in Bingham's ear when this is all over. It just won't do, that sort of thing. Can't have a whole swarm of amateurs running about and muddying the waters. I've enough to deal with as it is." Both men turned at the sound of heavy footsteps behind them. Richard Capstick's bulky figure was striding toward them across the roof. "I thought you were on watch," said Liddell.

"Not to worry. I've got a man in the car in case this doctor of yours shows up." Capstick paused. "It just came over the radio. They've found the Fordson."

"Where?" asked Liddell.

"Hampstead. Holly Walk next to the Catholic chapel. A patrolman spotted it and rang up Central. They want to know what they should do now."

"Shit," said Liddell. "We can't be in both places at once."

"I could go," Fleming offered.

"One more thing," said Capstick. "There's going to be a

raid. Word just came in from the coast. Heinkels and 88s, more than a hundred of them coming in from the Channel Islands and Cherbourg." The big man lifted his face and tested the air with his large, wide-nostriled nose. "Could be nasty with a breeze like this, especially if they use those candlesticks of theirs."

The first sirens began to moan, one high-pitched wail joining its nearest neighbor, no one matching another, until the air was filled with the sound of a hundred different, wavering tones spread out across the darkened city like a sinister spider's web of warning. In the distance, toward the center of the city, a weak array of searchlight beams flickered into life, roving vainly across the empty sky.

"Christ!" Liddell sighed. "The perfect bloody ending to a perfect bloody day." He shook his head wearily. "What next? I wonder."

"Hell," said Fleming, glancing upward. "Death from above."

CHAPTER TWENTY-EIGHT

Sunday, December 29, 1940
7:00 P.M., British Standard Time

MORRIS BLACK STOOD ON THE TOP STEP at the rear of 31 Mount Vernon Street and waited. Ignoring the distant echo of the sirens, he concentrated on the door in front of him. It was slightly ajar, and he could detect a faint light coming from somewhere deep inside the house. Straining, he held his breath and listened. He could just make out a strange, muffled sound, slowly repeated. It was steady, like the regular dull beating of a drum, a monotonous thumping. Grotesquely, he had the sudden image of a hanged man's hammering heels.

Using two fingers, he pulled the door open and stepped inside. There was enough light to see that he was in a scullery, the shelves on either side of him empty. Up three steps there was another door, also ajar, and from somewhere beyond it a deep, rich scent, dark and sour like newly composted earth mixed with an overly sweet incense. Shit and sandalwood.

He'd seen the dark, closed front of the house, then come around to the rear searching for an easier entrance. Now, standing there, nerves stretched to the limit, he found himself drawn farther in by the dim light and the dark hypnotic sound.

He went up the second set of steps, acutely aware that he was unarmed. He knew he was a fool for not using a call box to summon assistance, but somehow he knew he had to confront Queer Jack alone. Katherine had exorcised his past; Queer Jack would give him the future.

The detective eased through the open door and found himself standing in a kitchen. An electric torch was on a counter beside an enameled sink, its fading beam the source of the light he'd seen. From somewhere high above, the thumping sound continued. The smell was even more pronounced now, the sweet incense unable to disguise the rank, foul odor beneath.

Black took three quick steps and picked up the heavy torch. Not much of a weapon, but better than none at all. He swung the torch around the small, bare room, the beam picking up the glint of metal on a cutting table. A cleaver, leather-handled with a strap, the blade pitted with corrosion, the flank of the metal stained with flecks of dark rust, or something rusty red.

He went over to the cutting table, moving quickly and silently on the balls of his feet. He picked up the cleaver in his free hand. The leather handle was cold and cracked and dry, as though the instrument had gone unused for a long time.

Directly in front of him was a door leading toward the front of the house, and to his left there was the dark bottom step of a narrow staircase. Far above his head the pounding went on, and listening, he could now tell that it was actually two sounds, a firm mechanical progression followed by something else, a sound that was barely a sound at all. Ignoring the door ahead of him, he turned and began to climb the stairs, following the oddly patterned noise and the terrible, terrible smell.

He reached the first-floor landing and paused, his grip tightening on the cleaver. The door here gaped widely, but a quick flash with the torch showed him only an empty hall and great dangling wisps of dusty cobweb. A rotted carpet runner on the floor, stained wallpaper; empty and abandoned years before.

Black went on, his back against the stairwell wall, the torch held so that its beam shone dimly upward, showing him his path, the cleaver ready in his other hand. He paused again on the next landing. The door here was shut, but behind it the beating rhythm was much louder. A cold heart, calling to him.

The wood panels of the door had been painted over by a madman, filled with a bizarre motif of twisting snakes, oddly shaped stars, and roughly drawn creatures that could only have come from the depths of some horribly twisted mind. Half were male, their genitals huge and engorged, eyes monstrous and bulging, sores dripping from crippled limbs, mounds of coiled excrement piled beneath withered buttocks. The other half were hermaphrodites, penises small and immature, breasts huge and sagging, each face looking upward innocently, roughly splashed halos of yellow paint around their heads. The background to the writhing tangle of the figures was a fuming hell of flames in pink and red and orange that licked and framed the hideous scene.

Black fell back against the wall and closed his eyes for an instant, turning the beam of the torch away from the door. The stench here was overpowering, thick and palpable like the killing floor of a slaughterhouse. His mouth filled with saliva and he swallowed, gagged, and swallowed again. He could hear a new sound now. The harsh whispered buzzing of a thousand swarming flies. Turn back now, he told himself; turn back before the madness draws you in.

He turned the torch around the landing and almost vomited. In one corner there was a crumpled nest of old newspaper, soiled with excrement. Lines and daubs of shit climbed up the walls around him, dried and caked over everything. A few steps away another flight of stairs led up to the attic floor. The muted pounding mocked him from the far side of the door. The flies buzzed. Black reached out with the hand holding the cleaver, turned the knob, and pushed. He stepped back quickly, raised the weapon, and shone the torch beam into the room beyond.

He looked through the open doorway and into hell on earth. He stared, instantly aware that this was something that no man's or woman's eyes should ever have to see, a tortured, screaming horror more vile and obscene than the most blasphemous imaginings of any demented Brueghel or Dante Alighieri whispering, "All hope abandon, ye who enter here!" The entire third story of the house had been transformed into a single, glowing chamber, lit by a hundred candles fixed to rudely made tinplate sconces screwed into the walls and scattered from floor to ceiling. The walls themselves were primitively painted, depicting scenes a thousand times more ghastly than the ones splashed onto the door.

Chasms swallowed entire flaming cities whole; white-hot tongs pricked lolling, pink-wet tongues; rutting boars, tusks red with blood, tore entrails from infants in the midst of being birthed by headless, limbless women; blood boiled in pools; flames rose everywhere, fueled by squadrons of childishly executed, bat-winged aircraft, raining terror onto the orgy of violence and death below. Pale and fine as spider's silk, a thousand careful lines connected one image to the other in a monstrous cosmology. A demon's chart and guide.

The ceiling was dull black, and from it hung one hundred lengths of bright, stiff copper wire, the ends of some hooked to impale small, leathery things that might have once been flesh, while dozens more were twisted to hold larger, splintered lengths of bone. On a wire close to Black's right hand a new-looking revolver had been hung as a final trophy.

Black's quick opening of the door had disturbed the air, and the fresh currents set the wires moving, bone tapping dully against bone like a terrible wind chime, flies thrown from their meaty perches and whispering in angry muted counterpoint. The flickering candle shadows danced, and Black thought he saw small scuttling insect movements amidst the other hideous artifacts cast across the dark, oilcloth-covered floor.

In the center of the room stood the worst of all.

A dozen metal poles stood at clock-hour distance from each other in a large circle on the floor. Atop each pole was a skull, wax flesh built up upon human bone, eyes made of bits of colored glass. Below each poorly sculpted head was a small metal square, and on each square, neatly printed with a draftsman's hand, there was a name, twelve in all—Christ's apostles, clockwise in alphabetical order.

"*Gottenyu!*" Black whispered, speaking in his mother's tongue. "*Gottenyu!*"

In the circle, on the floor, drawn symbols. A crude pentacle in yellow chalk, a snake in white, and over everything, counterclockwise in bright scarlet, a swastika marching backward, the letter *Z*, inverted, four times over. Above the symbols a terrible device, Raymond Loudermilk's savage realization of deus ex machina, its application witnessed by the blind bottle-glass eyes of the surrounding saints and the buzzing, swarming flies.

A metal frame rose tall as a standing man, forming a cage above the runic images. Scaffolding bolted to the cage held cogs and cams and wheels and pulleys, all powered by a huge, crank-wound mainspring in a boxlike framework of its own. The strange, oil-gleaming system of descending gears, looking for all the world like the works of some enormous clock, drove a piston through a long, angled tube that ended at the back of a high wooden throne. A rod of tungsten steel, sharpened to a chisel point, was being steadily pushed forward by the piston, each movement marked by the metronome swing of a weighted pendulum attached to the spring. This was the source of the thumping sound—the impact of the piston on the rod.

The target of the slowly moving spear sat rigid on the throne, facing the door. A man, dark haired, a soft purple bruise at his temple, green-eyed and naked, palms flat on the chair's broad arms, hands hideously pinioned by a pair of heavy spikes hammered flush between the bones. Some crushing tool had been used to tear away the nails, and the ends of the curled, talon fingers were chewed to bloody stumps.

The eyes bulged madly, held open by gleaming, curved taxidermist needles threaded through the lids, and the man's spine was arched away from the seat of the throne in a final, desperate attempt to escape the descending rod. It had pushed through the flesh of his neck, one fractional movement at a time, digging slowly down through fat and muscle, narrowly missing the spinal cord, eventually cutting through the esophagus, silencing the tortured screams that had caused the man to bite through his tongue, then rupturing the madly beating heart. It had continued beyond the death throes, slicing onward and then coming out through the chest wall, letting a thickly flowing apron of blood ooze down across the belly and the groin, gathering to form a sticky puddle in the dead man's lap.

Oh, God, how long? thought Black, staring numbly at the clockwork killing chair. How long had it taken for the man to die? He would have felt the first cutting stroke, knowing what was to come, felt it puncture his screaming throat, and then...

A glitter of light reflected from the array of candles caught Black's eye and he stared upward. It came from the ceiling, high above, and back from the throne. Eyes. Flashing chips of deep red glass. Eyes in the yellow wax face of the last apostle, staring down, Queer Jack's avenging angel—St. Paul: The Final Judgment.

Morris Black swayed where he stood and then stepped back, shoulder brushing against the wire that held the dangling revolver. He whirled at the cold touch, then, almost without thinking, dropped the cleaver, reached out, and grabbed the weapon. He tore it away from the wire, turned, and ran. Behind him the oiled gears ticked on, the weighted pendulum swung steadily, and the thumping piston slid forward smoothly once again.

At precisely 7:10, with the sirens still moaning through the windblown empty streets of St. Paul's Precinct in The City, The Number entered the cathedral through the small crypt entrance of the northwest tower, using the key he'd made to turn the ancient lock. He climbed confidently up the narrow circular stairwell in pitch-darkness, sure of every step, counting his way upward until he reached ground level and the heavy wooden door that led into the Kitchener Memorial Chapel.

Here there was light, provided by a chandelier dangling from the vault above, and electric sconces set around the large, circular room. Closing the door behind him carefully, he turned and began to cross the patterned marble floor.

"My, we're quick then, aren't we? Raid hasn't even started yet."

The Number stopped and looked around. On the far side of the room he saw a tiny, rotund woman sitting on a camp chair underneath the massive altar between the pietà of Christ and the Virgin Mary and the prostrate figure of Horatio Herbert, Lord Kitchener, in white marble. She stood and came forward, walking toward him, carrying a book, its place kept with one extended finger.

She was very small, the shoulders of her firefighter's canvas jacket heavily padded. A delicately sculpted face looked out from beneath a regulation tin hat, her small, Cupid's-bow mouth painted with bright red lipstick. Long gold earrings dangled down below the hat, swinging as she walked over the echoing floor. Beneath the jacket she wore a short black skirt, black stockings laddered almost into oblivion, and a pair of heavy workman's boots. The hands, he noticed, were wonderfully small. Doll's hands.

"Brought your own supper, I see," she said, stopping in front of him and gesturing with her book at the leather briefcase in his hand. In contrast to her small size, the woman's voice was rich and strong with a deep, almost seductive harshness.

"Yes," said The Number. He hadn't expected to find anyone there, and for a moment he was confused. He took a deep breath and let it out slowly, keeping the count in his head as the woman's intelligent eyes looked him over. A false step or word and he'd have her, split her like a Christmas goose, her hot fat spurting, and her blood.

"Where've they put you tonight, then?" she asked finally. The Number breathed again. She'd taken him for a member of the Volunteer Watch, of which she was obviously a member. He shrugged and said nothing, counting, listening as the sound of the sirens outside faded, the silence before the terrible storm to come.

"Don't know," he muttered finally.

"Head for heights?"

He nodded and she nodded back.

"Probably the dome then," she said. Frowning, the woman turned. She'd noticed the silence now as well. "Better cut along. Sounds like the fun is about to begin."

"Yes." He tried to smile, then turned away, leaving her behind. He went through the arched entry leading to the side aisle and the nave, then vanished around the corner.

The woman listened to the silence and the man's receding footsteps for a moment, then went back to her seat between Kitchener and Christ. She sat down beneath the cold stone figures and began to read again. In the book, the hero, Robert Hunter, was armed with a high-powered rifle. He had just tried to pot Hitler from two hundred yards away and missed.

"Twit," she muttered, then turned the page. "Might've saved us all a lot of trouble."

Ian Fleming sat on the running board of the Flying Squad Wolesley, hunched over, head in his hands. He'd been violently sick and his breath was ragged and uneven.

"Christ! I've never seen anything like that," the young man whispered, looking up.

"Madness," said Liddell, standing beside him. The Wolesley was parked at the rear of 31 Mount Vernon Street, uniformed policemen moving back and forth along the narrow lane. From far down the long slope leading to the city and the winding ribbon of the Thames, he thought he could hear the growling, distant approach of the bombers. The raid had almost begun.

Dick Capstick pushed open the high garden gate and approached the car, hands jammed into the pockets of his overcoat. The man's broad face was set like stone, emotionless.

"Well?" Liddell took out his pipe, then thought better of it. He gripped it tightly in his hand and waited for the broad-shouldered detective to make his report.

"Your man right enough. Found his clothes in a heap behind the kitchen door. Wallet, money, everything. Some blood on the back stairs. From the looks of it I'd say he was coshed, then dragged up to that room." The big man raised a bushy eyebrow. "Gobs of other stuff. Three or four great whacking things that look like teleprinters in the basement, all taken apart. Shelves filled with electricals and such. Whole bleeding wardrobe on one floor filled with coveralls and uniforms." The Flying Squad man shook his head. "Saved his shit as well, by the looks of it. Great stacks of little boxes, nasty things all dried up in shredded paper like so many birds' eggs in their nests. Worst I've ever seen in all my time."

"That's it then." Liddell sighed. "We'll go back to the boat and see what he left behind."

Capstick shook his head. "Sorry, Captain, I'm afraid that's not it at all."

"What do you mean?"

"Someone's been here, after your man was done over."

"You're sure?"

"Certain. Boot marks in the blood on the steps, up as well as down. That chopper thing on the floor. Torch on in the garden, dropped there by someone running." Capstick frowned. "That's how we knew where to look. A warden saw the torch beam, saw the rear door was hanging open."

"Queer Jack?" said Fleming, getting to his feet.

"No. Not him. Not leaving things behind and running like that. Not our Jack. He'd have none of that. Methodical, his sort." Capstick grinned. "Like coppers."

"Then who?" asked Liddell.

Capstick looked at the two men standing by the car. "I think it was Morris. I think he finally put a proper name to Jack and tracked him here. I think he came too late and now he's taken up the chase again."

"You can't know that for certain, man," Liddell answered. Capstick lifted his shoulders and then tapped a thick index finger along his nose. "I'm sure of it. Who else could it be?"

"Where?" asked Fleming.

"Morris showed me the postcards," said Capstick. "All cathedrals, weren't they?"

"That's right."

"I know my saints. You saw that room yourself. Jack's put one of them up there above the rest. There's only one place he could be, I'll bet my reputation on it."

Fleming stared, then turned, looking toward the southern darkness of the city. Suddenly the sirens began to moan again. "St. Paul's," said Fleming, suddenly understanding. "He's going to St. Paul's."

CHAPTER TWENTY-NINE

Sunday, December 29, 1940
8:15 P.M., British Standard Time

MORRIS BLACK REACHED the underground station at St. Paul's just as the first bombs began to fall, the giant, whistling containers of incendiaries splitting open in midair, spreading hundreds, then thousands of the four-pound canisters across the densely packed buildings and the crowded rooftops, making a sound like a coal scuttle emptying itself across a marble floor. Screaming death, white-hot.

Panting and out of breath, Black reached the upper exit and found his way barred by an ARP warden who was peering out at the raid from the safety of the exit doorway. He held his arm across Black's chest and shook his head, stopping the detective's headlong run.

"You don't want to go out there, mate!" the man yelled, lifting his voice above the bellowing of the bombers and the chattering of the impacting bombs.

"You're right, I don't," Black answered, fishing for his warrant card. He flashed it in the warden's face, then pushed the man aside. He ran out into Newgate Street, then turned south, running past the narrow entranceway to Paternoster Row. A

485

few seconds later he reached the broad open plaza of St. Paul's Churchyard, the cathedral itself a massive rectangle of towering stone, topped by the monumental dome.

A dozen fires were already blazing. Flames were spreading across the roofs of the cramped buildings around Ludgate Hill, and the ornamental trees around the main west entrance of the cathedral were alive with gushing, white-hot light that threw dancing, grotesque shadows across the high stone walls of the church.

More of the bombs were raining down, cracking loudly as they slammed into the buildings all around him. Every few seconds there was a larger detonation as high-explosive bombs found their marks. Black pressed himself against a wall and closed his eyes, seeing Coventry again, feeling the heat blasts and the terror once more.

For an instant he considered turning back to seek the welcoming shelter of the underground station, but then he opened his eyes again and forced himself to go on. A moment later he crossed the roadway, dodging the blinding beacon of an incendiary, half-buried in the street. He ran up the broad set of steps leading to the imposing, multicolumned entrance and pushed open one of the massive doors.

The cavernous interior of the cathedral was dark except for a few faint winking lights and the bright, wildly moving beams of torches being carried by running men. All along the enormous nave, Black could hear the sound of pounding footsteps and yelled instructions, meanings lost in the roundabout echoes scattered back from the arches, vaults, and semidomes above.

A torch beam struck him in the face and he put up his hand quickly, almost blinded.

"There's no shelter here. You'll have to go!"

"Put out the bloody light! I'm not looking for shelter!"

The light clicked off, and in the gloom and dancing motes in front of his eyes, Black could see the short figure of a woman, tin-hatted, bundled up heavily. She had a book in one hand and a huge electric torch in the other.

"Who the hell are you?" Her voice was both harsh and sensual; a rusty nail wrapped in silk, an East Ender Marlene Dietrich.

"A policeman. Detective. I have to see the person in charge immediately."

"In charge of what? We've got a dozen or more in charge here, more's the pity." She snorted. "Sadly, not one of them's in charge of the lights. Power's down. All we have is the jenny now."

Black bent over wearily, hand to knee, trying to catch his breath. There was a sudden huge explosion and he was rocked off his feet, thrown into the woman's arms. They fell to the floor in a tangle. Black pushed himself away.

"I need to speak to someone in authority," he insisted.

"You'll be speaking to my authority unless you get your hand off that particular bit of goods," the woman snapped. Black realized he'd been clutching the woman's stocking-clad thigh. He stood up, helping the troll-like warden to stand as well.

"I really must see someone. Now."

"Why?"

"Because it's bloody important!"

"Isn't everything these days?" She shook her head. "All right," she said finally. "Follow me."

The little woman in her gnomish costume and flat tin hat led Black along the towering main aisle toward the high altar, a football field away. The checkered marble floor was awash in lengths of dripping canvas hose, and lengths of flex and rubber cable ran everywhere. They reached the edge of the dome, its yawning upper reaches lost in the smothering dark. Black's guide turned to the left, bringing him to the foot of a broad spiral staircase. From outside, the dull explosions of more bombs shook the air within the cathedral. Hell without and seeking death within. Black could actually feel the edges of his sanity begin to fray like a rotting paper tissue. All he wanted now was sleep, and freedom from the terrible noise. Rest from it all.

"Up we go, darling," said the woman. "His deanship's in the library."

Eventually they reached the top of the staircase, a hundred feet and more above the cathedral floor. Stepping through a small, bare vestibule, they entered the library of St. Paul's. Both the lower and the upper gallery shelves in the high-ceilinged room were bare.

The Very Reverend Walter Robert Matthews, Dean of St. Paul's, stood in the middle of the room, sorting through a pile of stirrup pumps, counting them into piles. He was a small man, although not as small as the woman beside Black, white-haired, pink-cheeked, stripped down to a flannel undershirt and flopping, too-large trousers held up by suspenders, cuffs tucked into rubber Wellingtons. He looked up as Black and his guide entered the room.

"Good Lord, Helen, don't tell me you climbed all those steps just to pay me a visit?" Black leaned on the doorpost, fighting for breath after the long climb.

"All one hundred and forty-three."

"Keep that up, my dear, and you shall do yourself a mischief."

"Not bloody likely," she muttered under her breath. In a louder voice she introduced Black. "Constable's come to see you."

"My name is Detective Inspector Morris Black."

"I'm Dean Matthews. Come to help?" Matthews beamed; he looked more like someone's dotty grandfather than dean of the largest church in England.

"Someone means harm to the cathedral," said Black, still fighting for breath. "Terrible harm."

"Other than our friends up there?" asked Matthews, looking up toward the ceiling. Overhead, the droning bombers were clearly audible, a great vibrating roar that pounded in their ears in a thundering maelstrom of sound.

"Yes."

"You're sure of this?"

Black nodded. "He's insane. I think he means to burn down St. Paul's. He has the ability to do it. He calls himself John Martin. He was a bell-ringer here."

Matthews stared. "You must be joking!"

The detective fought to keep his tone calm. There was no time for explanations now. "I'm afraid not, sir. He may already be in the building."

"This fellow round the twist, what's he look like?" asked the short woman in the tin hat.

"I've only seen him once. I'm not really sure."

"Your age? Year or two younger? Small, wears specs? Thin on the top?"

"It could be."

"Bloody hell," the young woman muttered. "I knew there was something wrong with him."

"You've seen him?"

"Hour and a bit ago. Erkish type. Soft, weak little voice. Carrying a briefcase." She shook her head. "And I asked him if he'd brought his supper in. Jesus bloody Christ!" She flushed brightly. "Sorry, Reverend Matthews. Just slipped out."

"Quite all right, dear, under the circumstances."

"Where would a man like that do the most damage?" Black asked quickly. "If he had a firebomb with him?"

Matthews didn't have to think. "The dome. Without question."

"How?"

"There are two domes. The inner one, which you can see from the floor of the cathedral, and the outer one, which you see from outside. The outer dome is relatively thin lead supported by an inner framework of wooden beams. A brick cone above the inner dome supports the lantern above, and the ball." Matthews knew the brief lecture by rote; he'd obviously explained it many times before.

"What would cause the damage?"

"The wooden beams. There must be thirty or forty tons of timber between the lead dome and the brick."

"Old? Dry?"

"It's been curing peacefully for the last two hundred and forty-three years," said Matthews calmly. "Dry is hardly the word." He paused. "It's been our biggest worry since all this began. If the beams ever caught fire, the lead dome would almost certainly melt. It would be the end."

"Shit."

"Precisely," the dean responded blandly. He paused again. "What do you propose to do?"

"Catch him."

"You'll need help," said Matthews reacting quickly. "Wait here and I'll—"

"There isn't any time, sir. It's too late for that." Black took a long shuddering breath. "How do I get up there?"

The dean stared hard at Black, worry visible on his face. Worry and something deeper. He nodded. "From the whispering gallery. I'll take you."

"I can do it, Reverend," said the woman.

Matthews shook his head firmly. "I think not, Helen. This is my responsibility. Go down and fetch as many volunteers as you can from the crypt. Explain the situation to them and tell them to meet me here."

"Right away, sir." The woman turned and left the library the way she and Black had come.

"This way, Inspector," said the dean.

Black followed the white-haired man through a small door to the right and down a long, narrow corridor. The huge stones on either side were cool to the touch, and Black found it hard to believe that such strength could be destroyed at the hands of a single man. They reached another door, stepped through, and Black found himself standing in the whispering gallery.

Half a dozen small, curved doors were set into the wall around the gallery, each one giving access to a series of narrow corridors and staircases that ran up between the inner and outer supporting piers as well as to an entirely separate group of passages leading up the circular "drum" of the dome and then outside to the open roof. From Matthews's complicated description it appeared to Black that the dome and the drum supporting it were honeycombed with hidden passageways.

Matthews took Black to the fourth door around the gallery. It stood open, snaking hose running up into darkness. "Useless," said the dean, kicking the hose. "The Nazis picked their time well enough. Lowest tide of the year. The hydrants are all dry, or spitting mud."

"Is there any other water?"

"Just what we've got on hand. Buckets and tubs spread all around. Anything we do will be done with stirrup pumps."

"Are there any of your people up there?" the detective asked, gesturing toward the doorway.

"Not yet. Betjeman and half a dozen others are on roof sentry duty outside, but that's all so far."

"Keep it that way for the moment, Reverend. The man is horribly dangerous. He's killed. Many times. For years."

The dean paled. "Are you armed?"

"Yes." Black unbuttoned his jacket. The revolver was jammed securely into his waistband. He'd already checked the chambers; the weapon was fully loaded.

"And what about the man you're after?"

"I have no idea. He might be." Black thought about the weapon Queer Jack had used on Trench in the Magpie and Stump, again saw Spilsbury fishing for the metal barb in Jane Luffington's back. The silent scream of the dead man in the chair.

"Perhaps you should wait," the dean said quietly, seeing Black's expression.

The detective shook his head. "No. He has to be stopped." He turned toward the doorway, but Matthews put a hand on his shoulder.

"May the blessing of God and this church be upon you, Inspector."

Black managed a weak smile. "I doubt your blessing will have much effect, Dean Matthews; wrong faith, if I've got any left to speak of. I'm a Jew."

The old man shrugged. "So was St. Paul."

The flights of bombers continued to march across the sky, dropping their bombs into the growing pall of smoke and flame. Within the first twenty minutes of the raid more than a hundred tons of incendiary bombs had been thrown into the flaming cauldron, and by the time Morris Black entered the first passageway leading upward to the inner dome, two hundred separate fires were burning across the One Square Mile.

More than eighty incendiaries dropped into the tinderbox of Paternoster Row, no more than a hundred and fifty yards from the cathedral. Unattended, the concentrated books and papers of a dozen publishing houses began to burn as roofs collapsed and glass exploded. The flaming debris from these fires was carried aloft on the gusting wind, tossing firebrands across entire city blocks. Night became day, and in the center of it all the dome of St. Paul's could be seen for miles in every direction, surrounded by boiling clouds of smoke and flame rising like a fuming maelstrom hundreds of feet into the air.

At street level, piles of brick and timber blocked the narrow streets, making it impossible for the men of the Fire Service to reach the flames. Even had they been able to do so, it would have made little difference; the Thames was a streak of mud, and the long pump hoses were mired and clogged. There was no water, and The City was left to burn unchecked.

Two hundred feet above the street, Morris Black finally reached the end of the dimly lit lower stairways and pushed up through the small wooden hatch that led into the space between the inner and outer domes. His ears rang with each explosion outside, the sound magnified by the amplifying outer skin, and Black could feel the heat as well, pouring in through the stone vents ranged around the dome's base and pressing through the scalloped openings of the light well another hundred feet above his head.

Closing the hatch behind him, Black stood up cautiously and stared. It was surprisingly bright. Light from the raging fires poured into the well and shone, hot white and flickering, through the circle of inner-dome windows. More light came through age-old widening cracks in the lead sheets where they met the rolled-metal ribs and iron-string courses of massive cable that gave the dome its shape.

He was standing at the base of the dome, one foot on a gigantic link in the iron chain that circumscribed the tall brick cone, rising at an angle above him. By craning his neck, he could see through the complex pattern of timbers to the light well and higher still to the spreading massive piers that served as the lantern mounting, that structure rising another fifty or sixty feet into the raging sea of fire. There was no sign of Queer Jack.

He began to climb up through the scaffolding of timber, slowly edging around the tall brick beehive of the cone. Pausing for a moment to catch his breath, he reached out and touched the skin of the outer dome, expecting to feel metal.

Instead his hand brushed over thick wooden planks, black with age and terribly dry. A single incendiary, unseen, would be enough to turn the space between the outer dome and its hidden counterpart into an inferno. He remembered a vague statistic, forced on him at school. The dome weighed seven hundred tons, as much as a small ship. Seven hundred tons of melting lead and blazing oak. Hell's forge, hot enough to turn diamonds into steam, hot enough to finally cleanse a madman's soul. This was Queer Jack's madness and his savage dream—the entire dome was a single, gigantic bell.

Black moved on, circling the brick cone and always climbing, shuffling across longer and longer timbers that stretched across to the thin, sheet-lead outer dome. He glanced down once and almost lost his balance, slipping on the beam beneath his feet. Squeezing his eyes shut, he gripped an upright timber and waited for the dizziness to pass.

As he reached the upper regions of the scaffolding, a small movement caught his eye. Moving slightly he saw a figure, twenty feet away, and fifteen higher up—a small bent figure eyes down on something he was doing. Drawing in his breath, Black eased the revolver from the waistband of his trousers. He cursed silently. He was a less than adequate shot at the best of times, and with all the uprights and beams, there was no way to get any remotely clear line of fire.

He moved again, edging forward until one foot and his free hand rested on the crumbling brick of the cone. The figure was still bent low, now no more than a dozen feet away and just above him. Black held his breath again, raised the revolver, and sneezed.

The sound reverberated incredibly in the confined space, rising above the roaring of the flames. Queer Jack looked up, firelight sparkling on the lenses of his eyeglasses. He saw Black, and in the flickering half-light the detective was almost sure he saw bared teeth. A mad smile or the sudden rictus of fear and rage? Listening, Black thought he heard a wild-animal howl rising above the furious din of the exploding bombs.

Queer Jack scooped up the foot-long tube he'd been wiring to a joint within the wooden structure and stuffed it into the pocket of his long gray coat. He moved swiftly upward,

dancing wildly across the beams, gripping the overhead supports, swinging over the dusty, empty holes in the air with the
agility of a monkey. Black fired, the detonation cracking across
the space between them, but it was far too late. Queer Jack was
gone, lost in the twisting shadows.

The detective jammed the revolver back into his trousers
and gave chase, keeping close to the brick and using it to guide
him. Less than a minute later he found himself at the top of
the cone and saw the man again.

The tip of the tall brick inner structure was built of stone,
broken by huge curving panes of thick, leaded glass at its summit, inserted to allow natural light to reach the inside of the
cathedral. Queer Jack crawled across the skylight windows,
nothing more than the thickness of the panes between him
and a spiraling descent, three hundred feet to the marble floor
and the circle of Wren's epitaph. He paused, then looked back
over his shoulder. The eyeglasses flashed again, then he scuttled off, the long wings of his coat beating around his ankles.

"Loudermilk!" Black yelled. The spitting roar of the fires
and the booming passage of the bombers was much louder
here, so loud in fact that Black could feel the last timbers of
the scaffolding vibrate beneath his hand. "Loudermilk!" he
yelled again, but the man kept on. Directly ahead of him, at
the summit of the cone's stone cap, Black could see a metal
ladder, bolted both to the cap and the footing of the lantern
overhead. Queer Jack crawled the last few feet across the glass,
stood, and began to claw his way up the ladder. A few seconds
later he was gone.

"I'll have you, Jack," Black groaned aloud. "Oh, yes, I
bloody well will." For Rudelski and Talbot and the others. For
Gurney's lifelong pain. For the child Bernard Timothy Exner.
For Katherine, and for himself. With a last burst of effort he
threw himself forward, keeping away from the glass, following
the thin ribs of stone that lay between them. Halfway up the
glass cap of the inner dome, a thunderclap of noise suddenly

threw the detective painfully to his knees. He shook his head to clear it, then stumbled to his feet.

Out of the corner of his eye he could see the tip of a high-explosive bomb poking through the lead sheeting of the outer dome, the rounded nose of the canister painted an idiotically cheerful blue. A creaking noise came from no more than twenty feet above his head, and a huge slab of lead and timber broke away; tumbling down to the window on his left, smashing it, and falling through.

Horrified, Black stared at the grotesque object hanging above his head. The bomb was about three feet in diameter, a third of it wedged firmly in the outer skin of the dome. Dud? Time fuse? Some sort of trembler booby-trap? At a guess it was a five-hundred pounder. More than enough to blow him to kingdom come and set the dome alight without Queer Jack's help.

He looked away. It didn't matter now. He stood and without hesitation simply walked the last few feet up the stone rib, reached the ladder, and began to climb. A few seconds later he reached the base of the lantern observation platform and stepped out onto the Golden Gallery, 312 feet above the ground. London lay beneath him, a seething cauldron of boiling flame and whirling smoke.

The world had been set on fire. From where he stood, Black could see the entire length and breadth of The City from the Thames and Fleet Street to the south and west, to Liverpool Street and the Tower, north and east. It was all alight, blocks of it consumed by fires that grew larger even as he watched.

Below him a hundred buildings were burning so hotly that he had to look away. Cinders trailing glowing tails of sparks spun past like bright swarms of locusts, and walls of smoke rose everywhere—yellow, red, and furious pink. More buildings crumbled, blasted instantly into charred piles of rubble by the endlessly falling bombs, the noise blasting at his eardrums like something alive, the moaning air so hot he could feel it burn his skin. Above Black, so close it seemed as though he could reach out and touch them, the bombers were still coming—dark, broad-winged shapes in silhouette, bellies glowing with all the colors of hell as they cut through the erupting clouds. He had climbed to Armageddon.

Ten feet away, Queer Jack looked out over the railing at the hellish vision that had been his own for so long, locked safe and waiting in his tortured mind. Realizing that he was no longer alone, he turned to meet his pursuer, the two-foot-long canister of thermite and magnesium held tightly against his chest. Black stepped forward, raised the revolver, then hesitated as he saw the position of the man's left hand. Like claws, two fingers were hooked through a wire loop threaded into the top of the firebomb.

Black shouted over the roar of the raging fires all around them. "It's over. Give it up."

"It's never over." The voice was dry and faint as though not often used above a whisper. Black took a single step forward. The wind hummed through the railings around the lantern overlook like the moaning of dead men.

"Let me have it," Black ordered, holding out his free hand. He took another step. Queer Jack moved back against the railing. From somewhere below them in the inferno there was a massive explosion, and Black could feel the base of the lantern shudder beneath his feet. The entire cathedral seemed to creak and shake, a great ark sinking into a hellish ocean. Above them the bombers came on and on, rolling and bucking through the furious sky. The air around them screamed.

"No closer!"

The detective could see Raymond Loudermilk's fingers tighten on the wire. If he managed to detonate the device, they would almost certainly be killed outright. If only a small part of the bomb's contents reached the softening lead of the dome, St. Paul's would become their funeral pyre. The two men stared at each other, separated by no more than four or five feet. Loudermilk's eyes were blank, hidden by his eyeglasses, their lenses reflecting only fire. For a moment he looked away, tempted by the gigantic, cataclysmic fire all around them. Black used the moment to take another shuffling step, but stopped again as Loudermilk whirled around. The man's small mouth opened, then closed again.

"Tell me," said Black. "Tell me what you want to say."

"I loved him," whispered Raymond Loudermilk. "I loved them all."

"I know," Black answered soothingly. "I know." He paused. "But it's over now, Raymond. It's time to end all this." His throat had gone dry as ash and his eyes began to water from the cinders that flew around them like whirling flakes of burning snow. His finger took up the tension on the trigger of the revolver. It would take no more than an instant to aim and fire, but if he did, the incendiary in Queer Jack's hand might detonate. Black forced himself to stand rigidly. He could feel the long muscles in his thighs begin to shake, and his heart was in his throat. All he needed was a single step, a single rapid movement.

"It will never end," said Loudermilk. He took one hand away from his chest and felt for the guardrail at his back. His right heel lifted, looking for purchase. Dear God, thought Black, he's going to jump. The madman raised his face to the burning sky. "See," he whispered. "See what I have done." He lowered his chin and looked directly at Black again. His heel was firmly on one of the lower rails now, his free hand gripping the upper. The muscles of his jaw and neck were tensed. There was no time left.

Black fired as Loudermilk boosted himself up onto the railing, the bullet tearing into the cartilage and bone around his knee. The man screamed, almost losing his already precarious footing, and Black surged forward, tossing the pistol away to give him free use of both hands. Before Loudermilk could pull the detonator wire of the incendiary, Black was on top of him, tearing the hooked fingers away with one hand and grappling for the canister with the other. Their faces were only inches apart, and Black could smell the foul, acidic odor of the other man's sweat. Fear and death combined. The scent that would have been in David Talbot's nostrils as he died.

"It will never end," hissed Loudermilk. Black rammed his elbow into the man's side, torso twisting, bringing the ruined knee around to smash into the guardrail. Loudermilk screamed and Black reeled back, wrenching the canister away. For a final instant Loudermilk stood perched high on the railing, and then his leg gave way.

Still clinging to the canister, Black lurched forward, but it was too late. The murderer stared at Black, his eyes on fire. He spoke once, lips twisted into the terrible semblance of a smile.

"You knew my name. Remember me!" and then he toppled backward over the rail.

Stumbling forward, the detective watched him fall. For a moment it seemed that Queer Jack was flying, borne up on the fiery winds that raged wildly around the dome of the cathedral, the long tails of his overcoat spread around him like a demon's wings or a winding shroud. He plummeted down, coattails trailing fire, smoke wreathed around his head and flailing arms. He struck the bottom edge of the dome, and in the blazing light that had turned night into day, Black was sure he saw one broken hand reach out, fingers gripping desperately at the heat-softened lead.

And then he was gone.

Sobbing for breath, Morris Black sagged down against the railing, hearing Raymond Loudermilk's final words, and faintly, madly, the distant sound of small chapel bells. He closed his eyes, willing the ghostly bells, the voice, and all the other raging sounds of death away. He'd had enough of all of it. No more, he thought, no more.

After a moment Black dragged himself to his feet and

made his way to the lantern stairs. The fires still burned on every side, and in through the cinder-swirling clouds the bombers still flew on, but tonight his own battle had finally come to its end. Queer Jack was dead, and all his secrets were dead with him. Ultra was safe and both it and Raymond Loudermilk would be forgotten, less than footnotes in the unraveling course of time, lost in the flames below. In time, perhaps, the bells might even ring again. He climbed down into the darkness, moving toward the light, thinking of the future and of Katherine.

EPILOGUE

Sunday, May 11, 1941
5:00 P.M., British Standard Time

Leaving London, Capt. Guy Liddell drove toward the Channel coast, skirting Southampton and taking a series of lesser roads that eventually took him to the New Forest and the town of Brockenhurst. He was happy to be out of the city; the night before, the Luftwaffe had launched an enormous raid against London, even larger than the one that had led to the death of Queer Jack a few months previously.

Rumor had it that the previous night's raid marked the beginning of a new Blitz offensive against London, but Liddell knew better. If anything, the raid was a swan song for the German Air Force. Signals picked up and decoded at Bletchley indicated a steady movement of Luftwaffe aircraft and materiel to the east. It was May, and with the threat of a Russian winter fading, Hitler was turning his attention toward Stalin; England was fast becoming a stage too small for the Nazi leader's mad ambitions.

After stopping for a late tea, Liddell continued on his way, turning east along a narrow, winding road that took him through Setley Park to Ladycross Lodge and Hatchet Pond on the northern edge of Beaulieu Heath. It was a strange landscape: half a godforsaken wilderness of brooding woods and harsh, bare rocks, like something out of a novel by one of the Brontës; half a fairyland vision of rolling lupine- and heather-covered hills, all of it sinking into a gathering dusk as a red-gold sun set at his back.

Several times during the journey the darkening air above Liddell's head was shattered by the angry, insect buzzing of low-flying Spitfires and Hurricanes from their base at Middle Wallop, hurrying toward the coast on some unknown, urgent mission.

Liddell found himself smiling; the night before, coincidental with the raid on London, Rudolf Hess, Hitler's deputy, had taken it upon himself to bring an olive branch to Churchill. He'd flown out of Germany and bailed out over Scotland, right into the hands of the local constabulary. From what Liddell could gather, the high-ranking Nazi had been taken to Latchmere House and was now in the less than tender care of Tin Eye Stephens. Perhaps the swarms of fighters overhead were hoping for even better luck tonight; maybe even Fat Hermann himself, wobbling buttocks squashed into the cramped seat of his favorite Messerschmitt.

Liddell reached the village of Beaulieu shortly before seven and stopped in front of the Montagu Arms, a large, red-brick building on the main street that looked more like a country house than a village inn. He had called from London to arrange for accommodation, and McEntee, the proprietor, came out to greet him personally as he climbed out of the car. McEntee was a bluff, red-faced man in his mid-fifties. The two shook hands.

"Welcome to Beaulieu, sir, and the Montagu Arms." McEntee used the local pronunciation of the name, "Bewley," a custom that dated back to the thirteenth century. "I'll just take your automobile to the garage and then see to your dinner, if that's all right, sir."

"Thank you. I'm meeting a friend. He's living at the Abbey."

"Oh, yes?" The hospitable smile faded slightly.

"Can you tell me how to get there?"

McEntee nodded. "Of course. Just go straight down the street here and cross the bridge." The frown deepened. "Someone will take you on from there, I'm sure."

"Thank you."

McEntee nodded. "Supper will be in about an hour, sir, if that's suitable."

"Fine."

"Afterwards I could show you the garden, if you like. We're quite proud of it. The polyanthus in particular. It's just coming into bloom."

"I'd like that very much."

McEntee's smile returned. "Very good, sir."

Leaving McEntee to attend to the car, Liddell walked down the broad village street to its end, then went over a narrow stone bridge. To the left he could see the dark blotch of a small, marshy lake. Beside the bridge an ancient stone weir controlled the flow of water that led to the widening course of the Beaulieu River on the right.

The Beaulieu was an ocean estuary, and the low tide had left a few small boats stranded on the muddy banks, the last rays of the sun tinting them every shade of saffron and gold. A skittering flock of waterfowl jumped into the air, small, anxious shadows rising above the silhouetted shapes of the Abbey ruins on the opposite side of the bridge. Liddell paused and lit his pipe, leaning against the stonework. It was a scene of utter peace and charm, without the slightest hint of war. No wonder Morris Black had chosen this place.

"Sanctuary," said a voice out of the gloom. It was Black. He stepped forward, joining Liddell on the bridge. The policeman was dressed like a gamekeeper, complete with shooting jacket, corduroy trousers, and rubber Wellingtons.

"Hello, Black." Liddell extended a hand, but the policeman turned away from it and crossed his arms on the bridge rail, looking downriver.

"It really is a sanctuary," said Black. "Officially, that is. One of the four or five places in England that could offer someone full rights of sanctuary within its grounds. Every other church in England could offer sanctuary for forty days; at Beaulieu it was offered for the life of the offender."

"I didn't know that."

"Queen Margaret of Anjou, the Countess of Warwick, and Perkin Warbeck, the Pretender, all stood sanctuary at Beaulieu. Rather ironic when you consider what goes on here now."

Liddell nodded. That was the point, of course; he wasn't entirely sure what *did* go on at Beaulieu these days. Officially the Abbey and an unspecified number of cottages and country houses in the area were being used by the euphemistically named Inter Service Research Bureau, a cover term for the equally obscure Special Operations Executive, or SOE. The organization had been established on Churchill's direct authority as a means of aiding and collaborating with resistance movements in occupied Europe. Its director was an obscure former Conservative member of Parliament named Frank Nelson, who had recently been made privy to the work being done at Bletchley, but other than that had no connection to the British intelligence establishment. The independence of SOE was already causing a degree of internecine jealousy, especially since its mandate was disturbingly close to that of MI6.

"You're happy here?" asked Liddell after a moment.

"*Content* would be a better word I think," said Black, still staring out over the dark water. "I'm away from London, at any rate."

"I never thought of you as being the country squire."

"Nor I. But it's better than being an out-of-work detective." Black paused. "I didn't really have much say in the matter, actually. Knowing about your bloody Ultra secret made me something of a pariah at the Yard." Which, Liddell knew, was at the root of Black's anger. For him, Ultra was the mark of Cain, and that mark would remain until war's end, and perhaps longer. His knowledge of Tennant's involvement was almost as dangerous; Morris Black was one of the few people in England who knew how close England had come to civil war sparked by Kennedy and a band of British turncoats, not to mention losing the war against Hitler because of their failure to realize the importance of Queer Jack and what he knew.

Liddell spoke finally. "So what do you actually do here?"

Black shrugged. "Teach interrogation techniques, occasionally playact at being a Gestapo agent." He paused and glanced at Liddell. "I'm really not supposed to say too much."

"Is that why you met me here?" Liddell smiled. He tapped out his pipe on the stonework. "Horatio at the bridge, defending his companions within?"

"The people I work for are a little suspicious of their sister organizations. I doubt I would have been able to bring you much further than this without a paper storm of authorizations." Black gestured toward the shaded buildings and the woods behind him. "The ruins back there are full of little men with large weapons who'd like nothing better than to potshot at a passing MI5 officer." Black smiled coldly. "A foot or so across the bridge would be as far as you'd get, I'm afraid."

Liddell ignored the veiled threat. "Join me for dinner, then?"

Black hesitated for a moment, then nodded. "Is that why you came all this way?" he said at last.

"I can fill you in on Queer Jack and the rest of it."

"I'm not sure I really want to know. But I'll have a glass of something with you."

They walked silently back to the Montagu Arms and went through the spacious, oak-paneled lounge into the dining room. The two men made small talk while Liddell ate and Morris Black worked his way through a decanter of sherry. The meal ended, Liddell sat back in his chair and filled his pipe again.

"Do you hear anything from Miss Copeland?" he asked, putting a match to the bowl.

"No." Black shook his head. "She went back to Washington. Presumably she's working for Donovan and his people."

"Interesting woman. Attractive."

"Yes."

There was a long pause. Liddell realized he was on dangerous ground. "Well, at least things seem to have settled down with the Americans now that Kennedy is gone. This fellow Winant seems to be on our side."

"So I hear." Black nodded. There was another pause. "You were going to tell me about Queer Jack."

"Ah, yes." Liddell blew out a plume of smoke. "In the end it appeared that you were right all along. He'd worked with half the people at Bletchley at one time or another, either that or played chess with them."

"Chess was always part of it. Almost from the beginning. It was the connection to Bletchley as well as his entrée into the Correspondence Chess group."

Liddell nodded. "Which was how he chose his victims. It was also how our friend Tennant found him out."

"How long had he known about Ultra?"

"From the start, I'm afraid. He'd worked with Turing on the first decoding machinery. Actually machined some of the parts for it. A mechanical genius. It wasn't much of a leap from there."

"You seem to have done a good job keeping it out of the press. It's been almost five months."

"Officially Queer Jack never existed. The only record is in Spilsbury's personal autopsy notes, and he's not named in those. Everything else has been expunged."

"What did you ever do with that fellow you brought back from the Isle of Man? The one who identified Tennant? Did you 'expunge' him as well?"

"Masterman has him working for Double Cross as an interrogator. I wouldn't be surprised if he was down at Latchmere with Tin Eye and Herr Hess."

"I heard about that. Unbelievable." The detective smiled blandly. "That should have Kennedy's fascist friends in an uproar, wondering what Hess is going to say. He was part of their little plot."

"Yes, I should think they'll be running for cover just about now. Low profiles all around and some rousing patriotic speeches in the House of Lords to prove their loyalties." Liddell smiled. "We still have that cine film of Knight's, though, in case they get out of line. Not to mention Tennant's records, or the threat of them."

"What about Tennant? Your elusive Doctor?"

"It's driving Maxwell Knight mad," said Liddell, smiling around the stem of his pipe. "There was enough material in the man's files to bring down half a dozen governments. It's been taken out of his hands entirely. Sealed forever, thank God. We've seen the end of Tennant and Queer Jack both; their secrets are safe."

"Secrets don't last forever, and The Doctor and Queer Jack won't be the last," Black answered quietly. "Treason and madness are universal constants, I'm afraid."

"I suppose you're right." Liddell smiled. "Which makes people like you and me constant as well."

"Is there anything else? I really should be getting back."

Liddell shrugged. "No, not really. I just thought I'd see how you were faring out here beyond the pale." It was a lie, of course, but then again, very little of what Liddell said or did these days had any truth to it. He pushed back his chair. "I'll walk with you back to the bridge."

"If you like," said Black mildly. He didn't seem to care one way or the other, and Liddell knew that something had gone out of the policeman. What the intelligence officer had originally taken as cool defensiveness he now recognized as indifferent calm. Assaulted by emotion and event, Morris Black had made himself an emotionless castaway in the eye of the storm of war that raged around him.

The two men left the inn and walked back to the bridge leading onto the Abbey grounds. Halfway across, Morris Black stopped and turned. "Why did you really come here? It wasn't to give me the gossip about Queer Jack and Tennant, or to ask me about Katherine."

"I wanted to find out where your loyalties lay."

"You want me to spy for you," Black said flatly. "Is that it? Your people want to know what SOE is up to and you want me to provide the information."

Liddell let out a small sigh. Black was still too good a detective. There was no point in lying to him. "It had occurred to us."

"Which would make me as much a traitor as Tennant and as mad as Raymond Loudermilk."

"Hardly. Tennant was working for the enemy and Queer Jack was a homicidal madman."

"From what I can tell, everyone is potentially an enemy and the definition of madness can change on a whim. If Loudermilk had been murdering Nazis in Berlin, you would have called him a patriot or a hero."

"Which doesn't answer my question."

"No, I don't suppose it does." Black's voice was cold.

"Just think about it." Liddell let the offer lie. If he said too much, too soon, the tenuous connection between them would disintegrate.

Eventually Black spoke. "I make no promises. Not now. To you or to anyone else. Not anymore."

"I'm not asking for any."

"But you will. Eventually. Your sort always does."

"Perhaps."

The two men looked at each other for a long moment, Black's expression lost in the darkness surrounding them. Liddell extended his hand again and this time Morris Black took it. The grip was firm and dry.

"Good-bye, Liddell."

"Good-bye, Morris."

The detective nodded once, then turned away. He crossed the bridge, feet ringing dully on the stone, then reached the path beyond. He paused, turned briefly, and raised a hand in faint salute. Liddell responded in kind, then watched as Morris Black vanished into the shadows of the Abbey.

Liddell stood on the bridge, then turned, looking out over the rippling water of the river running below him. He breathed deeply, taking in the scents of a dozen different wildflowers and the faint salt tang of the estuary where sea and river merged. There was no sound except the whisper of evening air through the trees. A haven of peace and calm that seemed inviolate, while a hundred miles away, on the far side of the narrow channel that stood between England and Europe, war was raging, a tempest of death and devastation. Liddell shook his head sadly; Morris Black had his refuge from the storm, at least for now—his sanctuary—but how long would its protection last?

The intelligence officer glanced down, realizing that his pipe had gone out. He dropped it into the pocket of his jacket, then made his way back to the inn, knowing that it was a question with no answer and that only passing time would give it meaning.